THE 7TH VICTIM

NANCY CHURCHILL

ISBN-10: 0615677630
ISBN-13: 9780615677637

Library of Congress Control Number: 2012914029
CreateSpace
North Charleston, SC

DEDICATED TO
My dear husband, Jack. Thank you for your love,
devotion, and support during the writing process and
our thirty years together My grief, over your passing,
is frightening. Rest in peace, honey.

ACKNOWLEDGEMENTS

What an amazing adventure, writing my first novel. There are so many people to thank, not only for the technical aspects of the book, but for the patience exerted when I would run by "another idea."

Colleen Dwyer, with the Bureau of Reclamation in Nevada, took a few seconds to recover from my initial question of "how long would it take a body to float down to Harrah's Casino after being thrown over the Davis Dam." When she realized I was a writer, rather than a terrorist, she and her coworkers calculated the water flow and spent time to help me with the answers.

Chris Rogakis of Sheble Aviation talked me through the process of how to throw a person out of a seaplane without killing him. I'm sure the two security guards at Davis Dam, Jerry McGovern and Mike Ellsworth, also thought I was a terrorist when I did my cloak and dagger research at the dam. Thanks guys. The friendly dealers and especially Jessica, a pit boss at the Riverside Casino, all listened intently as I described the latest pseudo crime happening in their city.

Dr. Jay Han, cardiologist, lent his expertise to the excising of the human heart, and was a little more than surprised to experience my dark side.

Jeff Jacques, Orange County Sheriff's Department, helped me sort out the appropriate weapons to use during battle. Lt. Jerry Duke, Bullhead Police Department, advised on police protocol, and filled in some blanks.

Huge thanks go to Jean Jenkins, editor-extraordinaire. She spent hours fixing my point of view and other miscellaneous problems which haunted my initial manuscript. Thanks also to the project team at CreateSpace for its instant feedback and help in the publishing process. A special thanks to Tara, the editor. I had no idea how stingy I was with commas.

Then, there are the Corner girls, Sharon, Gladys, Carolyn, Trisha, and Hermie. Four o'clock wine at Kelly's Bar kept me focused and on course to finish the novel. Thanks for the support.

Can't say enough about family support. Jack, my husband of thirty years, was thrilled when I began writing. During the time he was still aware of his surrounding, he would walk by my writing room, pause, and walk on to give me a little more time. I'm so sorry that Alzheimer's' took my love away before he had a chance to see it completed. And then, my girls...Suzie, Cindie, Karen and Becquie. Always ready to listen to the new twists and turns that the book was taking, ready to help in research and encouraging me to those final words—the end. Love ya kids.

THE 7TH VICTIM

FRIDAY, JULY 26

A thin layer of sandy grit settled on the police cruiser as it pulled to a stop in the wash. Rachael Pennington relaxed her grip on the steering wheel, turned off the engine, and unsnapped her holster. She waited.

The man was well over six feet tall with long, stringy hair, an old T-shirt, and cutoff jeans. He glanced over his shoulder and then returned his attention to his gun. He slowly broke open the barrel, pulled out two shots, and snapped the gun closed. Leaning the gun against a nearby rock, he turned toward the blue-and-white patrol car.

He raised his hands in the air. "Officer." His walk was steady. Shade from his cowboy hat concealed his eyes.

Rachael, a detective with the Bullhead Police Department, stepped out of the car without taking her eyes off him. "I'm responding to a 'shots fired' call. Don't suppose you know anything about that, do you?"

"Maybe." The man's walk turned to a swagger. Their belt buckles almost touched, but she didn't back down. "You're looking hot today, Officer."

"Yeah, right, you old redneck." Rachael shoved him backward. She looked around at the spent shells. "This your mess?"

"Nah. They was here when I got here. Just cleanin' my gun."

Rachael scooped up a shell, put it in her pocket, and reached for the shotgun. "Smells like it's been fired recently, Clayton. I'm probably mistaken 'cause you know that's against the law and all. Street sweepers are illegal."

"Ain't no dumb blood flowin' in your brain, Rachael." He paused, looking her over. "You married yet?"

Rachael mouthed a crooked smile, knowing that the conversation about the gun was closed. "Not yet. Not too many prospects sniffin' around since you got away."

Clayton grinned at that. He knew he'd never been in the running. "The boys say you hang out with that Hal guy after work. Sure you want to hook up with another cop?"

"Like it's really your business?" Rachael should have known about the gossip. Bullhead was a small town with an active pipeline.

They leaned against a boulder, shading their eyes from the brutal sun, comfortable with each other.

"OK, lay it on me, Clay. What's with bringing Old Lucy out of the closet? That sawed-off shotgun was retired years ago."

He reached for his Skoal, put a pinch between his cheek and gums. Chewed a little.

"Well, seems like Bullhead cops can't keep our women safe. Some of the guys are makin' plans for the killer. Supposed to show up next week, right? We're just getting our shit together."

"You know I'll haul your rank ass to jail if you try any vigilante stuff, Clay."

He thought about that for a minute and then spit. She was serious. "Rach, we're tired of letting this crazy bastard get the best of us. He's kidnapped three, killed two. When he dumps Melissa's body, he'll be out looking for another one of our women. We aim to stop him."

"OK, hotshot, what's your plan?"

"We catch him, strip him naked, drag his sorry ass across the desert behind my Jeep, for starters. Then we tie him to my hood and drive up and down the Ninety-Five so everyone can see the asshole. A regular Bullhead parade." He spit through his grin. "After we castrate him, I reckon we'll hang him from the bridge. Now that would be river justice."

"Listen. For starters, we aren't sure he'll take anyone else. The FBI profilers think he'll return Melissa's body but may move on. That's his regular MO."

"What the hell do they know? They show up and flash a few badges around. That's how it looks to us."

Before Rachael could reply, her radio squawked. By the time she got to it, another cop had answered the call. Looking at her watch, she decided to cut the conversation short with Clayton. Handling the vigilantes would come later.

"Well, I'm feeling generous today, Clay, so I won't be writing you up for shooting a firearm in the city. Next time, get the hell out of Dodge for your practice. Put Old Lucy back in the closet before someone gets hurt."

Rachael started to hand the shotgun back to Clayton but hesitated. "Ya know, I think I'll take Lucy for a ride in the blue-and-white. The guys in the department would like to meet her. Quite a legend behind her punch."

"Ah, come on, Rachael. No need for that."

"Go see the Captain next week. He'll probably want to store her for a few days just to keep you out of trouble."

"Ah, shit." Spit.

"See ya," she said, elbowing him in the ribs. She slid the gun in the trunk. "Behave yourself."

Clay grumbled an annoyed good-bye.

With less than an hour before the end of her shift, Rachael parked the squad car at the top of Silver Creek Hill, watching the traffic crawl by on the 95. *Damn fool*, she thought.

But Clayton did have a point. The department had been unable to catch the killer. She let her mind circle around what information they had but then decided to drop it before she went heat crazy. Rachael drove the squad car to the yard and turned the shotgun into the evidence room.

Roberto, a detective with the department, spotted her on her way out. "Hey, isn't this your day off?"

"Does it look like my day off?"

"Wow, sorry I asked."

She hit the door hard and headed into the penetrating heat. Sorely in need of some river time, she steered her Camaro toward home. The air-conditioning went out within two blocks, adding more antagonism to her already annoying day.

Rachael shared the river house with her younger sister, Meg. They both felt the river was their solace. Once inside, she left a trail of sweaty clothes in her wake as she tromped down the hall, the knot in her bikini top not cooperating as she struggled to switch from cop to girl. After throwing an inner tube over the balcony, Rachael tucked her cell phone into a plastic bag, grabbed a beer and the latest copy of *People*, and hurried down the circular stairs to the beach. It was Friday—supposed to be her day off. She knew there would be no time off until the killer was caught.

The river was calm—no weekend warriors screwing up the water with their boats or personal watercraft. In midsummer, the Colorado River, which forms the boundary between Arizona and Nevada, is typically only sixty-two degrees, in spite of the intense desert heat. The primal shock she felt upon entering the water was no different than yesterday's frigid encounter. She cushioned herself into the rubber tube.

But even the water couldn't bring relaxation today. Clay was right. Bullhead cops hadn't caught the monster, and now there were only days left before his return. *Oh, come on, brain. Switch off.*

The 118-degree temperature bore down, adding another coat of tan to her well-toned body. She stretched like a cat and was finally relaxing when her cell phone vibrated. Rachael groaned. Probably the department again. *Forget it, I'm not picking up.* When she looked closer, she recognized the phone number of her older sister, Amanda. *What's with this?*

Amanda's voice came cracking through the phone, "Hi, sis. What are you up to?"

"Well, trying to take a day off. Where are you? Last time we talked, you were at Quantico."

"I'm closer than you think," Amanda said. "I've been thinking of you and Meg and wanted to check in."

"That's a switch," said Rachael. "I mean, thinking of me and Meg? Usually it's your boy toy of the month that keeps you busy."

Silence.

Why did I say that?

Finally, Rachael heard a muffled sigh of exasperation. Amanda continued. "Rach, there's something I need to tell you."

"What? Is Mom OK?"

"It's not Mom. I called to tell you that I'm going to—"

Before Amanda could continue, Rachael interrupted her. "Hey, hang on a minute. I've got another call coming in." Amanda sputtered her objection, but Rachael, seeing it was her partner, Hal, took the call. "What's up? You know I came home to float."

"Car chase," he clipped.

"Routine," she snapped back. "Let someone else take it."

"It's Carlos. He jacked a car, and he's on the run."

Rachael could hear the sirens coming her way from the Laughlin Bridge upstream. "Damn it. We might catch him this time. Where are you?" she asked, prying herself from the tube. She scurried from the water and headed for the stairs. "Jeez. Can't I ever get a day off?"

"Sorry, princess. Duty calls. If he's got body parts on board, we'll nail his ass." Hal gave her his location and direction of travel.

"I'll be in my car in five minutes. Lemme know when you're close to El Palacio. I'll fall in. Who else is responding?"

"Roberto."

"Shit." Roberto was Carlos's cousin and would go easy on him if he got there first.

Rachael snapped her cell phone closed, completely forgetting about Amanda.

2

Carlos watched the old lady park her new SUV in Harrah's two-story parking structure and head for the elevators. He followed her through the casino and sat next to her as she ordered a drink, pulled out her player's card and twenty dollars, and started playing video poker. Carlos did the same, chatting with her about his luck at the games. After ten minutes, he nudged his baseball cap to the floor and, while picking it up, managed to lift her car keys. Piece of cake. An old-fashioned jimmy bar would never work on this car, and he wouldn't be able to hot-wire it without use of a laptop and blank keys, either. Too much time would pass, so lifting the keys was the best solution. He sauntered out the front doors of the casino, tossing the keys in the air like the proud owner of a powerful car. The interior smelled new, and he beamed with delight as he adjusted the seat and mirrors to his liking.

He drove to his parked car and transferred a small amount of cocaine and four medical containers into the Suburban. Rolling onto Casino Boulevard, he leaned back into the comfortable seat, feeling like a manly man.

Carlos didn't notice the unmarked police car fishtail as it made a U-turn. When Hal Jensen recognized Carlos in the stolen SUV, he gave chase. He flipped down the visor, activating the red lights, no siren, and called for backup. Hal hated to bother Rachael. She had been overly cranky as the dreaded anniversary for the serial killer to reappear approached. But they'd been trying to catch Carlos for months, so he made the call. Weaving in and out of heavy traffic on Casino Drive was tricky. Carlos was now approaching the Palms Casino, seemingly unaware of Hal's presence. *Good,* Hal thought. *Three more blocks and the pedestrian traffic will clear up.*

Carlos had been driving for the criminal element in town for a year but was growing impatient to get ahead. El Jefe, his boss, would promise more but deliver nothing. So Carlos, tired of being the patsy, decided to show his girlfriend just how her macho stud could hit the big time. He struggled to connect his Bluetooth but finally dialed her number.

"Hey, Sasha, I jacked me a Suburban, baby. Ripped off some of El Jefe's shipment. I'll be by soon to change the plates and stuff. We'll take off."

"What the hell you doin'?" growled Sasha. "It's daytime. They'll catch your stupid ass."

"No, baby. No one seen me. Hey, I got contacts in Tijuana. We can start our own business. Make real money. Maybe move to someplace that has grass for our baby."

"What? You gonna sell those nasty body parts? Where? Home Depot? Dump that car before they catch you. Tell me where you are. I'll pick you up."

The siren started up behind him, and Carlos jerked to full alert. His eyes switched to the mirror. "Oh, shit, baby. I'm busted."

The Suburban ripped around the corner on two wheels, careening onto the Laughlin Bridge ramp. Slamming his foot down on the accelerator, he crossed the centerline and squeezed the Suburban through an impossible opening. Getting caught with a stolen car and body parts was fast becoming a reality. If they caught him alive, even his cousin could not help him.

3

Amanda, the oldest of the Pennington sisters, winced when Rachael disconnected her. *I guess she'll finally get my message when I show up on her doorstep.* Her hands tensed on the wheel of the seven-year-old Mustang, the FBI-allocated car for her mission. The white dividing line leading to Laughlin was hypnotizing. Seventy-five more miles from Las Vegas to Bullhead. Enough time to thrash out any kinks in her first FBI undercover assignment.

Her main objective was to identify and take down the mastermind behind a money-laundering racket involving the Mexican Mafia. The money was delivered by seaplane, landing at different locations on the river around Davis Dam. But yesterday, Quantico called and expanded her assignment. Black-market body parts were now showing up in

Henderson, and it was believed that the two cases were connected. Her once-simple assignment was now getting complicated. Before leaving Quantico, Amanda addressed a more personal question.

"Sir, my sister is a Bullhead City detective. Should I coordinate with her? Also, she is hell-bent on catching the notorious serial killer. Is the FBI helping with that case?"

"The Bullhead chief is aware of the money-laundering assignment, but I haven't called him about the body parts. Will do that next. For now, you should share intel with your sister. Another task force will be helping with the serial killer. Not your job."

"OK, got it."

"You all right? First assignment and all."

"Good to go. Thanks for asking. I'll be in touch." Amanda was itching to get started.

The Oasis Casino was the target casino, and Amanda had received an e-mail from Len, the assistant manager, to come in for an interview. Cocktail waitressing and a possible opening for a dancer in the line were available.

A few miles out of Las Vegas, she got a call from Len. "Hey, Amanda, how ya doin'?"

"Oh, wow, just great. Thanks for calling me. I'm almost to town and not sure where you want me to go."

"Ask for me when you get to the Oasis. You'll have to fill out some bullshit forms and get fitted for a uniform. We'll nail down all this shit today. Where are ya gonna be stayin'?"

"Probably at the Oasis 'til I find an apartment or condo."

"Good enough. I'll call the front desk and book a room for you. Two nights on us."

Her phone went dead, and within seconds, it began playing the USC Trojan fight song.

The voice at the other end said, "We listened in on the tap. It's a go. Your partner is special agent Matt Duran. He's already staying at the Oasis. He'll contact you today." Then, once again, her phone went silent.

As her Mustang pulled up to the signal at the corner of Casino Drive, Amanda's eyes searched up the street to locate the source of the siren she heard. A black SUV ripped around the corner onto the bridge, followed by an unmarked cop car. *Welcome to Laughlin*, she thought.

4

Leaving her temporary office at Davis Dam, Meg Pennington marched toward her orange Mini Cooper convertible, yanked the large barrette from her hair, and unleashed a barrage of thick blonde curls. Shaking out the tangles, she drew in a long sigh of relief. Working for the Bureau of Reclamation was more challenging than she had anticipated. Most of the time, she felt like she was working beyond her expertise and everyone knew it. Fortunately, the position did have some positive incentives. The other employees were young, unmarried, and a lot of fun.

The day had not gone well. This afternoon, it had been: "Crap, Jerry, come help. The computer doesn't understand my brand of English." Earlier in the day, she had run into yet another problem and wondered if her mother's push toward continuing her college education might be a good idea. Meg didn't usually agree with her mother about anything, but now that Meg was twenty-three years old, her mother somehow seemed to be getting smarter.

Mike and Jerry, Meg's close friends, were also employed by the dam as security guards. Driving back to the dam office, they spotted Meg's Mini Cooper heading toward the gate and charged forward in the Cushman cart to block her way.

She honked the horn. "Out of my way, peasants. It's Friday. Party time."

"See you tomorrow," yelled Jerry.

"Hey, wait a minute. Tonight we're going clubbing," said Mike. "Did that change? And then tomorrow we're going skiing. That's still the plan, isn't it?" Mike switched from Meg to Jerry suspiciously. "Are you trying to ditch me?"

"Well, if we were, it was Jerry's idea." Meg laughed, knowing that the two men would be arguing for an hour after her comment. "But now that you caught us, the plans haven't changed. I'll pick up Paula, and we'll be at the Oasis by seven o'clock." She threw them a teasing smile. "We'll party hardy." She dug around in her purse, found the security key card, and inserted it into the slot. The gate squeaked open, and she squealed, "TGIF" as her orange bomb exploded through the gate.

The catastrophic events of 9/11 had mandated a tight security overhaul at the dam. No longer was the public allowed to drive across the dam or participate in self-guided tours. The dam had once bustled with sightseers, but it now was eerily quiet, like a forsaken child.

The Mini Cooper sputtered across the open section of the dam and headed toward Highway 95. It was Friday, and long lines of traffic idled at the Laughlin Bridge signal. Waiting her turn, Meg thought about the upcoming fun. Fun was her passion. No fun, no Meg. Waterskiing down to the Topock area and then floating through the serene gorge toward Lake Havasu, drinking with friends, all added up to an awesome adventure. Hopefully on Saturday there would be tons of people at Copper Canyon diving off cliffs or playing naked volleyball. She drummed her fingers on the wheel, anxious to get started.

Meg's Mini was the third car back when the light changed in her favor. The first car started forward but then abruptly stopped. The noise of approaching police sirens halted all traffic. She could hear the sound of a helicopter hovering across the river.

Meg cried out in surprise as two cars zipped by, "Oh, my God, that's Hal's car and…jeez…he's chasing Carlos. What the hell's going on?" She watched the SUV swerve on two wheels onto the 95 and grabbed her phone to call Rachael.

5

Gazing out the twenty-seventh floor window of the Oasis Casino, Beckett pondered his future. His dark brown eyes, half-hooded from too many nights of drinking, vacantly searched the bright desert skyline. His eight-year job as manager of the Oasis had been adequate but mostly boring. Was it just a year ago that he had sold his soul, his integrity, to the devil? That damn El Jefe. Who was he? The beginning of their association was simple: a little money laundering on occasion. But now their partnership involved transporting members of the Mexican Mafia from Rosarito Beach, Mexico, to Laughlin, Nevada, to facilitate their business. Millions were being processed each month. Beckett arranged for Carlos to pick up the men from the seaplane landing, drop them off at the Oasis, and the next day Carlos would drive them to Las Vegas.

When the exchange was complete, the procedure was reversed. Simple arrangements, but what if? Elliott vacillated. *Not too bad. A million bucks that Uncle Sam didn't know about.* But now there was talk that his partner was dealing in stolen body parts and cocaine. Rightfully, he was concerned about his relationship with his own boss in Chicago. There might be too much exposure. Beckett knew the casino owners wouldn't hesitate to dump his mutilated body in the desert if they suspected any outside criminal involvement. A low profile was a prerequisite to maintaining his position.

Beckett's life had involved years of bowing to the Chicago mafia, working as a grunt, bartender, dealer, and pit boss. Finally, they sent him to Laughlin to manage the Oasis. Life had been simple and prosperous until now. His conscience was unnerving his normally placid existence. Fear was surrounding him. Thinking his greed might erode his lifestyle, he contemplated ending the relationship. But would El Jefe allow that? Whispered words were ominous. No one crossed El Jefe and lived to talk about it. Would that apply to him? No, probably not, so he decided to move on. The money would be missed, but death as an alternative was not that attractive. The next drop would be his last.

And then there was Carlos, who was starting to screw up. He complained daily that his cut was too little, and he was starting to use drugs again. What a shit head. Drivers were cheap and expendable. Carlos should know that. The business was fracturing. What else could go wrong?

Out of frustration, Beckett turned on his computer, checking the personnel roster to see which cocktail waitress was on duty. Scanning the list, he noticed Angie's name. "Oh well, same ole, same ole," he muttered. He dialed his handyman.

"Leonard, I need some company. Looks like Angie is working, so get her up here. Pig that she is, she's better than nothing."

"Not much better."

"Agreed. Hasn't learned any new tricks lately, either." His face grew dark. He usually had a good read on people, but when sex was involved, his scrutiny could fail him. "Ya know, I'm worried about her. Last time when I finished with the chippie, she thought I'd gone into the bathroom. I watched her in the mirror. The bitch was trying to pull some shit off my computer. Stupid whore. After I'm through with her today, follow her. See if she's up to anything." He paused, realizing that a more permanent solution was needed. "Oh, hell, just get rid of her. Run her out of town. She looks frumpy. It's time I pick up someone with more class."

Ten minutes later, Angie arrived, still wearing her cocktail uniform, her heavy makeup suffering from exposure as the afternoon sun shining through the massive windows crossed her face.

Beyond tired, she gave a weak performance of being happy to see Beckett.

"Tits are looking good, Angie. Come on over here," Beckett said as he leaned back in his opulent chair and unzipped his pants. "I need a little distraction while I watch the monsoon gather."

Angie wanted to scream, "Go to hell, you pervert," but instead clumped across the room in her tattered high heels. She had been servicing Beckett for three years. Her teenage son always needed something, so she took the abuse. On some occasions, Beckett was nice, even offered her a drink afterward, but other times his dark side roared through and she would end up with a black eye—or worse. On those occasions, he would always give her a few black chips, or she might even score some coke. Angie hated Beckett with a passion, but needed the job.

When he was satisfied, Beckett grabbed her by the hair and snarled. "You don't seem too happy to see me anymore. Why is that?"

Angie wrenched away from him. "Ah, Beckett, ya know I love you. What do you want from me?"

"You ugly bitch, what do you know about love? You keep dreaming of landing a whale. Ha, what a joke. If he looks close, he'll see the dark roots and the fat that wiggles when you walk. Get the hell out of here—you make me sick." He grabbed a handful of hair again and smashed her into the wall. Her head cracked when it hit the doorjamb.

As Angie ran sobbing from the room, Beckett picked up the phone to call Len. "She's gamin' me. Get rid of her. I don't care how. Buy her a ticket on the bus, anything, but make it happen now."

Len grunted a reply. He tired of Beckett's orders. His boss never wanted to get his hands dirty but didn't mind asking Len to throw the muck around. As Beckett started to hang up the phone, Len exclaimed, "Boss. You need to turn on the TV, Channel Forty-Two. Metro's interrupting the news. There's a car chase in Bullhead."

"So what," said Beckett. "That's nothing new. There's always some wacko trying to beat the cops."

"They're chasing Carlos," Len responded breathlessly. "The camera from the Channel forty-two news copter zoomed in, and I could see his face."

"Fuck."

6

Another cop car joined the chase at Fourth
Street. Highway 95 was always crowded, but by five
o'clock on Friday afternoon, it was a parking lot.
Hal radioed ahead. Carlos would probably take off
for Oatman when he reached North Oatman Road.
"Set up a road block. Tell the sheriff's department
that we need backup."

As the chase snaked through the traffic,
weaving in and out of oncoming cars, they neared
County Club Drive. Hal spotted Rachael's red
Camaro in the El Palacio parking lot. He transmitted, "I see ya, partner. Fall in after me."

Rachael's car swung onto the 95, tailgating
Hal. She loved a high-powered pursuit. Adrenaline
kicked in as she hit the gas pedal. Her tires spewed
hot rubber in response. The Camaro leaped into the
middle of the chase.

The convoy continued down the 95, leaving a legacy of fender benders and blaring horns. Carlos sideswiped a pickup truck that outweighed the Suburban. Instead of heading for Oatman, he spun around the corner and headed for the river.

"Carlos is headed down Ramar," Hal radioed. "Anybody in the vicinity?" All cops checked in with a negative. "He's probably heading to Miguel's house on Miranda. They've got guns, so proceed with caution. We could use some more backup. Where the hell is everybody? Roberto?"

Roberto transmitted back instantly. "I'm rolling. Still behind you. Catch up in three."

As Hal predicted, Carlos pulled up sharply in front of Miguel's well-known drug house. Braking and turning the wheel at the precise time slid him into the side yard of the old sun-beaten frame bungalow. Shredded drapes moved inside the house as his friends peered out.

The Suburban stopped. Carlos bailed out, hesitating to throw something back into the car. Half running, half sliding down the slope to the river, he jumped into a skiff tied to the dock. With three pulls of the sun-frayed rope, the motor started. Carlos untied the dingy and steered the boat upstream.

Rachael and Hal arrived at the house in less than a minute, followed by Roberto seconds later.

"There's his car! I'll go left, you take the right," Rachael yelled to Hal. "Roberto, you call for more backup. I don't like the way this is going dow—"

Before she could finish, Carlos's car exploded, throwing both detectives onto the junk-covered ground. Body parts and trash whirled around overhead as they plowed face first into the dirt. Rachael grabbed her knee and pressed hard to stop the flow of blood. *Minor*, she thought. "You OK, partner?"

Hal yelled, "Yeah, you?"

"Just pissed. Let's go."

Roberto, standing beside his car, missed the fury of the blast. "I'll call for Fire," he shouted.

Rachael and Hal circled the house, guns drawn.

Rachael yelled, "Any sign of him?"

Hal rounded the south corner. "I hear a boat motor." He rushed to the top of the hill and peered down. "Yeah, shit, there he goes. Damn." Disbelief crept across Hal's face as he watched the dingy trudge through the water. "I thought we had him this time. Where is that chopper now that we need it?" He searched the sky for the Channel 42 helicopter that had dogged their chase but was now mysteriously absent. "They must've got another call. Something even nastier than ours." He turned and walked back toward the cars. Disgusted.

"Another day," said Roberto as he watched his cousin chug up the river. "I'll have a talk with my aunt. She's tired of his crap. She'll be happy to turn him in if he shows up at her place."

"Yeah, right," muttered Rachael as she dusted off remnants from her spill.

"You got something to say, Rachael? Spit it out," said Roberto.

"Ah, forget it." An exhausted Rachael walked back toward the house, pulling debris from her hair, not wanting to get into it with Roberto.

"Let's wrap it up," said Hal.

Roberto nodded. "The fire department's on the way. They'll handle the car—or what's left of it. Whatcha think? Maybe a frag grenade?"

"How would Carlos get hold of something like that?"

"God only knows."

"We'll get a search warrant for the house. Enough probable cause for that. Call CSI in for the rest of the stuff," Hal said to Roberto. He turned to Rachael. "Come on. Let's go celebrate today's failure. I'll buy ya a beer."

"What the hell's the matter with you? CSI won't take care of all of this. God, Hal, we've got reports to turn in. Do your job." She stood there, shaking her head. "I'm calling water patrol. Maybe they can catch him."

Hal didn't know what was behind Rachael's outburst. She should have known he wasn't serious. He was nearing the end of his patience with her. The awesome, spontaneous, caring Rachael that he loved was nowhere to be seen. Hadn't been for weeks.

Rachael stared at him in disbelief, still wiping the junkyard dust off her clothes. She hadn't had time to change into anything that even resembled professional. Her bloody knee was beginning to ooze again. She calmed down. "Later. We need to get back to the office and write this up so we can pull the warrants. I'm out of here." She turned abruptly, leaving Hal and Roberto with open mouths. Maybe it was the aftereffects of the chase. She wasn't sure what was really bothering her. *Hell of a day.*

"What the hell is eating her?" asked Roberto.

"Shit, who knows. Was supposed to be her day off. You know Rachael. She needs her river soak to wash off the department stink. Apparently didn't get it. It'll pass."

"Glad you have to deal with her, not me."

Driving away from the crime scene, Rachael had time to replay the earlier events.

Logic told her that Roberto had had ample time to catch up with or even head off Carlos because he, more than, anyone, could predict where Carlos was headed once they were on that side of town. Perhaps Roberto didn't want to be responsible for arresting his cousin. Had there been other times that Roberto didn't play square with the department? Maybe this was something she needed to explore with Hal.

Pulling up in front of the police department, Rachael met Hal again. "Hold up, partner. I need to run something by you before we go inside."

Hal slammed the door of his Explorer. "Can't it wait? We just about had our effing heads blown off back there. I need to cool down."

"No, it can't," Rachael said.

Leaning against the building, a tired Hal groaned. "Go ahead, shoot. What's bugging you now?" The exasperation in his voice was clear.

"Roberto's actions. Aren't you curious about the sequence of events? He had plenty of time to catch up with Carlos because he probably knew where he was headed, yet he came up empty-handed."

"He wasn't in on the chase from the beginning," Hal countered, "yet he still got there pretty close to when we did. What's the problem? Don't get paranoid on me."

"Maybe, maybe not. But it won't hurt to keep an eye out. We're getting closer to cracking this case. No slipups now."

"Ah, shit, Rachael, let's go inside. It's a hundred eighteen degrees out here. I need some water. Shelf this for a while, damn it. We can talk about it tonight if we have to." He turned and walked away.

Inside, the cool air hit both detectives as they headed for their desks to start the paperwork. Rachael, still angry and smarting from Hal's dismissal of her suspicions, told everybody she encountered that she was sick and tired of covering for them. Walking past Hal's desk, she said, "Here, partner. You think you know everything, so you do the paperwork." She slammed her pile of forms on his desk and headed for her car.

Hal glanced around the room to see who had heard her onslaught of angry words. Only Roberto looked up, smirked, and went back to work at his computer.

"Well, here we go again," Hal grumbled to him.

Driving home, Rachael glanced at her watch and realized that she had hung up on Amanda over two hours ago. If Amanda was coming to town, she would head for the house, which meant she would run into Meg, who would be incapable of welcoming her oldest sister. That scene was a catastrophe in the making. Sibling rivalry, along with eight years in age between them, was a lethal combination. *How had Mom stayed sane through all of that?*

And indeed, the scenario was much as Rachael had predicted. In the living room sat a despondent Meg, stripped down to bra and undies, munching Fritos. Next to the entryway was a travel case that Rachael recognized as belonging to Amanda.

"Where's Amanda?" Rachael asked. "Did you kill her already?"

"*Your* sister has gone to the Oasis for an interview with Beckett or Leonard, I don't know which. She's going to be a cocktail waitress. Ha. Imagine our brilliant, overly talented, ex-cop sister applying for a waitress job."

"What? You must have heard wrong."

"Actually, it kind of fits her disposition, slutting around and all." Meg switched channels on the TV.

"Come on, Meg. Give her a break."

"Yeah, right." She turned up the volume. Meg knew Rachael would be pushing her to befriend Amanda, and she wanted no part of that. Amanda had played pseudo mom all of her life, and Meg certainly didn't need another overprotective mother.

"She must be on assignment. Did she say anything about being undercover?"

"Undercover or under the sheets? Who cares? Maybe she'll hook up with Beckett. I heard he's a pretty good lay."

Rachael was tiring of Meg's blistering criticism. "Is she visiting or is she on assignment? Did she say?"

"Who cares? She doesn't get to breeze in and take over. She dumped her stuff by the front door. I'm not picking it up. It can rot there until she comes back for it. Said she might start working tonight if they hire her."

"I give up." Rachael retreated to her bedroom. She felt exhausted. Amanda had been off the family radar for about six months after she left the LAPD. The family decided it was best to give her some space to sort out her issues over her failed romance. In hindsight, Rachael wondered if that had been the most supportive position. Either way, Amanda had kept her distance, and they knew little about her professional or personal life these days. They heard she had graduated from Quantico, but no word from her. Showing up in Bullhead and getting a casino job in Laughlin? It made no sense unless it was FBI oriented.

7

The interview with Leonard had gone as planned. While looking just sleazy enough for the part, Amanda still allowed her sensuality to shine. She had fictitious letters from previous employers and a bogus social security number, and she indicated to Leonard that while she had been busted for drug possession one time, it was all a big mistake. The FBI had gone to great lengths to build a new identity for her. Now it was time to prove herself.

"Hey, Len, how about dating the customers?" she asked. "Any rules against partying with the whales? And my uniform. I'd like a size smaller than I usually wear. It seems to get me more tips. I really can't figure that one, but it works, so, oh well." Amanda wondered if she was pouring it on too thick.

"No problem," said Leonard as his eyes wandered down to her cleavage. "Let me call Beckett and see if he wants to meet you. Sometimes he likes to size up the personnel, if you know what I mean."

"Meeting the boss would be really cool. Let's go and surprise him."

"The boss don't like surprises." Leonard picked up the bar phone and dialed Beckett's number. Out of earshot of Amanda, Leonard described her salient points. "You know, with Angie leaving us, you might need a new friend. Anyway, she's going up to change. Auditions for the show are in an hour. She says she can dance. Who knows? With her knockers, she could just stand there."

"Any class? Or just the typical leftover garbage?"

"She's around an eight. That's better than we usually get. Wants to try out for the chorus line. Come down and see for yourself."

"Shit, I don't have time. What I need to know is what happened to Carlos. Did he get away?"

"I'll make some calls, boss."

"If he screwed up, I'll have to get a new driver. Was he hauling those damn body parts? Get hold of El Jefe. We need to know if we're still in business for the next drop." Nervous about Carlos, he wondered if this would be the opportune time to quit the operation.

Contacting El Jefe was complicated. No one had his phone number, just an answering service to contact. He accessed the service daily and returned only the calls he deemed important. Leonard made the call as directed with no high hopes of connecting.

Beckett slammed the phone down. While he really wasn't in the mood to watch some wannabe dancer, he decided to join Leonard in the theater. Who knows? Maybe Angie's replacement is waiting for me on stage.

Elliott Spencer, Bullhead's TV newscaster, stopped by to see Beckett and joined him in the theater. When Amanda marched down the aisle, heading for the stage, both men eyed her, keenly aware of her beauty. She tossed her soft brown hair back and gave Leonard a radiant smile as she passed him. Her provocative hips moved the whole beguiling package onto the stage.

"Mine," Beckett whispered to Elliott.

"We'll see."

No one danced like Amanda. Picking up the various routines was easy, and she captured the spotlight.

"Hey, new girl. Pull it down a little. You're chorus, remember?"

Amanda shot the director a quick smile and reduced her amplitude. Elliott and Beckett both nodded their approval.

"OK, I've seen enough," said the choreographer. "Check the board this afternoon for callbacks. Good job, ladies."

Amanda grabbed a towel and started up the aisle toward the exit. Leonard called her over and introduced her to both Beckett and Elliott. *Double whammy*, Amanda thought. Two promising suspects in one fell swoop. *This works.*

Beckett moved right in on Amanda, and after dismissing Leonard and then Elliott, he pushed for a meeting to finalize her job. "Drop by my penthouse after you change, and we can discuss your employment. If everything works out all right, then I must insist on taking you to dinner for your first night here in Laughlin."

Amanda wiped the small beads of sweat from her upper lip and the corners of her eyes and gave Beckett a seductive smile. She was somewhat surprised by his pleasant manners. Placing the towel around her neck and flexing appropriately, she replied, "Do you treat all new hires so great?" Throwing on her most convincing southern accent, she continued, "Why, you old rascal, I'd be delighted to join you for dinner." She laughed and gave him a friendly wink. "Later," she said and flitted away.

Beckett watched her until she was out of sight. He knew that stunning women were his weakness, and Amanda topped the scale in that category. Too smart to be a waitress? Far too beautiful for a two-bit hooker. *She'll need watching. Guess I'll have to volunteer for the job. So there, Elliott.* He liked to initiate the new girls before he and Elliott began tossing them back and forth.

Amanda returned to her room to change before meeting Beckett. After removing her stage makeup, she took a quick shower. While toweling off, she dug through her suitcase and found her sheer, lace thong underwear and the new push-up bra. She pulled a sea-green sequined tank top over her head. Looking in the mirror, she applied a moisturizer and a light tint of blush. Nothing else needed to be added except mascara. She gunked it on thick and flirty. She sighed at her reflection. *Who is this high-class party girl who was raised as trailer trash?* She hoped she could pull it off.

Her four-inch heels echoed across the terrazzo floor as she stepped off the elevator at the twenty-eighth floor. Spiked heels and shorts—what a combination. She was very focused on her assignment and decided to portray herself as a little needy and nervous. *I'll let Beckett come and save me,* she thought.

Beckett's suite was breathtaking. A 180-degree view of the Colorado River greeted her. The foyer opened to an expansive living area decorated with large overstuffed sofas that faced the hearth. Superb jade-colored Italian marble swept across the room, met by the expansive windows that accentuated the glimmering river below. A Greco-Roman bar was situated to the left, with seating for eight facing the river. An oversized flat-screen television accompanied a complicated-looking sound system. No expense had been spared to complete the ambiance. Beckett had nice toys.

To Amanda's surprise, Beckett was more than attractive, a fact that had eluded her when they first met in the darkened theater. His graying, thick hair complemented a perfectly chiseled face. Dark brown eyes, deeply set, moved slowly across her body. The scan didn't seem tacky to Amanda but more like a compliment. Tall, but not too tall, his presence was formidable in the room. Dressed casually, he seemed self-assured. Beckett noticed that Amanda gave him a second look and returned the look with a knowing smile. He knew she approved.

"So you're our new cocktail waitress and dancer, are you?" Beckett said.

She smiled and glided across the room. "Up to you. Is this a continuation of the audition? What happens if I don't pass?" She faced him and waited.

"Well, Leonard approved your application, and I approved your dancing. But why would a girl with your potential leave Las Vegas? Surely the tips are better there?" He took her hand and led her to the sofa.

"Las Vegas wasn't for me. Too fast. I was in a relationship with a jerk who ended up drinking and using drugs. Made him crazy." She slid her hand out of his soft grasp and sidled up to the bar. "When he decided to stalk me, I decided to split. I left before he killed both of us." Her eyes met his. "I'm keeping a low profile for a while, praying he won't show up here."

With her most seductive walk, she brushed past him and headed toward the windows. From her brief exposure to Beckett, she decided that a "needy" persona wasn't entirely the right fit, so sexy it would have to be.

"Give the chief of security his picture, and he'll keep an eye out. Now, Leonard mentioned you had a question about dating the whales?" Beckett walked behind the bar and reached for the vodka. "Our casino rarely attracts the Las Vegas–type whale, but we do get our share of big spenders. As long as you're discrete and don't end up hustling the customers, what you do on your own time is your business. We have no problem if you want to gamble in this casino, either, but watch your drinking and don't be using drugs when you're here."

"No problem," Amanda said. "So should I leave now and get my uniform? Maybe start working tonight instead of waiting 'til tomorrow? I could use the money." She turned to Beckett. "Oh, I did pass, didn't I?" She asked the question to try to get a read on him. If he looked only semi-interested, then she would have to work a little harder to set the hook and possibly even have to come back for dinner, a thought that didn't please her. *Handsome, yes. Letch, yes. Roll in the hay, no.*

Beckett didn't answer right away. Amanda turned him on, but he was seasoned with show-girls. He was uneasy about her motives for pushing so hard for the job. It would take some finessing to fill Angie's role since she had more class. But all things in due time. Beckett wasn't stupid. He registered a mental note to have Len run a complete background check on her.

"Hired? Yes, but I have a plan. Go with Leonard. Get your uniform and locker. Sign up with payroll, and then come join me for dinner. Leonard will take you on a tour of the casino, give you your assignments for the rest of the week, and make sure that you're on the clock for the rest of the day. Be back here by eight o'clock. Lobster OK?"

Amanda nodded. "You're the boss."

As she started to leave, Beckett took her by the wrist. She pulled away. "A little touchy, are we?"

Amanda turned to him and met his stare dead on. "Sometimes a little touchy with strangers. Comes with the job."

He gently opened her hand and placed an object inside. With a caressing move, he folded each of her fingers around the object, smiled, and said, "Welcome to the Oasis Casino."

Following Leonard to the elevator, Amanda knew exactly what she would find in her hand. *He's taking the bait in a big way. Step one is complete. Now on to step number two.*

She slipped the black chip into her handbag without looking at it.

8

The skiff trudged along, fighting the swift river current. Carlos steered the ancient craft close to the shoreline where the current didn't tug at the boat so hard. He was impatient to reach the beach. *Come on, come on.* Time was not on his side. If the cops radioed ahead and the water patrol guys were around, they could catch him at any minute.

Sasha, Carlos's girlfriend, was sweeping the patio of her rented trailer when she heard him yell from the boat. "Sasha, come help."

She dropped the broom and started toward him, holding her belly as she tried to run. Being eight months pregnant slowed her movements, but she grabbed the boat as it slid onto the sandy shore. "You ass. What? You runnin' from the cops? You bring 'em to my house?"

Carlos jumped out of the skiff, left the motor running, and shoved it out to the rapidly moving river. He grabbed Sasha's hand and pulled his resisting girlfriend toward the trailer. "Hurry. I'll explain later. Get your car keys. We gotta get out of here."

"There's no hurry left in me. Slow down." She leaned against the trailer and supported her overripe stomach. Frustration drew heavy lines across her young face.

Carlos dashed into the trailer and grabbed some bottled water. "Where's your purse? We need money. Damn it, Sasha, hurry up. I stole his shit. The cops are right behind me."

She pulled her keys from the tattered maternity jeans and followed him to her junky Toyota, mumbling all the time. "Slide down in the front seat. I'll drive." A trail of dust floated through the trailer park from their hasty retreat. She slowed to an average speed when they reached the 95. Sasha glanced over at Carlos, who was trying to hide something from her. "Whatcha doing? Whatcha got? Is that a gun?" Horns honked behind her as she pulled the car three lanes over to the side of the road and stopped.

"Drive. Don't stop."

"How come you got a gun? You never said you got a gun."

"Sasha, for God's sake, drive. I really screwed up. I have to protect us. El Jefe will kill me if he catches us."

"You just stole a damn car. He won't care. Turn yourself in to your cousin. Say you was joyriding. What's a month in jail? No big deal."

"God, no, Sasha. I stole his drugs, you hear me? I blew up the car. They'll find the drugs and body stuff. I'll go to prison."

The severity of the problem finally hit her. She wasn't a crier, but tears gathered in her eyes. She glanced at her lover, struggling to find the words to console him. Reaching over, she touched his knee, drawing his attention away from the gun. "Carlos, we'll make it. The baby needs a dad. I need you." She felt her dream of a happy life fading. "We'll figure it out. Maybe Roberto can help. Let's call him."

"Roberto can't help. I'm a dead man. Just drive and lemme think." Carlos slumped down in the front seat and stared across the desert…barren, like his life had become. He knew Sasha deserved better than this, and he felt tired, sad, and older than his twenty years.

El Jefe was thinking about Carlos at the same time. The mystery man was faced with two explosive problems. Carlos was a huge liability—a situation that demanded immediate attention. Trujillo, his seaplane pilot, also had to be handled. Recently, in a Tijuana bar and way past drunk, he spewed out secrets that could jeopardize El Jefe's business. If Carlos could be convinced to take out Trujillo in exchange for forgiveness, part of the problem would be solved. Carlos was aware of El Jefe's wrath and would easily acquiesce in exchange for mercy. Getting rid of Carlos would be easy when the time came. For this plan to work, swift action was crucial. He dialed Carlos's cell.

Carlos recognized the number in his cell phone display. "Oh shit. Shit, Sasha. What should I do?" Sweat formed on his brown skin as he studied the number and listened to the insistent ring.

"You got to answer it, fool. Be a man. Face the asshole."

"No, we need more time to hide. Just keep driving."

Sasha grabbed the cell phone from his hand and opened it. "Answer the damn phone," she said, thrusting it at him. El Jefe heard Sasha's voice and mentally added her to his hit list.

"*Si*, El Jefe. It is Carlos."

"I've been watching you on TV, Carlos. The only reason you could be running is that you have my drugs. Where are they?"

Carlos admitted to having some of the shipment in the stolen car, but he assured El Jefe that he had destroyed the car and the cops wouldn't find any evidence. "Oh, senor. I'm so sorry. I'll do anything to make this up to you." He knew he was groveling, but he continued. "Please, don't kill me."

"Carlos, your time to leave this earth hasn't come yet, though someday I could change my mind. But now, I have a job for you and a place for you to stay. Drive to Oatman. There's a house at 4392 Flower Street. The key is in the backyard, hidden in the ficus tree. The house is vacant, and you'll be safe. Go now. I'll call later."

Carlos was still shaking when he closed the phone. "Sasha, I don't trust him, but we have to do what he says for now. We got no place to go."

"Who is this El Jefe? Have you seen him?" Sasha asked. "He sounds like he's got two pounds of *masa* in his mouth. What's with that?"

"He has some kind of a Radio Shack thing on his phone. I don't know. I never seen him, but I know that he's mean—a killer."

Sasha turned her attention back to driving. One hand slid off the steering wheel and touched her swollen belly. Concern crossed her face. Would they make it through this? Tough, practical Sasha. She used to hate the thought of this baby, but now…

Tears never came easy to her. "Carlos."

"Yes?"

"I'm scared."

"I know."

9

Meg took special care getting ready for the evening with her friends since a new man was joining the usual gang tonight. Paula, her girlfriend, had met him Wednesday night at the Let It Rip Dance Hall at the Sunset Casino.

"What a catch," Paula exclaimed to Meg. Derek hailed from Los Angeles and was a graduate of Cal State Northridge with a major in finance. "Nice biceps, too," Paula mentioned, along with the fact that he had a new Eliminator jet boat. A perfect combination for the weekend, they all agreed. Paula warned Meg that she had dibs on him, and Meg agreed to leave him alone.

Pulling up to the valet-only parking area, Meg put the car in park and jumped out at the Oasis Casino. She stuck her perky face in front of the side mirror for a last-minute makeup check and hailed her friend, George, to park her Mini.

George yelled, "Gotcha covered, girl. No use lookin' in the mirror. Can't improve on perfection, I hear."

"I swear, George, if you weren't married, I'd be all over you." She laughed as she entered through the automatic doors. Theirs was a standing joke.

The other three members of her brat pack were sitting at the river bar, sipping apple martinis and investing some money in the video poker machines. A smile of approval ran across Meg's face when introductions to Derek Manning and his friend Arnie were made. Meg's eyes widened in admiration at the sight of Derek, a gesture not lost on Paula. *Oh dear, here we go again.* She touched Meg's arm and shook her head.

Arnie wasn't in the mood to hang out anymore and left, so the brat pack took Derek casino hopping for an hour. Realizing that Meg and Derek had connected, Jerry and Mike took off, agreeing to meet in the morning at Davis Dam. Paula heard them grumbling about the newcomer as they left.

"Well," said Paula, "I might as well call it quits, too." *The guys always like Meg best,* she thought. Why they remained such good friends, she didn't know. But below that vivacious, fun-loving, misbehaving, gorgeous exterior, Paula knew there was a loving, caring person who would do anything for her—or almost anything. Clearly, she was Derek's choice as well. Meg hadn't flirted or acted outrageously.

She couldn't help it that guys were drawn to her. Helpless fish dangling on the line. Guess those good thoughts about her friend would have to suffice for now.

"So, Meg," Derek began once they were alone, "where do you work?"

"Oh, for the Bureau of Reclamation," she started. "Most of my job is fieldwork, setting up and updating the computer systems. Right now, I'm assigned to Davis Dam as a GS-Seven. That means I'm supposed to know lots of stuff, but right now, I'm way behind. Takin' some classes, though. Soon I'll be an IT specialist, you know, like a network security specialist. Then I'll be making more money."

"IT," Derek said. "What's that stand for again? Incredible tease? If that's the case, you look like a graduate student to me." He lifted her chin and shot a grin her way.

She liked his smile…a lot. "Yeah, right. Davis Dam doesn't have any openings for permanent computer staff on site, so I'm on loan right now. I think I like it that way. It never gets boring, and there's lots of great people to work with."

Derek was getting tired of gambling. Conversation was difficult over the din of the other gamblers. He reached over and took her hand. "Let's go outside for a while—maybe take a drive down the strip. Just talk."

Meg was attracted to this new arrival in town, but she knew better than to be alone in a car with any stranger. Going to some less populated place was out of the question. Everyone in Bullhead was on high alert. The serial killer was scheduled to dump last summer's victim and seek out a new one within the week. It happened every year like clockwork. Rachael had pounded that fact into Meg.

"There are some benches along the river right outside. Let's go there. It's cooled down to about ninety-five degrees, and the breeze across the river should make it feel even better. Come on."

Few boats remained on the river at this time of night. Lights reflected off the water from the brightly lit casinos, and all seemed perfect. It had been a while since Meg had been attracted to anyone, and she sorely missed the intimacy.

Derek rubbed her fingers as they walked. "Nice fit, nice girl." They found a bench and settled in. "So, have there been any problems at the dam since nine-eleven?" he asked. "I mean, can you drive up to the spillway or across the dam now?"

"No problems as far as I know," she said. "Anyone can access the dam from the Arizona side, but they can't drive all the way across anymore. That's too bad, 'cause we used to spend a lot of time parked on the dam as kids. If you look north, you can see the lake all the way to Katherine's Landing. When you turn the other way, you see the river two hundred feet below. It's a blast to anchor your boat at the bottom of the spillway when they let out the water. The spray's refreshing, but cold. The water temperature is still in the low sixties this time of year. Makes you think twice before bailing out. And when the monsoons hit, wow—talk about scary to watch from up there."

Realizing she was talking too much, she said, "OK, now it's your turn. What do you do in LA?"

"Just boring stuff. I work for GE—in acquisitions, most of the time. We're always looking for new land to augment our company. Mostly boring, like I said. I've been looking into the entertainment business. I have a friend who works for ABC Studios, and he thinks there might be an opening coming up in my field. That sounds a lot more exciting than what I'm doing now. Gorgeous women, celebrities, and all."

"Sounds fun. Would you be scouting for locations to film?"

"That might be part of it. So, about the dam. How do you gain access to work each day? Go up to some impenetrable door and yell 'open sesame' or some other innocuous code, and the dam doors open up for you?" Derek asked with a smirk.

Meg twitched a little. *Why all the interest in the dam?* "God, you are really weird," she teased. "Quite easy. I drive up to this huge sliding door and insert a coded card. Big wow, huh? There's a roadway between the spillway and the actual dam—which, by the way, is earth filled, FYI. A swarm of armed security patrols the spillway area. Guess they do a good job 'cause we don't seem to have any problems. Actually, Mike and Jerry are both guards— you know, the two guys you met tonight." *Why all the questions?*

"Oh, yeah, those guys. They'll go with us to Havasu tomorrow?"

"Sure. We're indivisible."

"I heard there's a monsoon coming. Will that mess up our day?"

"I'm the local monsoon expert. I promise to keep you and your boat safe."

They shared nonintimate information, just getting-to-know-you details. Derek dropped enough female names to let Meg know that he'd been around. That didn't bother her too much since she had experienced her share of guys. Meg was still a little curious about all of his questions concerning the dam. Living with a cop for a sister did that to her. *It all seems mighty dull to me*, she thought, *but maybe that's his idea of small talk. Mom would probably think he's a terrorist.*

"Want to come up to my room for a drink? It's only eleven o'clock."

"Sorry, handsome. We're getting an early start tomorrow. Remember? Huge day planned for you, so I'm taking off. I know a shortcut to the valet parking from here, so bye for now. It was really fun meeting you." She gave him a quick kiss on the cheek and lunged away before he could catch her.

SATURDAY, JULY 27

The next morning, Paula and Mike were waiting for Meg and Derek at the Davis Dam Campground's launch ramp. At eight fifteen, without a cloud in the sky, the temperature already registered 102 degrees. The boat ramp was crowded with weekenders trying to get an early start. No wind. Perfect boating day. The group was quite impressed with Derek's boat. He had underplayed its size and worth.

"You've got some kind of righteous horsepower there," Jerry said as he joined the group. "What's under the hood?"

"Well, it's a two-thousand-eight Commander Twenty-Five Millennium Chevy with twin pipes," Derek said. "She'll do sixty-five or so on flat water—something you don't have too much of around here on weekends, I hear."

Meg knew all about this boat model and checked the transom to see if he had a jet engine and swim step. *Yahoo. It's a jet.* Happily, she came to the front of the boat and yelled, "Climb on board, Derek. Get her started, and I'll turn you around. Let's go."

Jerry backed the trailer into the water and stopped as the boat began to float. Although the current was swift, Meg had no trouble unhooking the boat and holding it in place as the others climbed on. With great agility, she turned the boat and popped onto the swim step as the current pulled the boat downstream.

"We'll get some flat water before we hit the gorge and check out this sucker," Meg exclaimed as she threw her bag over the transom. She grabbed her thick hair and managed a quick ponytail.

When everyone was settled, Derek kicked the foot throttle and punched it. The engine gave a thundering roar, leaving everyone on the beach staring as the sleek white boat zipped away.

As they cruised along at twenty-five miles per hour, Meg asked Derek if he would like a verbal guided tour by a local know-it-all.

"Would that be you?"

"It would. I've spent weekends and summers at the river since I could crawl."

"Go for it," he said.

They passed the no-wake zone fronting the eight casinos and continued south. "On the left, just before the beginning of the island—see it? That's my house. Well, I do share it with my sister. In the early morning, before the dam people let the damn water out, you can walk to the island."

"Are you suggesting you can walk on water?"

"Well, almost. The water's only about ankle deep sometimes, which, of course, means that our boat and boat dock are sitting in the mud. Pretty gross. Next, on the right, is the ghost casino."

"Now we have spirits?" Derek said, mocking her every word.

Ignoring his snide remark, Meg continued. "When the banks were folding in the seventies, the builder went belly-up, and thus we have our ugly reminder. Every now and then, someone decides to buy it and finish it, but it doesn't happen. Now it's a refuge for the homeless, coyotes, and other creatures, both bad and good."

Meg glanced over at Derek. She found him attractive, especially in the daylight hours, and she liked his sense of humor. His blond, wavy hair was complemented by his startling blue eyes. *Sinister? Hope not. Sexy? You bet. Great abs; not too much hair on the chest. Probably six-foot-one and looks like he can pump some serious iron. Hmm, the overall picture is not too shabby—and, of course, the mega boat doesn't hurt, either.*

She realized with a shock that he had mistaken the upcoming rippling current as deep water, instead of underlying rocks. "You'll need to swing to port here—er, left here," Meg said.

"There're no boats coming. This looks like a good line," Derek replied, giving her a sharp look. *Bossy bitch*, he thought.

Meg leaned over and firmly turned the boat's wheel to the left. She met with some resistance from him but finally snapped, "Don't be such an ass. There's a huge sandbar straight ahead, and unless you want to redesign the hull of your boat and throw us all overboard, you'll turn left. Damn it."

Derek kicked the throttle and twisted the wheel, sending everyone tumbling in the boat.

"Well, thanks, I guess."

No one talked while the heated exchange cooled down. Approaching the Avi Resort and Casino, the group decided to beach the boat and go swimming. A small, crescent-shaped beach area had been excavated to allow a swimming spot for guests and boaters to anchor and contribute some money to the casinos. The temperature had climbed to 105 degrees, and it was only nine thirty. Beaching the boat, they dashed into the cold water for a quick fix. Derek watched as Meg triumphed in chicken fights and held her own with the Frisbee. After buying more beer and water, they climbed back into the boat, heading south again.

"Mind if I drive for a while?" Meg asked.

"Can you handle my boat OK? I own it with a partner, and he'll be pissed if some strumpet I met screws it up." He laughed.

"Strumpet, indeed. You've been reading too much Shakespeare. I can handle it a lot better than you," Meg said. She bumped him out of the driver's seat with her hip, turned on the exhaust, and yelled at Mike to turn the boat around. Following the new captain's command, Mike headed the boat downstream and quickly crawled onto the swim step as Meg started the engine.

"Everybody set?" Meg yelled. "Away we go." They quickly passed the WWII Veteran's park, the overhead gas line, and slowed at the Needles Bridge to check out the expensive houses on the waterfront. No one talked because of the noise from the engine. Meg was in her element. Every once in a while, she would have to dry the tears from the outer corner of her eyes. Tears of speed, tears of joy—she was in the zone where life had real meaning. Orange County friends would often ask what she saw in the desert, where the temperature sometimes reached 126 degrees. The river was her other family, she would explain, and a speeding boat was her moment in time.

They reached the opening to the gorge, and the striking contrast from flat desert to jagged rising rocks was surprising. Derek leaned over and turned off the engine. "Let's float a while. It's beautiful here."

"Told you so."

The desert disappeared behind them. Now, unfolding in front were the multicolored sheer cliffs, dotted with a few scrub plants and endless clear water. Ancient Indian petroglyphs could be seen near the top of some of the abutments, and a sense of serenity prevailed.

"Only one more part of the tour remains," Meg said. "And here we are."

Around the curve, there appeared a cluster of boats, all sizes and colors, either tied together or beached—a regular regatta. A throng of young bodies scantily clad in bikinis—some with tops and some without—clamored around the volleyball net. Derek yelled, "Now this is more like it."

Twelve or so couples shouted a greeting from the beach, encouraging their participation. It was volleyball time on the sandbar. The current game had started an hour earlier, and the girls were ready for substitutions. Meg beached the boat on an adjoining sandbar, chairs and cooler were shoved onshore, and the crew took sides for a rousing match. Derek encouraged Meg and Paula to play topless, but the girls declined on the basis that they didn't want to make the other girls look bad.

After an hour of volleyball and beer drinking, Meg and Derek called it quits. Everyone agreed it was time to head back to Laughlin.

"Grab your stuff," Meg said as she folded the chairs. "Anyone see my beach bag? I thought I left it here by the cooler."

"Here it is under the beach towels," Derek said as he picked it up and put it in the boat.

As they climbed onboard, he noticed Meg staring at the clouds. "What's up with the weather change?"

"It looks like you might get introduced to our monsoon season tonight. Clouds are really peaking over Havasu."

She didn't want to worry Derek, but she had lived through many monsoon conditions and knew how quickly a disaster could strike. "We'll be OK if we leave now before the winds start. The gorge will protect us for part of the way. We need to be out of the water before it hits. Your boat hasn't got a lot of freeboard."

Reading the clouds was a family tradition. Often, Meg, her mom, and her sisters would sit on their patio and bet how soon the monsoon would hit. Meg knew her clouds and would usually win the bet, much to the feigned chagrin of her mother.

It took over two hours to get back to Laughlin, and by then, Mike, Jerry, and Paula said they were "heat beat" and wanted to call it quits for the day. Derek and Meg looked at each other and said, "Fine," sensing alone time was their mutual desire.

The weary travelers finally reached the grounds of Davis Camp, and the boat was beached and unloaded. The five gave hugs all around and headed toward their cars.

"Did you bring along a change of clothes?"

"Always," said Meg. "Why do you ask? Tired of looking at me in my thong bathing suit?"

"Like that's going to happen," Derek said. "I really don't want to cut the day short, and the casinos get too loud and boring after a while, so…I was thinking if you wanted to take a shower and clean up, then I'll go over to Chili's and get us some dinner. We could eat on the boat until this mysterious monsoon arrives. How does that sound?"

"As a matter of fact, this lady is fully prepared for anything and everything. Sounds like a deal." She studied the clouds forming to the east. "The only problem is this weather. It's really building. Havasu is probably getting their share of wind right now. We've only got about two hours before it breaks loose around here." Throwing caution to the wind, Meg said, "What the hell—let's go for it."

Derek grabbed a towel and sprinted for the men's room. In and out of the shower in a flash, he jumped into his car and drove to Chili's to pick up some takeout.

The public showers at the camp were marginal at best, but Meg was used to camping out, so they didn't bother her. She thought about Derek as she showered. *I think I could like him. Yet, is this another weekend romance with a weekend warrior?* It brought to mind a quote from a long-ago English class: "full of sound and fury, signifying nothing."

The warm water slowly snaked down her body. Her soapy blonde hair tangled past her shoulders, and her breasts tingled in anticipation of the touch from her newfound warrior. *Down, girls. Don't get too excited.*

***

Shade being a premium at the campground, Meg looked around until she found a picnic table under a tree and close to the boat. She looked up as Derek approached. He looked great. Almost squeaky clean. She stood and gave him a quick kiss and asked, "What's for dinner?"

"A surprise, but I think you'll be happy with my choice. Grab your stuff and throw it on the boat." His movements were manly and fluid. She knew she was in romantic trouble.

Meg hesitated. "You know, it's really not a good time to go boating. Besides the winds, we'll have rain and ungodly lightning if we get a full-blown monsoon. Not a good idea at all." Her better judgment was beginning to take over. She walked to the shore, looking for whitecaps.

"Oh, come on. I thought you were the adventurous type. We can go upstream and tie off on the cross rope by the dam. When it starts to get really bad, we'll head back. Maybe take five minutes."

"The dam?" Meg said. She hesitated. *How does he know about the security rope?* "God, you're a madman." She studied the water. Still flat, no wind surges. She could hear her sister spewing out a lecture on caution. "You know, my sister would warn me against going—have a regular shit fit. A stranger in a monsoon." She struggled for a minute. "But, well, OK. We can't anchor there, but we can tie up like you said. If you promise I get the final decision on leaving, then it's OK with me." She grabbed one of the Chili's bags from him. After looking inside, she said, "Oh, great, an Awesome Blossom and Chili burgers. I see you even bought some excellent wine. Wow, what a guy. Let's get this show underway while we can." She raced Derek to the boat with her devil-may-care attitude once again in command.

After attaching the boat to the cross line, they attacked their dinner.

"Nice stemware you have," said Meg as she reached under the transom and pulled out two plastic stem glasses. With a smile, she also found and displayed four condoms, waving them in the air to get Derek's attention.

"Hmm," he said with a sheepish look on his face. "I don't know where those came from. Arnie must have been entertaining without me. Bring the glasses over, and I'll fill your plastic ware with some rare vintage chardonnay, circa today, with an exquisite screw-on cap."

Meg laughed as she put the condoms back into their hiding spot. She engaged in another momentary thought about his potential. *He really hasn't tried anything yet. What a crackup if he were gay—but no way.*

Small gusts of wind caught the boat, tugging it against the temporary mooring. The conversation was going so great that the building monsoon went unnoticed. Background information on the two poured out with the wine, and soon they realized that they had grown up a few miles apart and that their high schools had competed against each other in all the major sports. One glass of wine led to another, and soon, there was a longer pause between each sentence.

The weather turned dark. Meg blinked at the gale-force winds. Whitecaps tossed the ski boat, and the boat strained against the mooring. The rain pounded down, and lightning illuminated the eastern sky. Meg struggled and tried to focus, but now her words seemed like gibberish. She shook Derek.

How could he be asleep? She should start the boat. She fell over his inert body. *Too tired to drive. I'll just rest for a minute.* She pulled herself back to his side and fell into a deep, black cavern.

II

A weekend date was not unusual for Hal and Rachael, but dining at Granny's certainly was. On Saturday nights when they both had time, they would go to Earl's Castle, eat too much, and end up at Lazy Harry's, the local watering hole. Their spat earlier in the day certainly didn't warrant Granny's. The restaurant had a semiformal dress code, so Rachael rummaged through her closet and found her white spaghetti-strap dress. White pumps—no nylons, since it was still 110 degrees—pearls, minimal makeup, and her long brown hair swept up and back completed her look. She finally located the pearl earrings Hal had given her on her birthday.

Rachael hummed to herself while putting the finishing touches on her makeup. She was still a little annoyed at their fight but was attempting an attitude adjustment. It was nice to look in the mirror and see something other than a cop looking back. *God, I really get bitchy sometimes, and how do I get repaid? Dinner at Granny's? Men. Their sense of timing is only compensated by the size of their...oops.* Rachael laughed.

Hal banged on the garage door and walked in. His usual good looks were amplified by the light dinner jacket and open-necked shirt, which allowed for just enough of his deep summer tan to show. He passed the first bedroom and walked into the bathroom, finding Rachael applying her lipstick.

"What's so funny?"

"Oh, nothing. Just getting in the mood for a great date."

"You're a knockout. Turn around, and let's look at the whole package," he said as he grabbed her hand, turned her around, and kissed her on the neck. "Hmm, nice."

"Thanks." *That was almost demure,* she thought. *Where the hell did that come from?*

Since Meg wasn't around and Amanda was at her interview or who knows where the two left for the car without small talk. "Monsoons are coming later," Hal started. "We should be fine for a while. Where the heck is Meg tonight? I thought you'd be keeping a tight grip on her."

"Oh, she's out with the brat pack. I'll start bitching at her next week when the bastard returns."

"God, you'd think she'd be smart enough to worry about this. Oh, hell, Meg is Meg. Given a chance, she'd party through the Holocaust."

They drove on in silence, neither ready to finish the conversation about the serial killer. They both needed a break.

They pulled into valet parking at the Edgewater Hotel and Casino. As usual, the casino was packed with weekend gamblers. The variety always amazed Rachael. First were the locals, who laughed at the weekenders. The smartly dressed women really belonged in Las Vegas, not Laughlin. Then there were the real gamblers, some down on their luck, who were on a marathon binge to win back their losses. With fear in their eyes, they placed their bets.

The smoke lingered heavily in the casino like a thick layer of LA smog, but as Rachael and Hal walked through the crowded casino and climbed the stairs to the restaurant, the air magically cleared and the deafening sound of the slot machines subsided. Hal quickly buttoned his shirt and slid on the required necktie.

Henri, the head waiter, acknowledged the couple as they approached the entrance and seated them at their favorite table, away from the kitchen and entrance. He sensed an importance to the evening, greeted them warmly, and handed them menus. "It's been far too long since I've been able to serve you two. Would you like to hear the specials for the evening?"

Glancing at Rachael, who shook her head, Hal told Henri that they would rather take a few minutes to glance at the menu. Henri nodded and walked away.

"Do you want your favorite, Rachael, or would you like me to surprise you?"

Tempted to order the poached salmon as usual, she decided to play out Hal's fantasy date and allow him to order. "Surprise me," she said, praying he wouldn't order escargot.

Taking charge, Hal motioned to Henri. Consummate waiter that he was, Henri did not have to write anything down.

To Rachael's dismay, Hal started with the escargots Bourguignonne, the Granny's salad, and Chateaubriand for two. *Oh, no.*

"Excellent choice," said Henri. Knowing that the couple never had cocktails before dinner, he continued, "May I suggest a bottle of Caymus Cabernet Sauvignon, say, an o-five, to enhance the dinner?"

Hal gave Henri a smile and thanked him for the suggestion. With all the basics for a perfect meal out of the way, Hal turned his attention back to Rachael. A short silence followed.

Finally, Rachael looked up and with a wry smile asked, "So, what's up?"

"What do you mean?" Feigning ignorance, he continued. "Can't I take my favorite partner out for an elegant night in Laughlin?"

"Hal," she replied, "our nights usually consist of going to Earl's or Applebee's, ordering the special with a carafe of their house wine that comes in a box. While I'm totally flattered and should probably wait until you decide to tell me, I can't. You know how curious I am, so come on. What's up? Did you get a raise or something?"

They both leaned back as Henri appeared with their escargot and uncorked the red wine. Pouring a sample into Hal's glass, he stood back as Hal sipped the wine and gave his nod of approval. The wine was poured.

"Not until we finish our salad. So tell me about Amanda. You mentioned she was in town. What's she up to these days?"

"Who knows? She dropped by the house, unannounced, and she and Meg launched into their usual fight. Luckily, I wasn't there. Why wasn't I there? Gee, let me think. Oh, yeah—a stupid car chase."

Hal shrugged, hoping she wasn't going to go there.

"But maybe that was better. I get tired of playing ringmaster at their bouts. Amanda—well, you know her. I have a feeling she's probably working undercover, but for whom? She's so secretive.

She must have finished her probation at the FBI, but who knows? All the silence and secrecy drives Mom crazy."

"How is Grace? You don't talk much about her these days. Is she OK?"

"Mom? Oh, yeah, always looking for new projects. Publishing her first two books in one year wasn't enough for her, I guess, so she's working on number three. She has a new boyfriend, too, so I hear. No one in the family has met him yet."

"She is a wild one. Is that where Meg gets her off-the-wall genes?"

Hal helped himself to the escargot as they talked. He hadn't noticed that Rachael had yet to take a bite of the several that Henri had dished onto her appetizer plate. Henri appeared with the salads, and with Hal's nod of approval, he left, taking her untouched appetizer plate with him, to Rachael's great relief.

"She is a free spirit, isn't she? Wish I could have a portion of her gusto, but I am what I am. Good old, solid, reliable me."

"Don't sell yourself short, Rach. You're the salt, and Meg—well, not everyone wants pepper all the time."

Rachael was getting uncomfortable with Hal's words. He was being overly attentive. Like a boyfriend. Had he been reading more into their relationship again? Companionship and sex—that was it. That was their agreement. Surely, he wasn't reaching for anything more. They had traveled down that road before.

No encouragement was needed for the two to lunge into their salads. Rachael kept glancing up to see if Hal was ready to resume the conversation. A taste of dread was mixing with the salad dressing.

"Rachael," Hal began, while dabbing his chin with the linen napkin, "you know I love you, although I probably don't say it enough. We've been more than friends and partners for over three years. I'm ready to make a commitment to you—to us." He had wanted to wait until after dinner to talk to her because he wasn't sure how she would react. She would either jump across the table and passionately throw her arms around him, or she would throw the dinner at him.

Not wanting to lose his nerve or momentum, Hal continued. "Rachael, will you be my partner forever? Will you marry me?"

Magically, a ring appeared. The two-carat diamond sparkled in the dim glow of the chandelier and loomed closer and closer to her. Shocked, she gasped and reared back.

Hal jerked in response to her reaction and pulled the ring back toward his plate. He stiffened in his seat and stared at Rachael. Anticipation turned to stunned realization across his face.

"Oh, my God, it's no, isn't it? How could you have led me on like this?" Hal stammered.

Rachael reached for his hand that held the ring, but he yanked it back and shoved the ring in his pocket. "Hal, it's not no. It's—well, it's just I can't marry anyone now. It's not the right time." She knew in her heart that it would never be the right time with him and that their connection, although often sexually and emotionally fulfilling, was not the real thing. But theirs had been a trusting and understanding friendship, far beyond the meaning of those words. Now, all of that had changed with one quick utterance. Their old partnership was not an option now. Rachael knew that. What an idiot. She should have seen this coming and stopped it.

"What the hell was I thinking? Great detective work on my part. I totally misread you, Rachael, damn you." His anger was mounting—anger that Rachael had seen directed at others in the field; anger that she always feared might someday come to be focused on her. The room fell silent, and the other diners quickly tried to center on something other than the scene that was unfolding. Rachael couldn't breathe.

Waving to Henri, Hal pushed his credit card to the edge of the table. "Sorry, we just got a call to go to work."

Henri took the card and was back instantly with the folder and bill. Signing the check, Hal threw his napkin on the table. He stood.

Rachael stood. *Not good...really not good.*

Hal stripped off his necktie as he stormed down the stairs from Granny's. Rachael tried to keep up with him, but her heels slowed her momentum, and she grabbed the handrail to keep from falling.

"For God's sake, Hal, we have to talk about this. Don't be such an ass," she hissed, trying not to project her voice across the casino. Hal continued down the stairs, shoving the tie in his pocket, unbuttoning the top button of his shirt, and finally yanking off his coat. Reaching the door first, he pushed his way through and told the doorman to order a cab.

"We don't need a cab. Please, Hal, we have to deal with this now." She wanted out of this parade of horribles.

A waiting taxi was hailed. Hal gave the driver the address and twenty dollars and shoved Rachael into the backseat. "Yeah, we'll deal with it. Tomorrow, either you or I will transfer to Metro. I don't want you to be my partner anymore. Not now, not ever."

Rachael mumbled something as he slammed the cab door. How could this have happened so quickly? The perfect evening had gone perfectly wrong. *Surely, he will come around,* she thought, but her inner self told her otherwise. It was over. Three years of building this wonderful

73

friendship—this perfect working relationship— was wiped out. Her partner, in every sense, was gone. *How will he handle this? Sarah needs him to lean on during her illness. Now what?*

12

Everything jelled. El Jefe picked the lock on an older SUV parked at the Oasis Casino and reached under the dashboard to hotwire his ride. His youthful training always came in handy, and now, he, a graduate of all things criminal and perverse, managed the task in seconds. He watched her exit the employees' entrance. "Angie, over here," he said as he left the running car to meet her.

How lucky can I get, Angie thought, *finally scoring with someone of significance, for a change.* After her horrible encounter with Beckett minutes ago, she ran to the employees' locker room and found her bottle of tequila. Four shots later, she began to relax as she changed out of her uniform into her backless dress. She knew the bruises from Beckett's violent attack would be showing by tomorrow, but not tonight. Tonight's date didn't have to know about their kinky sex. The two men were friends, so she didn't dare complain.

Before, the ugly, seedy men would always take Angie out after her shift as cocktail waitress. She represented an easy and cheap lay to them, and they represented extra cash to her—money she needed to help raise her son. But tonight, fortune had smiled her way. Tonight's date—handsome, close to rich, and definitely well-known—was going to change her life. Wow. She couldn't wait to share the news with her girlfriends.

"Hi, there," Angie said. She staggered. "Glad to see ya. Where's your hot car? Where ya wanna go?"

He knew small talk in the parking lot was dangerous since he might be recognized. Her intoxication was going to make the job easier. The monsoon, ready to unleash its mighty force, was an integral part of his plan, so he grabbed her as she walked up and said, "How about a kiss to get started?"

Surprised by the offer, Angie cooperated, watching his dark eyes. Just like in the movies. "You got it," she said, pressing her mouth to his.

Once their lips parted, he held onto her and steered her into the passenger seat of the SUV. "Buckle up; we're going for a little ride before the monsoon hits. Have you ever seen Davis Dam during the storm? It's magical."

"Sounds kind of freaky to me. Are you sure it's safe to drive there during the storm?"

"It's fine. It'll give us a chance to be alone. You'll love it."

Angie twitched. Her mental vision of their date was veering off course. First, the kiss was totally unexpected and didn't fit the gossip she'd heard about him. She expected suave, not forward. But her excitement over the prospects for the evening overcame her usual street smarts. *Oh, well. Might as well go with the flow.* She swallowed her concerns and nestled back into the passenger seat.

El Jefe drove the SUV to the signal. He took a right on Casino Drive and then another right across the Laughlin Bridge just as the first light rain started falling. Next came the wind, strong enough to move the bridge, as the SUV continued on its course. Left on the 95 and another left toward the dam. He turned off the asphalt road to a secluded spot overlooking the portion of the lake called Katherine's Landing. Whitecaps were cresting on the normally flat surface of the lake. Lightning appeared on the eastern horizon somewhere near Lake Havasu, and the wind increased to an intense crescendo.

"God, it's glorious. I could spend hours here, waiting for the storm to hit. The pure anger vitalizes me." He paused. He needed intel from Angie but didn't want to spook her. "Oh, by the way, there's some talk in town that I wanted to run past you."

"What's that?" Angie said. She wanted to light up a cigarette but thought her date would object. Her hands were getting jittery in her lap. She started sliding her sapphire ring around in circles to release some of the tension.

"Word has it that you know something about the illegal immigrants being dropped off here at the river by seaplane. Any truth to that?"

Angie pulled a few inches away from him and sucked in a silent breath. Her eyes focused on the river, not willing to look at him. She knew the penalty for talking out-of-school in this town but really didn't think that this man posed any threat because of who he was.

"Have you been talking to Beckett? That son of a bitch is such a letch. I don't know anything other than what everyone talks about. Like maybe he's laundering some money for the Mexican mafia? Don't know for a fact—just gossip." She took a breath and glanced at him.

"Yes, go on."

"I really need to look for a new job. He doesn't treat me like a lady when I go up to his penthouse. He's got the manners of a toad, and his Johnson is crooked, too." She laughed nervously. She realized her ranting was dangerous and decided to shut up. Maybe he thought Beckett was a creep, too.

Her date reached in the backseat for something.

"Whatcha looking for?" asked Angie.

"Oh, I brought along some booze. Wanna drink?"

"Sounds good. It's been a long day, and I could use a stiff one." She smiled her best three-dollar smile, slid her hand across his lap, and hoped he might pick up on the hidden meaning. Nothing there.

Laughing at her apparent attempt at humor, the man reached into the black medical bag stowed in the backseat. He found the hypodermic needle and, with only a slight move toward Angie, thrust the needle into her neck. She gave a temporary jerk. The ketamine took effect instantly, and Angie fell limp against his shoulder. *Oh, such a wonderful drug*, he thought. Little leftover residue in the bloodstream, can be given intramuscularly, and takes effect immediately. He smiled at the simplicity of it all. Those semesters in premed certainly were paying off. Such an effortless plan, and he was the best in his field. El Jefe…never a mistake. With the dosage he had administered, he had only a few minutes before the medication would wear off. Hustling, he prepared for the next step.

No guards were visible on the stretch of road between the dam and the spillway. Their usual means of transportation, a Cushman cart, was garaged because of the storm. Using his newly acquired card, El Jefe slipped it into the lock, and the heavy door began to open. He steered the SUV through the employee parking lot and onto the gravel and then dirt surface close to the precipice of the spillway. The raging storm dropped visibility to twenty feet. Again, no guards. Everything was working. He'd checked the newspaper and knew the generators would be coming "on line," releasing one unit of water. That would be forty-five hundred cubic feet per second, and when the spillway was opened, any evidence of the crime would be washed away.

Parking close to the spillway, El Jefe quickly opened the passenger door to remove Angie's relaxed body and, with a bit of effort, rolled her on her back. The sizzle of her bare skin coming in contact with the hot hood of the SUV excited him. He strapped diver's weights around her ankles and waist as the first bolt of lightning struck to the east. The weights were untraceable since he had stolen them off a diving boat in Santa Cruz, his last hometown. *People should be more careful with their equipment*, he thought. *They make it too easy.*

The rain pelted down, stinging his face. He picked up Angie. Her black mascara was beginning to run down her rain-soaked face. He kissed her forehead. *There, you old crow, you ugly old hag—a kiss good night. How could you believe I wanted a date? Have fun on the way down.* With that, El Jefe heaved Angie's now struggling body over the slanted spillway. He loved this part. He enjoyed inflicting pain. It stimulated him sexually. Angie screamed on the way down, the effects of the ketamine wearing off. The scream only added to his sexual pleasure. "Scream, you bitch. Let the world know what happens when someone screws with El Jefe."

Angie's arms and legs flailed. She looked like she was trying to climb the wind. He imagined her skin scraping back, her neck snapping, the breaking of bones, her nose and eyes launching off in different directions, and finally, at the bottom of the two-hundred-foot spillway, her plunge into a cold, watery grave.

Checking his watch, he realized it was time for the water release and for his departure.

Satisfied that he had disposed of any possible evidence, he returned to the SUV. To complete the perfect crime, he reversed his driving pattern and parked the car back at the casino.

Before abandoning the car, he leaned back and closed his eyes. No more Angie. Life was good. He envisioned the next few days. First, he would dispose of Melissa's body and kidnap his new love. The thought brought another erection, which quickly softened because, of course, there was still Carlos to contend with. El Jefe wiped down the car of prints. His exit was erased by the monsoon.

SUNDAY, JULY 28

"I got a phone call from the dark one, Beckett," said Len as he entered the office.

Beckett glanced at his watch. It was almost one in the morning. Not a good sign. "What the hell did he want?" replied Beckett.

"He was using that weird voice box. Said to tell you to relax. Angie won't be talking to anyone. Said for you to be more careful."

"Pretentious bastard. Any problems?" asked Beckett. "How'd he handle it? Give her some cash to leave?"

"Something a little more permanent."

"Shit, did he kill her? He didn't need to kill her, for God's sake. She had a kid. What the hell does permanent mean?"

Len knew that El Jefe considered Beckett a wimp, incapable of making the hard decisions. A slap on the wrist would have been punishment enough in his eyes. He was only tolerated because El Jefe needed his casino for the Mafia's overnight stay—and also because of his connection with Carlos.

"She was drinking and slipped over the spillway."

"What do you mean, the spillway? What was she doing there?" Beckett internalized the remark and finally said, "I just checked the recording for the Davis Dam. They aren't going to release any water until nine o'clock in the morning. It was supposed to be tonight. They changed it because of the monsoon. Is that going to be a problem? Did he consider that?"

"Don't know. That's all he said, except I'm supposed to let Elliott know, too." Len realized that the water release might be an integral part of the overall plan. El Jefe had lied to him when he said, "No problem." The situation had to be completed at that precise hour in order to work for the monsoon rain to cover up any trace or forensics on the spillway. El Jefe said it was handled, but was it?

14

Camp Davis was a complete mess as a result of the monsoon. It looked like a war zone. Campers were out of their tents and trailers early, trying to find their lawn chairs, coolers, and tarps that had been blown around by the wind.

"Come on, Harry. Get a move on it before the rest of the weekend idiots get out there and screw up the water. I want a chance to wakeboard before it looks like the Atlantic Ocean," yelled Sue, his wife.

"OK, already. Unhook the bow and get your rope ready. Jeez, you're a pain in the ass. Who's going to observe?"

Sue looked around and located her kid brother, Randy, munching on a Hot Pocket.

"Get over here, Randy. We need an observer," Sue said. Seeing his frown, she yelled, "Don't be such a brat. You're not doing anything. Get your butt over here."

Randy sauntered over, put on his water shoes, and waded into the river. "Crap, it's cold," he muttered.

"Quit being such a baby," Sue said as she tried to untangle the ski rope. "This is the wrong rope. Where's the single handle?" she yelled at Harry.

"In the bow of the boat," he snarled, still working on the anchor tie-down. "This rope is all screwed up, too." He decided that next time, they would buy a better anchor and a quick-release latch for the bow. This setup, along with his family's attitude, was a pain in the ass to deal with. Following the line underwater, his hand ran into something that was tangling the anchor hookup. Muttering profanities under his breath, he dove headfirst into the chilly water to locate the problem.

He came up spewing river water and screaming. "Holy shit, Sue! Holy shit!" He shrieked again as he ran out of the water. "There's a body down there. Call the cops."

15

Last night's fiasco with Hal haunted Rachael. She dreaded making the first phone call. On top of that, Melissa's body was due to appear, and her department would be on full tactical alert all day waiting for the Heart Collector to strike again. The serial killer had picked up that nickname along the way. His victims' hearts were always removed before he returned them to the city.

Passing by Meg's room, she noticed the door was ajar. Interesting. Sunday was always Meg's morning to sleep in, and the door was never open. She peeked in, hoping her sister was awake so they could discuss last night's disaster, but Rachael was surprised to find the bed empty. It hadn't been slept in. Who had Meg been out with yesterday? Where were they going?

Meg always called Rachael when she was going to stay out the whole night, but she hadn't this time.

Concerned about Meg's timing, Rachael continued on toward the kitchen. Meg was a big girl with an insatiable appetite for fun. She had probably partied all night with her friends and would end up at the IHOP for breakfast. When the coffee was ready, Rachael poured a steaming cup and opened the slider to see what a beautiful morning of ninety degrees had to offer. The river water was really low. The buoy was sitting on top of the mud, and Rachael knew no water was coming down from the spillway just by looking at the minimal flow. The mud flats looked like brown polka dots poking up through the shallow water. *I hope the dam releases some water today*, she thought. *The weekenders will be furious if they don't have any water to play in.*

On most mornings, she could walk in ankle-deep water to the small island in front of her house. Later in the day, according to downstream demand, calculated amounts of water would be released. It took an hour and fifteen minutes for the water to leave the dam and arrive at her beachfront. This was always the fun part of knowing the system. Guests would ask, "How long before we get water today?" and Rachael would call the recording at the dam, calculate the time, and tell them to come back from the island by a certain time if they expected to walk.

Shading her eyes as she stepped onto the balcony, she saw a boat teetering on the mud flats. *Oh, for Pete's sake. What idiot is stuck on that sandbar? Guess they weren't smart enough to come in out of the monsoon.* She picked up the phone and called the Bureau of Reclamation and heard that two units of water were going to be released at nine o'clock, followed by three units at eleven. That would be plenty of water to float the boat. Water should arrive around ten thirty, she calculated. She decided to wade out and see if there was any identification.

Changing to a pair of cut-off shorts and a tank top, Rachael sidled down the iron staircase adjacent to her upper patio, coffee in hand. She headed for the scuttled boat.

"Hey, boat. Anyone aboard?" she called.

She approached the boat from the stern and stepped up on the swim step, pausing to wash off her mucky water shoes. *Nice boat*, she thought. She stopped abruptly when she saw two bodies slumped on the floor. The second look chilled her to the core.

Rushing to the still form, she cried, "Meg, Oh, my God, Meg. What happened?" She immediately felt her neck, looking for a pulse. She grabbed Meg with both hands and turned her over, inspecting the back of her head. No sign of trauma, thank God.

Meg started to stir. She tried to shade her eyes from the morning sun and pulled back from

Rachael. Her attempt to sit up was unsuccessful, but she finally focused and peered at her sister in surprise. She acted woozy and incoherent.

Rubbing her eyes, she slurred, "What the hell you doing here, sis? Trying to mess up my love life?" She glanced over and saw Derek lying prone on the deck. "Is he dead?" She squinted. Realizing her situation, asked, "How did we get here?"

Rachael leaned over Derek's prone body and felt for a pulse. "He's just out. What the hell happened, Meg? Who is this guy? What the hell are you doing on a sandbar at sunrise? You knew the monsoon was coming last night. Were you out on the water? You know better than that."

"Hey, slow down." Her tongue was thick, and words were hard to form. "The last thing I remember, we were in his boat, hooked up to the tether line."

"By the dam? You idiot."

"We were having dinner and bottle of wine." Her words were incoherent. "Dale, no, Derek was watching the weather, just like I was. I remember… what do I remember? Oh, being tired. I closed my eyes for a minute. Next thing I know, I'm here."

"Think about it, Meg. Anything else?"

"I remember the wind came, and the rain. I knew we should leave, but, jeez, Rachael, I couldn't do anything about it."

"Were you drunk?"

"No. Two glasses of wine, maybe. Then, nothing."

Rachael checked Derek for injuries, but nothing was apparent. Turning back to Meg, she gave her a quick look over. "This is too bizarre. I'll call the EMTs and have someone come and check you out. They can help you pull the boat up to our beach." She opened her cell phone and punched in the private number for the water patrol.

Meg slumped back and rested on the seat. Trying to focus her eyes and thoughts was difficult. She looked at Derek but was too tired to go to him.

"Hey, Steve, I've got a weird situation and need someone to come over and take a look with me. Maybe have to dust for prints and tox screen? It's my kid sister and some guy who are stranded in their boat on a sandbar by the island."

"Hey, Rach, can't do. Just got a call from Davis Camp. There's a DB there. Think that one takes priority."

"A floater?"

"No. From the call, it sounds like this body has been torn apart. ID is going to be tough. The face is all mangled. It's a woman—that's all I know."

"Have you called Hal yet?"

"No. Do you want to call him instead?"

Rachael thought for a minute. "No, you go ahead. I'll go directly to the scene. Tell him that, OK?"

Turning to Meg, Rachael said, "Call Gus at the fire department. Have him send an EMT over to check you two out. Get out of the boat without touching anything else, if possible. Wear your water shoes. You're in the worst part of the muck. Davis Camp has a dead body. Gotta go." With that, Rachael eased herself off the swim step into the watery slime.

"Sorry, sis," Meg yelled. "Don't know how this happened." She looked back at Derek, who was beginning to show signs of life. "Great date, huh?"

***

Traffic was light on the 95, and within a few minutes, Rachael was pulling into the entrance of Davis Camp. The camp was filled with summer vacationers wandering around and bitching about the lack of river water. Some were in tents, but because of the sizzling temperatures in July, most had large RVs with air-conditioning. Twenty boats were moored offshore, along with a smattering of Sea-Doos. The fortunate families that had escaped the monsoon unscathed were enjoying the early morning, eating pancakes and sipping coffee with their temporary neighbors. Rachael was surprised that there wasn't an undercurrent of excitement regarding the body. As she drove to the guard gate, she smiled at Ron manning his station.

"Hey, Ron. Heard you have a little excitement. Thanks for keeping it under wraps. Where's the body?"

"It's pretty gruesome, Rachael. I've seen worse in my time, but not by much. Hey, before you go…" Ron came out of the booth. "When I opened this morning, I found Meg's car here, but no Meg. Everything OK?"

"Short version: She ended up on the sandbar by our house. Strange boat. Strange guy. Go figure."

Ron gave Rachael directions to the uppermost part of the camp. Larger RVs, and the commuter seaplane that landed on the river every weekday, usually occupied this area. This location was prime and a little more isolated from the general camp. Accommodations included all necessary hookups and a modern shower and bath for the campers. Sandy beaches offered a perfect playground for the smaller children and instant access to waterskiing and floating for the older generation. The spot was less than a mile from the dam and spillway.

As Rachael approached, she saw a flurry of activity. Two blue-and-white squad cars were nosed into the area, and the coroner's van had also preceded her. She stepped out of her car, catching a glimpse of Hal coming down the dirt roadway. Putting last night out of her mind, she headed for the yellow crime tape and slipped under.

Pete Perez caught up with her and said, "God, Rachael, this is really raspy. Looks like someone either beat the shit out of her or ran over her a bunch of times with their propeller. Really nasty."

"Any ID yet?" asked Rachael.

"God, no," Pete replied. "We might be able to get prints off her, but nothing else. Her face looks like a peeled lobster."

The ME had been doing a cursory exam and nodded to Rachael as she approached. "I'll have my hands full with this one."

Rachael had been exposed to dead bodies for years. Usually, it was the kids that bothered her the most, but this body was an exception. Part of the vic's scalp had been torn off, showing her skull, while the opposite side of the head oozed with gray matter seeping from her brain. One eye was missing; the other was still connected but idly dangling from the rectus muscle. The woman had witnessed life through green eyes at one time. There was something oddly familiar about the corpse, but Rachael couldn't pinpoint it. Maybe it was the eye. She felt that she had looked into that eye. Somewhere, they had crossed paths.

The nose was stuck to some bone fragments next to her ear. Only one ear. The face seemed to vanish into mush after the nose. No lips or chin. From the neck down was a tangle of bones attached by some muscle or ligaments. One breast implant was still in place; the other was missing, with only a hole remaining. Compound fracture of legs, one arm missing, clothes in shreds. Rachael bit her lip and could only fight back the anger. Who could have mutilated another human being like this? Overkill.

"Jesse," Rachael addressed the ME. "Can you tell how long she's been in the water?"

"From the looks of it, I'd say she's been dead about six to eight hours. Hard to pin it down because of the water temperature. She's somewhat bloated, too. I'll know more when I finish the autopsy."

Rachael called Ron at the guard station. "Call the Bureau of Reclamation and ask them not to release any water from the dam. Tell 'em we'll explain later, but get Search and Rescue up to the spillway before any water goes over. Our vic had to have been thrown from up there. There's no other explanation. We'll need two guys to rappel down for hair and fibers. Send CSI to the spillway and dam area. Look for tire marks and trace evidence at the top of the spillway. Get someone to cover your post and meet me. Hurry, before they start generating."

Hal joined the scene. "We'll need our patrol boat here to check the float lines across the bottom of the spillway. Let's get a diver out there, too. Check the catch basin. I think you're right. She must have been tossed off the spillway last night during the monsoon. Son of a bitch."

Rachael turned to measure Hal's expression. Intense and professional. There was serious carryover from last night. "Look, Meg and some guy were out here last night, apparently hooked up to the tether line crossing the spillway. They washed up on a sandbar in front of our house sometime during the night. I wonder if there's any connection."

Hal gave Rachael a glancing smirk. "Ya think?" He chose to disregard her comments and headed toward the ME instead.

Walking over to a small group of boaters, Rachael asked, "Are any of you the owners of this boat connected to the homicide?"

Harry was quick to push forward. "Yes, little lady, I'm the one who found her." He smiled a toothy grin and waited expectantly.

"I'm really sorry to spoil your weekend, sir, but unfortunately, your propeller, tie-downs, and anchor will have to be confiscated as part of the ongoing investigation."

"The hell, you say. I'm on vacation. You might as well take the whole damn boat, trailer and all," he yelled, turning red.

Rachael turned as Ron approached. "Full cooperation here. I like that. Get his trailer, and pull the boat out of the water. Use gloves. Don't let anyone touch it, and call the guys at the impound yard to come and pick it up."

"Screw you, lady. Nobody touches my boat."

All 230 pounds, six foot two inches of manhood moved in. "I think the officer is asking for your cooperation. Do you have a problem with that?" asked Ron.

The situation was quickly defused.

Rachael made a note to follow up with Colleen at the Reclamation Department to find out when the last water had gone over the spillway and get an exact temperature to help the ME with time of death. She would also need a record of everyone who had used their access in the last twenty-four hours. This could narrow down the number of suspects. Colleen would have the answers for her within an hour. Efficiency was her middle name.

Today was July 28; in two days, Melissa's body was supposed to appear. Coincidence? Could this be Melissa? No, Rachael felt sure this was not the woman the killer had kidnapped almost a year ago. He was meticulous with his timing. Despite all of the vic's missing body parts, the heart was still in place. The serial killer always removed the heart before leaving the victim to be found by the terrorized town.

She knew the answers would come. Right now, she had to deal with Hal and this scene—and also find out what was going on with Meg and her new boyfriend. While Meg could sometimes act like an airhead, she was usually a responsible person when it came to the river. Usually.

16

Taking the elevator from his penthouse to the casino floor, Beckett started on his morning rounds, checking with his floor managers, pit bosses, and security personnel. Since the hotel rooms were totally booked, he anticipated a huge profit for this weekend. The monsoons had actually driven people indoors, particularly the less hardy campers, so the owners should be pleased with the return. Soon, the boating season would be over, and the snowbirds would arrive. They never gambled as much, but it was enough to keep the casino afloat. In spring, the city would host the Harley Davidson fiasco, and then on it went with the summer crowd again.

Beckett's thought process was interrupted upon returning to his office when he noticed movement across the river. Squinting to capture a more accurate picture, his gaze settled on Davis Camp. Picking up the intercom, Beckett called Leonard. "What the hell is going on at Davis Camp? There must be ten cop cars over there."

"Gossip is they found a body. A floater. No ID, apparently, but it was a woman," said Leonard.

"Get your ass up here now," Beckett demanded.

Flipping on the TV, he tuned to Channel 42. Elliott Spencer, the network news pundit, had just started hyping the morning news.

"Another floater has been found in the river. When are these crazy weekenders going to get smart and not drink and drive boats? Oh, our on-the-spot reporter just called in, and I might be a little off on this one. Looks like a suicide or murder. The only information we have right now is that it's a woman. We'll be in touch with Bullhead police and follow up.

"One other item of local interest, since we're discussing dead women. It's time for the return of our local serial killer. We need to give him a name. Some say that he'll be moving on to another city after he delivers last year's victim to the police, so everyone, mark your calendar. If the killer is on schedule, our femme fatale will mysteriously reappear—dead, of course—on July thirtieth, which is—guess what?—only two days from now. Maybe I'll have a contest. If the winner picks out the spot where she'll be deposited, they can volunteer to be this year's prey. Too gory? I think the whole thing is a bunch of police propaganda, anyway. What a way to keep us lining their coffers with taxpayer dollars." He was winding down his typical inflammatory monologue now. Anything to boost the ratings, which kept his pockets lined as well. "You know if it's news, we'll report it. That's all for this morning. See you on the afternoon show."

Beckett reached for the phone. When the network secretary answered, he said, "Beckett here. Gimme Elliott."

"Hey, Beckett, how's it hanging?" said Elliott.

"I just tuned in. What do you know about the floater at Davis Camp?"

Elliott fought the instinct to call Beckett a stupid fool. "How the hell should I know? I got the same call from Len you did. Might be El Jefe's answer to the Angie problem. Why are you so concerned?"

"I just wanted to know if you heard anything else. This is totally fucked up. I told Len to take care of her, but now Jefe's involved. I meant to pay her off and put her on a bus. He's such a damn liar. Is this Angie's body?"

"Shit, how do I know? Doesn't make any difference now. If it is, then the problem's solved. Just drop it."

Beckett didn't like what he was hearing but decided to let it go. He was on the verge of ending the relationship with Elliott. Always drawn by the money, he glanced at the computer, which showed his bulging offshore account. During a drinking bout with Elliott, Beckett had shared small details of his business arrangements with the Mafia. Once sober, he realized his mistake. That had been months ago, and there had been no repercussions. Later, Elliott had disclosed that he, too, was working with El Jefe. Beckett was feeling the walls close in on him.

Beckett knew now that he should have asked more questions when El Jefe needed a small money-laundering job handled through the casino. It was supposed to be simply a place for his clients to hole up for a few days. The penthouse was always available to them at a premium price, and there was no need to register. An envelope with cash was waiting for Beckett when the men left.

"So, just what is my job?" Beckett had asked.

The modulated voice had replied, "When the seaplane lands, you will be notified. Your driver will take the passengers to your casino. They are to be treated as VIPs but with little fanfare. Take them to Las Vegas, and within the week, pick them up and reverse their travel arrangements."

"And why would I want to do this?"

"Money is always a good reason for actions. An account will be opened in the Bahamas. Your name will be on it."

After the first trial operation, there was no turning back. The money was beyond Beckett's anticipation with little effort on his part. That was then. Now, more was expected of him. The seaplane would now make two landings a week. Beckett was not told about the other cargo, but Carlos knew.

When he realized that black-market body parts were also being transported, Beckett froze. Where were they coming from? Of course, he knew, pedestrians on the streets of Mexico supplied the answer.

I can't keep doing this, Beckett thought. *Bringing attention to the casino is exactly why the bosses will kill me.* The operation was small, but El Jefe was pushing him to increase the amount of money to be traded, along with the frequency of the visitors. How deeply was the Mexican mafia involved? Maybe it was time to reconsider the partnership. If the owners of the casino were tipped off about his money laundering, he would be toast. This worry was consuming more of his waking hours. Yes, the risk may not be worth it anymore.

After finishing the conversation with Beckett, Elliott called Leonard. "What the hell is going on across the river? Beckett just called me, all nervous about that body. Is it Angie? You said El Jefe would take care of her. No body, no worry. Who screwed up?"

"I'm trying to reach him. He never screws up. It can't be Angie 'cause if he killed her, they'd never find her body. Maybe it's that Melissa chick. I'll find out and call you. And what about the illegals that're supposed to arrive? If you don't want them, I've got to call off the plane and vans."

"Give them another landing site. Go upstream from Katherine's Landing. Tell Carlos to lie low; the cops are still looking for him. I may have to get another driver for the van pickup. How many will be on board this time?"

"Six, but one's a kid," Leonard replied. "And we got container boxes again."

"You're pushing it, Len. Three was going to be the max. That plane is only set up for four passengers. I'm looking into buying a seaplane, maybe larger, and going out on my own. Jefe keeps pulling us into deeper shit, and I don't like it. Like those body parts. I'm happy with the money laundering and illegals. Screw El Jefe, and screw Beckett, too."

"That's bad talk, Boss. Beckett's too paranoid to complain if he gets dumped by you. But, jeez, El Jefe is mean and don't like nobody messin' with his business. He'll kill you—and me, too, if we cross him."

"Nobody's that tough."

"Look, I'll need two weeks if you want to do this by yourself. I have to find some new coyotes. They'll want more money if we're going to cross El

Jefe. Every coyote knows he's the devil. Maybe we should wait."

Elliott was tired of the argument. "OK for now, but let me know on the Angie thing. Call back with the exact illegal count and the arrival time. I'll make arrangements with the hospital in Henderson for the body parts. Beckett doesn't know about the containers, does he?"

"Not from me. I keep my mouth shut."

17

By the time Rachael and Hal finished analyzing their part of the crime scene, the crowd was dispersing and starting on their busy day of boating and drinking like nothing had happened. The sun had slipped through the clouds and was now casting a horrific stream of heat. All remnants of the monsoon had passed. As Rachael left the campground, she called Meg's cell phone, looking for an update on their boat situation.

"When are they sending water through the dam? The recording says nine o'clock, and nothing is happening," Meg said. "We can't get Derek's boat to float without water."

"Calm down. What's happened so far?"

"The patrol was here but can't help us move it. Crap, what a mess. Derek's got to leave and head back to LA. You know, some people have to work for a living."

"I'm afraid that's not going to happen. Did the medics get a blood sample from both of you yet? You know it has to be done now. I'm not altogether convinced that the murder at the dam and your mishap aren't somehow connected."

"What do you mean?"

"We'll talk about it later. Leave the boat where it is, don't touch anything else, and drive to the precinct. We'll take your statements."

"Oh, great," Meg said. Covering her mouth so Derek couldn't hear this part of the conversation, she continued, "Sis, I really kind of like this guy. What are the chances of him showing up on my doorstep again when I tell him he's got to give it up for the police department?"

"Can't be helped. Be there in a half hour," Rachael said and closed the cell phone.

Turning to Derek, Meg shrugged and said, "Want to play cops and robbers with me?"

They were still sitting in the stranded boat, the full sun now beating down on them. Both agreed that they felt a little strung out—almost like a hangover, but not exactly. Not being used to the desert weather, Derek said, "I'd do anything to get out of this heat. When is the water coming down?"

"Rachael said there's going to be an investigative team at the spillway, so they can't send any water down until after Search and Rescue does their thing. It could be hours."

"Then let's abandon this sinking ship and head up to your house. Hopefully, you have air-conditioning. I'd like to take a shower, too."

They collected their personal items, crawled over the transom onto the swim step, and jumped. The mucky water came up to meet them. "Glad we have our water shoes. It's about one foot of water and two feet of squish here."

They trudged their way across the hundred-foot expanse and were glad to meet up with the sandy beach. They took turns hosing off before they ascended the stairway.

"Just a second, and I'll unlock the slider," Meg said as she fished in her beach bag. "That's strange. My house keys are missing. Not to worry—we have a key hidden by the gas meter for such emergencies. Hang on. I'll go around and let you in from inside."

"Hurry." Derek was feeling the effects of the sun and last night's disaster. Hanging out with Meg had been more trouble than anticipated. When she reappeared, he took in a full breath of cool air. "God, it must be a hundred and ten already. OK if I take a shower first?"

"No problem," Meg said. "Clean towels are on the baker's rack next to the shower. Use the hall bathroom. We keep that one clean just in case we get stranded on sandbars all night with handsome strangers," she added with an impish laugh.

Derek grabbed her arm as she walked by. "You are some outrageous broad, my Megan girl. Is there nothing that upsets you?"

"Since you asked, yes. I didn't even score a good-night kiss last night. At least, I don't think I did. I had big plans for you, handsome. And now look at us. We had a glass of wine and then both passed out for eight hours. Lightweights, huh?"

He pulled her close, but she pulled away from him.

"Hmmm, guess I read you wrong," Derek said. "Do you think maybe I could make up for some lost time? I have depositions asserting that I'm a pretty good kisser."

"First, I have to go back to the boat. I can't figure out where my keys are, and the security pass to the dam is with them. I'll be up shit creek if I lost them. Last time I remember seeing them was when we were playing volleyball at the gorge. I tucked them away in the bottom of my beach bag so they wouldn't fall out. Did you see anyone messing around with my stuff?" Meg rattled on, not giving Derek an opportunity to answer. "After I find them, I'll be a second in the shower, brush my teeth and hair, and then…well, then, you'd better watch out." She headed back to the stranded boat.

Searching the boat didn't take long as there weren't too many places for a set of keys to hide. When she didn't find them, Meg reached for her cell phone. "Hey, sis. We may have a problem. Does that dead body involve the dam for sure?"

"Looks to me like she was thrown over the spillway during the monsoon last night. Why?" Rachael said.

"My pass to the dam is missing. Damn. I had it yesterday morning when we launched the boat and when we were playing volleyball, but I haven't seen it since. My house keys were on the same set. I really didn't miss them until I tried to get in. God, I'm going to get fired for this."

"Don't get paranoid, Meg. I'll call the guys at the dam and have them check to see if your pass was used last night. In the meantime, come down to the office ASAP. We really need to see if someone drugged you and what's-his-name last night."

"What's-his-name is Derek," snapped Meg, "and I like him. I promised him a good time before he had to leave for LA, and that didn't include a blood test. A girl can't even catch a break."

"Sorry, sis. Don't be such a baby. It's a police investigation now. Get your butt down here," said Rachael.

Meg kicked the side of the boat and slammed her phone shut. "Shit."

Derek looked ruggedly handsome wrapped only in a towel when he reappeared in the living room. Water trailed down his neck. He walked to Meg. "Your turn, gorgeous. I left lots of hot water for you, but guess you don't really need hot water here with the temperature what it is," he said with a laugh.

"Thanks. I'll take a shower, but, oh shit, I guess you might as well put on your clothes. The Tarzan-Jane towel scene just got interrupted."

"What?" Derek drawled. "It took untold minutes wrapping this towel just right to turn you on. Should I flash you now? Guaranteed you'll like what you see."

"Has to be later. We might be involved in a murder case. My sister, Rachael—the one you met earlier—is a detective with the Bullhead Police. There was a body found by Davis Camp, and someone may have stolen my pass to get to the dam last night. Since we can't account for our whereabouts last night, we have to go in and give the PD a statement."

"Now?" Derek asked.

"Now," Meg said. She grabbed him around the neck and gave him a long, passionate kiss. Her hands slid down his back and onto the soaking towel. After feeling his strong butt, she grabbed his towel and raced down the hall to the bathroom. "First peek looked good" she yelled.

"Smart ass," Derek yelled back as he watched her dash into the bathroom. He walked outside onto the balcony, buck naked, to check on the boat and considered the fact that he hadn't been completely honest with Meg. It might not be the best discussion topic for later—if there was going to be a later.

The water patrol arrived and was on his boat to collect fingerprints, bag the wine bottle, and the rest of the trash. Seeing them, Derek quickly ducked back into the house and put on his shorts. No need to get arrested for indecent exposure along with whatever else was going on. Derek went out again as the cops collected the remains of the Awesome Blossom and trash from Chili's. *What a friggin' mess. Dating this girl might prove to be more trouble than it's worth.* And, of course, since he was already involved at the moment, he realized that Meg might be more trouble than a fling would entail.

The patrol yelled at Derek and said they would also need the clothes he and Meg were wearing, along with their swimsuits and water shoes. He waved an acknowledgement and made a quick call on his cell. "I have a problem. Might not be able to get home for a while."

Initially, he had perceived Meg to be an easy date, a potential one-night stand on this Laughlin weekend. But after spending the day with her, his opinion changed. She seemed bright, articulate, and excessively fun. Being gorgeous didn't hurt, either, but currently not in the market for a relationship, Derek decided to cool it and officially drop Meg when she had finished her shower. She had served her purpose.

As Derek waved to the cops leaving in their patrol boat, he was oblivious to Meg's presence. Coughing loudly as she stepped up behind him, she caught his attention. Derek froze when he saw her. Her tasseled, wet hair hung past bare shoulders.

"You're naked," Derek said.

"You noticed." Meg laughed. "It was only fair since I got a peek at you." She darted down the hall again, leaving wet footprints in her trail.

I may have to revise my thinking, Derek thought. She was breathtaking.

A taxi picked up the two, and on their way back to Davis Camp, they had time to input their cell phone numbers into each other's phones. Meg's car was found intact at the camp. She used the hidden key under the fender to open the car door. Her attempts to pay for overnight parking fell on deaf ears. Ron gave her a hug and said, "No way would you pay. We're just glad you're all right. Had us all worried."

Meg drove her Mini Cooper through the gate and, tossing a wave to Ron, headed across the bridge to the Oasis Casino to pick up Derek's SUV.

"After you check out of your room, come to the police department in Bullhead," she told him.

"Here's a map on the back of this envelope. Sorry to be such a pest. My sister has some questions about last night. They may have to take fingerprints to eliminate yours on the boat."

"My partner's prints will be there, too, plus God knows how many others. What's the point?" Derek asked.

Meg looked at him quizzically. "Any problem with submitting your prints? What, are you the serial killer or something?" She pulled the car to a quick stop at the casino entrance.

Derek smiled. "No problem. But you know, if you hadn't run down the hall so fast a few minutes ago, I could have been a serial rapist. You have one fine body."

"Glad you noticed." Meg gave him a quick kiss good-bye. "Maybe we can discuss that this afternoon. I might let you look for my tattoo. It's tiny. See ya," she said as she drove off in her sexy convertible.

Derek rushed to his room. He packed his overnight bag. He considered wiping down the bathroom counter and phone but hastened to the cashier to pay his bill instead. Time was not on his side. He needed to get back to Orange County.

"Hope you enjoyed your stay at the Oasis, Mr. Turner," the clerk said.

"Not exactly the weekend I had planned," he replied.

Derek hadn't used valet parking, so he headed for his SUV. Where had he parked it last night? Clicking the alarm button, he was surprised to find his car parked halfway up the hill, pointed toward the river. *That's strange.* Derek threw the bags into the rear seat and headed south on Casino Drive. *Four hours until I get home. Better call the firm and let them know I'll be late for the deposition.*

18

"Hi, Hal," Meg called as she entered the police department. Hal gave a grunt and a slight nod. *Grisly old bear*, Meg thought as she headed for Rachael's desk.

"Hi, sis. Reporting as requested. Want me in the interrogation room?"

"That works. Where's Mr. Wonderful?"

"It's Derek," Meg growled. "He'll be here pretty soon. I told you he had to check out of the Oasis first."

"Rachael," Hal said as he pushed his way into her cubicle. "What the hell do you think you're doing? You can't interview Meg. Right now she's a suspect."

"What?" Meg snapped around. "What are you talking about? A suspect in what?" She turned in dismay to her sister. "What's he talking about?"

"Well, for starters, it's definite that the body was thrown over the spillway, and I just got a call from your buddy, Jerry, at the dam. Looks like your card was used last night at eleven. Your excuse of sleeping on the boat is rather weak. We need to talk about this."

Rachael lashed out at Hal. "You shithead. Just because you're pissed off at me doesn't mean you have to take it out on Meg. You've been like a brother to her. You know she's not involved." Rachael turned back to Meg and said, "Don't talk to him right now or else call our attorney. He's way off his rocker. Stupid ass."

Meg looked back and forth between the two warring partners. She was curious about their bitter exchange but thought twice about getting involved.

"Call this Derek guy and find out how soon he'll be here before Hal has a meltdown."

Meg touched the number that Derek had loaded into her cell phone. "The number you called is no longer in service. Please try your call again," was the mechanized reply. Meg quickly redialed and heard the same message. She closed her cell phone with a disgruntled look on her face.

"Looks like he gamed me, Rachael."

Rachael took Meg's hand, sensing the hurt her sister was hiding. She flipped a back-off look to Hal.

"Why don't you call the Oasis, Rachael? They'll have something on him. Derek Manning is his name, and he had a room there. Hal, is it OK if I go home while you check everything out? I don't feel so good right now."

Hal glanced first at Rachael, then back at Meg, whom he did adore like a kid sister. "Yeah, it's OK for now. Sorry it played out like this. We'll call if we need anything else, and if you think of anything you missed, just call me. You know the drill. Sorry I came on so strong." He walked over and gave Meg a hug. Hugging Meg was easy for Hal. He knew as well as Rachael how Meg had a penchant for latching onto the wrong guy. These past few years of dealing with Meg had helped him in raising his own daughter as a single parent. The emotional side of girls and women was almost more than he could handle at times, he thought, as the pain of rejection from the night before returned with a sharp stab.

As Meg left, Rachael was already on the phone with security at the Oasis. Within minutes, they told her that there had been no one registered at the hotel under the name of Derek Manning. There were three guests who had checked out within the last hour: a couple, and a single man registered under the name of Derek Turner from Yorba Linda, California. Information regarding his address, phone number, and credit card was given to Rachael. *Could that be the friend that Meg had talked about? What about the boat that was now tied up to her dock? Was that going to be another wild goose chase? Looks like she picked another loser.*

"Hal," Rachael said, "I'd like to go home to be with Meg for a while. I'll call in the boat AZ numbers and follow up on that. Not too much we can do 'til Search and Rescue gets through with their part." She maintained a professional attitude.

"OK with me. But don't compromise the boat any more than you already have."

"Sometimes you're really a prick," Rachael fumed. Grabbing her purse, she left.

***

Rex and Sam of the Search and Rescue team were immediately dispatched to the dam. After outfitting themselves, they rappelled down the forty-five-degree concrete slope of the spillway. Twenty feet down, Rex found blonde hair evidence, a large piece of scalp still attached. With some difficulty, he bagged and tagged the evidence. Farther down, Sam found an arm separated from the victim's body at the elbow and a diver's belt dangling from the humerus. Since no water had been released over the spillway, there was a fair amount of blood and tissue that had coagulated, which would no doubt prove invaluable to the forensic crew. Nearly two hours elapsed before the team had collected twenty-two bags of evidence. The other arm, the head, and the torso were not located on the spillway, so water rescue was notified to be on the lookout. The bags were separated into spillway evidence and Davis Camp evidence and transported to Kingman for analysis. The CSI senior officer called the Kingman lab and informed them that the evidence would be there within the hour.

Additional S and R officers were still working the bottom of the spillway, accumulating evidence. "Looks like someone tied up to the buoy line recently. There's evidence of a tie line being cut. I'll bring a sample of the rope showing the cut marks. Looks pretty generic. We're going across the rope barrier now to the spillway basin. Holy shit," an officer said, "an eyeball is floating in the basin along with a...well, it looks like a boob." The officers moved to the basin and then reported again. "Only one silicone breast implant, and the other item turned out to be a grape. Sorry for the confusion."

"Bag and tag it," came the directive over the two-way. Hal was monitoring the operation. "Lab's going to be busy today. If the DB's prints are registered in AFIS, then we'll be notifying her folks tomorrow. God, who wants that job?"

19

From her sixth-floor room at the Winding River Hotel and Casino, Amanda watched carefully through her Bushnell binoculars. With the Record button on, she dictated notes into her miniature recorder. "Crime scene is breaking up. Don't know if this DB will have anything to do with our investigation, but I'll follow it through my Bullhead informant. Still have not been contacted by my backup. Per instructions, I have rented two rooms. Room four-eighty-six, at the Oasis, is where I'll be sleeping. I've hooked up a camera in case someone gets curious about me. Winding River Casino, room six-ninety two is the room where my partner can stay, or we'll just meet here to coordinate.

Amanda removed the tape from the recorder and labeled it with the time and date.

Without knowing when her partner would arrive and retrieve the tape, she decided to hide it in the air vent. Pulling an envelope from the desk, she wrote, "Mystery man, find me if you can."

Leaving the cryptic note on the desk, she deposited the tape into the air vent and left.

The time was approaching for her date with Beckett. Selecting her favorite sequined dress, she threw it in her packed suitcase and headed out for her room at the Oasis. As she opened her parked car, relentless heat poured out of it, sucking the air out of Amanda's lungs. *Who in their right mind with any choice in the matter would want to live in this hellhole?* With a smile, she realized that her two sisters lived here full time and loved it, while her mom would only visit six times per year, usually during the fall or spring. It had been years since Amanda had been back herself, but she did have fond memories of the many childhood trips to Grandma Nora's house, now the home of her two siblings.

Parking her old Mustang in the Oasis parking lot, she glanced around to see if her silent partner was lurking. No such luck. Usually, the FBI didn't want agents to start any undercover work without initial contact from a partner. At that time, they would discuss strategy and embark on the scenario with all the groundwork covered. This operation, however, had opened up so quickly that no one had had time to contact her. She had a dinner date set up with Beckett and decided to move forward with the project since this beginning step was simple and seemed safe enough. As she stepped into the elevator, a man quickly jumped in with her.

He smiled and asked, "Win any big jackpots yet?"

"Honestly, I really haven't had time to hit the tables. How about you?" Amanda asked.

"Same here. Just got here and checked in. Oops, my floor. Good luck at the craps table," he said, exiting the elevator.

"How did you know that's my game?" Amanda asked.

"Must be psychic, I guess," he replied. Contact had been made.

20

Registration on the boat was called in to the PD. Hal called Rachael on her cell phone. "Is the kid doing OK?" he asked.

"We haven't had time to talk yet." She was relieved to see that he was calm, professional, and almost friendly. "I think she's still a bit woozy from last night. Anything come in on the boat?"

"It's a rental from Havasu City. Rented by some local guy, but he reported it missing two days ago. Some big talker, this new boyfriend of hers."

Rachael moaned. "The Oasis had no Derek Manning registered. Besides the front desk, I checked with the valet service, and no one fit his description. Must have parked in the lot. We've temporarily ID'd him as Derek Turner. He took up with Meg's friends on Friday night. Then, Meg joined the merry group. She said that Derek had

122

a buddy with him but that he sort of disappeared after a while. Said it was all just fun. They liked to dance, casino hop, drink, waterski."

"What's not to like?" Hal remarked, thinking of the old days.

"She remembers that the other guy's first name was Arnold, or Arnie. Wasn't sure if Derek and Arnie were friends. Didn't really act like it. Strange, but I guess what happens in Laughlin…"

"Shouldn't happen at all," Hal said, finishing her sentence. "Does Meg know what kind of car he was driving?"

"Don't know."

"There were forty sets of prints from the boat. That's going to take a while."

"Probably a waste of time. Was a rental."

"Yeah."

"She's sure he touched the wine bottle and the screw-on top that was collected by the water patrol. Try to put a rush on it and also on Meg's tox screen. That might shed some light on this," Rachael said. "From the way she was acting, seems like she must have been slipped something. She's up now, sitting on the boat dock. I can see her from the kitchen. Not a good sign."

"So what are you thinking?

"Too early to say. I haven't got a clue if all of this is connected."

"Maybe he drugged Meg, lifted her gate pass, picked up the chick, murdered her, threw her off the dam, got back on the boat, and faked being knocked out. Busy night, but it might have happened that way," Hal said.

"I guess it could have," agreed Rachael, not wanting to start another fight. *Fat chance*, she thought.

21

The seaplane had been redirected to land north of Katherine's Landing. At the appointed time, the plane, with its cargo of six Mexican illegals and a number of labeled Styrofoam containers, landed on the flat waters of Lake Mohave. Within minutes, it idled into the deep cove known as Hard Luck Landing. As the Mexicans were transferred off the seaplane into jet boats, Trujillo, the pilot, collected gas cans from the boats and began to refuel.

"*Necesito mas gasolina*, asshole," said Trujillo.

"Speak English, buddy. You're in the good ol' US of A now." The boat driver laughed and punched his partner.

"*Mas* gas, *mas* gas. I need more to fly," Trujillo managed in his broken English.

"Call the boss on your cell. This is all we have. Not our problem."

Once the men were on board, the two jet boats carrying the illegals bounded away, heading to the Arizona side of the lake, where a minivan waited to take them to their new destination in California. Conversation was forbidden. The parties to this operation could only communicate with El Jefe on an electronically altered throwaway cell phone, which he supplied monthly to each of them. It kept them in the dark about each other and added to El Jefe's ability to control them. And, much to El Jefe's satisfaction, it enhanced their collective fears.

El Jefe had always timed the operation to within minutes of completion. Knowing that Trujillo would be concerned over the amount of gas, he called him.

Trujillo immediately voiced his fear. "Hey, man, you make me fly too far. Now I no got enough gas. Your asshole man say he no take the ice chests. Now what I do?"

"Shut up, amigo," started El Jefe. "Food has been left on the beach for you. Stay the night, and then tomorrow you will fly south, toward Needles. There's a wide expanse of water eight miles north of the Avi Resort. Land there. Arrangements have been made for a yellow-and-white boat to meet you on the Arizona side. There's a sandy stretch of shoreline. Enough gas for your flight home will be waiting. Carlos will meet you and take the ice chests. I'll call in the morning to give you the time schedule. When you get back to Mexico, I'll transfer the money to the Bank of Mexico. Have the illegals been transported yet?"

"*Si,* they gone, but amigo, is no good now. My government working with the Anglos, so I have to move outside of Tecate. But, senor, what is in the big boxes? I told you I no do the drugs," Trujillo said. "I tell Maria maybe *drogas* in package, and she say the cartel will kill me for this. They no care about coyote work, but they kill me over *drogas.*"

El Jefe was quiet. "How does the cartel know about my small dealings? Did you tell someone?"

Trujillo tried not to voice his fear. He knew he had made a mistake. Hesitantly, he said, "No senor, I tell no one. My wife tell no one."

The man stiffened, hiding his seething hostility. "You told your rot-gut whore of a wife? She's nothing but a *prostituta* with a big mouth. Make sure she tells no one, otherwise…"

Trujillo managed to stammer, "*Si,* senor."

While El Jefe continued with the conversation, his mind was concocting a new plan to solve the looming problem. It would be necessary to make contact with his other coyote to see if there was any gossip on the street regarding Trujillo and his big mouth. "I may want to increase the amount of containers and decrease the number of peasants. Do you have a problem with that?" El Jefe asked.

"No, senor. My wife is crazy in the *cabeza*. No worry, she likes the money. We are fine. No worry. No drugs, no worry."

"Don't disappoint me, Trujillo. Others who have made mistakes end up with their dicks stuck in their mouth. You sure we don't have a problem?"

"No, senor," said Trujillo, who suddenly found himself holding a dead phone. As he reached behind the backseat to find the tie-downs, being a good Catholic, he crossed himself and then dialed his wife. "Maria, pack our clothes," he said in Spanish. "El Jefe's going to come after us because of your big mouth."

22

Nearing the appointed hour, Amanda began to fidget. Her skimpy dress looked great, and simple costume jewelry highlighted her long neck. She had elected to put her abundant dark auburn hair in an upsweep with a fashionable twist. This was a new color for her, and she was pleased with the way it complemented the natural blush of her skin. Mentally, she ran over her contrived background as she pressed the elevator button for the penthouse.

Beckett was standing in his foyer when the doors opened, and he quickly extended a hand. "Hope you don't mind," he said, "I thought we could eat in. By the way, you look ravishing."

"I'm fine with that," said Amanda. "But for some reason, I thought you were the playboy type. Maybe go clubbing?"

"I can do that anytime with anyone," he replied, continuing to hold her hand. He led her across the travertine floor to the living room and the spacious bar that overlooked the river below. "Quite a beautiful view at night, don't you think?" Stepping behind the bar, Beckett asked, "Any requests?"

"Manhattan would be fine. Can you handle that?"

"Bartending put me through college. That and gambling," he said, mixing her drink. He then poured a double Grey Goose on the rocks for himself. "Here's to us. For this moment in time and perhaps many more to follow," he said as he toasted Amanda.

Sipping her drink, Amanda acknowledged its perfection with a smile and noted, "What a boss— only on the payroll for four hours and already in the penthouse. What's a girl got to do to get ahead? Oops, I don't really want to hear the answer to that one yet."

"Your company is reward enough for me," said Beckett. With a practiced eye, he scrutinized her every move. *Classy...nice.* "Let's sit and sip. Gazing at the river with a glass of vodka and a beautiful woman by my side brings me ultimate pleasure."

They moved slowly to the sofa that was strategically placed to enhance the overtly romantic scene. Both slipped into a peaceful reverie, or so it seemed to Beckett.

When the magical moment passed, they fell into an easy conversational repartee. While Amanda had read the full profile on Beckett, she acted completely engaged and feigned a little starry-eyed pleasure in his elaborate lies. It was hard to stay enthralled with some of his deletions and embellishments.

After an evening that featured lobster tail, sautéed asparagus, potatoes au gratin, and the perfect wine to complement the gourmet meal, Amanda prepared to leave. She found Beckett to be a very smooth talker, a skillful liar, and quite a gentleman to be with on a first date. Next time, their meeting should be less formal and hopefully would present an opportunity for Amanda to be left alone to check out his computer and desk drawers. Now was not the time to go for the jugular. The groundwork had been set for another date, and this was all that she meant to achieve tonight. *Now to get out of here intact.* She gave a small yawn and smiled at Beckett.

"I hope you don't mind if I call it quits. The evening's been perfect, but I'm totally exhausted. It's been a long day. Forgive me?" Amanda turned as she was leaving the penthouse and lightly kissed Beckett on the cheek.

Smiling as the elevator door closed behind her, Beckett thought, *Sweet.*

Smiling as the elevator door closed behind her, Amanda thought, *Gotcha.*

23

Elliott, sitting behind his desk piled high with folders, correspondence, and sticky notes from the station's secretary, yelled out, "Sharon, call the Bullhead Police Department and see if the captain can come in for an interview tomorrow morning. I need some better material than what we've had recently. Hey, and get some cats or dogs here from the animal shelter. The old broads in town always like that." He shuffled some more papers. "Oh, and see if we can get anyone here from the city council about the new bridge they're talking about."

Elliott leaned back in his swivel chair and contemplated the direction his daily TV show was taking. He peered into the mirror on his desk and squinted. *New wrinkles.* His comb-over 'do was standing up. *Maybe I should look into implants.* The four years in Bullhead had added too many pounds to his middle. He scoffed. *What the hell, no one to dress up for, anyway.* He ached to report more exciting news than the weather and the occasional car or boat chase. *Probably should push the floater story and maybe the car that blew up in Bullhead two days ago.*

Elliott had never been satisfied with his minor role in the huge world of TV. Running a station with three technicians, one secretary, and one rookie newsgirl wasn't what he had envisioned when he graduated from the University of Nevada Las Vegas Journalism Department. But here he was. Free booze and cheap women. An unfulfilled life. *Oh, hell*, he thought, *I might as well make a call and cover the drowning victim myself.* Picking up the phone, he called BHPD and asked for Roberto.

"Yo, Elliott, what's up?" Roberto asked. "I suppose you want some update on the DB—or half-body floater, as we're calling her around the office."

"Anything new that you can share? My gal is getting in touch with your captain to see if he'll come on the show tomorrow, but just in case he's too busy, I thought I'd give you a call. So lay it on me."

"Nothing much. I'll share what I have, but use some diplomacy in the telling, please, so you don't scare the hell out of the community. Since Melissa's body is supposed to get dumped soon, the town is already edgy enough. Apparently the vic was around five-foot-nine and weighed a hundred and thirty pounds or so. Boobs weren't hers. She had delivered a kid at one time. Forensics has all kinds of shit they're working on. Not much other than that unless you want to get into the boater and his family who found the remains of the body."

Elliott thought for a minute. "OK, I'll take their names for a follow-up interview later. Well, I'll clean it up a bit, maybe not talk about the boobs. Can't the PD get a number off the implants? I heard that was possible."

"It'll take time to locate the source of the implants. I don't know what condition they were in."

"Any suspects yet?"

"Not yet. Although, off the record, Rachael's kid sister and some guy were found this morning by Rachael, stranded in his boat on a sandbar right across from Rachael's house. You know her sister—Meg. The sassy blonde. Well, Meg came in to give a statement already. She doesn't know much. Boyfriend of hers has disappeared. They're trying to track him down. He didn't show up for a statement at the PD. More than a little suspicious."

"OK. Well, let me know if anything develops on that. And, by the way, what's the deal on the car chase? Did they ever catch that guy? Have they identified what blew up the car yet? Rumor has it that the driver was your cousin. Anything to that?" asked Elliott.

"No comment on that one," said Roberto. "Except that we've got lead on the case. Hal wants Rachael off the drowning because Meg's involved, but I think the captain is going to have them work it together. Man, those two are fightin' like cats and dogs. Don't know what's going on, but the whole department is staying out of their way. Not much else to give you, Elliott. Gotta go now. There's some new info on the car bomb coming in."

"One more thing before you go."

"Hurry."

"Why do they think Meg's involved?" Elliott pushed. "She's an airhead."

"Looks like her pass was used to get onto the spillway during the monsoon. Not for publication, ya hear?"

"Hmmm. That could be serious. Thanks, Roberto. I'll catch ya later. I owe you one."

Elliott leaned back in his chair, absently tapping out a beat with his fingers, lost in thought.

Might need to do some follow-up on this. He reached for the phone and started dialing.

24

When Rachael first arrived home, she expected to find Meg sprawled across her bed, crying and sobbing over a potential lost love. To her surprise, Meg was sitting on the boat dock, dangling her feet in the cold water. Rachael poured two glasses of chardonnay and headed for the dock.

"Thought you might like some company," Rachael said, handing her a plastic wine glass as she sat down. She took off her shoes and joined in the soaking time.

"Oh, I'm OK. I just thought Grandma might drop down and give me some advice."

Rachael sighed and glanced toward the stratus clouds.

The house, now occupied by the sisters, had been willed to their mom, Grace, and the girls by their grandmother. They all seemed to find solace in returning to this spot when they were having problems. Grandma had delighted in telling them that in times of trouble, she would be perched on the nearest cloud. When they needed her, they just had to sit with their feet in the water, and she'd show up. She'd never tell them what to do when she was still around, but answers would become apparent with time. Of course, Grandma also had a book of two thousand spells and remedies that she would share with the kids when something required more than her trivial intervention.

"You know, Rachael, life was much simpler when Grandma was around. We were just kids, and our family was so filled with love and caring. I tell you, it's really different in the big world. People lie and cheat and think nothing about walking away from responsibilities. I don't know if I'll ever get the hang of that—or even if I want to. What's wrong with me? You and Amanda seem to cope and always move on with your life, but me—well, every guy who comes my way just ends up being a disaster."

Rachael was silent. She knew there was more to come.

"Derek flat-ass lied to me for no reason. That really pisses me off." As Meg stopped to take a breath and a swallow of wine, both girls studied the water silently. An old carp slowly swam by, came up to the surface, mouth gaping wide in an attempt to catch a gnat. Rachael felt suddenly helpless sitting with her sister, looking for the words to console her. She wasn't sure she was doing so well in the coping-and-moving-on part of her life, either. Words didn't come, but surprisingly, tears did.

"Oh, God, Rachael. What's the matter with me? You've had to go through so much more than any of us. I'm sorry I get so self-absorbed. Please forgive me," said Meg. "I'm such a jerk."

Rachael put her arm around her little sister and pulled her close, in the process experiencing pain so naked that they both cringed. Finally, Rachael laughed and said, "Look at us. Four bare feet in the water and two crying women trying to talk to a dead grandma about the world. She would love it."

Perking up, Meg said, "And damn, I just got her message. Why the hell am I sitting around here feeling sorry for myself? If you can't locate my loser boyfriend, I'm going to find him myself and do a citizen's arrest and bring him in. Who does he think he's dealing with?"

"Now don't get crazy on me, Meg. The department is on this, and we'll track him down. Why do you think he was being so deceptive with everyone? Do you think he's hiding something? Could he be involved with the dead woman?" Rachael asked.

"I honestly don't know. I didn't pick up any weird vibes from this guy. I know I'm a pushover sometimes, but he really didn't strike me that way. You'll have to ask him, I guess, when I bring him in."

Rachael finished her wine and stood up, rocking back and forth as small waves from a passing boat rolled by. The dock undulated. She hesitated. "I'm really sorry to tell you this, but we got a call from the Bureau of Reclamation. Until your name is cleared, they're putting you on a five-day paid leave. After that, they'll give you a call about your future employment with them."

"Why are you telling me this? Why didn't they call me?"

"I told them I was heading home and would rather tell you myself."

Meg grimaced. "Oh, great. Not only do I lose a potential boyfriend, but now I may not have a job. He's going to pay for this." Meg headed toward the house in full pout mode.

MONDAY, JULY 29

Rachael left for work. Meg banged around the house—nowhere to go, since she couldn't go to work like the rest of the world. She was fuming. *What kind of a fool does he take me for? Jerk.* Patience was not one of her virtues. She stomped, she cussed, she stewed. Finally, she grabbed the phone and called Rachael. Meg was put on hold. Her sweet disposition was imploding.

"Detective Pennington here."

"I *hate* being put on hold!" Meg yelled into the receiver.

"What do you need, Meg? I'm really busy right now."

"Have you identified my mystery man yet? I'm really pissed about being used. Who is he? For God's sake, Rachael, give me some help here."

"OK, OK. The guy who checked out of the Oasis is Derek Montgomery Turner. It looks like he told you part of his name, huh? And guess where he lives," said Rachael.

"He told me Anaheim Hills. Our high schools were crosstown rivals," Meg said, exasperation oozing from her voice. "Was that a lie, too?"

"Wow, cool down. He was close to honest about that. How about Yorba Linda? Quite a coincidence, I'd say."

"Oh, my God. I can't believe he lives in our city. Why would he lie about that? Did you get an address or anything about where he works?"

"Last address is on Via Marwah. Expensive part of town. No lead on where he works. I'm waiting for a call from the local PD. I can't get a read on this guy. Do you think he had anything to do with your missing key?"

Meg felt the slap of surprise.

"And if that's the case, how about anything to do with the dead woman? Come on. You've had time to think about that. What's your gut feeling?"

Meg was slow to answer. She felt like saying, "Hang the bastard," but said, "I don't know him well enough to guess, but the timing's weird. You've lectured me many times on coincidence. I'm still foggy about the night, but I'll think about it." She stopped. "Even if he's innocent, it doesn't mean that he's off the hook with me."

"I should have more answers in a couple of days."

"Days? Crap. Since I don't have anything to do this week, I'll go see Mom. I'll go stir-crazy if I have to sit around here watching TV."

"Oh, no you don't, Megan. It doesn't take an Einstein to know what you have planned. Seeing Mom is OK, but hunting down a witness or suspect in my crime investigation is a no-no. Promise me you'll stay out of it," Rachael pleaded.

"Sure, no problem. I just need a break from this whole cop scene. I'll throw some stuff in a bag and head out now. Don't call Mom. I'll surprise her. I'll call ya when I get there," she said as she closed the cell phone. *OK, Mr. Turner. Now it's my turn.*

Rachael sighed as she replaced the receiver. "Yeah, right."

***

The trip to Orange County took exactly four hours and five minutes. Driving down the asphalt driveway of her childhood home, passing the avocado tree she used to climb and the flowerbeds where all the Easter eggs used to hide made Meg sink into a happy-sad mood. So many memories were there with all the relatives, aunts, uncles, cousins, and the huge parties that Mom loved to throw.

Escrow, the family Lab, barked ferociously while wildly wagging her tail. Throwing the gear into park, Meg raced to greet her.

"Hi, puppy. Meg's home." Recovering from the friendly dog attack, Meg tried the back door and, as usual, found it open. *Right, Mom, no one locks their doors in Yorba Linda.* She walked through the family room showcasing her mom's sixty-two-inch television, black-and-white photos of old movie stars, statues of the Blues Brothers and Betty Boop, a dance floor, a bar, and a jukebox. A decorator's nightmare. Sliding open the French doors leading to the pool area, Meg stepped through, smiled, and waited. Her mom, oblivious to the outside world, was sitting in the shade of the liquid amber trees, fingers flying over the computer keyboard, engrossed in her writing.

"Mom, are you going deaf on me? I've been yelling for five minutes."

Grace Pennington looked up from her writing with surprise, which was quickly replaced by a huge grin. Pure joy escaped from her gray-green eyes. "Well, look what the cat drug in," she announced. "Did you call and tell me you were coming and I somehow totally spaced?"

With a laugh, Meg said, "No, Mom. It's just a spur-of-the-moment visit. I can only stay the night, and then I have to get back to Bullhead."

"Come over here and give me a hug. Why aren't you working at the dam today? Did they switch your days off?"

"No. There was an incident, and I...well, I guess I'm suspended for a day or two. Nothing serious," she said.

"Bullshit," Grace said. "Sounds serious to me. Did the phone system become obsolete since you left town? Why didn't you or Rachael call me? Or for that matter, why didn't Amanda call me? I got a message from her saying she was on her way to visit you two."

Meg decided to let this part of the conversation go for a while. "We can talk about that later, but right now, I've got a little job to do for Rachael while I'm here. I might as well get it over with. Let's see. It's about five o'clock—a perfect time—so I'm out of here. OK if I use my old bedroom for tonight?"

"No need to ask. It's the same as you left it, minus some trash." Grace paused. "Uh, Meg. Rachael did call me about an hour ago and gave me a heads-up about your visit, and I'd like to talk about it for a minute."

Irked, Meg heaved a huge sigh and replied, "Go for it. I should have known. God, I hate this interference."

"You're here to track down some jerk. Really. Listen, young lady, don't be pulling an attitude on me. All your life, you've had any boyfriend you wanted. We'd have to beat them away from the door, but in all of that history, I've never seen you chase any guy. What's going on?"

"Mom, I'm not chasing him. He stood Rachael up. He was supposed to go in for an interview, but he skipped. He used a bogus name and phone number on me, and since I'm not employed at the minute, I decided to come and check it out. He might be the very reason that I've been suspended, for all we know."

"Don't kid a kidder. Rachael said you really like this guy. Get off your high horse and tell me what's really going on."

Meg pulled a lawn chair over next to her mother. "How do you always know? It's been a long time since I've been interested in anyone, Mom. Derek, besides being handsome, is witty, intelligent, and spontaneous. He likes the same things that I do, and well…I need to know what happened. Why he left like that. If there's something wrong with me, I think he'll be honest enough to tell me. Maybe it's time I start getting a little more serious about life."

"Meg, you should never have to chase a man. The way you described this Derek is what everyone sees in *you*. Both your sisters adore you and have a certain amount of envy for your exuberance."

"Not both. Not Amanda."

"You're an original, a classic, and yet you sell yourself short. Get over it. Now if you want to track down this guy, go for it, but do it for the right reason. I'll be interested in the outcome. I told Amanda—"

Meg cut her mother off. "What's Amanda got to do with me?"

Grace quickly realized her mistake. The relationship between Amanda and Meg had been so strained. Keeping the secret for all these years had been a mistake.

"Is that the real reason she's in Bullhead? To keep an eye on me? Did you send her? She gave me some cock-and-bull story about a waitress job. I should've known that you sent her spying."

Grace bristled.. "Oh, don't get so paranoid. She told me what she was doing there, but I forgot. Senility in its prime."

"Senile, my ass. What aren't you telling me? This family gets so secretive sometimes. Don't you think I'm old enough to be on the inside track of her career? You've shielded me from Amanda for years."

Grace leaned back and sighed. "You're right. We haven't told you the whole story. You were too young when the tragedy happened, and as time went by…well, it was her decision to keep it a secret."

"What are you talking about? How her fiancé turned into a drunk? What's the big deal about that?"

"No, not that. Do you remember when Amanda was involved in a car accident? She was in college?"

"Yeah, she came home for a few weeks. All beat up and crying. Shit, she never stopped. That's when I decided she wasn't worth my time. Just looking for attention from you, which you gave her."

"There's more to the story than that."

"Like what? There are car crashes every day. Sometimes fatal ones. What was the big deal?"

Grace stood and walked away. When she finally turned, she met Meg's curious face. "Amanda was raped and beaten."

"What? What are you talking about?"

"After the USC basketball game, four students from UCLA grabbed her and threw her in their van. They took turns with her, raped her, beat her up, and dumped her in front of the sorority house. Near dead."

"God, Mom. You should have told me. I could have helped. All of these years, I've been a rotten sister."

"She understood. It was her story to tell, and she didn't want to burden you. She idolizes you, Meg. Maybe now you can take it easy on her."

"Does Rachael know about this?" Meg demanded.

"Yes. Remember, she was in high school when it happened. She helped me get Amanda through the trauma."

Meg turned away from Grace and sobbed. "I am such a self-centered shit. Mom, I'm so sorry. Is there anything I can do to make it up to her? I've been more than cruel. I'm so sorry."

Grace leaned over and gave Meg a hug. "It's OK, honey. You didn't know. But maybe give her a hug when you see her. Be a sister. She's on assignment in Laughlin, so you'll have a chance."

"Right." Meg's softer side was squeezing her heart. "I won't know how to start since I've been so mean. I had no idea. You let her know that I know, 'cause if I just try to hug her, she'll think I've lost it."

"I will, sweetheart. I'm really glad it's in the open. The secret has been hard to keep." Grace walked to the edge of the pool and sat down, dangling her feet. Meg joined her.

"Amanda tried to tell Rachael about her assignment on Friday, but Rachael had some emergency car chase and had to hang up on her. Sounds like your sisters are busy chasing the bad guys. The river has called all of my girls back again. Maybe when I finish this book, I'll start a new novel based on you three. Wouldn't that be a hoot?"

Meg threw her arms to the heavens. "Please say you're kidding."

"You kids would love that. I always get so busy when I write that I quit trying to micromanage your lives. It must be quite a relief for you three," Grace said with a laugh.

"We love ya, Mom, but you are quite a handful when you focus on us. Listen, I do need to get started on my detective business. What I need now is a trench coat and a spyglass." With that, Meg stood and, leaning over, gave her mom a kiss.

"Trench coat, indeed. Just another item to add to my Christmas shopping list. Please leave the thirty-eight at home."

"You're the greatest, Mom. Love ya. I'll be home late, so don't wait up."

The drive to Eastlake Village took five minutes. Via Marwah was easy to find, and after locating the address for Derek, Meg parked her car across the street. It was after six o'clock, and if he worked in Santa Ana, the drive would take approximately thirty minutes on the 55 freeway. No car was in the driveway, but she saw movement in the house. *What if he's married? Hey, maybe that's what all the secrecy's about. The jerk—he deserves to have his wife know that he messes around on weekends.* With that, Meg marched up to the front door and rang the bell. Before she had time to change her mind, the door opened. A striking brunette smiled, asking, "May I help you?" Drying her hands on a dishtowel, she waited for an answer.

While Meg was somewhat taken aback, she finally stammered, "Yes, is this the residence of Derek Turner?"

"Yes, but he isn't here right now." When Meg hesitated, the lady repeated, "May I help you?"

"Yes, my name is Megan Pennington, and I need to see Mr. Turner on a legal matter."

"Megan, hmmm," the brunette said. "Why does that name sound familiar?"

Oh, my God, he confessed to his wife. What an idiot. We weren't even intimate. No wedding ring, no wedding ring. She tried to see beyond the woman, checking for signs of children. "Beats me," Megan said. Ready to shove a fake subpoena into the woman's hand, she stopped when a car pulled into the driveway.

Oh, great, Megan thought. *Now the shit is really going to hit the fan.*

Derek put the car into park, stared with curiosity at the scene, and thought, *What is she doing here? Can't be good.*

Walking toward Meg, he removed his Oakley sunglasses and said, "Well, it looks like you found me. A little help from your sister, possibly?"

"Beside the point entirely. Why don't you introduce me to your wife? I'm sure she'd like to be in on this conversation," said Meg.

"My..." Derek smiled at the lady in the doorway. "Yes, of course. How rude of me. Megan Pennington, I would like you to meet Marisa Turner. Marisa, this is Megan Pennington from Bullhead City. I told you about her."

"No wonder I remembered your name. Derek told me all about you. But what brings you here?" Marisa asked.

"I am making a citizen's arrest and intend to take him back to Bullhead with me."

Derek laughed. "Did you bring handcuffs, or is that too kinky for you? Actually, I'd prefer pink fuzzy cuffs, myself, if you happen to have any with you."

"Kid me all you like, Derek. The fact is that you left a murder investigation in which you were implicated as a possible felon. The Bullhead PD requires your prints, a blood sample, and a statement to clear your name. I, too, am under investigation and have been put on leave until this matter is concluded. Your testimony will clear my name, unless you are indeed the perfect villain and refuse to tell the truth. Now, pack a bag and come with me." She cocked her head sideways, completely satisfied with her eloquent soliloquy.

Derek replied, "I'd like to see the paperwork from the PD authorizing you to take me into custody. And, by the way, I am an attorney, and I know my rights. Taking me across state lines won't sit too well with the judge unless I waive my rights pertaining to extradition." He smirked.

Meg realized that he was enjoying this repartee. *What a scoundrel.* "I thought you were working as a financial manager, acquisitions or something.

Another lie? What's this attorney shit? And Derek Turner, not Montgomery? What, a different name and phone number for each innocent you try to pick up?" She took two steps forward and, pushing her face to within inches of his, growled, "Why don't you play nice and pack your bags?"

"Well, you know, Meg, I would be glad to accommodate you; however, my sister is only here for a week. She's from Seattle and down here on business. Now, that wouldn't be very hospitable of me if I were to leave town right now." Derek said this with tongue in cheek, pushing the irony of the situation. Before Meg had an opportunity to digest the whole picture, he leaned forward and kissed her on the mouth.

Jerking back, Meg wiped her mouth. "Your sister. You creep. Why didn't you say so?"

"You really didn't give me much of a chance. Why don't you come in, and we'll sort this whole thing out? Don't be a hard nose. Come on in."

Realizing she had made a total faux pas and now looked like a complete fool, Megan almost said no, but within seconds, she recovered and defiantly threw her head back as she trudged into the living room. "Sure, why not. How many more times do I get to be humiliated in one day? Let's go for a record."

Megan saw Marisa whisper something in Derek's ear, and then she left the room, leaving the two lovebirds alone. Derek headed for the wet bar and fixed two apple martinis. "If you promise not to throw this drink in my face, I'll hand it to you."

Megan knew her face was still flushed, and she was fighting for control of her temper. The smirk on his handsome face added to her frustration. Determined that he wouldn't get the best of the situation, she nodded and, with a show of civility, said, "Thank you. I could use a drink right about now. What did your sister whisper? Get rid of the crazy bitch?" She reached for the glass.

"Let me begin with why I left town. I was scheduled to take two depositions on Monday. I called my office to see if they could be postponed, but since we're going to trial in two weeks, the arrangements couldn't be changed. I tried to call you when I got on the freeway, but my cell phone was dead. Anyway, by the time I got back to town, all hell broke loose, and I had to go to the office. I did call your sister at the PD this afternoon and made arrangements to go back to Bullhead tomorrow. Just for a day. That's the best I can do."

"Well, it looks like I might have jumped to a few wrong conclusions along the way," Meg said. Her lips were pursed so tightly that the words were barely audible. She sipped her drink, glanced his way, and saw he was giving her that crooked smile. *Oh, he is enjoying this far too much.*

"Is that an apology?" Derek asked, trying not to laugh.

"Apology, my ass. Since you and Rachael have made these arrangements, I guess I'll be going. You know I'll be checking with her as soon as I leave, and if you have lied to me, I'll come back and drag your sorry ass out of the house," Meg said challengingly.

"Hey, wait a minute. Since you're in town, why don't I show you around my neighborhood?"

"I grew up in Yorba Linda," Meg said. "What could you possibly show me? In fact, what do you know about, say, the Canyon Inn? Or even the graveyard?"

"I was thinking maybe we'd go to dinner at the Heritage House. Does that compare to the Canyon Inn?"

Meg laughed. "Go change out of your monkey suit and put on some shorts or jeans. I'll give you a tour of Yorba Linda that you won't forget." *Is this like a second chance?*

Eating dinner at the Canyon Inn was a different experience for Derek. They munched on juicy hamburgers and chili fries and tossed back several shots of tequila. Everyone knew Meg and asked when she was coming back home. Truckers and businessmen alike would meet for a drink after a long, tiring drive on the 91 freeway. The local watering hole attracted all types. Derek and Meg fit right in.

"Another round of tequila shots for my new friends," yelled Derek, already feeling the results of the last two. With that, the bar was ready to adopt him.

"Have you lived in Yorba Linda long?" asked Meg.

"About two years. Transferred down from San Francisco with the firm."

"Frisco? Oh, bet you miss all your boyfriends." She smirked.

"Yeah, it was tough at first." He leaned over and kissed her on the neck and pulled the barstool closer. "They weren't my type."

The evening lingered on. Meg enchanted Derek with historical stories of Yorba Linda: how the Quaker settlement would not allow any bars, so the Canyon Inn opened up one block out of town.

"Our city has a resident ghost who shows up June fifteenth each election year."

"Sure."

"I'm not kidding. She's registered. Check her out online. She was killed going to the prom in a buggy and is buried right across the street in the historical cemetery."

Finishing off the remains of his tequila, Derek stood. "Show me."

"You're on."

After wandering through the cemetery, they headed back to the car. "I really hate to cut the evening short, but I should get back to my sister. She's leaving tomorrow. We'll make up for all this lost time after the interview tomorrow."

"Oh, sure. I understand." Her disappointment was visible. "What about tomorrow? Are we taking two cars?"

"I'll come along with you. No handcuffs required. Then catch a plane back. Let's leave early."

When Meg left Derek in front of his house, she felt he seemed distracted. No long, passionate kiss? A quick hug was all? The curtain moved slightly in the living room window. Was Marisa watching? Strange behavior for a sister. He tossed a wave to her and rushed through the door.

Marisa was waiting for him. "Well, that was unexpected."

"Don't start on me. We underestimated her curiosity. I need to make a phone call after I use some mouthwash."

26

TUESDAY, JULY 30

As directed, Carlos was holed up at the safe house in Oatman. Spending the night there with no TV and an anxious, pregnant Sasha proved to be trying for Carlos. The bed was lumpy, and the room reeked of cigar smoke.

Sasha blamed all of her frustrations on Carlos. She spread her legs for him in the ninth grade and had never looked at anyone else. Her youthful beauty had faded into an angry replica of her homely mother. Now she needed someone to blame for her pitiful life, and that job rested on Carlos. Sasha was close to her delivery date, and they were on the run. No money and no plans. She feared her baby's first cries would be heard in the back of some dingy bar with no one to help.

"I'm pregnant, homeless, and hungry. This hole-in-the-wall stinks. There's cockroaches everywhere. It'd be better to live on the streets—at least there'd be some fresh air. What is that awful smell? It's coming from that shed out back. There's probably dead bodies rotting inside. Go get me a hamburger or something. This baby is kicking the hell out of me." She continued walking around in circles, spasmodically throwing her arms skyward—complaining, complaining, complaining.

Carlos hesitated. His usual response to her railings was to backhand her, but just looking at her size and considering that the baby was due in a week, he finally gave in. "OK, OK. I have another cell phone that El Jefe left for us. I can take that with me. I'll get you some food." He headed for the door. "Shut up. I'm going."

Carlos was tired of her whining. This was not how he planned his life. He should have listened to his cousin. Now everything was screwed up. He still loved the fat, bitchy girl—had since grammar school—but the pressure was getting to him.

Sasha threw her purse at him. He stopped and looked at her. "Sasha, stop. I'll make this up to you. We'll have a good life. I only have one last job to do, and El Jefe said he'd give me some extra money so we could leave town. I'll work hard to get your dream."

Sasha growled. "El Jefe this, El Jefe that. He's going to kill you, and maybe he'll kill me and the baby, too. Don't be such a fool." Now the fear was giving way to tears. The baby moved hard under her ribs, and she doubled over in pain.

"No, he won't. And we're going to move to Las Vegas next. That's where his operation is headed, and he still needs my help. You'll like it there." He picked up the car keys and walked toward the door. "I'll get you your damned burger now, so stop whining." He was torn between wanting to hold her or run. As Carlos reached the door, the throwaway cell phone rang.

"*Holà,*" Carlos said. He listened as instructions were given over the phone.

"*Si,* senor. I can get there in one hour. *Si, si.* No problem. Do you want me to come back to the safe house with the cargo? No problem."

Sasha stood. "So we're leaving now? I'm still hungry."

"Not we. You stay here and wait. El Jefe doesn't like women knowing anything about his business."

"Screw you. I'm going with you, and we're getting my burger on the way. He won't know if I go along."

"Jesus, just get in the damn car, bitch. I'm tired of listening to you." He threw open the door and stormed outside.

As she awkwardly angled her huge belly into the car, Carlos said he'd forgotten something and went back to the house. She waited. He made two trips to the car with containers. She saw the medical insignia on the side but didn't want to know what was inside. Carlos had to do what he had to do. He had to get them out of this trouble, and whatever was in the trunk was no doubt their ticket to freedom.

Carlos drove down the dirt road to Boundary Cone Road and then took a right heading up Highway 95. Sasha yelled to pull into the Carl's Jr. when she spotted it. At the drive-through window, he ordered her two hamburgers, a vanilla shake, and fries.

He shoved the bags at her. "Now shut up, bitch. I have to think. El Jefe's giving me one chance to make up for my mistake. I have to be careful."

They passed Fort Mohave and then headed toward the river. An undeveloped area located down a winding dirt road was adjacent to the river's edge. Driving through the brush, they quickly came in view of the water. The meeting place was directly across from the old twenty-story vacant structure that in years past was to have been a hotel/casino. The skeleton structure stood vigil, overlooking the river below as a beacon of despair, a sinister reminder of greed and failure.

Carlos parked the aging minivan under a scrub tree and waited for the seaplane to arrive.

"It won't be long now, Sasha. Enjoy your burger. Next week, I'll take you out for a real steak dinner at the Mirage in Las Vegas." They waited. The car was stifling. He turned and studied Sasha. There was little resemblance to the pretty girl he had fallen in love with. Swollen from the pregnancy, worried, scared. Just a pitiful rendition of his young love. *Will there be a future for us? Jesus, I'm having a kid. Will El Jefe let us live? God, if I could only run from all of this and start over.* He looked at Sasha and then quickly looked away.

The seaplane circled and prepared to land.

27

Meg and Derek left Yorba Linda early in the morning and drove directly to the Bullhead Police Station to see Rachael. Roberto, the first to greet them, said, "Well, it looks like you got your man. Your sister's pissed about going over her head. Better stay out of her way. Yeah, like that's going to happen."

Trying to change the subject, Meg said, "Hey, Roberto, have you got anything new on the car explosion? Was your cousin involved?"

Roberto grunted. "My aunt's looking for him. Really pissed. She thought he had blown up her car, but it turns out he stole one off a casino parking lot. He's holed up someplace with Sasha, his knocked-up girlfriend. Fine mess he's in. We'll find him. Just a matter of time."

"What's going on with that? What car explosion? Is that why I'm here?" Derek tried to pump Meg for more information, but she told him to mind his own business, at least until he was cleared.

Rachael came bustling into the room and stopped when she saw Meg. "I'm so glad you didn't take the situation into your own hands, Meg," she said sarcastically. "Did the witness come along easily, or did you have to cuff him? Did you use your pink, fuzzy cuffs that you use on most of your arrests?"

Derek turned to Meg and smiled. "See, I figured you for pink, and I was right." With a smirk spread across his face, he held his hands out for Rachael to cuff him.

"I'm out of here. He's all yours," said Meg. "I'll be over talking with Roberto when you're through with him. And by the way, Mom said to say hello."

"You and Meg can play with the cuffs. Hope they won't be needed." Rachael led Derek to an interrogation room. She squared off at him the minute the door closed. "If you think I'll go light on you because Meg thinks you're cute, guess again. Let's take it from the top. Explain the different name you used, the boat that doesn't belong to you, leaving town abruptly. Start with these questions. What's the deal?"

"Well, the name is easy. I was introduced to Paula in the Oasis by Arnie. She didn't hear my full name, and later when introduced to Meg, I didn't correct her. Figured that I'd only be spending an evening with them and it didn't matter. The boat… well, I met this guy Arnie on Thursday, and we spent the day on his boat. Friendly guy. He had to go to Las Vegas on Friday and said I could use the boat for the day. I tried to impress Meg by saying it was mine. That's all."

"Not quite. The boat was stolen."

"I didn't know that."

"Convenient. You gave Meg a wrong phone number and also skipped town before coming to the station to make a statement."

"The phone number was a mistake. Just one number off. We were driving in her Mini Cooper, and I just screwed up. Meant to call you on the drive back to Orange County, but my phone was dead. I did call you when I got home."

"Why did you skip town?"

"I was scheduled for depositions and couldn't get excused. I explained that to Meg. You can call my office to verify."

"I will."

Rachael concentrated on his face. She knew he was not telling her everything. "What do you recall about the monsoon?"

"We tied the boat to the cross line at the dam. Ate our hamburgers, drank some wine, laughed a lot, kissed a little, and then I went to sleep. Hot date, huh?"

"Did Meg fall asleep before you? Were there any other boats or watercraft around?"

"I don't remember who fell asleep first. It just happened. No other boats that I recall."

"What was your purpose here in town?"

"Gambling and girls. Now, if you don't have anything else to ask, I'd like to go."

Rachael stood. "We're good for now. I'll need your correct phone number. The clerk will print you on the way out."

"Is that really necessary?"

"Yes. Any problem with that?"

Derek stood up and looked her straight in the eye. "None at all."

"Thanks for your cooperation. You might be called once we catch the perp."

After heading down the hall, they stopped and shook hands. Rachael grabbed Meg by the arm. "Excuse us for a minute." Rachael pulled Meg into a vacant interview room and asked, "Is Mom OK? Did she tell you anything about Amanda's assignment?"

"Oh, yeah. Amanda's in town on an assignment for the FBI. Hush-hush. Mom also told me the real story behind Amanda's so-called car crash. Wish you two could have trusted me. I've been really mean to Mandy for so long."

Rachael was surprised. She always felt that it would be a family sit-down presentation when it was time to tell the story. "She understands. It was a hard time for all of us. We'll talk about it when she comes over. But, look, stay with me on this. First, damn it, I don't want you interfering with my investigation. You take too many chances. I want you safe. Now, about Derek. He seemed forthcoming with his reasons—or excuses—for his actions. But watch him. I'm not convinced about his sincerity. He's a little too smooth. Be vigilant, sis. You really don't know much about him."

"Well, I do know that he doesn't kiss like a serial killer…well, not any serial killer I've kissed lately."

"Meg."

"OK. Sorry. I'll be careful."

Rachael could see that her words weren't sticking to Meg's gray matter, so she moved on. "Keep Amanda's assignment to yourself. Don't share with Derek." They walked down the hall and rejoined Derek. Rachael gave him a terse good-bye.

"Let's go celebrate. We still have most of the day to play." Meg latched onto Derek's arm and dragged him out into the beastly heat.

Roberto received information from his car-bombing investigation regarding his cousin and was anxious to share it with his partners. Detonation had been from a grenade, as previously believed. Prints from Carlos had been identified, and there was also trace amount of blood that did not match his. There were no bodies found after the explosion, but the crime scene investigators found a partial kidney with a rare blood type. *Body parts,* Roberto thought. While at first, smuggling body parts was just a theory, it had now moved to the top of the list of crimes. And Carlos was totally involved. He glanced over at Hal. *Wouldn't it be great to find an extra kidney for Hal's daughter?*

"Hey, Hal, I wanted to give you a heads-up on our car-bombing case. Some of the blood found in the car came from a partial kidney. It looks like it was being transported in a foam container of sorts. Weird, huh? Any connection with the body parts floating down the river?"

"Not sure. We just got an ID on the vic. She was that nice middle-aged waitress who served drinks at the Oasis. Angie. You knew her. Too bad. She had an eight-year-old kid. Looks like she might've been alive when the asshole threw her off the dam. Hell of a way to go. I don't know if they found her kidneys or not, but we'll check it out. What blood type did they find?"

"Type B negative and then some special kind of other blood markers. Very rare. Do you have a time of death on the vic?"

"Around midnight on Saturday. That doesn't fit in with the car bombing, does it?" asked Hal.

"Nah, the car blew up the day before. What the hell is going on in this town?"

Hal smirked and said, "I don't know for sure, but if you find another kidney, let me know. Sarah needs a type A negative. Wouldn't that be something to pick up a matched kidney at some anonymous drop on Highway 95 in the middle of the afternoon? No questions asked? Hey, that would work for me." Walking away, both men let their imagination run with the previous conversation.

Reentering the interrogation room, Hal met up with Rachael.

"What do you think of this Derek guy? Is he on the up-and-up, or has Meg picked another loser? His answers were pretty pat. I listened in on your interrogation. Sounds like any other pretty guy in a suit."

Rachael was relieved that Hal had left his attitude out of the room.

"You know, Hal, usually I can nail one of her boyfriends really fast. But you're right. He's smooth, but that comes with the territory, being an attorney. His answers seemed straight and forthcoming, but I still feel there's something going on. I'll act like I approve of him; otherwise, Meg'll get all defensive and not share anything with me. I'll keep you posted. I still think he might be involved with the missing key."

"How so?"

"He could have passed it off when he went to Chili's."

"That means we're looking for an accomplice, for sure."

Rachael took her time thinking through his remark. "'Fraid so. I might be stretching a little to get Derek on this. We'll see."

A quick look passed between the two. "Now, back to Angie. Who's going to tell her folks about her death? And her poor son. Do you have any idea who the father is?"

"None," Hal replied grimly. "Beckett would have personnel records. Do you want to handle that part?"

"Good place to start," Rachael agreed. "I'll head over there now. Why don't you give Elliott a call at the TV station? He usually keeps up with all of the bullshit in town. Maybe he's got some gossip on Angie's dating habits."

Rachael took her gun and badge out of her desk drawer and threw them into her purse.

"I'll take my own car to the Oasis and go home afterward," she called out to Hal. "Need to catch my breath before we go on tactical alert tonight. Gimme a call when you finish with Elliott." She headed out the back door of the PD and into the 118-degree heat. As usual, it took her breath away. *Only crazy people would live in heat like this, so what does that say about me?*

The trip to the Oasis Casino took ten minutes. She traveled through Old Town Bullhead, glancing at the river's edge to catch anything out of the norm. *Where will you show up tonight? How will you dump Melissa's body? No one deserves to be tortured for a year.* A chill shot through her body.

Valet parking was always the easiest. She pulled into the covered area by the front door of the Oasis. Rachael was immediately met by a young man she hadn't seen before. She flashed her badge at the parking attendant. He smiled.

"On the clock today? I'll park it close by."

Rachael headed toward the interior bank of elevators. Beckett's office was a treat to visit—one of the best views of the river. She wondered what his penthouse looked like. While Beckett had come on to her many times, she had always rejected his passes. *If I had any other job, he might be worth a whirl. Polite, handsome, and rich. Not a bad combination. But also sleazy.*

Rachael called Beckett's secretary on the house phone to arrange for the impromptu visit. Beckett was interviewing a new employee, but she could go up to the penthouse to meet with him. "He will only be a minute more, Detective."

Rachael immediately pressed the penthouse button in the elevator and inputted the code she had been given. The express elevator swooped her up to the top floor. She was arranging her gun and blouse when the elevator door opened and she stood face-to-face with her sister.

28

Meg laughed at Derek's huge presence in her little car as they went on their way, eager to have some fun before he headed back to Orange County. Once inside the house, she dug around in the closets and found a suitable bathing suit for him. The two changed clothes and met in the kitchen.

"I'm taking you for a real boat ride, and this time, we won't get knocked out on wine or stuck in the mud," Meg said as she threw some crackers, cheese, and apples into an ice chest. A decent chardonnay was added to the picnic basket.

"Promise?"

"I never make promises. Grab two squatty chairs from the garage. I'll meet you downstairs with the rest of our stuff," Meg said.

Meg and Rachael had pooled their money one summer and purchased a six-man rubber Zodiac with a motor. It was a perfect size to cruise the river, go to the casinos, and occasionally fish when the mood struck them. All the locals knew the Zodiac by sight and would try to swamp the girls. Meg and Rachael would carry a bucket filled with water, and when the Sea-Doos or small boats would attack them, they would let the water fly in return. Nothing like good times on the river.

"I'll get in first and start the motor. When it's going strong, just untie the bow line and jump in," Meg said.

Completing the task was not as easy as it sounded. Derek struggled to untie the boat while fighting with the current and trying to "jump in." Meg was hysterical watching his antics. Finally, he was safely on board, and they headed downstream to her favorite cove.

"This is Willow Cove," she said as they arrived. "My fave spot." The entrance to the cove was narrow and rocky, but the Zodiac managed to float through with Meg's expert driving. Thick willows were everywhere, presenting a complex maze of openings. "We're protected from the rush of the river, and the water temperature is always about ten degrees warmer. There's a sandy beach just around the next rush of willows. See it?"

Derek marveled at how a small beach could bring such huge joy to Meg. *She's an enigma,* he thought. *Sophisticated, yet simple. An airhead at times and yet very grounded at others. Ultimately, a person to be reckoned with.*

Floating around in inner tubes, eating and drinking, laughing and kissing, the two each shared stories of their present love affairs and a few from their past. Derek seemed to have more to brag about in that category than Megan. His affairs were short and torrid and ended with an agreement of stony silence when they were over. The opposite belied Meg's relationships. Her affairs were sensual, lengthy, fun, tender, and always ended with the two parties maintaining a unique, close friendship.

"You're getting toasted…and I don't mean from the wine," Meg said. "The SPF thirty is wearing off. We'd better get back to the house and into some air-conditioning. It's past noon. By the time you shower, it'll be time for your flight back to the OC."

"Air sounds good, but the OC sounds like work. I'd rather stay in your tiny paradise."

Reluctantly, the two packed up the Zodiac. They were comfortable with each other now and didn't need to communicate all of their thoughts. Instinctively, she packed the cooler, he picked it up, she washed off the chairs, and he packed them in the boat. Everything was relaxed. Everything seemed just right.

Starting the motor was effortless, and the two snaked their way through the willows, heading out the small opening between the rocks into the fast-flowing river water. They reached the opening as a seaplane taxied to the opposite shore.

29

El Jefe had stationed himself on the third floor of the abandoned building across the river from the designated meeting site. He had been there for twenty minutes awaiting Carlos and the seaplane. His M-2 rifle was set up with the Bushnell Elite 3200 scope that he had purchased online. When he spotted a Jeep driving down the dirt road across from the river, he tensed. About two hundred yards downstream, a man exited his Jeep and made his way upstream, carefully concealing himself behind the underbrush as he walked.

The drone of the seaplane approaching from the south announced its arrival, and El Jefe readied his rifle as the scene unfolded across the river. The Renegade 410 was a new addition to the fleet of planes that El Jefe now owned. This trip was the first time Trujillo had flown the plane, and being stranded overnight on a sandy beach had not been part of the plan.

El Jefe leaned the rifle on a rusty rail, raised his binoculars, and adjusted the lenses. He focused on the plane landing and watched as Trujillo started unloading the Styrofoam boxes. A swirl of dust announced the arrival of Carlos's car. El Jefe checked his watch. Carlos was late. He watched as Carlos jumped out of the minivan.

"Hola." Carlos greeted the pilot nervously. "Let me open the van, and I'll load the stuff."

"*Si, si,*" was Trujillo's response. He moved with nervous intent, still concerned over El Jefe's threat. He searched the area for a shooter. "Who's the bitch?"

"What?" Carlos turned to see Sasha waddling toward the water. "I told you to stay in the car!" he shouted back at her.

"It's too damn hot. I'm going to explode in there. The baby's trying to kick out my sides. I'm going to wade in the water. Mind your own business. Hurry up so we can get out of here."

El Jefe cringed. *What the hell is that whore doing here? Carlos, you fucked up again.* He realized that his plans had to change immediately. There were too many witnesses. He dug into his gun case and pulled out an object similar to a garage door transmitter. He pushed the button. Sasha was hurled into the air by the explosion.

Smoke obscured the shoreline. "Shit, who blew up my car?" yelled Carlos. Turning, he saw that Sasha had been knocked down. Her belly was stained with blood, and she was twitching. He ran to her, screaming her name. Her fingers dug into the sand. A few more steps and he could help her. A piercing sting in his back crippled him. "Oh, God, Sasha, Sasha. What have I done?"

Sasha tried to respond. Only a sucking noise emerged. Shrapnel from the explosion had ripped a hole through her upper torso.

Carlos tried to crawl to her, but another shot resounded from across the river, and this one exploded through his head, ending his journey. Carlos died as he had lived, struggling to overcome what he had never fully understood. "Sorry, *mamacita*," he whispered with his last breath.

Trujillo watched in silent terror as the bodies fell before him. He ran, zigzagging through the watery underbrush and then across the sand toward the desert. Trying to outrun El Jefe was futile, so he stopped and faced his tormentor across the river. "Take your best shot, you son of a bitch."

Two more shots and Trujillo's lifeless body dug a trench in the sand as he fell. A concealed stranger now came out of the brush and headed for the seaplane. Blood and bodies covered the ground. He stepped over the carnage as he headed for the plane. His job was simple, and he was focused on it—he was to fly the empty plane back to Mexico.

Meg and Derek emerged from the willow cove just as the shooting began. Meg let out a piercing cry before she could stop herself. The sound carried downstream to El Jefe's hiding place. He lowered the rifle, picked up his binoculars, and turned his attention to the Zodiac visible up river.

"We've got to get the hell out of here."

They started upstream. The current was strong, and their progress was slow. Meg guided the boat, trying to put distance between the shooter and them. Bullets pinged in the water.

"We're out of striking distance. Thank God. Give me my cell phone. Hurry," Meg yelled.

30

While Meg and Derek struggled to put more distance between the shooter and themselves, Amanda and Rachael fought to keep their composure. No one flinched. The two sisters stood there, inches apart, minds whirling, but keeping their cool. Rachael cleared her voice as Amanda took a step toward Beckett.

Beckett spoke first. "Oh, Detective Pennington, what brings Bullhead's finest to my casino today? Need some tips for betting the ponies?" He smiled suavely. "Excuse my lame jokes. Amanda Roberts, let me introduce you to Detective Rachael Pennington of the Bullhead Police Department."

Oh, crap, Amanda. I should have called you.
Oh, sis, don't blow my cover, for God's sake.

The two women shook hands. An awkward silence followed, so Amanda smiled at Beckett and headed for the elevator. "I'd better get to work, Mr. Beckett. I'll be back after the lunch shift for that tour you promised me."

"Until then, Amanda. Congratulations on landing such a good part in the show. You'll certainly be an asset to our ticket sales. And by the way, it's just Beckett."

Turning, Beckett addressed Rachael. "Looks like you have something on your mind, Rachael. How may I be of service? And I mean that in a nonprofessional way as well." His eyes, ever roaming, traveled up and down her body, just as they had checked out her sister's exit moments ago.

"Oh, give it up, Beckett. Your chance with me passed years ago. Looks like you've hooked up with a newbie, anyway."

"No hookup yet, but I plan on trying. There are so few pleasures left in life that when an opportunity presents itself, well…"

"OK, Beckett, got the point. Now, I'm here officially, and I'm on the clock. Angie Perkins has been identified as the victim thrown over the spillway on Saturday night." Rachael watched closely for a reaction to the news. No tell, but of course, he was a gambler. "I know you two were an item for a while."

"Oh, God. I was afraid that might be her. She hasn't been to work for almost a week now. The night of the monsoon, someone said."

"Again. Your relationship?"

"My relationship with Angie was, say, sporadically spontaneous. I would call when I wanted to see her. The rest of her social life is unknown to me. Anything else?"

"I'd like you to check her personnel file for next of kin. Did she have a steady boyfriend? Who did she hang out with from the casino?" Still no reaction to the news.

He crossed the room and sat behind his desk. Rachael could see that he was a little nervous, intertwining and releasing his fingers and then making a steeple with them as they continued to twitch. Was this guilt, remorse, or a sincere gesture of concern? It saddened her to see that a human life was reduced to such a shallow conversation.

Beckett leaned back in his expensive leather chair and rotated around until he was facing the river. Rachael gave him time to collect his thoughts but wondered if he was just using the time to contrive an appropriate reaction. Time passed, and he made no attempt to continue the conversation. Rachael stepped around the desk and blocked his view.

"Come now, Beckett, don't overdo the scene. She was just another easy lay, and everyone in town knew that. So, what gives? Who was she hanging with? I'll need names. Was she into drugs or gambling?" Rachael asked.

Beckett swiveled around again and lifted the intercom. "Betty, the detective will need a copy of Angie Perkins's personnel file. Oh, and Betty, you were tight with Angie—who was she dating, and who were her buddies? Give that info to Rachael on her way out." He stood to usher her out the door.

"If you think you can herd me out, guess again," said Rachael. "I'll need an alibi for you the night of her murder, between, say, ten p.m. and three a.m." She wanted to take this opportunity to catch him in a lie. She pulled out her notebook to start taking down the statement when her phone rang. "Excuse me, Beckett."

As Rachael opened her phone, Meg's terrified voice came pouring out. "Rachael, we're in the Zodiac. A sniper is shooting at us. God, oh God. A seaplane landed across from the skeleton building." Meg spurted out all the facts. She was almost incoherent.

"Meg, calm down." She walked away from Beckett and muffled her voice. "What?"

"Send an ambulance...across from the skeleton casino. Now." The line went dead.

"What's going on, Rachael?" Beckett asked.

"Later," she yelled as she ducked into the elevator.

When out of earshot of Beckett, Rachael called Hal. "Meg's in trouble. Sniper on the river." She quickly filled in the sparse information. "You take care of the ambulance, bodies, and whatever else on the Arizona side. Have someone check on Meg. I'll call Metro and head down Casino Drive. Maybe I can cut the shooter off on this side. I'll check the River Rat Bar, too. Someone may have seen or heard something. Call me with what you've got. Be careful."

"You too, partner."

Rachael ran for valet parking, bumping senior gamblers out of the way as she aimed for the exit. She called Metro, asking for her counterpart in the Laughlin Police Department, Gary Temple. Rachael filled him in on the details of the crime, knowing Gary would react immediately.

Peeling out of the parking lot, she slammed the red light onto her dash. Dialed Meg's number. Voice mail. Not a good sign.

River Rat Bar's dirt parking lot was crowded with Harleys. Although she knew that one of the bikes could belong to the shooter, Rachael continued down the highway toward the abandoned building. She called Gary and asked him to have one of his officers stop at the bar.

"Check any warm engine, get the license numbers on all the bikes, and follow up inside the bar. Bill will help."

When Rachael pulled onto the dirt road leading to the abandoned building, she was careful not to run over the fresh motorcycle tracks. From the ruts in the dirt, she knew that he was probably long gone. She continued on. Metro would take over this part of the investigation because it was on the Laughlin side of the river. Since it was a cross-river shooting, the two police departments would have to sort out the jurisdiction later.

Rachael quickly opened her ringing phone when she saw it was Hal. "Go," she said.

"God, Rachael. It's a friggin' mess. Carlos is dead, and his girlfriend is dying. Roberto is here working CPR on her. EMTs are on their way. Carlos's car blew up, but there are some body parts here in containers. Probably what that plane was delivering. The pilot took off before we got here. There's another car uphill, a Jeep. No tags. No driver. There's another male body. Mexican. No sense to all of this. Shit. What the hell is going on? Too many kidneys floating around to be a coincidence, and all of these are in medical boxes ready for transplant."

"Have you heard from Meg? Is she all right?" asked Rachael.

"She's back at the house. Shook up," Hal said, "but not injured. She's worried that the perp got the AZ numbers on the Zodiac. We'll need to stake out a patrol car at your house. How's your end going?"

Rachael told Hal that the shooter had gotten away. "I found two rifle casings. No signs of the rifle. Sniper probably broke it down and stashed it. I'll leave one casing here. CSI can deal with it." She took a picture of the evidence, bagged and tagged one of the casings for their office, leaving the other for Metro.

"Metro should be here any minute. I asked Gary to check the River Rat for any new activity. Maybe twenty-five bikes in the lot."

"Recognize any of them?"

"Going too fast. Didn't have time. I'm through now. Gotta head to the house to check on Meg."

"Derek's with her."

"I figured. Oh, listen. Just met Amanda with Beckett. She's on assignment."

"What's she working on?"

"Don't know. You'll probably run into her. Stay cool."

"Still looking sweet?"

"You horny old fart, back off," Rachael said. "One Pennington girl is enough for any man." She walked away from the crime scene.

Hal scoffed. "As I see it, I don't have one Pennington girl anymore. Guess I never did."

Rachael closed her phone.

31

Yellow tape had been stretched around the crime scene, covering a square mile down to the water's edge. Stacked along the shore were several medical containers. This was the second shipment that had been seized, so Hal recognized them as organ transplant receptacles. He carefully stacked the boxes. He always held out hope that a miracle would float his way.

Hal noted each organ description, the blood type, and the expiration date. Heart Type AB-8/02; kidney Type B negative-8/03; liver Type A-8/02; kidney Type A-8/01. Hal froze. Sarah's blood type. It's viable until tomorrow. He paused, looked around, and carried the medical boxes to his SUV, replacing the containers with cones for the CSI team to find. *Play it cool. Play it cool.*

Walking over to the other investigating officer, he said, "What's your take on what went down here?"

"Beats the hell out of me," he replied. "It's going to take all day to clean up this mess. Anybody checking on the seaplane that took off?"

"I'll call headquarters. They'll get on it right away. You know, there are some organs here, ready for transplant. I'll rush them over to Mohave General. They're still good."

"Hey, it's evidence, man. Better check with the captain. You know how he gets about chain of evidence."

"Right, sure. Last time we stopped a shipment, they went to the hospital, but...yeah. You're right. I'll check in with the old man first." With that, Hal hurried to his car. A crazy plan was forming. He felt all eyes were on him as he pulled the SUV away from the sandy beach. As he took off toward the department, he grabbed his personal cell phone.

"Sarah, how do you feel, honey?"

"Oh, OK, Daddy. Are you on your way home? This is the day for my dialysis."

"Well, honey, there's been a little change. There's a new doctor in Henderson who might be able to help you. I have to stop by the department for a few minutes, but I want you to pack a small bag. PJs, your toothbrush, hairbrush, robe, and slippers. I'll be there in an hour. Oh, and don't eat or drink anything. Love ya, baby."

"I'm spending the night there?"

"Just this once. Hurry up, now. I gotta go."

Hal closed his cell phone. He drove up Ramar and parked next to a dumpster behind the TV appliance shop. He retrieved the one container that matched Sarah's blood type and placed it on the backseat, covering it with a jacket.

As he headed toward the PD, he made a second call—a call that hopefully would change his daughter's life and quite possibly ruin his career.

32

After finishing her investigation of the derelict building, Rachael stopped at the River Rat Bar. There were two Metro cop cars parked out front. The bar was established in 1958. Long overdue for some tender loving care, it looked seedy, and likewise, so did the clientele. It was built within fifty yards of the river, and no matter what kind of inbreed was knocking down a beer, the view was majestic. Bill, the bartender, was part owner, and he didn't take kindly to fights when they would inevitably erupt. Being a retired Navy SEAL and never hesitant to brag about it, he found his reputation kept fights down to a minimum. His persuasion was hidden behind the bar, a heavy baseball bat with lots of DNA on it.

Bill greeted Rachael with a roaring hello over the din of the patrons. Past lunchtime, the crowd had settled in for serious drinking. He motioned his head toward the rear of the room.

Rachael saw the two cops talking to a small group of bikers. She moved toward the Metro guys to see what kind of leads they were picking up. Since nothing too important was being divulged, she headed back to sit at the bar and quiz Bill.

Rachael and Bill had been friends for years. He liked to be in the know and in return would act as Rachael's quasi snitch. Most of his information was drug related.

"So what's going on?" asked Bill. "Shit, we haven't seen this much activity since the Mongols and Hells Angels shoot-out at Harrah's."

"Oh, some maniac was shooting from that abandoned casino building. It looks like they shot someone across the river. There was a seaplane involved. A holy mess. Hal's covering the scene on the Arizona side. Have you seen or heard anything?"

"You know, Rachael, you might want to talk to Elliott. He was in around lunchtime. You know how he is. He can get info out of a can of vegetable soup if you give him enough time."

"What time did he get here?"

"Lunchtime. He didn't order any food. Didn't stay around too long. One beer."

"Was he on his Harley?" asked Rachael.

"Probably, but don't know for sure. That's how he usually gets here. It was a weird time of day for him to drop by. Usually it's late afternoon, after his second newscast. Anyway, he was by himself."

"Thanks, Bill. Call if you hear anything else."

"Will do."

"Gotta go. Heading home. Meg's got herself in another pickle. Oh, and also a new male companion of sorts. Not too sure about this one. Anyway, call me if you see anything suspicious. OK?"

"What? Meg found another loser boyfriend? Why am I not surprised?" Bill said with a smile. "And she doesn't even pick them up here."

Rachael looked around at the bar's scruffy inhabitants; most of them lived on a singular diet of beer and had the bellies to prove it. "Well, the guys here are really not her type, but who knows with that girl?"

"Tell her hi for me. Next to you, she's my favorite."

"Well, I'll be sure to let Amanda know you said that when I see her."

"Oh, shit. I'm in trouble already."

"Not to worry. Your secret is safe with me. Gotta go." Rachael was getting itchy to leave the bar. Meg needed some counseling, and night was closing in on the town.

33

Hal quickly finished logging in the evidence from the crime scene. He stopped by the Captain's office. "Hey, Cap. I brought some kidneys or whatever from the scene. Someone should take 'em over to Mohave General. Still might be good."

"You take 'em. We're short staffed."

"Sorry, Cap. Can't do. I've got to check out for a few hours. Sarah is having another bout. I need to take her in for dialysis."

"Jeez, Hal. We're in perp mode. You know that Melissa's body's supposed to show up tonight. Everyone's on duty."

"Only need a few hours. I'll be back to cover my regular shift."

"You're pushing me. Shit. OK." He motioned for Hal to leave. He knew Hal would never leave the department for any personal matter other than his daughter's health. Loyal and honest should have teen tattooed on his forehead. The captain wished he had more cops like him.

"Have you heard anything else about Carlos's baby?" asked Hal as he was leaving. "I heard his girlfriend didn't make it."

"I talked to Roberto, and he says the baby's got a fighting chance. They kept Sasha alive long enough to do a C-section. He's on his way back to help out tonight."

"That's wrong in so many ways."

"Carlos's mom is on her way to the morgue. Sasha has some relatives who'd probably take the baby. Roberto thinks he and his wife would like to adopt her. God, it's a shame, a real shame. Roberto's worked so hard to get Carlos to go straight. He was a good kid, but the money was too much of a temptation. Really sad."

Hal nodded and took off. He stopped at the Wells Fargo Bank to withdraw ten thousand dollars in cash, as instructed by the hospital. Arriving home, he took the kidney and transferred it into his personal car, helped Sarah with her overnight bag, and headed to Henderson.

Crossing the Laughlin Bridge, he spotted Rachael's car coming toward him. He knew she would see him—couldn't be helped—and of course she did. Immediately, his cell phone rang. Viewing her name in the display, he elected to ignore it. *I'll deal with her later. The less she knows, the better.*

34

Amanda made a date for early afternoon with Beckett to get the grand tour of the casino, including the surveillance rooms, cashier booths, and his office. She told him she planned on moving up in the casino world and her current occupations of cocktail waitress and dancer were short-lived. Elliott was a little hesitant about sharing casino secrets. Angie had to be disposed of for that very reason. Ultimately, his personal desire to impress this beauty won out.

Amanda arrived at the appointed time, and the tour began in the cashier's cage. He explained the various holding areas, the pick-up procedures, including the checks and balances, the counting room, and the vault.

"Sorry I can't take you into the vault. Very few people allowed. I'm sure you understand."

"No problem. What I'm looking forward to is the surveillance area. How about now?"

"Why the interest?"

"Always wondered how much cleavage is really taped." She smiled and flexed.

Dozens of monitors lined the walls, with technicians scrutinizing every move of the gamblers down below. Other cameras were installed in the shops, theater area, dining rooms, and all other areas excluding the bathrooms and guest rooms. Amanda acted impressed with the setup when Beckett mentioned that much of the security was a result of his design.

Beckett was growing weary of being the perfect host. He checked his watch. "Your afternoon rehearsal starts in less than an hour. Let's go to my office for a drink."

"Sounds good."

Counting on perfect timing from her partner, Amanda acted excited about their forthcoming alone time. They passed Matt at a bank of slot machines. He nodded as she walked by. Entering his office, Beckett took time to introduce Amanda to his secretary, Betty.

Amanda began, "The view is breathtaking—almost as nice as your penthouse. I'd be ecstatic to do the nine-to-five here, although I probably wouldn't get too much done."

"Oh, after a while it's old hat. Besides, my hours are nowhere near nine to five—no, usually four in the afternoon until whenever the casino quiets down. On weekends, I make an appearance and usually have to settle some ridiculous fight about three times a night. Mostly drunks."

"Do you throw them out personally?"

"If they're not guests, they're escorted to the coffee shop for a free meal by security. I kick out a few drunks per shift. All in a day's work," said Beckett.

Betty interrupted. "Beckett, security wants you to turn on your monitor. Table twelve. A drunk. He made the lady in first position move 'cause she's getting the good cards. He wanted her chair. She's still getting the good cards, and he's cussing everybody out. Now he's yelling that the casino is prejudiced 'cause he's Mexican. You know how the gaming commission feels about being 'colorblind.' What do you want me to tell the pit boss?"

Matt was doing his job. Beckett turned to the computer, switched the screen over to table 12, and watched as the man began shoving the lady's chair. "He doesn't look Mexican. Oh, shit, it's probably one of Elliott's customers. I'm on my way. Get Elliott on the phone when I get back. This agreement is starting to piss me off."

Beckett stormed out of the office. Amanda moved to his computer. Cash irregularities, offshore accounts, or evidence of other illegal dealings was her primary mission. Beckett had left without logging off, so all she needed to do was locate Beckett's personal file. She took the flash drive from her purse and started copying the information.

"Amanda, are you coming out? Beckett doesn't like anyone in his office," yelled Betty.

"Well, I guess so. Beckett said he was going to fix me a drink, but it's getting late. I'd better get ready for practice."

A few files hadn't been copied, but she had enough to take back to the FBI for analysis. Returning Beckett's computer to its original screen, Amanda walked past Betty.

"Betty, tell Beckett we'll have to get together later. See ya."

35

Halfway to Henderson, Hal called ahead to the private hospital and asked for Dr. Hendricks. Per his earlier instructions, he used a prepaid, disposable cell phone.

"Use the delivery entrance when you arrive. There will be a nurse and wheelchair waiting. Give the kidney and envelope to the nurse. Stay with Sarah while she gets prepped for surgery. The nurse will give you a set of post-op instructions. You will get a phone call when it's time to return. Any questions?"

"None. And thanks, Doc." Hal loosened his grip on the steering wheel and continued driving. He glanced at Sarah and noticed she seemed troubled. "You OK, honey?" he asked.

She was slow to answer. "I guess so, Daddy. I worry when we do something different. Tell me again why we're going to Henderson instead of Mohave Valley Hospital? I like all the people at Mohave. They know my name and give me extra ice cream."

Hal stifled his emotions. How simple it was to please his daughter. He had to hold it together, but his emotions were running raw. Deceiving Rachael, stealing a kidney, and praying the doctor could save Sarah's life was his new reality. Now he had to lie to her. Secrecy was, of course, all important to the success of this venture. No one could know that Sarah had a new kidney. She was way down on the national registry list. Everyone knew it, and she knew it. He didn't want Sarah to carry this burden, but...later, when she was old enough to understand his actions as love-propelled, he would tell her.

"Well, honey," he began, "there's a wonderful doctor in Henderson who has developed a new treatment for your type of problem. Dr. H. When we get to the hospital, a nurse will take some blood. They want to make sure you're OK. This time, you will be going to sleep for a while. I'll be with you all the time so you won't have to be scared."

"How come I have to go to sleep? We never had to do that before."

"I know, sweetie, but this time they are going to make a small cut by your belly button area so he can do his magic trick and save your kidney.

When it's all done, you won't have to go for dialysis anymore. Won't that be great?"

Sarah sat for a while, staring out the window at the barren desert. "Will I have a big scar that'll show when I wear my bathing suit?"

"Naw, no one will ever see it." He laughed, happy that she seemed to be handling the situation. He glanced over. How very grown up she was for a wannabe teenager. "It's best that you don't tell anyone about your new scar."

"How come? You mean not even Rachael?"

Shit. Especially not Rachael. "Well, Sarah, this new treatment is not approved by all of the hospitals. Since I know and trust Dr. H., he said he would do it for you. We don't want to get him in trouble, do we? You know, when people do favors sometimes, you can't tell anybody. Some favors have to stay a secret."

With that, Sarah sat back, seemingly satisfied with her dad's explanation. After a few more miles, Sarah broke the silence again. "Will I still be on the kidney list?"

"For now, yes, until we see how you do."

"Dad, if something happens to me, then you wouldn't have anybody to take care of you. I don't mind the pain that much, daddy. I'd rather have the pain than not to be around to make your breakfast."

Hal's lips turned inward as he fought to control the tears. *Poor baby, poor baby.* "I guess I didn't realize how grown up you are. You'll be fine, honey. This isn't anything risky. Dr. H. has done this lots of times, and everyone always gets better. Don't worry. I love you like crazy."

"Love you back," said Sarah as she leaned her head on his shoulder and worried.

36

Amanda inserted the key card to her room and stepped inside when it opened. She froze. The TV was on. Someone was in the shower.

What the hell? *I know the door was locked when I left. It's automatic.* She slipped over to the bed and lifted the edge of the mattress, looking for her gun. Gone. Now what? Glancing around the room, she saw a badge. *Matt wouldn't show up like this. He has his own room.* She decided to storm the bathroom, but as she turned, she stopped short.

"How the hell did you find me?"

Trent, her old LAPD partner and ex-lover, was standing in the doorway, a towel wrapped around his naked body. "Easy enough when you have friends in high places," he said and moved toward her. In his right hand was her gun; in the left, his.

"Unloaded your friend just in case you weren't too happy to see me."

Amanda could tell that he had been drinking and knew that the next few minutes might be fatal for one of them. "Surprised comes to mind."

"When you left without even a note, I figured we had some unfinished business. Am I wrong?"

Amanda smiled. "Let's put all of our guns on the table and talk about this, shall we? I'll feel a little more comfortable that way."

"No problem." Trent walked over and put Amanda's gun on the table. He put his Glock next to it. Clips had been removed.

"How about your backup?"

"Oh, yeah. Forgot. Mine's in the bathroom." He walked over to her dresser and pulled out another gun. "Can't forget yours."

Now what? I can't call security. He'll blow my cover. "I'm on an assignment, Trent. You really need to go. I'll meet you somewhere in town and we can talk."

"I think not. I like my odds here. We'll stay."

Amanda knew if she offered him a drink, he would take it. "I don't have a mini-bar in the room. If you insist on talking now, I need a drink. Let me call room service and order up some drinks and food. I'm starved."

"No tricks now, sweetie. I know the way your mind works."

She picked up the room phone and quickly dialed Matt's number. "Hi, this is room four-oh-two. We'd like a pitcher of margaritas and two ham sandwiches delivered, please."

Matt answered. "You need help?"

"Rye bread for one and the other white with no mayo."

"I'll be there in three minutes. Guns blazing?"

"No, that will be all. Oh, just a minute. Trent, do you want anything else?"

"No, and for God's sake, hang up already."

Amanda made small talk with Trent, and when Matt knocked on the door, she walked over, commenting that room service was really fast these days.

"Matt, what are you doing here?" Amanda said. "Our date is for seven o'clock. You're super early."

Matt picked up on the ruse. "Couldn't wait to see my girl. Oops, looks like you have company...naked, with guns," he said as he entered the room.

"Well, that didn't take long, Amanda. What? Did you have this guy lined up before you left me?" Trent crossed the room, and before Amanda could duck, he punched her across the face, opening a crack on her lip. She moved in close and kneed him in the groin, giving Matt enough time to collect the guns.

Trent bent over with pain and grabbed his crotch. "You bitch."

Amanda took her gun from Matt and loaded it. "If you didn't know it before, get the picture now. I've moved on. If I ever see you again, I'll file a restraining order with LAPD, and your career will be toast. Now get your sorry ass out of here before I decide to shoot you myself. Matt, you get his clothes. Make him dress in front of us. I don't trust him."

Trent glared at her. Towel now around his ankles, he grabbed his dick and thrust it at her. "Last chance to ride a big one," he said with a painful smile.

Amanda raised her gun toward him. "Put it away, or I'll blow your balls off. You were never that great, anyway."

"This isn't over." Trent dressed, shifting his stare between Matt and Amanda. "Count on it." He slammed the door as he left.

"What do you think? Is that the last of him?" asked Matt. "Do you want to call the Bureau or let me handle it for you?"

"I'll do it. I'll fill them in today in case they need to intervene. Thanks for showing up. I was about ready to wrestle him for my gun."

"No problem."

"Wow, I really picked a winner when I dated him. I thought Meg was the only one with poor taste in men."

"I've had a few of those myself. Don't beat yourself up. Looks to me like you can handle yourself, anyway. Nice knee job." He smiled.

Amanda looked at Matt, really seeing him for the first time. "Thanks again. I'd better put some ice on this split lip and get ready for work."

37

Traffic was heavy on the 95 as Rachael headed home. Glancing to her left, she smiled with a heavy heart at all the new construction. Life seemed less stressful when there was just a gas station and an airport that would barely handle a Piper Cub. Now, the big dogs all clamored to get their spot on the tarmac. Home Depot was open, along with a Lowe's, IHOP, Chili's, McDonald's, Panda Express, and on and on. The south end of town now featured a Kohl's, Marshalls, Apple Haircutters, Target, and some other outlet stores. Was this really progress? The town seemed more and more to resemble any other town, losing its folksy identity.

Rachael reminisced about the early days, days when youth was wasted on the young. Grace always said the best days were when you were a kid, with free room and board and no responsibility except making your bed. How right she was. Sister rivalry tore through their home life when they were young. Grace was a teacher then and had all summer to spend with her daughters. June 13, the swimsuits, shorts, tank tops, makeup, and sunscreen were packed, and the four would jump into the car, heading for Black Meadow Landing at Lake Havasu, where they would spend most of the summer. A cabin on Catalina Island was also rented each summer. A cool break from the desert heat.

Watermelon days. Every day was filled with waterskiing, chicken fights, horseshoes, and other games that would end with everyone rolling with laughter. At night, the girls would sneak out of camp for a party on the hill. Grace was a great provider, but often she would hire someone to take care of the girls and disappear for a few weeks. Rachael often wondered if she had a second life going on.

Back to reality. Meg's car was parked in the driveway. No Derek's car? The garage door opened and swallowed Rachael's car. Finding the house empty, Rachael put her gun and badge on the closet shelf. She glanced out the family room slider toward the boat dock. *No Derek—good.* Stopping to kick off her shoes, Rachael poured a glass of chardonnay for Meg and some apple juice for herself. She headed down the stairs.

Without looking, Meg said, "You'd better have two drinks in your hand. Both for me."

"Sorry, I have to go back to work tonight. But I do have a drink for you—will chardonnay do?"

Meg turned to greet her sister and immediately perked up when she saw the wine. "You should have brought the bottle. I've had a helluva day."

Rachael sat down beside Meg, put her feet in the cold water, and, leaning over, gave Meg a tight squeeze. It seemed like a replay of the day before, but so much had happened in between. How crazy their lives had become. "You OK?"

"Yeah, I guess."

"Lay it on me, sis. I need to know every detail to catch this bastard."

"Well, first, Rach. God, what happened to those people on the beach? It looked like the girl was pregnant. Was she? I didn't have a lot of time to look. Do you know who she is? Are they all dead?"

"It was Sasha."

"Sasha? Oh, my God. And Carlos? Was Carlos hit, too?"

Rachael shook her head. "Sorry, sis. He's dead. Sasha didn't make it, either, but they're trying to save the baby." Rachael gave her a quick recap of what she knew.

Meg sat quietly. She hated violence and never could understand why her two sisters had picked such brutal professions. "Sis, I'm pretty sure that the shooter got a good look at the AZ numbers on the Zodiac. Derek and I were leaving Willows Beach. We were really connecting."

"OK, about him, the shooter. What else?"

"I told Hal most of this. Rifle probably had a scope. God, the bullets were pinging around all sides of us."

"Well, if the shooter was good enough to flatten Sasha with one bullet, how could he miss a rubber boat?"

"That's your department. Anyway, we finally ducked behind the island, and then I heard a motorcycle. If he had a scope on that rifle, that means he got a good look at me, too. I made Derek hide on the bottom of the boat. He probably thinks I was alone. Now what'll we do? Holy crap, all I wanted was a nice afternoon with a great guy."

"Speaking of Derek," Rachael said, "where is your knight in shining armor? Boy, he spooks easy. Might be a lesson there."

Meg bristled, took another sip of her wine, and launched into a full-scale attack on her sister. "I can't believe that you would even think of giving me love advice. Look at your record lately. Speaking of spooking easily, what happened between you and Hal? He was a real jerk this afternoon."

"Later about that, too."

"Do you know what Derek said when he left?"

"No clue. What?"

"In a nutshell, he said that he likes me a lot, but in the four days or so that he's known me, he's been drugged, accused of murder, stalked by me, and finally was shot at by some wacko person while floating down the river. He said he knew all of it didn't have to do with me, said Bullhead was probably more to blame, and he never wanted to come back here. He's right, you know—nothing bad happened to us when we were together in Yorba Linda." Meg sighed and looked at her older sister with baleful eyes. "He said that if my life ever gets back to normal—whatever normal might be for me—that I should give him a call and we'll meet someplace, not here." She sipped more wine. "And…" she continued, "I don't have a job right now until they clear me. Add to that the shooter is probably looking for me. Could even be across the river right now. So how does that stack up against your day?"

Trying to reason with Meg right now was out of the question, so Rachael took another approach. "The captain was going to assign a patrol car to watch our house for the next twenty-four hours, but we decided it'd be best for you to get out of town. Since you can't go back to work yet, it should be pretty easy for you to disappear for a while. Besides, the serial killer has a due date in two days."

"Who the hell is 'we?' God, there you go again," screeched Meg. She stood up on the boat dock, feet spread apart and hands on her hips.

"Telling me what to do, living my life for me. No way, José. I will damn well do as I please. I'm capable of making my own decisions and taking care of myself."

Rachael, tired of Meg's outburst, also stood. Putting on her cop face, she said, "Look, you *will* leave town, but you don't have to go to Mom's. In fact, you can't. We're making her leave the Yorba Linda house, too. She doesn't know it yet, and she'll be just as pissed as you are. But too damn bad. This is a full-blown multiple murder investigation. I can't protect my family and get the job done at the same time."

"Too effin' bad."

"Now Hal is up to something that he won't talk to me about. I just passed him heading out of town, maybe to Vegas, right in the middle of our investigation. So I can't count on him to help me protect you, either. Then there's Roberto. His cousin's been murdered, and he's still working the case. He shouldn't be anywhere near that case. The captain's losing it, and to top it off, it's time for the monster to strike again." Rachael paused for a breath but, not wishing to lose her momentum, continued, "Now settle down and pack a bag. You *are* leaving. I'll call Mom. Maybe you two can meet in Palm Springs."

Meg realized that she had lost the battle. She leaned against the dock's pole, finishing her drink. They were both quiet.

"Not much water coming down the river today. That old carp is back. Nothing to swim in," she said as she watched the ancient fish circle the dock.

Rachael, satisfied with the direction of the conversation, glanced down at the clear water. "He swam by yesterday, looking for dinner." The carp circled a round object protruding from the murky bottom of the river. She looked closer, thinking it was a grape. "Oh, my God," she cried. "It's an eye. Get it, Meg, before the carp swallows it."

Meg looked at her sister in disgust. "Hey, I may be the one in a bathing suit, but I'm not a cop, and I'm *not* fishing a dead eyeball out of the water for you. That's the grossest thing you've ever asked me to do. Get it yourself, sis."

"Ah, come on," Rachael pleaded. "I need it for evidence."

"I'm going to pack for my lovely, lovely trip." Oozing sarcasm, Meg drank the last of her wine and started up the gangplank. Passing behind Rachael, she hesitated, and then with a quick move bumped Rachael with her butt and knocked her into the water.

Rachael went flying. The carp disappeared. When Rachael came up for air, she spurted, "I'll get you for this."

"Yeah, yeah," said Meg with a smile. "Be sure to rinse off before you come into the house."

After several attempts at retrieving the eye from the infinite layers of silt, Rachael finally came up with it. The passing boat wakes were coming in fast, but she touched bottom and slugged to shore. She carefully took the eye to the kitchen, bagged it, and stuck it in the refrigerator. She smiled at her sister's audacity and was not mad but more amused than anything.

"While you and Mom are in Palm Springs, please don't tell your friends where you are. Buy a disposable phone at Walmart on the way out of town and call me on the road with the number. Remember, you have to use your Bluetooth in California, and—oh, call and tell me the name of the hotel when you check in."

"OK, OK, OK," said Meg. "I know the drill. But it ticks me off that I can't call Derek while I'm gone. I don't want to lose too much ground with him."

"You are such a sicko," replied Rachael. "He's far too staid for your personality. He'll repress all your shameful giddiness if you let him."

Meg smiled. "Aye, my dear, and there's the rub. No one represses me."

When she finished packing, Meg headed for the car with Rachael on her heels.

"Disconnect your GPS right now and turn off your cell phone. I don't want anyone tracking you."

"Do you think the shooter has our address already? You know, maybe I don't have to go." She paused by the car. "He didn't get a real good look. Maybe he doesn't have access to that information. We might be giving him too much credit."

"AZ numbers on the Zodiac are easy to trace. He'll have access to the information, I'm sure. He's no dummy," said Rachael.

"Well, what about you? Are you going to be safe?"

"Hey, I'm the cop, silly. Everyone's on duty tonight, trying to catch the bastard when he dumps Melissa's body." She closed Meg's car door. "Look, get a move on. I want you to get to Palm Springs before dark. I'll call Mom right now."

In a flash, Meg disconnected her GPS, turned off her phone, and headed south on Highway 95. Rachael knew this was just a stopgap but felt better knowing that Meg and her mother would be out of danger for a few days. She was surprised that Meg had left without more of an argument. Maybe she was truly scared. Maybe, too, she had her own suspicions about who had taken her slot key from her purse and why. *Now that's something else to worry about.*

38

Though her lip was swollen and painful, Amanda shrugged off the inconvenience and applied extra concealer to hide the bruise. She changed into her dance clothes and dashed to the theater for rehearsals. The choreography was simple, and she quickly learned the routines. During the break, she headed to the dressing room for water. Backstage, she was approached by Elliott, who was on a break from his studio.

"Fancy meeting you here," she said as he walked up. "You lost or just a backstage junkie?"

"Not lost since I found you. I heard Beckett gave you a tour of the casino. Thought maybe you'd like to see a bit of *my* world."

"Are you hiring dancers for your commercials?"

"If you're looking to advance your career, I'm the one with the contacts in town. Besides, I'm better-looking."

"And more modest, too. I'm through rehearsing in an hour. How about five at your TV station? I'd like to start there, where you work."

While Elliott would have preferred to pick her up for obvious reasons, he agreed. "Sure, five sounds good. Wear jeans. We'll be on my Harley," he said with a smile. He gave her the address of the TV station on Boundary Cone Road.

At five o'clock sharp, Amanda pulled up in front of the Channel 42 Network TV station. As she entered, she noted the alarm system, including motion detectors. The station was small with only one reporter, three technicians, and one anchorman, Elliott.

Elliott walked out from the back room, zipping up his pants, and smiled when he saw Amanda. "Two minutes earlier, and you could have helped me with this," he said with a snide look. He began with a cursory description of his job. "We only broadcast two hours each morning. Local stuff, mostly. Usually a couple of interviews with Bullhead and Laughlin officials, new gripes in the community so people can call in and let off steam, about five minutes of national news, and we always have some animals from the shelter that need to be adopted."

"Do you get out in the field much?"

"That's the most exciting part of my job, interviewing people at the local watering holes and squeezing news from my inside man at the PD. That's where I get all the latest info. There's only one other station that services this part of the tristate area, so we've got to cover it all."

At Amanda's request, Elliott spent time explaining his computer system and how the facts are compiled and modified to meet airtime requirements. While she acted totally intrigued, Amanda was making mental notes on the whole scene in case she needed to break in. There was something about Elliott that was off the mark to her. "Trust your instincts" was a motto that had been instilled during her FBI training.

After touring the studio, Elliott handed Amanda a soft drink and a day-old cookie before they headed out to the Harley.

"You really know how to entertain a girl." Opening the door, Amanda paused. "It has to be one hundred and ten degrees out here. Are we really going on the Harley?"

"No better ride in the country," he said.

"Oh, and you cared enough to buy the very best. If I'm not mistaken, we are now about to climb on a Harley Springer—what year, two thousand one?" she asked.

"Love a lady who knows her bikes. Actually, it's a two thousand. I just had it detailed. Perfection in motion. Here's your helmet. Climb on. Your adrenaline'll kick in, and you won't even notice the heat."

"Yeah, right," she replied, sliding in behind Elliott. She kicked down the foot pegs and leaned into the backrest. "This bitch seat is perfect," she said as she settled into the firm seat.

"Like to keep my lady friends comfortable, whether they're riding my Harley or me."

"Nice paint job," Amanda said, ignoring his remark but thinking, *Eeek,* as she donned her helmet.

"I've owned it for five years now. The desert is tough on the paint, and the rocky terrain takes its toll, so I get it repainted every two years. I always have it ready for Harley Week."

"What's Harley Week?" asked Amanda.

With a roar, they took off down the street, heading toward the 95. "Every year," Elliott yelled over the howl of the engine, "the city of Laughlin sponsors Harley Week. About thirty thousand Harleys and other bikes pull into town for a rally. Sponsors and merchants line the parking lots with stuff to see and sell. The broads show up in their finest leathers—some topless—along with their newest tattoos. The tattoo parlors go nuts during the week. People get tattoos where you can't imagine, and after enough beer, they want to show them off."

Amanda yelled in his ear. "You got one you want to show off?"

"I'll show you later. The cops hate Harley Week and recruit a bunch of Las Vegas Metro cops to help with the herd. Back in July of two thousand two, there was a shooting in Harrah's Casino between the Mongols and Hells Angels. Two people were killed. That pretty much put a damper on the festivities."

"Ya think?"

"Since then, the number of bikers has dropped. The casinos raised their prices, the cops pull everyone over for everything, and the locals get hassled along with the rest. Not so much fun anymore."

By the end of this long conversation, Amanda had tuned him out since she already knew the details of Harley week. *Probably know more about Harley Week than you do, Elliott*, she thought.

Turning down a dirt road, the bike fishtailed in the sand. Elliott straightened it out with ease and headed down the rut-filled road. Amanda was side-swiped by the underbrush and was not surprised when they came to a clearing on the banks of the mighty Colorado River. Thirty-five or so bikes were lined up in front of a long wooden building, the River Rat Bar.

"Local watering hole?" Amanda asked. She tensed up.

"The best," replied Elliott. "Come on in and meet Bill, the bartender. He's been here as long as the building and knows everything that happens in town. Doesn't mind sharing it, either."

Amanda hesitated. *Oh, crap. Hope Bill's not working.*

Entering from the strong sunshine into the darkened bar, the two took a minute to allow their eyes to adjust to the dim light. The jukebox was playing Alan Jackson's song, "It's Five O'Clock Somewhere," and everyone was talking above the song, drinking and swearing. Only three women were in the bar. They assimilated into the rest of the seedy crew.

"Don't let the looks of the patrons confuse you. The guy over in the corner owns the car dealership in Bullhead, the red-headed guy is a Metro cop, and the woman he's talking to is the owner of a popular boutique in town. Most all are businesspeople just relaxing after work. Come on over to the bar."

Amanda and Elliott found two empty barstools and sat down. Bill was taking care of a customer at the end of the bar and finally came their way.

"Hey, Elliott, good to see you again—wow, twice in one day. I see you've brought some company this time." Amanda had taken off her helmet and was shaking out her thick hair, momentarily hiding her face.

"Amanda, meet Bill, and likewise. Bill this is Amanda. She's the new dancer at the Oasis. Beckett tried to hide her from me, but I got lucky and saw her audition for the new show. His loss."

Bill checked his immediate instinct. *Oops, sister number one,* he thought. *Rachael told me she's some sort of cop somewhere, and now she's pretending we've never met.* "Glad to meet you, Amanda. Watch out for this guy. First drink is on the house. What'll it be?"

Amanda relaxed and said, "When in Rome…" and ordered a draft. Bill returned with two beers. "So you're here covering the shooting, Elliott? Actually, you were in here about the time it went down. Come up with any hot leads yet?"

"Not much to go on. Guess I missed the action by half an hour or so. Bullhead cops are stonewalling me so far on details. You heard anything?"

"Well, Detective Rachael was nosing around. Told her you were here, so she'll be looking to talk to you."

"Thanks a lot. She can get pushy. Oh, well, won't be the first time we've sparred."

Amanda decided to shift the conversation. "Hey, Elliott, we still have some daylight left. Let's go see this mysterious Emerald building when we finish the brew. It sounds interesting."

"This is quite a date we're having. Why not?"

Bill watched as they left the bar. When he heard the Harley rev up, he called Rachael.

39

Understanding that the surgery would take approximately four hours, Hal decided to return to Bullhead and show the captain that he was still diligently working the case. Rachael was filling out forms at the department when he showed up. He tried to get to his workstation without crossing her path, but she spotted him when he entered. Not to be ignored, Rachael headed for his cubicle.

"Where the hell have you been? Since when don't you answer your phone when you know it's me?"

Hal turned slowly. "How's your day going, Rachael? Anything new on the case?"

Rachael was steaming. She wanted to verbally castrate him, but when she looked at his stern face, she decided to back off. Not the time to attack. "Talked to Meg. I've sent her out of town 'til this whole damn mess gets resolved. We don't need a car to watch my house, so I cancelled it. Now, if it's not too much to ask, why were you driving across the Laughlin Bridge when you should've been at the hospital trying to interview Carlos's girlfriend? And who was in the car with you?"

"That's my personal business, Rachael, so butt out."

The captain came into the office and told all three detectives to go to the bullpen. When everyone was present, Captain Hendry stood at the whiteboard and started writing. "We need to get together on some of these investigations. It looks to me like we have some overlap. Rachael, you're working on the Davis Dam floater, so line up the evidence for me."

As Rachael presented the facts, the captain wrote them on the board for everyone's consideration.

"First, we've collected about seventy-five percent of Angie's body parts," began Rachael. "Her full name was Angie Marie Perkins, and she worked at the Oasis as a cocktail hostess. The vic was divorced with an eight-year-old son. Parents have been notified and will be here to make arrangements for her burial. We won't ask them to identify the body, given the state it's in. That's already been done by fingerprint analysis. The rope that was cut, tying Derek's boat to the tether across the river, is being analyzed. It looks generic, so we aren't holding our breath on that. Hair and fiber was found in Angie's hand. Some skin was found under her nails. The samples are really compromised, but we've sent everything to the Kingman lab.

"Apparently, Angie had finished her shift and changed at the casino. Margaret, who worked with her, said Angie was excited about a date with an 'old friend' who she hadn't hooked up with for a year or so. No name, but she said he's well-known in town. The perp picked the most opportune time to commit the crime, right at the height of the monsoonal storm. Most evidence was washed away. Generic tire tracks were found at the spillway. Too much damage to the body parts to tell if there was sexual activity. Ketamine was found in her system. Rather unusual because it's what vets use on animals to keep them quiet during surgery. Just paralyzes them—doesn't kill."

"Not hard to get Ketamine these days, is it?" the captain asked.

"No. Just need to know the right person," replied Rachael. "The perp gained access to the dam's spillway with Meg's slot key that was stolen from her. Still checking on that. Could have been at the sandbar while she played volleyball, at Davis Park while she showered, or on board the boat during the monsoon. No answer yet.

"Chemical analysis from the bottle of wine on the boat came back as Rohypnol. Usual date rape stuff, but they ingested enough to knock them out overnight. Derek Turner hasn't been charged, but is still a person of interest, at least in my book. We don't know how that drug got in the wine. Either he did it himself or he bought it that way. He tested positive for Rohypnol, too. I'm still on the fence about him.

"We interviewed campers, and Ranger Ron is doing his part to assist in the investigation. It's not a dead end right now, but close to it. That's all on this case. Where do we go from here? Put this on the backburner? Does Melissa's body take precedence?"

The captain took over. "Yes, for now. Our serial killer supposedly will kidnap a woman on the Laughlin side of the river, if he doesn't break his pattern. We'll be watching both sides. There'll be a full briefing two hours from now, and it's going to be all hands on deck tonight and tomorrow. Clean up any other problems that you might be working on so we can all give this one hundred and ten percent. We'll get the bastard this year." The captain looked pointedly at Hal.

Hal picked up on his intent. "I'll be there, Cap, no worries. If he follows the pattern, we'll find Melissa on the Arizona side tonight, and he'll pick up his new woman sometime tomorrow. Can we pull in the sheriff's department for the night? We need extra hands. He might dump her outside of our jurisdiction. Shit, we are so short-handed right now. How can we cover all this desert territory?"

"But then, he might not show up at all," countered the captain. "The perp only stayed in Santa Cruz for three victims. Why would he change his ways now and go for another kidnapping in Laughlin? If he follows his usual MO, he should dump the body tonight and simply leave town. Maybe we'll get lucky."

Hal started to voice his objections, but the captain raised his hand to interrupt. "Look, we'll come back to this later, but right now, I need to know how your investigation's going." He wrote *seaplane* on the board and started with Hal's outline.

"Well," said Hal, "what we have so far is that the seaplane's ID numbers were fake. No big surprise. The man, identified as the possible pilot, was Hispanic, male, six-foot-three, two hundred and ten pounds. He was the third victim. Meg gave us the most accurate info on the scene. The shooter drove down the dirt golf path at the Emerald River golf course. Dead are Carlos, Sasha, possible pilot. One person got away in the seaplane."

"Yes, OK, I've got all of that, but now where are we? What do we have?" asked the captain.

"Two casings were found. Nothing else noteworthy. Tire prints are Metzler, which is typical for most Harleys. A cast was made of the tire prints."

"Did we get tire prints from the spillway?" asked the captain.

"They're ID'ing them as we speak," replied Rachael. "Poor Sasha. Never got to see her baby. Is the baby going to make it?"

"She's a little girl. Pretty healthy for such a tough beginning," said Roberto.

"Sorry," the captain said.

"Well, thank God for small miracles," replied Roberto.

Hal finished his part of the briefing. Everyone studied the whiteboard.

"Damn," said the captain. "So again, we've got nothing. Everyone is checking with their snitches to see if we can turn anything new. That's all for now. Keep me posted," the captain said as he left the room.

The three detectives sat for a minute, looking at each other, as the room cleared. Rachael said, "Is there any evidence to show that all three of these crimes are related? Could there be one serial kidnapper-killer who's also moving body parts? Can we tie Angie into this, too? Is the perp that clever, or are we just being stupid?"

Hal leaned back in his chair and stretched. Rachael could see his gears working. "There's something else that should be factored in. That seaplane…Ron at Davis Campground said that it had passed over the campground the day before.

He could see it descending around Katherine's Landing. The next day, it flew back over, apparently rendezvousing with Carlos. If the body parts are being flown in from Mexico, then why not fly in some rich Mexican illegals at the same time?"

The room fell silent as the three detectives worked through their questions, patterns of behavior and possible answers. Each person's mind was connected and a unity of thought flourished, similar to mild meld. Roberto broke the collective reflection. "I'm sure that Carlos was getting ready to leave town. He and Sasha were going to Las Vegas. Had a job offer in an auto shop. She was thrilled. She also said that when he talked to her, he kept mentioning 'El Jefe.' Must have been his crime boss. Mean SOB. You ever heard of him?"

"You know," Rachael replied, "Bill at the River Rat overheard that name mentioned a week or so ago. He wasn't sure what the context was, but two guys, not local, were saying they were going to work for him. They hadn't met him and felt he was some kind of a creep but had money. I'll call Bill and see if he's heard anything else."

"Why not Mexican Mafia traveling by seaplane to the US to launder drug money?" asked Hal.

"Why not, indeed," followed Rachael. "So, El Jefe, or whoever, charges the Mafia for an illegal flight into Laughlin and, while he's at it, brings along some kidneys for sale. Not a bad deal.

He would need transportation from Davis Camp for the Mafia, an overnight stay, and then a ride to Las Vegas. Probably lots of cash in hand to launder."

Hal broke in, "He also needs a hospital to take the body parts to. We need to follow all seaplane landings. El Jefe may be transporting body parts and the Mafia at the same time to Henderson or Vegas. Two for the price of one." Sensing a compromising connection to his recent actions, Hal continued. "Let me handle the body part involvement. Will Ron call us if any unfamiliar plane lands in his area?"

"Absolutely. You know he was a Tucson cop. He'll love to be involved. Roberto, do you know anyone down by Topock or AVI?"

"Another cousin," Roberto said with a smile.

Hal laughed first, followed by Rachael. "Another cousin?" she asked. "Hell, we'll add this one to the other nine. Pretty soon you'll have your own football team." With that, they all had a good laugh.

Rachael was still puzzled over the events of the shooting. "I can see where the shooter had to get rid of Carlos because he was leaving, and Sasha was just collateral damage. The Mafia and body parts make sense, but what about Angie? How does she fit into all of this? Or does she?"

"Easy. Maybe El Jefe or one of his cohorts was dating her a while back and let something slip. He got concerned that she knew too much and had to get rid of her," said Roberto.

"Well, if El Jefe is all of the above *and* our annual kidnapper, was Angie going to be his next kidnap victim, but something went wrong?" asked Hal.

"I don't think so. Our body snatcher—or Heart Collector—likes 'em young," said Rachael. "Look at his previous victims. The cute, perky high school dance teacher from Bullhead was his first snatch. Jump across the river to Laughlin for number two. She was twenty-five years old, a cosmetologist. Number three from Bullhead was the adorable clerk from Walmart. No, he likes them young and pretty. That part I can understand, but why does he take great care of the women for a year and then slaughter them and cut out their hearts? When we find the bodies, they're all in excellent health—no signs of trauma, except they're dead. I wonder what goes on during that year of captivity..."

"Ugh. Better hope you never find out," said Roberto.

Hal pitched in. "Trophies. Trophies—that has to be it. He probably collects them in some container and jacks off every night in front of them. Sick bastard."

Rachael's eyes met Hal's. "You're right, of course. When we find him, we'll have all the evidence we'll need to nail him. Good job, Hal."

"Are we through here?" asked Hal. "I need to take some personal time before we get going tonight. You can catch me on my cell." He stood up to leave.

Roberto nodded and left the room, feeling that each had their own direction to go.

Rachael stopped Hal before he could get out of the room. "Listen. Am I being paranoid about Meg's safety? The perp got the AZ numbers. If he's as smart as we think he is, he could be following her out of town."

"Well, if this El Jefe is the only perp, he'll be too busy to chase her. What about you?" Hal asked. "You both live in the same house. If he tracks one, he tracks you both. Are you going to stay there at the house?"

"Yes, I've made arrangements to borrow Fang from the canine unit. With the German Shepherd and my gun, I should be fine. Thanks for worrying," she said. Again, Hal tried to leave, but again Rachael stopped him. "Speaking of that, what's going on? I know you saw me on the bridge, but you didn't pick up your cell phone. What's the deal? Where were you going with Sarah? That was Sarah, wasn't it?"

"You asked me before. Same answer. My business. Drop it. I'll be back on duty in a couple of hours. We can talk then," he said and stomped out of the room.

Rachael stayed in the bullpen by herself. What was going on with him? She didn't want to consider the answer that nagged her.

40

Amanda insisted on driving Elliott's Harley. He tested her on the essential operations of the bike and was satisfied that she knew how to drive it. Amanda turned the key, the engine fired, and she peeled out, giving Elliott an excuse to wrap his arms around her. She turned back to give him a flirtatious look. When they arrived at the entrance to the Emerald River golf course, Amanda pulled up abruptly, staring at the huge No Trespassing sign, a padlocked gate, and yellow police tape that stretched around the long, ranch-type fence.

"What now?" Amanda said. "Got a secret entrance? I don't mind hopping the fence if the walk isn't over a mile or so. Otherwise, forget it. It's too damn hot."

"No worries," said Elliott. "Drive the bike down the fence line. That's where we'll get in.

The wood fence is broken—by the homeless, I guess. They think this is their own casino. No walls, of course, but why be picky?"

Rachael turned the Harley and followed his instructions. As the scrub brush kept hitting her in the face, she said, "Should have let you take this part. It's nasty down here." Ruts in the dirt kept messing with her steering, but she gritted her teeth and pushed forward.

Elliott laughed. "Thought you were tough."

Arriving at the opening, Amanda over-applied the front brake, throwing Elliott forward. He seized the opportunity to squeeze her breasts. Amanda recoiled and turned off the bike. "OK, Romeo, it's your turn. Take me on a tour of the mysterious haunted building, and watch it with the feelies."

Elliott maneuvered the bike around the dried-up greens and tees, pointing out the run-down clubhouse, the chained parking area for the golf carts, and his favorite spot, the nineteenth hole, where foursomes would gather to while away the afternoon, trying to outdo each other with tales of conquest, bravado, and sex. Finally, they reached the asphalt cart trail bearing toward the unfinished twenty-story casino.

The Emerald River golf course was situated on a four-hundred-plus-acre plot of prime land adjacent to the flowing Colorado River. The project was put on hold in 1990 when the original developer filed for bankruptcy protection. Development of the building was halted, but the golf course proper was completed and opened to the public. The original design included an eighteen-hole golf course, a clubhouse, a hotel/casino, a convention center, and 1,200 homes surrounding the area. The hotel/casino was to host 1,100 rooms, and the steel framing was completed on one tower and partially completed on the other when the bankruptcy occurred. Now the golf course was closed, and the steel frames had turned into a rusty reminder of better days. Over time, the homeless and teenagers experimenting with drugs and booze adopted the derelict building as their own.

Elliott parked the Harley, and they headed for the building. Ducking under more police tape, they climbed the steep slope to the concrete slab. As they wandered around the five-hundred-by-five-hundred square foot area that was strewn with trash, drug paraphernalia, remnants of bonfires, and a few used condoms, Amanda's eyes searched the area. The trash only reflected years of kids with bikes, homeless people, and curiosity seekers.

"How do you get up to the other floors?" Amanda asked. "I can see where they were going to build the elevators and the stairwells, but there's nothing there."

With a know-it-all smile, Elliott answered, "Only those in the know are privy to the secret."

He's really a jerk, Amanda thought.

"Most people don't know about the hidden ladder. It's spring-loaded, and when it's closed, it blends in with the ceiling."

Amanda made a mental note to tell Rachael in case Metro hadn't discovered the easy way up and was waiting for a ladder. Elliott led the way to the southeast corner of the steel structure. "There's a twelve-foot pole with a hook attached hidden in the bushes over there. Your turn—fetch."

While Amanda's reaction would normally have been to flatten any man who told her to "fetch," she played along. Striding over to the edge of the concrete, she wiggled more than usual, knowing that Elliott was inhaling all of her movements. Even though she had only worked a few days at the casino, the other girls had shared stories about both Elliott and Beckett. The overall opinion was that they were both macho guys, cock-sure, and egotistical as hell. Of the two, apparently Beckett was more of a gentleman and might even have some redeeming qualities. If you didn't put out for Elliott by the second date, he wouldn't darken your door again. Angie had dated both of them, most recently Beckett. Gossip was that the two men would pass the girls back and forth and make bets about what each girl would do in order to make the men happy.

When possible, they would tape the episode and watch the reruns on Friday night. *Totally gross*, Amanda thought as she jumped off the concrete slab, located the pole, and scrambled back to join Elliott.

"You're pretty agile," Elliott said. "I like that in a woman, and you certainly know how to swing your ass when someone's watching. Gimme a hand with the pole and watch out when the ladder starts to come down. It's like a freight train that's jumped the track."

Amanda was seething inside over his last comments but smiled and gave him a sexy look. "Yes, master sir. I'll be right there to help ya."

After Elliott attached the hook to the hidden ladder, the two started pulling. Amanda was not sure if one person could pull the ladder down. If not, that meant there was probably an accomplice to the murders. *Make a note. Tell Rachael to check for prints.* Finally, with a valiant effort from the two, the rusty springs cooperated, and the stairway came crashing down.

Elliott insisted that Amanda go first—so he could stare at her ass, she was sure. *He was sooo obvious. But was he harmless? He certainly knew his way around.*

"How many floors are here, did you say? Are there hidden stairways on each one?" Amanda, again taking inventory of the potential evidence, noticed a shiny object in the center exterior edge of the building facing the river. It looked like an apt spot for the shooter to hide. She distracted Elliott. She saw footprints in the dusty floor and didn't want them compromised.

"Hey, big guy. This could be a romantic setting. Why don't you whistle up a card table with a linen tablecloth, candles, and a beautiful steak dinner for me? Have a boatload of singers tie up below and serenade us while we eat?" She laughed and motioned for Elliott to join her. Thinking this was his opening, he walked to her and, putting his arm around her waist, pulled her into him. Trying not to gag, Amanda returned his wet kiss but pulled away immediately.

"Nice, but you don't want to get me started right now. Might not be able to turn me off. You know I've got to get to work in forty-five minutes. Surely that doesn't give us enough time for what you have in mind," she said as she broke away.

Elliott was pissed. "I thought we had the afternoon *and* evening. What's going on? There's a name for what you're pulling right now."

She could hear the irritation in his voice and had to defuse the situation. There was more to learn about this man to either leave him on the suspect list or eliminate him. "Now, now, don't pout. They called me in to work the evening shift. Beckett says it's going to be a zoo in the casino tonight because of some kidnapper thingy. Let's face it—you're lucky to have this much time."

Elliott smirked at that. "Self-confident—good show. And you should be. Most of the chippies that arrive in Laughlin are left over from some trauma, don't speak English, or else are all withered up like the snowbirds. Not much to pick from."

"Hey," said Amanda, "that brings up another subject. I hear all of the young women in town are staying in the high school gym for two nights. A huge sleepover. They're going to have pizza delivered, and no men are allowed on the premises. Has that got something to do with the serial killer? The girls at the Oasis say some spooky guy is going to dump a body tonight and pick up a new girl tomorrow. It sounds scary—I mean, shouldn't he wait for Halloween? Why aren't you out interviewing the young chicks? It would make for good TV ratings."

"I'll check with the chicks after the day passes and nothing happens. Or I'll take pictures of the corpse. Whatever."

Amanda decided to push him a little more. He might know something or might even be involved. He certainly spent enough time at the bars, hanging with the locals. Any information she could pick up, she would share with Rachael. Elliott portrayed a superior confidence and, given an opportunity, would probably brag about anything and everything he knew.

Besides investigating Elliott and Beckett as potential suspects, her partner was watching Jonathan Kemp, a hospital administrator in Henderson, and Gerald Swanson, who was in charge of the airport. So far, nothing seemed out of the ordinary for those two, but they had not been cleared by the FBI yet. Within the next three days, the two agents would switch subjects to evaluate their results.

"Is there really something to this serial killer thing? And, gosh, does the FBI show up in town tonight and start watching everybody? I hear they all wear black shoes. Gee, what a great disguise. Oh, and dark glasses too. This guy must be really good. Kidnapped and killed three women? Or else the police must really be pathetic. I met one of the Bullhead city cops today. She was with Beckett. Didn't seem real sharp."

"Oh, you must mean Rachael. She's OK. I tried to give her a look-see one time, but she didn't take the bait. Probably a lesbian."

"Probably," Amanda replied. "Lady cops, you know, they don't have the real deal, so they pack guns."

A few more playful remarks were exchanged, but Elliott was either innocent or careful. The two headed for the stairs, climbed down, and replaced the secret opening. The trip back to the TV station was uneventful, and upon arriving, Amanda excused herself, giving Elliott a quick kiss on the cheek.

"Later," she said. "You really are an exciting afternoon date. Gimme a call." She turned to retreat and tossed her helmet back to Elliott, who was rendered speechless by her abrupt departure.

Amanda scurried back to the Oasis and changed into her cocktail waitress uniform. Hardly room to breathe. *Guess I'd better lay off the chocolates for a few days.* Her partner had left a message that one of the other suspects, Jonathan Kemp, was a regular on Friday night, typically playing three-card poker at the north tower of the Oasis. Since she had a picture of him already, Amanda planned on serving drinks to him and maybe letting him escort her back to her room. Time would tell. After struggling to hitch up the last two hooks on her uniform, she located her FBI cell phone and gave a quick call to Rachael.

Rachael's phone rang as she was driving to Camp Davis to meet with Ranger Ron. She let out a sigh of relief when she saw it was Amanda calling. "God, I thought you'd died and gone to heaven. What a trip, bumping into you at the Oasis today. What the hell are you up to? And by the way, I am so sorry I put you on hold last Friday and never called back, but you would not believe my life since then."

"Actually, I have a pretty good idea how your life has gone lately," Amanda said, quickly relaying the details of her assignment to Rachael. "I've met with two of the suspects; my partner has met the other two. I'll size up number three tonight. Beckett is smooth, but not a murderer. If he's involved with money laundering, it's probably in an outsourcing way. One of the girls at the Oasis says she gets to serve drinks to the penthouse on special occasions. Rich Mexican types. I'll see if I can get a wiretap and surveillance cameras installed."

"Looks like our investigations are overlapping." Rachael filled her in on her staff meeting, including the new information on El Jefe. "Keep your ears to the ground on this guy."

"Will do. I was with creepy Elliott today. Tell Metro to check the second story of that building for a missed cartridge and footprints. Let me know if you hear of any new seaplane activity."

"Sure." As Rachael pulled into Camp Davis, her phone beeped. "Oh, I have another call. Damn, it's Meg. She's supposed to be driving to Palm Springs to meet Mom."

"Is she still mad at me?" Amanda asked.

"Not anymore. Mom told her."

"Mom told her about UCLA? Rachael, why?"

"It was time. Look, I gotta take her call. I'll check in later. Sorry."

Amanda was speechless. She always felt that it was her story to tell.

"What's up?" Rachael asked Meg. "You still on the road? And why didn't you pick up a throwaway cell like I asked?"

"I was going to, but I picked up the house phone messages, and I've been reinstated at the dam. They want me back at work tomorrow. I guess they figured out I didn't have anything to do with Angie's death. No lack of smarts there. They said I was just targeted because of the pass. They've changed all of the locks. So, yahoo, I'm on the Fifteen and I'm turning around this second and heading back home."

"Oh, no you don't. You know what's going down tonight and tomorrow. Just go ahead with my plan. I'll call the people at Reclamation and tell them you need to take a few more days off."

"Bullshit," replied Meg. "Already on my way north. Be home in two hours. I can take care of myself. I care about my job, just like you do, and I'd like to keep it."

Rachael's phone went dead as she made the left turn into the Camp Davis parking lot, where Ron was waiting for her.

"Beefin' up security, Rachael? The date is upon us," Ron said as Rachael left her car.

"Yeah, you know the drill. Vigilance throughout the night. We'll need your help on that, watching for the body dump, but I also have another job for you."

Ron was jazzed over the invitation to be part of an active investigation. Rachael felt confident in revealing some of the department secrets since Ron had previously helped on other cases. They discussed the possible use of the seaplane for transporting Mexican Mafia and harvested body parts. There were always two seaplanes at the camp that were in use daily; one was for hire, and the other provided transportation for an employee back and forth from Needles. Neither of these two was involved in the criminal investigation, but a third plane had been reported landing occasionally between Katherine's Landing, Camp Davis, Topoc, and Havasu City. Often, the plane would be disguised with different call numbers and paint, but it was always a Renegade. Since Ron knew the owners of the various aviation schools in the area, Rachael put him in charge of coordinating the effort to investigate this third plane but cautioned him not to let anyone know the underlying reason.

"No need to tell me, Rachael. I'll tell 'em that we're watching for suspicious activity like boat-napping." They both laughed at that.

As she was leaving, Rachael thanked Ron and said, "OK, it's heads-up time. Call me with any irregularities. Our full force is on tonight and also extra cops from Metro. Command center is being set up at Harrah's RV parking lot. Here's the number. Bullhead dispatch is being bypassed. We want all calls to go to one place."

"Makes sense. I got a long stretch of beach here. Anyone else to help me?"

"Sorry, we're stretched thin. But, hey, do you know Clay?"

"Yeah. Good old boy. I'll call him. And don't worry. I'll check his gun in when he arrives."

"Thanks. Gotta go."

Rachael waved as she left the camp parking lot. Now it was time to visit the command center and coordinate Bullhead Police with Metro and the sheriff's department, who were also involved. Night was approaching, and panic would soon encompass Laughlin and Bullhead.

41

Hal raced to Mercy Hospital in Henderson, realizing that Sarah's surgery had come and gone. The head nurse was there to greet him and gave him an update on Sarah's condition, which was excellent. After receiving post-op instructions, he went to Sarah's room, where she was waiting for him. Hal gave her a light kiss on her forehead and pushed her gurney toward the ambulance entrance. Arrangements had been made for a hospital bed and full-time nurse to care for Sarah at a neighbor's home.

"Dad, I'm really woozy. Where are you pushing me? What's the rush?" Sarah asked.

Hal had never told Sarah the full story of the river rapist, but as gossip among teens went, she was aware of some of the details. Parenting hadn't been easy for Hal. Prior to his wife's death, he was an absentee parent, leaving all of the supervision to his wife. Now, looking back, he knew what a mistake that had been and figured it was payback time now. Life had taken on new meaning. It was so enriched, but sometimes it did interfere with his work. No longer was he the hard-ass cop jumping first into any fray. Now, he had Sarah to think of—he was all she had left. This was not the best situation for any cop with a partner. One minute of hesitation could cost Rachael's life. He knew this—fought this—but a mental picture of Sarah would always win out. He didn't want her to be raised by anyone else because of some macho move on his part. Now, he was faced with telling her as much of the serial killer history as was necessary so she would focus on her surroundings for the next few days. This had to be done without scaring the hell out of her.

He had mentally practiced this moment, and most of the more horrific parts of the story were sugarcoated. Enough truth would be told to help Sarah recognize the difference between normal, good people and the likes of the maniac.

The ambulance pulled up in front of the Bullhead home, and the EMTs hustled to settle Sarah into the hospital bed that awaited her. She was hooked up to the monitors, and when everyone had left, Hal sat next to her. "Mrs. Granger is on her way. She's a nurse and will stay here for a few days."

"Is she that old grumpy one?"

"Nah, she's young and cute like you. But, honey, I do need to talk to you about tonight. There are some things you need to know." By the time Hal finished his second sentence, Sarah started to doze off. Between her friends, the Internet, and the local TV news, she knew about the sicko.

She mumbled, "I'm OK with this, Dad. I'll be careful. Just want to sleep." Her head tilted slightly to the left as she dozed off.

Hal stayed with Sarah until the nurse arrived. His alone time allowed him to visualize his future. His dream of having Rachael share his life was so one-sided, and he knew this. Being her partner wasn't fair to anyone. Changes were needed—quickly. Of course, if the captain learned the truth about the kidney, the decision could be made for him. Switching mental channels, he headed back to the station.

42

Assignments were being handed out at the command station in Laughlin during the joint-force tactical meeting to deal with the impending return of the kidnapper. Bullhead police had a long stretch of river to cover. The sheriff's department would handle the Oatman area, including both the major roads leading to and from the town. Boat launch areas would take four people, patrol boats numbered four, and the casino parking lots would involve another twenty cops, leaving only twelve to patrol the streets. One of these cops would be assigned to the Avi Casino, which was quite a distance from the main casino row. Slim pickings, but it was the best they could do. Rachael informed the captain that she had recruited Ron at Davis Camp to cover that area, which freed another officer.

Bullhead had sixteen officers lined up for the task. Again, like Laughlin, priority would be given to the boat launch area since the killer had floated the last two victims down the river on a grotesque barge-like float. No evidence was obtained from the float—no fibers, fingerprints, or DNA.

The victims had been extremely healthy— except for the fact that they were dead. The coroners who performed the autopsies found no signs of malnutrition nor trauma to the sex organs. Recent hair dye, manicures, and pedicures. Dental health was perfect. The only problem was the tiny needle punctures in the side of their necks and their missing hearts. Apparently, a syringe filled with morphine had been used daily for the past week, building up the amount of medication that ultimately caused each death. Then, the heart was meticulously removed, and the incision was sutured. The investigators believed the killer had some medical experience since the sutures were perfect. They could almost be categorized as the technique of a plastic surgeon. Dressing the bodies must have been difficult, but no button was left undone.

"The FBI has sent a profiler to assist us this year. Come on up, Morgan. He'd like to address you before we break up. Special Agent Morgan Wiley, they're all yours."

The FBI agent took the podium. All eyes watched him intently, searching for knowledge to further understand their killer. Within the next twenty-four hours, the information he would give them could help break the case. On the board, he drew columns reflecting his organized words.

"The unsub is male, Caucasian, between the ages of thirty-five and forty-five. Has a decent build, so he would be attractive to females. Probably works out. He's strong enough to carry the dead bodies for some distance before displaying them. He's well-known in our community—someone like a doctor, pharmacist, bartender, or someone outgoing. He moves easily in diverse social groups. In other words, he fits into the town on both sides of the river. He keeps the women hostage for a year, taking care of them, nourishing them, loving them, and giving them a chance to love him back. As their one year anniversary approaches, he evaluates them. When his expectations are not met, he murders them and searches for a replacement. He has yet to find his perfect mate.

"He's an expert in firearms and can handle a scalpel. Looks like some background in medicine. A smooth talker, fun to be around, but people see through him and realize that most of what he says is bullshit. He will talk out of both sides of his mouth. So, in essence, he's not going to be a stranger, nor will he be a homeless person. He's not a longtime local."

The profiler placed eleven pictures on the board, outlining the months of August through

July. The pictures had been taken monthly by the unsub, showing Melissa dressed in holiday fashions. She held a copy of the *Mohave Daily News* indicating the current date.

"Each month, the unsub mails a picture to the FBI. He committed these same crimes in central California. An officer from Santa Cruz has a sister who lives in Bullhead. She was bitching to her brother about the serial killer in town. Missing hearts, one year anniversaries, sounded too familiar. His city had undergone three years of attack by a similar perp. Well, he put two and two together and called Bullhead PD. We got a lucky break there. He may have been involved in other cities, but this is the only match so far. I believe that once we apprehend him, most of you will know this man. Any questions?"

The cops were pensive after hearing Morgan describe the killer, many of them reflecting on their acquaintances and mentally pushing around possible suspects.

"Thanks, Morgan," said the captain. "The only other thing is a password for this scenario. That will be 'monsoon.' I know the FBI can't memorize all of your mugs right now, so be sure and identify yourselves by the password if you meet. If no more questions, then let's get out there and catch this sick bastard. Let's make it a night to remember."

The captain finished giving out the assignments. Rachael's job was to cover the community center ramp and adjacent park. There were only two single-story buildings, an expansive parking area used to store boat trailers, and finally the long boat ramp. The area had been closed to launching and parking all day, so there shouldn't be anyone entering the facility, giving her greater visual surveillance. Rachael was grateful for the assignment, and her instincts told her that she might just be the one to catch the bastard. If he intended to float his victim down the river, either the community center ramp or the ramp at Davis Dam would be the most accessible. Hal walked in as the meeting was breaking up, and the captain assigned him to the Safeway/El Palacio area.

"Keep your eyes peeled, Hal. The killer could fit in with that bunch of crack heads around the Safeway dumpster." He turned to the rest of the assembly, which was swollen with all the guns from other precincts. "We'll be on Channel Twenty. Check in with me hourly, and I'll relay anything to the command center that needs to be investigated. All communications come here. We're shutting down the Bullhead center for the night. Heads up, gang. Be safe."

As Rachael rushed home to prepare, she called Amanda's cell phone and left a voice mail about her assignment for the night. "When you get off work, would you check in with Meg? Oh shit, you can't do that. No one should know you know us. It's getting complicated. Well, I'm hoping Hal can check on her tonight. His assignment is right around the corner. The captain pulled the canine from our house, so she'll be on her own. She's so bullheaded—trusts everyone. God, I'm rambling on. Talk to you soon. Love ya, sis."

Rachael changed lanes and continued toward home, only to realize that she was behind Meg's car. With a smirk, she grabbed her portable red light and stuck it to her dashboard. The switch was flipped, and the siren screamed out a warning. Meg's head whipped around like a figure skater doing a spin. When Rachael saw that Meg recognized her—how could she not?—she turned off the siren and merely followed her sister home. Pulling in the drive, they both catapulted from their cars, Meg ready to take a swing and Rachael laughing her head off.

"You crazy fool. You scared the shit out of me," yelled Meg.

"What a bullheaded brat you are," Rachael returned. "You could have waited a few more days to come home. Now I have to babysit you on top of this whole damn town."

"Screw you," replied Meg. "I have a life, too, and I'm a big girl, so butt out." With that, they laughed, hugged each other, and went inside.

"God, I miss you when you're not around," said Rachael. "But still, why did you come home so soon?"

"I hate the thought of some radical person running me out of town. Besides, need to get back to work. Mom is great, but I can only take small portions at a time, and I just saw her on Monday. Too much—what does she call it?—directional conversation gets to me."

Rachael brought Meg up to speed about the FBI profiler and the surveillance setup for the night, including her assignment. "The captain pulled the canine from our house. Needs him at the beach."

"That's OK. If I stay home, I'll load the gun. Quit worrying."

"You know what's going on tonight. I need to know every move you intend to make. Give me your word that you'll call me when and if you change your location. I'm getting the feeling that you don't plan on staying home tonight. Maybe you should check into the Oasis. How about that?"

"Big surprise—you already have a plan for me. Well, it just so happens that Paula and I have already booked a room at the Oasis. Great minds, they say. We'll probably party 'til midnight and then flake out. I'm really kind of tired, and I have to work tomorrow."

With a sign of relief, Rachael hugged Meg again. "Awesome. You're way ahead of me, as usual. Gotta go, sis. "

"Hey, wait a minute. I still don't get why everyone's so uptight. If the killer is still doing what he's done before, then he should be on his way out of town after tonight. After he kidnapped and returned the third corpse in Santa Cruz, he headed out of town for good. Why would he change his MO?"

"Ah, I see you've been reading the local papers. In Santa Cruz, the cops were getting close to an arrest. Santa Cruz PD pulled into town Monday to help. So, OK, here's the drill. Have a fun evening, and say hi to Paula for me. Is Derek back in town?"

"Might come back tomorrow. Just waiting to hear. So, OK, already. I've got my instructions for tonight. I won't open the door unless it's Hal. Later, I'll go directly to the Oasis Casino and stay there all night. Now, get your crap together and get out there and catch the creep. I'd like to go partying sometime soon without all these safety instructions. Yeah, yeah, I know. Just not tonight."

Rachael's phone rang. "Hey, Rach. It's Ron. We've got a seaplane landing."

"Oh, great. That's all we need. Tell me."

"Blue-and-white Renegade. Landing across the river, up by the dam. Pilot plus three. And a bunch of luggage. There's a van. Gray. Can't see the plates. Sorry, I can't do much else from here."

"You did great. I'll call Amanda. She'll have to handle it. Thanks." Rachael started for the car. Truth be told, she felt excited. They might really get the unsub this year, and then life in Bullhead would return to a state of normalcy.

Rachael opened her car door. Turning, she smiled at Meg and said, "Love ya, sis," leaving Meg in the driveway with a puzzled look on her face.

"Love ya?"

43

"Matt," Amanda whispered into the cell phone. "There's been a drop-off. Seaplane just landed. I need two things."

"Name them."

"Three bugs for the penthouse. I'll plant them. Theresa's working the floor. Have to get rid of her. She delivers drinks to the suite. No one else. Tap into the Oasis personnel records. She's got a kid. Get the baby-sitter's name. Fake a call. Say you're the sitter's brother and she has to leave. Say she's sick or something. OK?"

"When?"

"Now. Where are you?"

"Oasis, north tower, ground level."

"Hang out by valet parking. Look for a gray van, three passengers, lots of luggage. They won't check in. Follow them. Call me when they get to their suite, and we'll figure the logistics. How soon can I get the bugs?"

"Ten minutes, in your room."

"That works. Thanks."

"Be safe."

44

Like the FBI and other contingent agencies, El Jefe was finalizing his own plans. He had hoped that Melissa, his present captive, would have been the one. But no, Melissa, like the other five women before her, when given an opportunity to live a perfect life with him, had not risen to the occasion. At the beginning, she showed signs of allegiance. He would come home daily, and she would be waiting for him with dinner and a smile. Wine was poured, and they would sit after dinner, talking about the news. She begged for a small dog, and he even bought one to keep her company during the day. Why had that not been enough? Oh, well. It was history now, and her yipping little dog was history, too. Tonight was to be the big night, and he needed to get started and stay on target.

His secret basement was divided into two compartments. One was for the initial stages of the kidnapping, where the hostage was kept in pitch-black solitude for three days. The other compartment was a small room equipped with a table, surgical tray, drain in the floor, and an assortment of chemicals and jars holding incised hearts. Mozart recordings always started when the door opened. Today, Sinfonia Concertante, his favorite, was playing.

Melissa had received the final injection to stop her heart yesterday. Now, it was time to remove the heart and get her dressed for her coming-out party. With a great deal of proficiency, he inserted the scalpel at the shoulder area. No bleeding occurred since the body had no blood pressure. Melissa's corpse was opened using a Y-shaped incision from the shoulders to the mid-chest and then down to the pelvic region. He separated the skin from the muscle, used his snips to crack the ribcage, tore into the pericardium, and exposed the heart. The inferior and superior vena cava were incised, and the aorta was severed, along with the main pulmonary artery and veins. El Jefe gently removed the heart and held the vessel up to the light, smiling at the size. Carefully, he placed the once viable organ into a jar of formaldehyde and sealed the top. After washing his hands, he took the marking pen and put Melissa's name and date of death on the label. Cautiously, he drew six blood drops symbolizing his sixth victim. *I'm getting quite a nice collection here. Melissa, darling, your heart is larger than Stephanie's. I think you were some kind of an athlete.* Once the heart was tightly secured in the jar, El Jefe meticulously closed the wound with size 5-0 Prolene thread. He was so thorough with his work. Even a practiced plastic surgeon couldn't do a better job.

He sprayed her body with a hard flow of water, removing all traces of blood and membrane. Putting on her Walmart uniform took more time than anticipated. He hurried to pull up her underwear and pantyhose, snagging the latter. *Oh, never mind the snag. No DNA there from me, you little wench.* Shoes came next and now he was ready to transport Melissa. Lugging her up the stairs was difficult, but El Jefe was muscular and quickly accomplished the task.

Makeup and hair would be done later.

It was approaching midnight as he pulled up to the Bullhead Police Department. He knew only one staff member was working. He parked the car across the street at City Hall with Melissa's body in the trunk. Iron gates enclosing the PD were open. He slid along the back wall and disengaged the security light and motion detectors.

El Jefe returned to the car and drove across the street. Only one car was in the lot. Next came the lock to the back door leading to the detention center. Bullhead didn't have its own jail, and its prisoners were shipped off to Kingman for long-term confinement. In lieu of this, Bullhead did have a small holding cell, with applicable bars to detain overnight guests. Well practiced in lock picking, El Jefe opened the door. He overheard the dispatch operator in the next room. He waited until her phone conversation ended. With stealth movements, he quickly slid up behind her and pushed the hypodermic needle into her neck. She would be out for eight hours. He knew no one would be calling in. He taped her mouth, wrists, and ankles.

Carrying Melissa's body into the holding cell was simple—no stairs and no sharp turns. He was surprised how supple she felt. He propped her up on the cot, crossed her legs, and placed her hands in her lap. Taking out the cosmetic bag, El Jefe started to apply some foundation. *Hope your mother recognizes you when she comes in to identify her precious daughter.* Next came the lipstick and a spray of perfume. It was Chantilly, like his mother loved. He stepped back to make sure the picture was perfect and returned to the office. A sheet of white paper was pulled from the fax machine. He drew a heart with six large drops of blood, symbolizing his six mistresses. A message that read *SHE LOVED ME NOT* was meticulously lettered. Finishing, he returned to Melissa and placed the note in her hands. He straightened her hair again and stood back to admire his handiwork. *Oh, what a nice surprise for the early shift of the great Bullhead Police Department.*

El Jefe retraced his steps and returned to his pseudo home located off the main road east of Fort Mohave. His own little hideaway. Now, it was time to remove all traces of Melissa.

His next princess was also a size four, so part of the clothes might fit her. He decided to wash, dry, and iron his bride's trousseau and hoped she would be pleased with the clothing inherited from her predecessor. Oh, yes, his new bride. Thoughts of his new bride, the blonde beauty, aroused him, and he smiled at his erection as he drove. *Not too long now.*

Pulling up to the iron gate, he rolled down the window and pressed his hand on the security pad. The massive gate opened. Two large Dobermans ran toward the car, eager to greet their master. "Did you fellows enjoy eating Melissa's dog?" he asked. *Quite a nice touch*, he thought. Why should his new partner have a leftover dog? A new dog could always be selected if lover number seven desired one.

"I hope you fellas didn't leave a big mess," he said, laughing at the thought of the tiny Shih Tzu being eaten by the Dobermans.

The compound was secure. Motion detectors were mounted at every critical point of the house, both inside and out. The entire property was enclosed by a twelve-foot metal fence wired with 220 volts to keep intruders out and his women in. The first two ladies had to be brought out to witness the swift death of a chicken tossed against the fence. The bird's poor, scorched body left nothing to the imagination. When it was Melissa's turn, he realized how much fun it was for him to witness the women's horror, so he smiled when he took Melissa on an early morning walk. She was curious when he reached into the small chicken cage and pulled out the hen. *Dinner?* But when he laughed and threw the bird against the electrified fence, she got the message. No one tried to escape after that. Anyone could see through the metal fence, so a stone wall had been constructed to provide privacy. El Jefe liked his women to have freedom around the property. They were expected to tend to any flowerbeds, keep the house clean, and always be available to satisfy his every whim. And whims he had—especially when the women were new and fresh. While he didn't torture them after the first week, he did restrain them during sex. That was the only way he could get it up. As months went by, most of the women lost their will to fight him. They merely acquiesced to his desires. Each girl knew and recognized the menacing history of El Jefe and understood that she would eventually be killed.

It took all night to ready the house for its next occupant, and by morning, the task had been completed. Driving to work in Bullhead the following morning, he started to whistle and then hum. Dreams of his new partner filled his mind, and savage pictures of sex tormented him.

45

"Visitors are in the penthouse," said Matt. "Your turn. You sure you're OK with this?"

"Got it covered," Amanda replied into the phone. "Where are the bugs?"

"In my pocket. We can take the same elevator up and make the switch."

"Great. Make your call to Theresa's cell now. I'm walking her way."

Amanda walked up to the bar. "Hi, Dan. Just comin' on duty. What area do I get today?"

"You've got the north tower river bar."

"Hi, Amanda," said Theresa. "How do you like the Oasis so far?" She held up a finger as her phone rang. Amanda waited.

"Oh, crap. That was my baby sitter. She's sick. Has to leave. Sorry, Dan, I've got to get home.

Who's working this shift? I've got a penthouse run to make."

"Amanda's just starting," replied Dan. "Help her get the trays set up. I'll call room service for their food. She can cover for you."

"Should we tell Beckett?" asked Theresa.

"God, no. He doesn't like to be bothered over this kind of stuff. He won't care."

Amanda and Theresa finished setting up.

"Wow, these guys like expensive booze," Amanda remarked.

"Yeah. They don't speak a lot of English. Look, smile a lot and get in and out. They may try to proposition you, but you just say no and smile. They're special clients of Beckett's. He handles the prostitutes for them."

"Got it." Amanda headed through the casino, pushing the tray. She slowed until Matt caught up with her for their elevator ride.

"Hey, let me hold the elevator door for you," said Matt.

"Thanks," said Amanda with a relieved look.

Both FBI agents knew there were surveillance cameras in the elevator, so they positioned themselves out of view. Passing the bugs went smoothly, and Matt got off the elevator on the next floor. When the door opened to the suite, Amanda was surprised to see Beckett there. "Oh, hi, boss. What are you doing here?"

"I might ask the same thing. Where's Theresa? She's the only one assigned to this suite."

Amanda could tell he was suspicious. "Baby sitter called. Guess she's sick. Theresa left, and the bartender told me to bring the stuff up. That's all I know." She put on a huffy air. "If I'm not good enough to serve some Patron, then call someone else." She waited.

"Hey, Beckett. Let the girl in. She's better-looking than Theresa," said one of the men.

Beckett moved aside, and Amanda walked in with a sexy smile. She set up the bar, mixed drinks, and served them to the nicely dressed Mexican men. Putting the bugs behind the bar and under the coffee table was discreetly accomplished. She started for the door.

"Come to my office when your shift ends." Beckett was not smiling.

"Whatever."

***

Amanda's shift ended at 7:00 a.m., and Beckett was waiting. The morning sun was already drenching the room. "I thought you were a smart bitch, but I guess I misjudged you."

"Look, I'm tired, and I don't deserve your shitty attitude. If you don't like the way I serve cocktails, then fire me."

"Don't play dumb with me. It doesn't become you. Everyone knows the upper suites are reserved for special clients. Those people like their privacy. Only the girls who have been here for years are allowed to serve. What the hell were you thinking?"

"I was told to take the trays up. Big wow. There wasn't an orgy or anything going on. The men were nice to me. You were there. So what's the big deal?"

Beckett looked at her, wanting to believe her, but his gut was saying no. "One more chance for you. Don't screw up."

"Or what? I get thrown over the dam like Angie?" Amanda decided to push his buttons. "Is that how you fire all your waitresses?"

"You've got one smart mouth on you, Amanda. You're walking a fine line, young lady. Put a cap on it." He grabbed her wrist and squeezed to the point of pain. "Now get the hell out of here."

Amanda called Matt when she got back to her room. "Did you pick up anything from the taps?"

"The men are headed for Las Vegas—the Mirage—this afternoon. I've made contact with our office in Vegas, and they'll set up their suite. The meeting's set for tomorrow morning. After the deal goes down, we'll bust the lot of them."

"What about Beckett?"

"Once we've made the arrests, you can take him down."

"You know he's not the brains. Can we deal if he agrees to roll over?"

"Not our call. You did good, by the way. First time out. Whatta gal."

"Well, it's not over yet. Save your accolades."

The morning news was just coming on. Amanda watched as Elliott started his show. *It looks like Rachael is going to have her hands full today, too*, she thought.

WEDNESDAY, JULY 31

By dawn, all police and FBI had reported in. Nothing unusual had happened during the night, and a sigh of relief swept through the neighboring towns. The Las Vegas news team had spent the night at the Oasis Casino, waiting for some huge news to break, but nothing was forthcoming. The local Bullhead TV news started at the usual hour of 7:00 a.m., and every household and business was tuned in to hear firsthand about any activity. Had a body been found?

Elliott started out sounding exuberant, as usual. "Good morning, Laughlin and Bullhead City. Elliott Spencer, Channel Forty-Two, with all the news as it happens. Flash: I just got off the phone with an unidentified caller. Says he knows the truth about last night. While most of the citizens of Bullhead and Laughlin woke up with a sense of relief that no new body was floating down the river, they were sadly mistaken. I was told that Melissa Gordon's body has been recovered. Yes, you heard me right. Found. You old-timers remember cute Melissa. She was your favorite checker at Walmart. No details were given to this reporter, but even with all of the heavy police activities last night—and, I believe, FBI coverage—nothing could protect our local citizens. Way to go, Bullhead. Maybe next year, we'll call out the National Guard. Hell, we might as well call out the Salvation Army. They could do a better job. Well, just look at all the phone lines lighting up. It appears we have the city ready to comment on last night's debacle." Picking up the first line, Elliott said, "Channel Forty-Two TV. You're live."

***

The first to arrive at the Bullhead Police Department was Roberto. He had spent the entire night in the Walmart store, awaiting the return of the perp. The duty hadn't been bad. The store manager said he could eat anything and watch TV on the sixty-two-inch plasma TV. He declined, saying he was on duty. With the loss of his cousin, a renewed sense of law was driving him.

Only one car sat in the PD parking lot when he arrived at 5:00 a.m. The car belonged to Eleanor, the nightshift dispatcher. He entered without giving any thought to the trauma that awaited him. Once inside, he called out for Eleanor. Receiving no answer, he headed to the dispatch room and discovered her unconscious on the floor. Roberto checked her neck. Finding a pulse, he called for an ambulance. Pulling his weapon out of the holster, he started searching the rooms. He called the captain, Rachael, and Hal. Each answered their phone in turn and replied that they were already on their way. As Roberto reached the holding cell, he was about to hang up on Hal.

"Oh God, oh God," he whispered. "I just found Melissa Gordon. Oh, sweet Jesus, she's here in the cell. Damn it." Roberto leaned against the jail wall, trying to gather his emotional strength. His breathing came in short bursts. He didn't need to check for a pulse. He knew she was dead. His gun hand dropped to his side as he stared at Melissa's posed body. The heavy makeup made her look surreal. They had gone to high school together. They were friends. She was dead, and her death taunted him in the most grievous way.

The whole department, notified of the findings, rushed to the precinct. The command center in Laughlin was notified, and the forensic team, CSI, and FBI profiler all converged on the crime scene. Rachael and Hal fumed at the discovery. What a slap in the face to the department. While it was their case, the two had to stand down while the medical examiner established the time of death, pictures were taken, and evidence was collected.

There was a bigger concern now. He was back, and he was on schedule. Speculation ran rampant. Would he or wouldn't he?

"Time is of the essence" shouted the captain. "Any personnel not involved with this part of the case needs to report immediately to the Laughlin command center. Get moving."

Rachael watched as Hal left the squad room and headed toward his car. He was responding to a phone call. *You're not getting away from me this time*, she thought. Giving him some leeway, she followed at a safe distance as he turned south on the 95, heading toward Fort Mohave. *Wrong way, partner. The command post is north, not south.* He turned into the Valley Medical Hospital emergency parking. Rachael became increasingly alarmed. She followed as Hal raced to the elevator banks. She watched as his elevator stopped at the third floor. The ICU unit.

Leaning over Sarah's bed, Hal was racked with guilt. Had he, in all of his haste to save his daughter, supplied the doctors with a bad kidney? Choking back his guilt, he said, "Hi, honey. I hear you're having some problems. Are you feeling any better now?"

Sarah looked pale and weak but managed, "Hi, Daddy. I'm doing better, I think. I just had a lot of pain. My body got hot. I want to go home. Will the captain give you a day off so you can stay with me?"

"Don't be worrying about that, honey. I'll take care of all that nonsense. You just take care of yourself."

"Hi, Rachael. I'm so glad to see you. Now I know I'm going to be OK," said Sarah.

Hal turned and glared at Rachael. "What the hell are you doing here? You following me?"

"I sure am. We're assigned to the command center, and I see you take off the wrong way. It makes a girl curious." She moved forward to Sarah's bed. "Hi, sweetie. What are you doing here?"

Sarah didn't know how to answer. She didn't want to lie to Rachael. "Oh, Rachael, just you and Daddy talk about that, OK?"

With a nod from Hal, Rachael left the room. Hal leaned over and kissed Sarah on the forehead. "Be right back," he said and followed Rachael. "Just had to butt in, didn't you? This is my life, damn it. You gave up the right to interfere. Just leave us alone."

"What have you done, Hal?" She didn't want to know the answer, but she had her suspicions. She felt Hal wanted her help but couldn't ask for it. It was his secrecy that gave her cause for alarm. She waited.

His voice was low and strained. "My daughter, my problem. Please leave."

"There was a type-A kidney on the seaplane, wasn't there? You stole it, and some asinine doctor did surgery on your baby. What, down some dark alley in Las Vegas? What were you thinking? Jeopardizing her life, let alone your career? You ass. I know that you're pissed at me right now, but I love Sarah. Tell me. Jesus, Hal."

They were both quiet for a minute. Rachael could see he was close to the edge. She sank into the vinyl couch and pulled him down beside her. Putting an arm around him and tugging him close into her shoulder, she waited.

When he gained control, he looked at Rachael. "God, Rachael, I really screwed up. I saw a chance to save my kid. A healthy life. You know I'm not a thief. I've been a good cop, but shit, I couldn't stand by while the captain pussyfooted around. You know he's slow. I took one that matched Sarah's blood type, and we went to Henderson. Don't ask me what hospital, 'cause I won't give them up. Then, the babysitter called after the meeting. Said Sarah was running a fever. I told her to bring Sarah here. That's it. Do what you have to do."

Rachael pulled Hal closer, fighting back the tears. "We'll take care of this together. Let's see what the doctor has to say. Come on. We're on a short leash."

After conferring with the doctor, the two were relieved that the transplant was fine. Sarah had caught a virus and would have to stay in the hospital for a few days. Hal and Rachael both kissed Sarah good-bye and headed for the parking lot.

"Thanks, Rach. I didn't mean to drag you into this. God, I feel so much better sharing it with you. I guess you're right. Maybe we'll always be best friends. I can live with that."

They left in separate cars for the Laughlin meeting. *Maybe you can live with it, but I should tell the captain*, she thought. *Should? What kind of a word is that?*

The FBI was delivering their opening statements when Hal and Rachael arrived. After going over the salient points of the crime scene, the profiler took over.

"The unsub thrives on the publicity. December was when the pictures started arriving. You had heads-up on that. The media wasn't informed. Every detail in the picture was scrutinized. Four rooms and a yard were identified. It seems the yard is left available to the victim because the electric fence has barbed wire on top, along with a block wall that also surrounds the fence. There's some kind of camouflage netting over the entire complex. We believe that the structure is somewhere between Bullhead and Oatman, maybe backing up to one of the old gold mines. We've done several aerial checks, but we've come up empty.

"We still believe he's a local. About the locals: we need to put a cap on the vigilantes that are organizing. We've heard talk. Too many civilians could get hurt. Do what you can to squelch it. Let Weaver know what you hear. He'll coordinate. We may have to declare a curfew."

The squad room became restless. A shout came from the back of the room. "Come on. This is a resort town. The casinos will have a screaming fit. Without the gamblers, this town'll dry up and get blown away with the next monsoon. Curfew is a stupid idea, and besides, any vigilante group in this town of weirdos would ignore it, anyway." Most in the room agreed with his remarks.

The FBI continued. "OK, you're right. We've called the casinos. All unescorted women will be urged to use valet parking, and employees will be walked to their cars. If you can think of anything else, bring it up now."

Rachael chimed in, "We should call Elliott at the TV station and ask him to minimize the coverage. He's got a good pulse on the community and could help rather than hinder the situation."

"Good point, Rachael. We all heard his program this morning on the way to work. He slammed us good. In fact, who called him with the news of Melissa's body? Roberto only discovered it at five this morning, and Elliott had it on his seven o'clock news show. What's with that?"

No one had an answer. Grumbling continued until the squad room cleared out. Emotions ran high. All personnel moved with committed intent to their assigned positions.

Rachael had to fill her gas tank before hunting for Elliott. When she pulled up to the Arco self-serve, she was accosted by three locals.

"Hey, Rachael, heard last year's catch was found in the jail. God, you guys just have to show up for work and you get fast-food body delivery." The men laughed hard at their own joke.

Rachael had known these river rats for years and knew that when the story hit the *Mohave Daily News*, she would be in for a good ribbing. There was not one person in the whole community, however, who didn't show her the utmost respect when she got down to business.

"You guys really know how to kick a gal when she's down," Rachael responded. Making her gas selection and hooking the lever to self-fill, she walked over to the three as Clay came out of the mini-mart. "I could use some help. You know the drill; the asshole will be out to get his next victim tonight. I've heard rumors of a vigilante group gathering, but I've got a better idea. Clay, why don't I elect you captain of the town's rednecks, and you get everyone together for a meeting? Hand out driving and surveillance assignments."

"Oh, wow. Look at me. Narc for a day."

His buddies bent over laughing.

"We don't want to shut down the city with an early curfew, so don't push us. Still, we don't want you local guys running around, pumped up on testosterone with no way to vent it."

"Vent my junk," one of the guys said. More laughter followed.

"Decide on a code word so you won't break the wrong neck. No more than twenty guys, 'cause some of you have to stay home to protect the women. Give me a list of the men with their plate numbers, and the cops will leave you alone. You'd be doing us a favor. Maybe cover Oatman, Fort Mohave, Walmart area, Old Bullhead, the community center, and then from Fourth Street and the Ninety-Five to the bridge. Swing by the high school. There's a ladies-only sleepover scheduled. Two men to a car with cell phones, checking in each hour from four p.m. to dawn, should cover it. And no guns."

Clay grumbled. "Well, you already put Old Lucy to bed. A guy can't have any fun around here anymore."

"Like she's your only girlfriend," said Rachael.

The men found another laughing point and exchanged knowing looks. Clay took over the conversation as Rachael turned to finish topping off her gas tank. Her last retort was to no avail, of course, but she felt it was her duty to tell them no firearms. Most of the guys in town had at least three guns, if not more; some were registered, some not. She really didn't want to know everything about their stash. She did know, however, that while they could be on the wild side on a Saturday night, they did love Bullhead and would take pride in protecting its citizens. With Rachael's approval, they didn't have to be covert about their actions that had already been planned. They would incorporate her suggestions and hand out her cell phone number, along with Hal's. Parting company, Rachael and her righteous warriors all shook hands, each knowing the other so well and making the most of it.

Rachael found a break in the traffic, headed north on the 95, and made a quick call to Amanda. She was updated on the Mafia activity. "Do you think Beckett is behind the money laundering?"

"Involved, but not the main man. Hey, look at us, sis. All dressed up with guns and a party to go to." While sounding lighthearted, the sisters said good-bye with dread in their hearts.

47

Following the discovery of Melissa's body, the city remained on high alert. Plans were checked and rechecked, and all loopholes were eliminated. Crossing the Laughlin Bridge and turning left on Casino Drive, Rachael could feel the tension in the city—or was that a reflection of her own tension? Bullhead and Laughlin were both rough around the edges—lots of transients—but the towns were also balanced with tons of great, down-to-earth people. She loved the common people most, which did not include Elliott. She was weary to the bone and ready for tonight to be over. Meg felt the killer would move on, but Rachael knew the bastard was out there, waiting, ready to grab another victim.

Meg always anticipated a happy ending, and Rachael admired her for that. But reversing the scene also meant that Rachael had to run interference for Meg, knocking down as many obstacles as possible before they could overwhelm or entrap her baby sister. She wondered if Amanda felt that way about her. Probably not, she decided. Their relationship was loving but not protective, since each of the two siblings was street-smart and physically strong. Their vulnerability was identical. They both lacked the ability to choose the right partner. When a promising man materialized, the girls would usually run them off. Lack of commitment? Possibly. Possibly? Probably.

Rachael parked next to Elliott's tan 2006 GMC SUV and noted that the hood was hot and the car was dirty. Elliott was usually meticulous with everything: his dress, his office, and especially his car. Fanatical came to mind, and prissy was rather a trademark for him. When he was going out on an interview, he would stick the magnetic sign on the side of his car that read, *KTVC News. Covering the Tristate Area. Elliott Spencer (928) 555-1234.* He was so suited for his job—a self-righteous blowhard who believed every woman in town would love to get laid by him. What a joke. Rachael pushed away the mental sarcasm and entered the small studio. "Hey, anyone around?"

"Yeah, right here, Rachael. Just shaking the lily," said Elliott as he finished zipping up his fly. "Suppose you're here to go over the news coverage for tonight's activities?"

"Got that right," said Rachael. She wondered if Elliott had timed her entrance to the precise second he was zipping up. Maybe that was a trademark? "We'd like you to play down the story. Let the public know the last time the jerk pulled the abductions in Santa Cruz, he left after three victims."

"Can you promise that he's gone?"

"Not really. OK to say that FBI, Metro, sheriff, Bullhead, and Laughlin cops will be out in case they're needed. We want the city to feel safe but alert. If you could help with that, we'd appreciate it."

"Yeah, I can handle that," said Elliott. "Metro chief is coming in for an interview on the afternoon show, and he's good. He'll be brief and give the folks a sense of security. What do you think? Is this guy going to show up or what?"

"No comment on that. Time will tell."

"Isn't this the year he's supposed to go looking for some virgin territory? Well, who knows. I'd rather put a gigantic spin on this, but I'll cooperate this time. I'm sure you're going to pay me back by slippin' between the sheets with me."

"Dream on, Elliott. Besides, I saw you with that new barmaid the other day. One ride at a time, I always say." Rachael smiled, but as she turned away from Elliott, she couldn't help herself. She grimaced, crossed her eyes, and wrinkled her nose. *What a creep.*

"She's a hot one. I may have to give her my full attention for a while. Really shouldn't cut myself out of the pack for one gal though, Rachael. We'd have too many women jumping off the bridge if I denied them too long."

"Yeah, right. Anyway, we're counting on you, and we really do appreciate your help on this. Gotta go. Big night coming up. Lots of ground to cover."

"You got it, Rachael. Say, I haven't seen your little sister around lately. Did she lose her job at the dam over that missing key thing?"

Rachael hesitated; she didn't like Elliott's interest in Meg, but she was here asking for a favor. "Just got back in town. I've got her stashed in a safe place for tonight, but she's been reinstated and back to work. Thanks for asking."

Elliott smiled. "It's easy to wonder about someone that hot. She going with anyone?"

Rachael headed for the door but paused. "Better change your interest in that one, Elliott. Anyone caught messin' with Meg has to account to the whole Bullhead Police Department. Go lookin' for another fish," she said with a serious look.

They walked out of the air-conditioned office and were greeted with 112 degrees of desert heat. Elliott walked Rachael to her car and opened the door.

As she got in, she said, "Hey, do you need to borrow a buck to get your car washed? I've never seen your car so dirty."

"Nah, I've got it covered. I went to Oatman yesterday afternoon. Supposed to be a hot story on some new donkey game they're promoting, but it was stupid. I had to do some off-road driving. Haven't had time to get it washed. That's my next job, and then I'm meeting with one of the neighborhood watch groups. I'll be the contact for the southeast section."

"Oh, good. Give me your cell number in case I need to call you."

Elliott jerked a little, so slightly that Rachael almost missed it. "Minor problem. I can't locate it, so I'll have to pick up a new one this afternoon. I'm going to change my number. Been getting some really weird voice mail messages lately."

"OK, call me when you get it. Here's my number." Rachael pulled out a preprinted flyer that included all of the contact numbers. As Elliott took it from her, she felt a chill in the unimaginable heat of the day.

"I'll tell the captain about those annoying calls. Maybe we can track down the caller. Changing your number is a pain in the ass." With that, Rachael closed the door, started the car, and headed toward Bill's bar, still trying to shake off Elliott's essence.

48

Meg spent most of the day catching up with all the new programs at work. She was behind in upgrading the computer network and felt the pressure of her two days off. Mike and Jerry teased her incessantly about her choice of boyfriends and how stupid she was to lose her security pass. Meg took most of it in stride.

"OK, you guys. Get off my back. I had a wonderful two-day vacation—*paid,* may I add—while you were driving your Cushman around, looking like security guards. My disappearing boyfriend left me a text this morning, and he'll be in town tonight."

"Right, just in time to kidnap someone for a year. He's probably the serial killer." Both men laughed. When Meg shot them a frightened look, they clammed up. Mike changed the subject and said, "Where ya hanging tonight?"

"Paula and I booked a room at the Oasis. It should be a blast. I know the locals are going to do some really stupid things. I told Rachael I would behave, but who knows? I might just want to join in. Most everybody thinks this crazy killer has left town. Anyway, come on by, and we'll go dancing."

There was no need to beg Jerry and Mike to show up. They adored Meg, and while they would love to make a move on her, they weren't that naive. Being Meg's best pal, instead of her boyfriend, was a happy second choice. She was special to everyone who knew her—the total package. Even-tempered, spirited, funny, and over-the-top gorgeous could only partially describe her attributes. There wasn't a vain bone in her body.

"Well, shit," said Jerry. "If dear old Derek shows up, then you'll probably drop us like a hot potato. You really don't need to look so far for a boyfriend."

"I don't see anyone applying for the job. Anyway, Derek and me? Not going to happen," said Meg. "When we were at the cemetery in Yorba Linda, I told him that he wasn't my type. I did tell him he was fun enough to hang with. He's just another groupie now."

No one believed a word she said.

When she got home after work, Meg put in a quick load of laundry. The sun was just about to set, but she still had time to put on a swimsuit and head down for a quick dip. The dam hadn't released a lot of water again, so she grabbed an inner tube. She popped the top of a Coors Light and took the wrought-iron stairs down to the lower patio. A roadrunner was sitting on the deck. The awkward bird showed signs of aging from the horrific heat. His feathers were ragged and faded, and his eyes were slow to recognize a person approaching. He remained motionless and stared at her blankly. "Well, aren't you too brave? That's what I get for feeding you and your family," Meg said as she slid by the large bird.

She tossed her inner tube into the water and started floating. The water normally seemed more soothing. *My troubles should be floating straight down the river.* But now, good thoughts refused to replace stressful ones. *Hey, Grandma, have anything to say?* She watched the sun finally give up for the day.

Why do I have this morbid sense of impending disaster?

49

Despite the flurry of activity, by far the busiest person in town was El Jefe. He went into the basement of his Oatman home and began filling empty boxes. He had finally decided that if he remained in Laughlin, he might be testing his luck. In lieu of staying, he would kidnap his victim and take her with him. The city would assume he was still there and would continue the search locally. That would give him more time to establish his new frontier without undue pressure. He knew this woman was the real thing and his search had finally ended.

He was annoyed that he had spent so much time preparing for number seven, but common sense told him the decision to relocate was a good one. His most important item was his collection of labeled jars. He had searched the Internet to find the perfect jars for his hearts. Only clear glass would do. On his computer, he had designed his own creative label for each heart; the basic part of the design was a childlike drawing of a heart with various drops of blood dripping from each. Dolores was his first love. The label showed her name and the date of her demise. She was a cocktail waitress, so he had included an olive in her jar. Preserving the heart was quite simple. Once the heart was rinsed with a saline solution, it was relegated to a jar containing formaldehyde. The jar was tightened and the label affixed. He was proud of his collection. If he was ever caught, the jars would attest to his brilliance.

Six jars were placed in the carton: three hearts from Santa Cruz and three from Bullhead/Laughlin. Each jar was separated by cardboard and an ample supply of foam peanuts. What a beautiful sight. Ah, but moving forward, his thoughts of the new home awaiting him were equally delectable. The desert heat would be replaced by a gorgeous view of the ocean again. His mother would have been so proud of his newly acquired wealth and homes. She would also be proud of the new woman he would be collecting tonight. The fair maiden.

Bundles of C-4 were placed strategically throughout the house, the timer set for 12:00 a.m., which would create another distraction for his departure from Laughlin.

Arrangements had been made with the Mexican connections that Laughlin would no longer be their destination. They would now be flown with the body parts from Mexico to Lake Mead, a short distance from Las Vegas. Continuing with the black-market body parts would be relatively easy. Only selecting another hospital and finding an unscrupulous doctor was necessary. One project at a time—and setting up his new home with *her* was the only thing on his mind.

One last examination of the grounds and house convinced El Jefe that all was ready. He would take the two Dobermans close to the new housing off the Parkway and let them go. Someone would adopt them if the dog catchers found them. Glancing at his watch, he knew it was time. He picked up the box of hearts and carefully placed it in the back of his stolen van. The outside of the box declared its contents to be fragile. Everything else had been prepared the night before and was now waiting in the van. The only other items to be carried to the van were his duffle bag with two changes of clothes, a wheelchair, personal items for his new mistress, and a scruffy beard and baseball cap that were to be part of his disguise tonight. It was time.

50

Sunset comes late in August. It was still 112 degrees at six thirty when Hal pulled up to valet parking at the Oasis. He left his keys in the ignition and walked over to the head valet attendant. "Hi, George. Leave my car close by in case we have to take off. Rachael and I will both be covering the casino tonight."

"No problem, Hal. Keys will be in it. I won't let any cars box you in. Rachael hasn't shown up yet, but her cute little sister has already checked in. How about setting me up with her?"

"Yeah, like I don't get that question about ten times a day." Both men laughed. "What's it look like in there tonight? Bunch of weirdos or just the normal few?"

"I caught this one asshole walking in with a noose around his neck. Bombed out of his mind.

His girlfriend flashed me with the biggest set of knockers I've ever seen. Her T-shirt read, *Take me, I'm easy.*"

"No accounting for taste, huh?" Hal entered the casino, passed the guest check-in counter, and headed for the bank of elevators leading to the security office.

***

Rachael loaded and reloaded her Glock, decided to carry her hunting knife, strapped the backup .22 to her ankle, and grabbed some extra ammo. She threw in the pepper spray, stun gun, and shotgun, and finally got into the car. She made the familiar trip across the bridge and pulled into the valet parking lot.

"Hey, Rachael. Hal just went inside. Leave the keys in your car, and we'll have it ready to go."

"Thanks, George. Have you seen Meg yet?"

"Oh, yeah. She came in a few minutes ago. I asked Hal to fix me up, and he said sure. I've got to win ten thousand dollars at the craps table tonight, and he said it would be a go."

Rachael smiled at that. "You guys just never give up. Wish someone would pay that much for me for a few hours. I might say yes."

George knew she was kidding. Rachael was the practical one—good-looking, great body, but had some kind of a wall around her. Rather unapproachable. "Well, I'll check with the whales when they show up tonight. You might get some action after all."

"Me with a whale? Well, if he doesn't mind someone with about twenty pounds of artillery strapped to her body, maybe we could be a good fit." He knew, and she knew that he knew, so enough was said. Rachael sprinted off and entered the smoky casino, thinking, *Here we go.*

Rachael checked in with security and asked what room Meg and Paula were occupying. She was told room 607. They showed her the camera footage of Meg and Paula, being their happy selves, entering the room. "Where are the elevator, emergency stairs, and ice machine located on that floor?" was her next question.

After studying the floor layout, Rachael felt comfortable about the situation and decided to call on Beckett. He was usually cooperative with the police, and she needed some reassurance that times had not changed. She found him in his office, grumbling at the computer monitor.

"It would be great if you could convince all the vigilantes, FBI, Metro, and Bullhead cops to gamble while they're here. Our whole clientele consists of ten busloads of senior citizens and a pot full of crazy locals who are acting up." He turned his monitor so Rachael could get a handle on his consternation and said, "Check out that weirdo. He's wearing Dracula fangs, and his T-shirt has a huge heart painted on it with a dagger through it. Sicko."

"Yeah, but you know he's not our guy. He wouldn't be that obvious. He'll probably be in disguise. Try to fit in with the crowd until he makes his move. And who knows if he's even still here in town? This is a pretty tough assignment with twelve casinos to cover and all the other areas. Oh, and don't forget the river itself. God, I'll be glad when this night is over."

Beckett agreed, and they started toward the elevator to check on the casino floor. "So I hear Megan is staying here tonight. Quite a feather in my cap to think that of all the casinos in town, you think ours is the safest for your kid sister. Just gives me more time to try and pick up on her. Think I'll send some bubbly to her room to get her in the mood."

Rachael was tired of all this testosterone flying off the walls at the mention of Meg. There was so much more to her sister than just the obvious.

"Hey, go for it, Beckett," replied Rachael. "Won't help your cause any. You might be better off spending the cash on that new cocktail waitress you were hitting on last week. What's her name again?"

"Amanda. Oh, well, she seems to be playing the field. She went out with Elliott twice. She's a looker, all right. She's a little too smart for her good-lookin' britches. We got into it last night. But you're right. I'll see what her schedule looks like. The gals have to wear those tight outfits and damn shoes. Maybe she'll need a massage by midnight." They both laughed at that—for very different reasons.

51

El Jefe had a perfect plan. There was risk involved, but it might be the only way to kidnap the woman. The previous day, he had checked into the Oasis Casino as Mr. and Mrs. Henry Jacobson.

Mrs. Jacobson was a blow-up doll dressed in an old-fashioned polyester pantsuit, a shawl around her shoulders, and a gray wig sitting on top of her head. Gloves hid the plastic hands, and black sneakers covered her feet. El Jefe practiced patience as he caked on the makeup. With a final touch, he placed his mockup wife into a wheelchair, strapped her in tightly, and transported her to the Oasis. His disguise coincided with hers. Padding across his back gave him a good widower's hump. Added to that was his gray makeup and gray wig, glasses, and partial buckteeth. They presented themselves as a nice, elderly couple. He was given a room especially equipped for the handicapped. He paid cash for the night and said they were just passing through on their way to Los Angeles. El Jefe inwardly laughed at all the fools who helped him through the doors and got out of his way when he pushed the wheelchair through the lobby. All necessary medications, tape, scissors, hair dye, sex toys, and rope were neatly packed in his overnight suitcase for the next part of his plan.

Other preparation included the rental of an eighteen-wheeler and parking it on the Arizona side of the river, across from the casino. This area was used by truckers as an overnight stop. He had practiced loading and unloading a car into the trailer of the rig and knew how much time it would take to perform the task. Oh, what a wonderful time he was having. The mastermind behind the perfect crime.

El Jefe had spent enough time in the casino earlier in the day so that no one would think twice about the elderly, gray-haired man whose shaky hands could barely hold the cards when playing blackjack. Most people would help him onto his stool and put his cane on the back of the chair. Stupid, stupid. How could there be so many victims in this world? He cashed in his winnings after each gaming session and returned to the room, where he had twice ordered room service for two. The extra food was dumped into an ice chest. All was set.

***

Amanda was getting ready for her shift, putting on the last-minute false eyelashes and powder to set her makeup, when there was a knock at the door. "Room service."

Since she had not ordered room service, she quickly checked her revolver and slid it under the pillow. "Coming," she said and opened the door without even looking through the peephole. "Why, Beckett, what a surprise. And expensive champagne, too. Does this mean I'm forgiven?"

"Not totally."

"I'm really sorry to piss you off. I was just doing what I was told to do."

"That was a mistake, and you only get one with me. We'll move forward. Thought I'd check in on you. Looks like you're getting ready for your shift. That means at midnight, I should be able to drop by your room to visit. How about I have dinner delivered here, and you can change into something more comfortable?"

Sleazy, sleazy. "Well, that sounds like a workable plan. I don't have rehearsal tomorrow, and, gee, I don't even have to serve drinks tomorrow. Don't order dinner; just show up. I might want to go dancing or do something else to unwind. Maybe a movie? How about that?"

"Works for me," said Beckett. He put an arm around her waist and pulled her close.

Amanda could feel the beginning of an erection and responded by pushing closer. She gave him a quick kiss. "Glad you're not mad anymore. You kinda scared me. Gotta get to work now. My boss might get jealous if he catches us together." She pushed even closer to him and continued. "Just hold onto that…hmmm…thought."

They both laughed. She ushered Beckett out of the room. After the door closed, she experienced an involuntary shake, close to a spasm. *What a creep. I'll be so glad when this assignment is over.* She wrapped a red fluffy boa around her neck and headed toward the casinos, cursing the damnable high heels.

***

Meg and Paula took great care in preparing for the evening. They each wore flimsy spaghetti-strap dresses. "Well, I think we look slutty enough to get someone to buy us a few drinks. Maybe take us dancing, don't ya think?" Meg asked as she flirted with the mirror.

"This is when I really hate you. I look mousey next to you. Guess that's why I always get your leftovers," Paula said as she joined Meg in gazing into the mirror.

"Not true. Greg was not my leftover, and he was awesome. You guys really had a good ride.

Me, well, I always go for the hunks that are either brainless or so self-absorbed that there's no room for me. Anyway, that's history. Tonight, we start on a new adventure. Where to first?"

After a few minutes, they decided to coat their stomachs with something, so they headed to the food court. The casino was starting to fill, and both girls laughed at some of the locals wearing freaky T-shirts and giddy women wearing shirts that read, *Serial or cereal, I'm yours* or *Let me be your number 7*. Both girls agreed that this was going to be a fun, wacky, night. After Chinese food, they sauntered over toward the north tower casino to locate Mike and Jerry.

The river bar was packed solid when they got there. Meg stood on her toes, trying to locate the guys, when suddenly someone grabbed her from behind, turned her, and planted a kiss square on her mouth. Meg pulled back and started to fight when she realized it was Derek. "You shithead. You scared the hell out of me. I thought I was going to be number seven."

"Sorry, sorry. I thought you'd recognize the slurpy kiss. Again, sorry. Just trying to have some fun."

"You are so lucky not to get my knee in your groin. You'll never know."

He looked rather sheepish by now, and Meg decided to back off. "Well, well, Mr. Mystery is back in town. I thought you were going to text me when you arrived."

Derek flashed his special smile, and Meg felt another of those heart twangs. *Down, girl. He may be handsome but really hasn't been on the level with me. Probably another loser, like Rachael thinks he is.* Derek had been sitting at the three-card poker table with a stack of chips in front of him when he spotted Meg. The adjoining seat was empty. He put one hundred dollars' worth of chips at that spot and asked Meg to join him. She felt her friends inwardly moan. The influx of the outsider meant their plans for the evening would probably change.

"Maybe four hands, and then I've got to go. We're going to party hearty tonight. You can join us if you want." Jerry and Mike weren't too thrilled with that idea. Someone else might get lucky tonight, but it wasn't going to be them.

Meg knew her friends were anxious to get started, so after winning four hands in succession, she gave Derek his original one hundred dollars and put the winnings in her purse. She joined the brat pack and headed for the craps table.

"Cocktails?" asked the dark-haired waitress as she greeted the group leaving the table. "Cocktails?"

Three men at the table readily placed an order with Amanda. "How about you five? Want to order now? I can deliver to the craps table if that's where you're headed."

"My, my," said Meg. "Who do we have here? A new cocktail bunny at the Oasis? Sure, sweetie, make mine an apple martini. The others like their Coors. Think you can remember that? Maybe you should write it down." Meg was enjoying this moment, bossing her oldest sister around.

Amanda gave her a half-assed smile and said, "I'll try, sweetie. Be right back."

All three men sucked in a huge amount of air as Amanda walked by with her cocktail tray held high. She couldn't help but flex a little and give them her sexiest smile. Meg was seething. The men recovered and moved through the smoky crowd to the craps table next to the poker room. Meg recognized the croupier and knew they would have their ration of fun with him. After the group had passed the dice twice and made a few dollars each, they decided to go to the Swinger's Lounge and do some serious drinking and dancing.

The lounge was already packed at ten o'clock. There was no place to sit. Meg said she was ready to go casino hopping but needed to change into some shorts and sandals for the trip. Paula agreed, and the two girls left the guys with Dan, the hot bartender, at the river bar.

52

Matt called Amanda at 11:00 p.m. "It's done. We nabbed six players in Vegas. Got the money and the head honcho when they exchanged the cash. Exciting. Went down without a hitch."

"Good job, Matt. Now it's my turn."

"Look, there's plenty of backup in Laughlin this week. Do you need some help with Beckett?"

"I'm fine. He's expecting me at midnight, but I'll go now. The casino's getting pretty rowdy. Maybe we should have someone come and cover his job after I arrest him. If that serial killer ends up in this hotel, we'll have a mess on our hands."

"I'll get someone there now."

A few minutes passed, and Special Agent Larry Hopkins met with Amanda. "OK, you go in and do your thing. Leave the door ajar. I'll know when to come in," he said.

Amanda had changed out of her uniform and called Beckett. He was expecting her.

Betty had gone for the day. "I'm surprised the pit boss would let you off early," Beckett said as she entered.

"Didn't have a choice."

Beckett looked puzzled by her answer. "Dressed rather casual for dinner, aren't you? What's going on?"

"You don't like my clothes? Actually, this is FBI-approved attire."

"FBI? What are you talking about?"

Amanda pulled out her badge. "You have the right to remain silent…" and continued on with the Miranda. She moved forward with her handcuffs as Hopkins entered the room.

"The hell, you say. What's going on? Who are you?"

"Amanda Pennington, FBI."

"Pennington. Pennington? You bitch. What are the charges?"

"We can start with money laundering for the Mafia. The rest will follow depending on your involvement and cooperation. Turn around, and put your hands behind you."

Beckett didn't argue. His facial expression changed from livid to concerned. "You know I'm a dead man if you take me in. The syndicate that owns the Oasis has nothing to do with this petty money game. But I'm toast."

"If you're willing to cooperate, we might be able to help," said Hopkins.

53

El Jefe had been tracking Meg and Paula all evening. He had watched and waited three years while the young, beautiful blonde matured, and now she was ripe for his taking. He broke his original pattern of three girls in one town because of her and was taking a huge risk. The rewards would be worth it. Anyone looking would wonder what an old gray-haired, stooped man was doing trying to hide the beginning of such a magnificent erection.

Earlier, as the girls were checking into the Oasis, El Jefe moved as swiftly as his disguise would allow and entered the elevator with them. They punched in their floor number. He nodded pleasantly and with a whisper said that was also his floor. He scuffled past them when they entered their room. Once he knew their room number, he went downstairs and changed his room to the same floor.

He transferred his fake wife and few possessions. Now, his room number was 623 and perfect for his plan. He returned to the casino and patiently continued playing cards.

When the girls went up to change clothes at ten forty-five, they were not surprised to be sharing the elevator once again with the old man from down the hall. "My wife's an invalid, and she's in the room by herself," he told them on the way up. "I need to put her into bed now. She likes to watch the late show on TV until I tuck her in. We've been married for fifty-eight years now. She was my first sweetheart." He smiled and continued his handshaking motion. *They think I have palsy and will be so happy to help this wonderful old man. Fools.*

"Your wife is very lucky to have such a loving husband," said Meg as the three stepped out of the elevator. When Meg and Paula stopped in front of room 607, El Jefe said good night and shuffled down the hall. He waited five minutes.

El Jefe walked back to room 607 and knocked gently. Meg opened the door. She had changed into her shorts, and Paula was in the bathroom. Pulling her hair into a long ponytail, she smiled at El Jefe.

"Excuse me, dear. I'm legally blind and can't get my key card to work. Would one of you mind calling housekeeping so they can help me? My wife is getting agitated. I can hear her on the other side of the door. Her wheelchair must be stuck. She can't help me. She confuses so easily these days." He trembled as he spoke.

"No problem. I can help you. Be back in a minute, Paula," she yelled. "Just helping the neighbor." Paula yelled back to hurry so they wouldn't keep the guys waiting.

Meg took the key from El Jefe's quivering hand and walked down the hallway in stride with the old man. She quickly opened the door. As she started to hand him the key, he said, "Oh, my God. Something's wrong. Martha's lying on the floor."

He had previously positioned the blow-up doll next to the bed, lying facedown. If the room had been brighter, it would have been obvious to Meg that something was amiss, but the only light emanated from the TV. "Oh, help. Something's wrong. Help me."

As Meg headed for the prone pseudo figure, El Jefe pulled the syringe from his jacket pocket. When Meg leaned over the decoy, he plunged the needle into her neck and forced the ketamine into her body. As she slumped onto the floor, he pulled her out of the way. Leaving the lights down, he went back to get Paula.

Paula was easy. When she heard that Meg needed help with El Jefe's wife, she rushed down the hall and walked in on the same scene. El Jefe injected her with the same drug. Too bad he couldn't take them both. That, indeed, would be a surprise for the police. Jefe stuck duct tape on Paula's mouth and, after taping her feet and hands together, dragged her into the shower. His movements were quick and precise. Escape time was running out. Returning to Meg, he put an old robe on her. After taping her hands down to the arms of the wheelchair, he covered her blonde hair with the ancient gray wig and applied some grayish makeup on her. He added padding to the back of her robe to look like a matching old lady's hump, taped her mouth with clear plastic, and headed out the door.

When the elevator opened at ground level, the security guard was standing there. "Good evening, Mr. Jacobson. You and the missus are out kind of late this evening."

El Jefe mumbled something almost incoherent about a call from their children and leaving for Los Angeles right away. The guard really didn't give a rat's ass.

"I don't like to drive across the desert at night; my eyes aren't good anymore. But this time, it can't be helped. Really enjoyed my stay, as usual. Good night, now."

El Jefe walked with measured footsteps toward his stolen van with the bogus plates. He knew the security system was on in the hallway of the casino and that the parking lot also would have cameras. The van was parked halfway up the lot, beyond the focus of the cameras. He opened the back of the van, pushed the button to lower the wheelchair lift, and shoved Meg's wheelchair onto the platform. Immediately, he raised the platform, pushed the chair inside, closed the van doors, and rushed into the driver's seat. As planned, that took eight minutes. Right on schedule.

While there were plenty of cops around, no one looked twice at the old man pushing a wheelchair and doting on his wife. The van displayed a handicapped license plate, and all looked ordinary. The wiring had been stripped, and he started the car. He crossed the bridge going to Bullhead and made a quick right turn onto Highway 95. A mile down, he made another right turn into a huge trucker parking lot. The cops didn't bother the truckers' lot. They would rather have the drivers sleep than drive when they were tired. El Jefe's eighteen-wheeler was waiting for him. He started the engine earlier in the evening so the trailer would be cool for his girlfriend. He opened the rear of the trailer, pulled out two planks, and, after setting them in the right position, drove the van up the ramp and into the refrigerated trailer.

He gave Meg another shot of ketamine, enough to keep her unconscious for the hour's drive. If she did awaken, she was still strapped to the wheelchair. Managing an escape would be impossible. Slamming the doors shut, El Jefe drove the truck out of the parking lot and headed across the

Laughlin Bridge again. He pulled the gray wig from his head, replacing it with a red baseball cap for his escape from town. It was midnight. Las Vegas was his next stop.

Another monsoon was approaching, and the wind slowed down the high-profile truck as it headed across the desert. A few minutes were stolen from El Jefe's precise plan, but he was still in the parameters of success as he parked the eighteen-wheeler at a warehouse area adjacent to the Amtrak Station. Reservations for two on the last train, leaving at 2:00 a.m., had been confirmed. He paid extra for a large sleeping compartment, including a bathroom with a small sink, toilet, and shower. El Jefe's luggage was almost nonexistent except for the well-packed box of human hearts. The gray wig went back on his head. He wheeled Meg from the back of the trailer, down the ramp, and onto the sidewalk. She was still semi-comatose as he pushed the wheelchair three blocks to the boarding platform. As anticipated, a porter was there to assist the poor old man and his sick wife. When he pushed Meg into their honeymoon compartment, El Jefe smiled at the excellent manner in which he had foiled the cops. The train started on time with an "All aboard" from the conductor. As the wheels turned, they seemed to be saying, "She's mine, she's mine, she's mine, she's mine."

54

Amanda and Agent Hopkins checked with headquarters. There was no place to transfer Beckett at the moment. They uncuffed him and escorted him to the surveillance floor. The FBI wanted to downplay his capture. An agent was assigned to watch him for the rest of the night.

"You don't need to cuff me again. For God's sake, where am I going to go?"

Amanda cuffed him to the swivel chair. "Oh, Beckett, you can't charm your way out of this one." She moved away and studied the monitors covering the north tower casino. Everything looked normal.

***

Rachael was making her rounds in the north casino and spotted the three guys sitting at the bar overlooking the river. They weren't having much luck with the video poker machines but seemed to be having a great time downing the booze. She walked over and tapped Derek on the back.

"Back in town for another visit, I see."

"Yeah, thought I'd give this crazy town one more chance…and your sister, too."

"I thought Meg and Paula were sticking close with you guys tonight. Where are they?"

"They went up to their room to change." He stood and looked around the crowd. "We were going casino hopping. I guess girls can't do that in heels."

Concern crossed Rachael's face. "How long ago did they leave?"

The three men turned to look at her. Jerry answered, "Must have been around eleven o'clock. The dealers were changing shift."

"Why didn't you guys walk them to their rooms? Jesus."

"God, Rachael. They weren't going outside. Just changing to shorts. They're probably still looking in the mirror. You know those two."

"Idiots." Rachael headed for the bank of courtesy phones and dialed room 607. "Come on, come on, come on, Meg. Pick up." No reply. Rachael called security to see if they could locate Amanda or Hal. Amanda was there.

"Meg's missing. I'm heading for her room."

"Shit. I just busted Beckett. I'm here in security. On my way."

Both sisters headed to Room 607. Amanda grabbed a security pass. Meg's room was empty. No signs of a struggle. They raced back to the security floor to review the surveillance tape.

They checked the sixth-floor hallway tape starting at 10:45. Fear began to mount. They saw Meg, Paula, and an old man exit the elevator at 11:05.

"Who's he?" asked Amanda.

"Just some old fart staying here with his wife," said a technician. "She's in a wheelchair. He comes down and gambles a couple of times a day. They order room service stuff. I guess she's pretty handicapped."

They watched as the girls entered their room and observed the "old man" fumbling with his key card. "Where's he going now?" asked Rachael.

"Shit. Back to Meg's room. The oldest trick in the world. God, Meg, don't fall for it," said Amanda as if her sister could hear her. As the tape played on, the women realized what had happened. The whole plot was unfolding in front of them. Meg was the intended victim all along. They continued watching, urging the tape to hurry up. At the same time, they feared what the next scene would show. When they saw the old man pushing someone in a wheelchair down the hall into the elevator, they both sprang into action.

"God, not my sister!" cried Amanda. "Rachael, finish watching the tape. Review the exit tape and any tape showing the north parking lot. I have to get my gear. I'll meet you there in five minutes. Check out the old man's room first. Hopkins, watch Beckett. Call the command post and fill 'em in. Heads up for an SUV that's handicapped equipped. Close down the parking lot. Set up road blocks. No outgoing traffic without being searched. Oh, no, not Meg." Amanda ran for her gear.

Hal joined Rachael in the security office and watched the tape showing El Jefe pushing the wheelchair through the parking lot and out of focus. "That's it. We don't know what he's driving but have a description of him now," said Rachael.

"He'll ditch that disguise in seconds, Rachael. Let's get to the parking lot. Maybe he dumped the wheelchair. Call water patrol. Check the boat ramp. There might be a boat waiting."

Agent Hopkins updated the command center. The FBI had a helicopter for their use.

When the car/van was ID'd, they would follow by air. Rachael and Hal hurried to room 623 to look for evidence. They found Paula bound and gagged in the shower. She still suffered from the effects of the ketamine. Paula mumbled something about an old man. They found the blow-up doll deflated on the bed with a hole cut in her chest.

Sick bastard.

THURSDAY, AUGUST 1

Once the train hit its stride, El Jefe turned his lascivious attention to the next part of his well-structured plan. Meg, still drowsy and strapped to the wheelchair, was oblivious to her surroundings, so El Jefe had free reign to chop off her long blonde hair.

"A little haircut, my dear—or, rather, how about an extreme makeover?" With just a few whacks, her hair dropped to the floor. "Just a little below the ears, you say? Fine, now when we put on the brown hair dye, you'll look very average. No one will notice you, especially when you put on these pitiful glasses." He was humming and smiling at his makeover.

Putting the dye on proved to be a mess. Plastic draped over her shoulders solved part of the problem, but rinsing was a real task. While the dye was setting, he cut the duct tape restricting her hands to the chair and laid her on the bed, which was covered by a plastic sheet.

El Jefe undressed her, delighting in her youthful anatomy. Another erection. She was fluid perfection. He stripped down and carried her drugged body into the small shower to rinse out the hair dye, the tape still on her mouth.

As the water flowed over her body, Meg's eyes fluttered. The catatonia was disappearing, but she still experienced visual distortions. She tried to peer through the fog.

Seeing that she was trying to speak, El Jefe pulled the tape from half of her mouth.

She grimaced, and then, recognizing the man holding her, she tried to smile. "Elliott, thank God you're here to help me." She heard the words coming out of her mouth, but they didn't sound like what she was trying to say. "Help me before that old man comes back." Again, she fell into semi-awareness and slumped against him.

Elliott smiled and placed the tape back in its original position. "Sorry, pumpkin. Welcome to your new life."

Meg sagged into his arms, her mind incapable of comprehending what was happening. Elliott returned her to the bed, dried off her petite body, rolled the fragile girl off the plastic sheet, and began to examine his prize.

***

By the time the train neared Los Angeles, Meg had been sexually attacked with barbaric strokes, sodomized, and ravaged again. He savagely inserted the sex toys. He amused himself by biting her body and then sucking on other parts until bruises appeared. He took pictures as he inserted himself into her mouth. He propped her up and inserted her fingers in her swollen vagina. He whispered in her ear that this was their wedding night. "On our anniversary, we'll look at these wonderful pictures and remember how excited we were." When he realized that the train was approaching LA, he had to abstain from more sexual pleasure.

The meds finally wore off, and Meg became aware of her surroundings. She was too tired and weak to fight back. The injections supplied relaxation to the skeletal muscles, which suited Elliott's madness but also threw Meg into a mental state that blocked the sense of time and pain.

As the Amtrak pulled into Los Angeles's Union Station, Elliott was ready for the next step. He dressed Meg in shorts, a tank top, and sandals for their later departure. She was apathetic to all her surroundings and didn't resist. Two business-class seats were reserved on the morning train heading toward San Diego.

Once Meg was cleaned up, he started to sanitize the compartment, removing all of the fingerprints that the FBI would be looking for. As he started this task, he remembered that in his haste to leave the casino, he had ignored the plastic doll. When the FBI dusted the doll for prints, his anonymity would be destroyed. He stopped the cleaning. The FBI could find any evidence they needed. He didn't care anymore. He had his final prize, the one woman who would satisfy all of his needs, and if all went according to plan, they would never be found.

Changing trains at Union Station was necessary, and Elliott managed to manhandle the stumbling Meg onto the train heading toward San Diego. "Your new name will be Sandra, or Sandy, if anyone asks. We're going to San Clemente for a day at the beach. Oh, you probably believe that I'm a fool for thinking you'd go along with this, but please, darling Sandy, understand that I know where your mother and sister live, and I will kill them if you cause any problems. You know by my history that this isn't an idle threat. I would relish ravaging Rachael. Oh, such charming alliteration." He started humming. "When we get to our final destination, I'll sober you up, and we'll have a wonderful year together. You are my ultimate trophy. I will keep you forever."

While her words seemed jumbled, Meg said, "When my sisters catch up with you, you're dead meat, Elliott. They'll carve you into small pieces for what you've done to me."

"What do you mean, sisters? I thought Rachael was your only sister. Do tell. Is there another sibling that I can play with?"

Meg was clearheaded enough to lie. "Older. Schoolteacher, but she'll take her pound of flesh."

Elliott thought he knew everything there was to know about Megan and her family. He had taken a trip to Yorba Linda to check out her mother. Rather a renegade herself. Well, a schoolteacher couldn't be that much of a threat, so while it bothered him that he might have overlooked something, he decided to let it go.

"Let's hurry, darling. We have another train to catch. Our love nest is waiting."

56

Rachael, Amanda, and Hal scoured the parking lot to no avail. The security camera showed ten vehicles leaving the parking lot in the past half hour. The license plates were visible and immediately checked. One plate came up as stolen but didn't belong to the car seen in the tape. This was their best lead. Rachael called Ron, who was assigned to the Laughlin Bridge. He ran the bridge surveillance footage for Rachael.

"There it is. Can't see the driver's face. He's old with straggly gray hair. The van turns south on the 95; then he's out of range. Check with Chili's or IHOP. They all have cameras covering their parking lots. Maybe some of them catch the 95, too."

The three split up. Amanda started at the corner of the 95 and the bridge, Hal drove two miles to the tattoo parlor, and Rachael took the middle ground. It was now after midnight, but the restaurant owners were eager to help the police.

The radios all started transmitting at the same time. Hal spoke first. "The van didn't get down this far."

Amanda said it had gone past her location at 11:35 but disappeared after that.

Rachael was the lucky one. "Meet me at the trucker's parking lot across from Home Depot. He pulled in there."

Time is always the most important factor when looking for a kidnap victim. The more time that passes, the less chance of finding the victim alive. They knew this and hurried.

As the three cars pulled into the parking lot, signs of the projected monsoon began to appear. The wind was gusting at forty miles per hour, and the dirt parking lot was like a sandy wind tunnel. The usual parking attendant, who charged the truckers forty dollars per night to park, was not around. Hal banged on a Swift Truck and awakened the sleeping driver.

"What the hell do you want? I paid my forty dollars already."

"Police business," said Hal, flashing his badge. "That crazy serial killer just grabbed another girl. We think he pulled into this lot. Seen any activity in the last hour?"

"Ah, shit, sorry. I've been sleeping, but ask Henry. He runs the joint. He usually takes a nap in that RV over there after midnight. He might be able to help you."

"Thanks," said Hal as the wind pushed him toward the RV. Rachael and Amanda joined him as he awakened Henry.

"Hey, man. I don't know. A car might have come in, but I made a special deal for tonight, so I didn't stay awake."

"What do you mean, a special deal?"

"Well, this guy paid for the whole parking lot. Didn't you see the Full sign out in front? Gave me a grand for it. I sure as hell wasn't going to turn it down."

"What did he look like? What was he driving?" asked Amanda.

"Older fella, kind of stooped over. Maybe seventy-five. Spoke good English and had cash. He was drivin' an old eighteen-wheeler. Parked it in the south end of the lot. Usually, I don't let the guys park facing that way 'cause it takes up too much room, but what the hell. Shit, I didn't care if he parked it upside down."

"Is the truck still here?" asked Rachael. "Come on, you old fart. Take us there." She grabbed his arm.

"OK, OK, don't get your panties in a twist." Henry slammed the door. The wind had kicked up so hard that the south end of the lot was no longer visible. Bucking the wind, the four trudged the quarter mile. "Nope, looks like he's gone. Truck was parked right here. Sorry."

"Shit," said Rachael. "You must have a license plate number or something. Describe the truck. Give me details. Any commercial names on the side of it?"

"No name on the side. Normal-looking. Aluminum with a bunch of interstate stickers. Regular shit."

Amanda was on the phone to the command post with the update. "Increase the search parameters to include an eighteen-wheeler, license plate unknown, possibly driven by an old, gray-haired man."

Hal took off down Highway 95 to do some investigating on his own while Amanda and Rachael rushed back to the Bullhead Police car.

"Let's think this through. He's smart. He'll know that we can track him this far, so what would his next step be? He'll have to get rid of the truck. And why a truck?" The sisters sat quietly for a minute while the wind pushed their car around. "Damn. Here comes the rain."

Quiet returned.

"He drove the van here immediately. This was part of his plan, not improvised at the last minute. Since the van isn't here, we have to assume that he pulled it into the back, closed it up, and took off. We'll have to look at the tapes again to see if we can track the truck. Did it go north or south? I'll call Ron. He can check the footage right now to see if it drove across the bridge. What time frame are we looking at now?" asked Rachael.

"Somewhere between eleven thirty and twelve thirty should do it."

The call to Ron proved productive. Three trucks had passed over the bridge during the time in question. Ron had identified two trucks, both of which were subsequently stopped and cleared, leaving a single eighteen-wheeler driving west.

"That means he has to be heading toward Henderson, Las Vegas, or going to catch the Forty West. God, there's nothing on the Forty." Amanda reached for her phone. "I'll have the FBI do a fly-over and report back. We'll grab a chopper and head toward Las Vegas. That trip takes an hour-plus by car. He would almost be there by now. Let's get a move on." Amanda flipped open her phone and ordered two helicopters from the FBI.

"Damn monsoon," she said. "Pilots won't fly in this. Chris would. I'll check. If we can't get a bird up, that'll give the creep another hour leeway. Let's call the weather station and find out which way the storm is headed. When it'll stop blowing." Rachael could hardly hear her sister over the wind. "Meet me back at the Oasis. I'll grab my backup shit."

Rachael grabbed her sister's hand. "Mandy, he's got her. You know what he does."

"He's been too busy to hurt her. We'll get the bastard before he can. Hurry, sis."

At 6:05 a.m., the Amtrak pulled out of Union Station, right on time. The train was nearly empty on its first run south for the day, but the Fullerton station would add a number of commuters and beachgoers. Several more stops were scheduled before its final destination, including San Clemente, where the surfers would unload their surfboards.

Meg watched Elliott through her swollen eyes. He seemed happy. Humming. Soft words of future plans were uttered. He was losing it.

Still bound, with her wrists duct taped in front and tape over her mouth, Meg moaned. Her body was showing signs of bruising already, and her inner thighs were scraped raw from whisker burns and digital mayhem. She tried to mentally transport herself to some other place where she was happy and felt safe, but her mind was blocked by the pain. *How could I have been so stupid? Mom and my sisters have told me all of my life that I am too trusting, but he was such a nice old man. God, please help me. Help my sisters find me. I can't go on like this.*

Elliott had left the compartment for fifteen minutes and returned with sandwiches and hot coffee. He propped Meg up. "You need to eat something. I got two ham and cheese sandwiches, the best they had. If you promise not to yell, I'll take the tape off; otherwise, you'll just have to watch me eat."

Meg knew she needed to keep up her strength in case there was an opportunity to run, so she nodded yes. Elliott started to pull off the tape a little at a time but realized Meg's lips were so raw that they were starting to bleed. With a jerk, he yanked the remaining tape, and Meg let out a muffled cry. A small stream of blood trickled down. She licked the blood and then withdrew again into her own special place. Her eyes went vacant.

"Sorry, darling. I know that hurt you, but it's temporary. I have some Neosporin that I'll put on your lips after we eat. These are just temporary setbacks. Soon everything will be as you desire."

Meg's eyes squeezed open momentarily but then rolled back into oblivion.

"I really can't trust you enough to let you hold your food, so just for this time, I'll feed you.

When you get a little more accustomed to our living conditions, then you'll be free to handle your own food, like the rest of my ladies. They all developed into quite nice partners, but not nearly what I anticipate from you."

He pushed the sandwich into her bleeding mouth. Meg took a bite and almost gagged, but forced herself to continue. A small tear trickled down her left cheek; she immediately disposed of it with her taped hands. "I can hold the sandwich, Elliott. Please."

"How sweet. Yes, of course. The hot coffee, however…I'll have to help you with the coffee for now."

The train rolled on.

58

It was 5:00 a.m. when FBI Special Agent Frank Bartello called Amanda with the results of the AFIS fingerprint search. "Amanda, we got hold of the portable fingerprint system, and we got positive results. You'll never believe whose prints match."

"Come on, Frank, hurry up. Who is it?" Amanda asked as Rachael listened in.

"Elliott Spencer. That's your serial killer. We're pulling all kinds of shit up on this guy as we speak. Besides Santa Cruz, he might be involved in some other murders up and down the coast. What's your next step?"

"Elliott!" Amanda cried out. "Oh, my God. That son of a bitch."

Rachael was stunned. She grabbed Amanda's free hand and squeezed it to hide her pain. Why hadn't she followed up on her suspicions of Elliott?

The dirty car, the bar. She had felt he was just a major creep, not a major threat. Guilt grabbed her body like a parasite taking a hefty bite.

Amanda did her best to stay calm for the rest of the conversation with Frank. "Rachael and I think he's headed to Las Vegas. Will probably change his mode of transportation. That leaves the bus—too slow, a flight—too public, or maybe the Amtrak. Four agents are covering the first two places. Rachael and I are going to the Vegas Amtrak. We've called ahead. There was a train headed to LA. Left three hours ago. Another just came through heading east. We need to interview the staff now. We're still in the midst of the monsoon, so we can't take the chopper. We'll head for Vegas in the car. Line up a chopper to meet us there when the weather clears. See if Chris is available."

Frank said, "Got it. Good luck. We all hate it that the bastard has your kid sister. Of course, you know you should take him alive, but sometimes that's not possible."

Amanda knew what he meant but couldn't say anything in response. "OK, Rachael, this is it. Let's take my car. Throw as much artillery in the trunk as you can. Let's hit it. Meg needs us."

Driving through the monsoon was always risky, but Amanda was oblivious to the danger. The torrential rains pounded down on her Mustang.

"Stop," yelled Rachael. "Flash flood in the dip." Amanda braked hard, and the car slid sideways, stopping inches before the wall of water.

"Thanks for the heads-up. Didn't see that one coming." The water subsided, and the Mustang exploded down the highway again. Visibility dropped down to fifty feet. The wipers worked overtime, losing the battle with the hammering rain. They reached Henderson and swerved onto the freeway. The monsoon subsided by the time they reached Old Town Vegas. Only short bursts of rain and wind hit the car as they parked at the Amtrak station.

The station was nearly empty. It was 6:30 a.m., and only a handful of commuters were waiting to buy tickets. Amanda and Rachael spotted the stationmaster and, after identifying themselves, started their interrogation. He did recall helping an elderly man and his wife, who was in a wheelchair. She seemed very dazed at the time, but he didn't think much about it. They had tickets in a sleeper compartment for as far as Los Angeles, as he recalled.

"Can you get hold of the conductor or engineer? We need to know if they're still on board the train," said Amanda.

The stationmaster said that could be arranged, but it would take a few minutes. While he began the task, Amanda checked in with Frank and asked about the helicopter coverage for them.

"Frank, looks like they're on the Amtrak train that left for Los Angeles. Should have arrived in LA at five thirty. If they're headed for Sacramento, they won't change trains. That's a long time for Elliott to be captive. He knows we're looking for him. I think they'll change trains and head south…maybe San Diego. Might be headed for Mexico."

"I'll alert the San Diego office."

"I'm trying to get hold of the conductor so he can tell me if they're still on the same train. The monsoon has passed. I need that helicopter. How soon will it be here?"

"We'll have it there by seven o'clock. Can't do any better than that, but I did get you Chris."

"Thanks. Gotta go, the conductor is on the other line," said Amanda. She briefed the conductor on the situation, and he said he would check the compartment.

The conductor called back within fifteen minutes and said that the compartment was empty but a total mess. "There was a bunch of blonde curly hair stuffed in the trash, a lot of plastic that had brown dye of sorts on it, and the sheets were a bloody mess. A wheelchair was found in the luggage area that no one seemed to claim."

Amanda sucked up her emotional response. "Don't touch the room. Wait for the FBI to search it. What about the man and woman? Did they exit the train? Did anyone see them?"

"I don't know anything else. They didn't get off as a handicapped couple, or the porters would have seen them. So they either got off regular or they stayed on the train and headed for Sacramento," the conductor concluded.

"Thanks." Amanda dismissed Sacramento. Too many hours, and the commuters would have to do part of the trip by bus. Elliott needed to move faster than that. "Where's your next stop heading south? How long before you get there?"

"We're just pulling out of the Fullerton station now. Next stop will be San Clemente and then on to San Diego."

"Bring your train coordinators up to date on all of this, please. Report back after your conductor's made the first sweep. Keep everyone on the train until the FBI arrives." Amanda closed her cell phone and looked at Rachael. "We may have caught a break. The chopper is three miles out of town on some desert road. Let's go."

"What about Meg? What did he say about the compartment?"

"The bastard's hurt her. Cut off her hair. There's blood…" Amanda's voice broke. She couldn't finish. "Come on, we've got to meet the chopper."

Rachael hurried, hiding her tears from her sister.

59

Elliott shoved Meg into the shower. "Wash your hair. Hurry up."

Looking around the small bath area, she realized she had no means of escaping yet. She dried with the rough towel. Pain encircled her body.

Clothes were laid out on the small bed. After she put on her underwear, Elliott strapped a huge pillow-like bag around her stomach. "Oh, I forgot to tell you. Now we're a married couple, and, gosh, you're already pregnant." He shoved a fake gold ring on her finger. Elliott read her repulsion by the scornful expression that passed across her face. "Not your dream of the perfect honeymoon?" He grabbed her left breast and twisted it.

There was a Lakers jersey and a pair of purple shorts on the bed, along with a Lakers cap. Elliott pulled a pair of tennis shoes and socks from the small valise and threw them at her. Now she was a married, pregnant, Lakers fan. Elliott dressed for the beach in walking shorts, a Hawaiian shirt, sandals, a baseball cap, and sunglasses. When he put sunglasses on Meg, Elliott knew no one would take her for anything but mousey.

For the last hour, they sat in the commuter section with all of the surfers and businessmen. The conductor came by to check everyone's tickets. Elliott knew that was the regular routine, but when he came back a second time with another Amtrak employee, he became increasingly concerned. He watched as they hovered and talked quietly at the exit. While it seemed uncanny to him that the FBI was smart enough to catch up so quickly, it certainly was within the realm of possibility. A change of plans had to be made. Elliott made two calls on his cell phone. He didn't have his phone modulator attached but had no choice. The calls had to be made. The first contact was to his new seaplane pilot, Gilbert, who lived in the small town of Escondido, north of San Diego.

"Fly the plane to San Clemente now. Land south of the pier. Keep the engine running. A small boat will meet you. Be ready to take off when I am on board. I will have one passenger. You got that?"

"*Si*, El Jefe. It will take me fifteen minutes. Maybe sooner."

"Make it sooner."

The second call was to a partner who lived in San Clemente. He was given instructions to drive his boat to the end of the pier and tie it to the landing. The man understood the gravity of the situation and said it could be accomplished within the specified time frame.

As the train pulled into the San Clemente Station, Elliott stared out the window, trying to locate his seaplane. Landing in the ocean should be no problem, especially today, with no noticeable swells to fight. He couldn't see the boat but knew it would be there. Running to the end of the pier could only be accomplished if Meg cooperated. He gauged the distance to be a solid quarter mile from the train to the stairs descending to the water.

"Just remember who will be hurt if you don't cooperate. You know me. I will smile as I torture and kill all of your loved ones, especially your mother." Meg nodded in reply. Survival meant still cooperating at this point.

The train came to a full stop, and the beachgoers began to depart. Elliott spied an FBI helicopter approaching. He knew a landing south of the pier was impossible. Beachgoers were already swarming like bees on the sand. His plan was still viable. As Elliott and Meg waited their turn to depart the train, the conductor made an announcement. "Sorry, folks, there's a problem at the station. We have to close the doors now. Please step back on the train. Sorry about the delay. Shouldn't take too long."

Elliott yanked Meg forward and pushed her through the crowd. With his shoulder, he pried open the doors and muscled through the opening. He forced Meg to jump over the second set of rails and head for the pier.

She stumbled and cried out, "Help me!"

Elliott scooped her up and said, "Of course, darling. Let me help you."

Other passengers smiled at the attentive husband helping the pregnant, plain woman.

The conductor relayed to the FBI that approximately thirty passengers had departed the train. "I tried my best, but some folks got out. Most of the debarked people are heading to the north side of the pier, it looks like. Some are still milling around the platform."

"Any sign of the couple we described?"

"Sorry."

60

Amanda and Rachael heard the communiqué from the conductor and told Chris to set the helicopter down on the north side of the pier. They watched the crowd emerge from the train but didn't recognize Meg or Elliott. When the chopper touched down, the women hit the sand running. Two FBI agents boarded the train to secure the crime scene and question the conductor.

Rachael elected to stay outside to look for Meg in the crowd. She questioned the passengers, and the only practical lead seemed to be a married couple. One witness said the girl was a lot younger than the man and was pregnant. "She didn't look too happy, and the guy was dragging her around like a rag doll," said the woman. When she pointed them out near the end of the pier, Rachael called Amanda.

"I see them."

"Same here. Near the end of the pier. Hurry. They're heading for some steps." As she said that, Amanda spotted a seaplane landing adjacent to the pier.

Four local fishermen had stopped to watch all of the activity. A helicopter, seaplane, and boat were all acting wild. Their attention turned up the wooden pier to a man pulling a pregnant woman along behind him. They were coming toward the fishermen. Now they heard him cussing and witnessed him strike the woman across the face.

"Hey, asshole. Wait up. That ain't no way to treat your wife. Calm down. Let her go before you hurt your kid."

Elliott brandished a gun, and the men backed up.

"Ain't none of our concern, fella."

"We've got a problem," yelled Amanda as they sprinted down the pier. "Stop. There's a seaplane landing. Damn. That's where Elliott's headed. Get back to the chopper ASAP. I'll call Chris to get ready. God, hurry. We can't let him get away." Both women turned and ran for the helicopter.

The boat roared up to the pier platform and idled next to the landing. A rope was looped over the pilings.

"In you go, darling," said Elliott as he pushed Meg on board. "Go," he yelled. "Those FBI imbeciles are right after us. Go."

Meg's hands were free, and as Elliott untied the mooring rope, she tried to throw herself overboard. Elliott grabbed her at the last minute and slapped her across the face again. A new wound opened over her right eye. He knew most of her strength and will had been depleted.

Meg became aware of Elliott's hysteria. She felt he was really losing it. *Were her sisters close enough to help? Could they get her before it was too late?*

Elliott and Meg were thrown backward into the small boat as it zipped away from the dock, heading for the seaplane. "Guess we can get rid of your big belly now," Elliott said as he pulled off the pregnant appendage and tossed it overboard. "You don't need the extra weight when we transfer to the plane. I want you to enjoy the trip to Mexico. I have a wonderful hacienda waiting for us with a magnificent staff. Anything you want, you can have," he babbled.

"Where are we going?" Meg whispered.

"Paradise. I know you'll like it." Elliott glanced back and saw the FBI helicopter taking off from the beach. Their boat had reached the seaplane, and as the side door opened, Elliott pushed Meg into the plane and quickly followed her. The boat driver turned the small craft, putting as much distance as possible between him and the seaplane.

Elliott yelled, "Take off Now...Take off."

The pilot rammed the throttle forward. The plane trudged through the water with the wind behind them. When the air speed reached sixty-five, the small aircraft lifted off, quickly extending their altitude to two hundred feet. To Elliott's surprise, there was now a Coast Guard helicopter approaching. They were flying toward the seaplane rather than chasing it.

Gilbert, the new pilot, turned to Elliott, alarm registering in his voice. "We have company. Do you still want to head to Mexico?"

"Shit. Looks like they have some help from the San Diego Coast Guard." Quickly formulating yet another plan, he shouted to the pilot, "Maintain an altitude of two hundred feet, but be ready to throttle back to sixty when I tell you. Turn and head back toward the pier. We're going to drop off the bitch."

"But we'll stall."

"Do it."

While Gilbert argued that his request was dangerous, he still obeyed. It was his first day flying for El Jefe. The man's reputation was so dark that no one in his right mind would challenge his orders. Elliott threw open the door of the seaplane, and the rush of air knocked him backward. He knew

Meg could survive the two-hundred-foot vertical fall, but the speed might kill her. He didn't want her dead.

"Bring your air speed back to sixty. When I yell 'OK,' drop the flaps for twenty seconds. Then take off like the devil was after you." Again, Gilbert voiced his displeasure but acquiesced.

"Looks like we're going to have to say goodbye for a while, Meg, my darling. When Rachael sees you floating through the sky like a wounded bird, I'm sure she'll stop for you. My trip to Mexico can go on. If you survive the fall, sweet girl, I shall find you. We'll rendezvous next August first. Our anniversary. If you're pregnant, be sure to name the baby after me."

He laughed, grabbed Meg, and untied her feet. She tried to grab a life preserver, but Elliott stopped her. Elliott struggled with her for another minute, surprised at her renewed strength. Wrestling her to the open door, he hurled her from the slow-moving seaplane into the cold Pacific. He yelled, "Mine, you're mine."

"Go to hell, you bastard," Meg screamed as she plummeted toward the ocean.

Meg heard the other helicopter as she fell. She knew that either Amanda or Rachael would be on board. Her only job was to survive the fall. *Point my toes. One hand over face. One hand between my legs.* She knew to take in a deep breath. She knew to enter the water feet first. She knew after entry to open up and swim like hell to the surface. She knew to let some air bubbles escape and to follow them up in case she was disoriented. She knew all of this until she hit the water at forty miles an hour and was knocked unconscious.

Everyone aboard the FBI helicopter saw Meg falling through the sky. They watched in horror as she tried to brace herself for impact.

Rachael let out a scream as she witnessed Meg enter the water in a splayed position. She did not resurface.

Chris mentally marked the area where she hit the water and headed there, hovering and searching. The circular churning of the water caused by the copter was like a wet whirlwind and inhibited the hunt for Meg. Amanda quickly took off her guns, Kevlar vest, and shoes. She was prepared to jump the minute they located her. Nothing. Life vests were readied. Seconds seemed like hours as they all peered into the ocean for any sign of life.

"There. Underwater. There!" yelled Chris.

The helicopter hovered at twenty feet. Amanda searched for the submerged outline of her sister's body. "I don't see her," yelled Amanda. "Are you sure this is the spot?" She was becoming frantic, knowing that a person could only survive a few minutes underwater.

Suddenly, Chris yelled again "Look, just below the surface. It's Meg. God, no, it's just a shadow."

Amanda yelled, "No, it's her."

He positioned the chopper over Meg's body. Amanda grabbed goggles and jumped feet-first into the ocean. She was immediately joined by the Coast Guard search and rescue team wearing their scuba equipment. Amanda's third dive was successful. She saw Meg's body floating upward in a grotesque dance-like position.

Hang on, Meg. We're here for you. Hang on, she mentally mumbled as she reached her sister and, with mighty leg thrusts, pulled her to the open air.

"Take a breath, Meg. Damn it, take a breath." Amanda grabbed two life vests that were floating nearby and pulled Meg's arm through one. The Coast Guard divers were there immediately and assisted Amanda through the process of hooking Meg to the FBI helicopter winch. Amanda tried to start mouth-to-mouth, but there was no room or time.

The wind picked up. The helicopter was having difficulty hovering. When she was ready, they hoisted Meg's unconscious body to the helicopter, laid her down, and started CPR. Now it was Amanda's turn to be lifted back to the chopper. The wind was blowing at thirty knots, and the chopper was being tossed around, unable to maintain a stable position. After the second attempt, Amanda grabbed the cable and, hooking it to her harness, was drawn up inside the FBI transport. Chris radioed the Coast Guard chopper that they would fly immediately to the San Clemente hospital. The Coast Guard helicopter hauled up their divers and took off after Elliott.

61

Calling their mother was not a task that either sister relished, but one that had to be done. Amanda volunteered.

"Mom, hi. How's it going?" Amanda said, trying to sound lighthearted.

"What's wrong?" demanded her mother.

"Why do you think anything's wrong? Can't I just call to say hello?"

"Sure," Grace said, "but that's not why you're calling. Get on with it."

Amanda told Grace the whole story about the kidnap, the chase, and the ocean catastrophe. When asked about Meg's condition, Amanda could only say that she survived. The doctors were still with her and contemplating surgery.

"What's the name of the hospital?" Grace asked as she packed an overnight bag and grabbed her prescription medication. Cell phone in hand, she set the house alarm and slammed the kitchen door after her. "You should have told me sooner. I am so mad at you and Rachael right now. Your most important job in life is taking care of that innocent child. I'll deal with you later. I'm on my way."

"Mom, you don't need to come now. We'll call you back in an hour."

"Meg needs her mother." Grace closed her cell phone and started the car, heading toward the 91 Freeway East. She didn't want to talk to Amanda anymore.

Amanda slowly closed her cell phone. While anticipating Grace's rage, Amanda knew that she was the only person who could get Meg through this crisis—if indeed Meg survived.

It took an hour to drive the freeway system and arrive in San Clemente. Grace noticed police activity at the beach but headed directly toward the San Clemente Community Hospital. Bypassing the admissions desk, she turned toward ICU. Both Rachael and Amanda were at the nurses' station. They felt their mother's presence as the elevator opened.

"OK, take me to Meg and fill me in on the way," said Grace, ignoring her daughters' attempts to hug her.

"Mom," said Amanda, "you can't see her yet. She's in surgery."

"Why? What surgery?"

"Has a broken arm and left ankle. Maybe a concussion. She hasn't woken up yet. They did a CAT scan, but we haven't heard the results yet. It'll take time, but she should recover as good as new."

"Stop it," threatened Grace. "You know better. She'll never return to new. She's been traumatized by that bastard, and you, of all people, should know what follows." They sat, mute with fear.

The doctor approached them and said it was OK to go to Meg's room. The surgeon had successfully set the bones. An IV was hooked up to her right hand. While all systems seemed to be working, she still had not regained consciousness. The three women thanked the doctor and headed toward Meg's room.

"Oh, God," cried Grace as she saw her youngest child. Her hand flew to her mouth to avoid more outbursts. "She's been tortured." She moved closer. "The bastard brutalized her. I thought Meg would be my one child to get through life without this kind of pain." She turned and left the room to mourn alone.

Meg opened her eyes later in the day. She tried to smile. Happy to be alive. "You all look like shit," she mumbled, and the room erupted in laughter. While the scars were ever so close to the surface, at least her personality hadn't been as deeply wounded, or so it seemed. Fragile hugs, kisses, and tears followed, and the family shared an innate sense of relief. Meg had now joined the sisterhood; she was officially a survivor.

Meg asked for a mirror, but no one supplied it. Her fingers traced across her face, and she flinched when touching her eye and torn lips. "Not too pretty, huh?" The mirror would attest to the trauma, and it was too soon to face that ordeal. Pushing back a tear, she said, "Elliott. Did you catch him? Please, God, say you did."

"Meg. When we stopped to pull you out of the water, he headed south in his seaplane. Word has it that he landed on a private strip close to Rosarito Beach. We're on it," said Amanda.

Meg ran her tongue across her swollen lip. She teared up. "I'd like to be alone right now."

"Not a good idea, honey," said Grace. "I just drove here to be with you...to support you. Please let me stay."

"Mom, just get out. All of you get out. I want to be alone. Leave."

When they left the room, Amanda said she had to report back to work. The FBI and Coast Guard were still tracking Elliott, and now she needed to do what she was trained to do: get the killer.

Grace found an empty room and, once alone, flipped open her cell phone. The international number connected immediately.

"Hello."

"Luke."

"Yes, Grace. What's wrong?"

Grace quickly told him of Meg's kidnap and torture. He listened intently.

"I'm available. Finishing up an assignment in Mexico. How fortuitous. I'll handle it from here. Are you OK?"

"Yes. And thank you. Someday…well, someday."

"I know." The phone went dead.

Searching the train turned up the obvious evidence, but it still had to be collected and processed for the trial. But for now, Elliott was long gone. The FBI and Coast Guard had observed him fly across the border and land. They were forced to abandon their mission once he was in Mexico. After his apprehension, they would deal with extradition. His day would come.

Amanda walked down the pier as the sun was setting. She stared south across the blue Pacific and thought about Elliott. Given the planning and effort he had demonstrated to get Meg, she knew it was not over. *Next time we'll be ready, Elliott.*

62

Amanda boarded the FBI helicopter and headed back to Laughlin. She met with the Laughlin Police and FBI the next day. Beckett had been held at the command center. The assistant manager at the Oasis was told that Beckett had suffered a mild heart attack and would not be in for a while. Total silence shrouded his arrest. He looked tired and worried as she observed him through the one-way mirror. The captain briefed her.

"He hasn't given up much. Maybe he'll talk to you."

"Probably pretty pissed at me, but I'll give it a shot."

He lifted his hooded eyes when she entered and then dropped his gaze back to the table.

"Beckett, how you doing?" She put a cup of coffee in front of him.

He shrugged in response. They sat quietly. He finally leaned back and returned her stare. "You're very good at your job, Amanda."

"Thank you."

"I haven't asked for an attorney yet. I figured you'd be back and we could talk. You owe me."

"That's a yes and no. We will talk, and no, I don't owe you." She sensed he wanted to tell her something.

"Did the crazy serial killer connect again?"

Amanda stifled a bitter reaction. "You haven't heard?"

"No one to spread the gossip around here. So?"

"He kidnapped Meg Pennington." *Apparently, he hasn't made the connection yet.*

"What? Oh, my God, Amanda, I'm so sorry. She was a great kid." His concern seemed sincere. "So, they didn't catch the killer?"

How to play this? "He's been identified but not apprehended. But, of course, you already know who he is."

"Why would you think that? I've been locked up. Elliott is probably blabbing about it on TV, but they wouldn't let me watch. So what gives? Who is he?"

Amanda focused on Beckett's tired face, concentrating on his immediate reaction to the answer. "Well, you'll hear about it as soon as you're transferred so, why not tell you. It's Elliott."

Beckett was out of his chair in a flash, slamming his hands on the table and leaning toward her with anger spewing from his mouth. "That son of a bitch. Is Meg OK? God, what an animal. Did he hurt her? He's the one who killed Angie. Oh, shit." He sat back down, dropping forward and covering his head with his hands. "I didn't know. Oh, my God, I didn't know."

"So what part have you played in this scenario? He was your partner, wasn't he?"

Beckett lifted his head and stared at her. "I think it's time for me to ask for an attorney."

"Before you do that, Beckett, think about it. If your involvement is minimal and you were unaware of the extent of Elliott's business dealings, we might be able to cut you a deal. No promises, but I'm sure the FBI would be interested in talking to you."

"Hold up. Let me get this straight. So, Elliott is El Jefe. That son of a bitch."

"Had us all fooled." *This is news. El Jefe. This ties up a lot of loose ends.*

"How is Meg? Is she going to be all right? How long did he have her?"

"Can't disclose much on that, Beckett. But it looks like she'll be OK." They sat. "Beckett, let's hear it. I can't make any promises to you, but if you can help us get Elliott, it might go easier."

"OK. I want to cooperate. Never really liked that bastard. Bring your boss in, and I'll tell him what I have."

"Let's hear what you have first. Shoot."

"Elliott called me. Said someone named El Jefe was looking for a casino suite for some high-level Mexicans. Just overnight. They didn't want to check in. Wanted to be picked up from a seaplane. Wanted women. I'd have to arrange for transportation to Vegas. Then, the scene would get reversed, and they'd leave town."

"When did you start?"

"A year ago or so. Got Carlos to be the driver."

"What were you paid?"

"Ten grand a head. El Jefe would pay Carlos and the pilot, so the five was all mine. Pure profit. "

"Did you ever talk to El Jefe? How did you know when the seaplane was arriving?"

"He'd call Carlos. I never talked to the son of a bitch. He was the one who killed Carlos, wasn't he? And Angie?"

"That hasn't been determined." Amanda knew he was pumping her. "Look, Beckett, we already know what you're telling me. If you want to deal, we have to have more."

"It must be obvious to you and your friends that I'm peanuts. I just rented a damn room. You caught the Mexicans. Let me stay on the job, and I'll be your snitch. I know everything that goes on in town."

"I'll pass it on. But you know Elliott won't trust you. He won't come back to Laughlin. Maybe Vegas."

"No one saw me getting arrested, so tell them you brought me in for questioning and let me go."

"What about Leonard? He witnessed your arrest."

"He took off. Was playing both sides of the game. You'll never catch up with him. I'll do house arrest and keep working. I'll be your snitch. That way, I can save my job and help. If the casino owners know what I've done, they'll waste me. Give me a year to straighten this up."

The interview went on for another hour. Beckett told Amanda what little he knew about the smuggled body parts. When asked if Elliott had a partner, Beckett hesitated.

"If Elliott is responsible for Angie's death, then he had to get Meg's key. Derek was the only unknown factor. Was it him?"

63

During her recovery period, Meg would fall into a funk, lying in bed, staring out the window. She turned away from all company and wouldn't take phone calls. Even the brat pack was rejected. The old Meg wasn't responding.

"First thing when we get to Catalina," Grace said, "we'll call to see if Tim happens to be at Apple Haircutters and have him bring back your original hair color."

Meg resented her mother's interference. "I don't remember agreeing to go to Catalina. Let's just go home."

"Out of the question," said Grace. "I've booked our old rooms. You weren't meant to be a brunette. And we'll have him style it, too. Short is in this year, thank goodness."

"How can you talk about haircuts? For God's sake, Mom. Tim doesn't go to that salon very often. It doesn't really matter, anyway. It'll grow out." She turned her back on her mother and pulled up the covers.

"Hey, don't be pulling that crap on me. We're going on vacation for a month or so. Enjoyment comes to mind. And you'll have to look good when you go back to work. Gotta support that swinging lifestyle of yours." Grace kept pushing. It was her job.

"We'll see," was the reply. Meg couldn't care less. It seemed nothing was important to her right now. Sleeping was her salvation, and while she really wanted to be left alone, she knew her mom wouldn't let that happen.

Near the end of the second week, Grace went to Yorba Linda for the day, packed some clothes and personal items for Meg and herself, and returned on the Amtrak to San Clemente.

***

Instead of going directly to Bullhead, Rachael requested a two-week vacation, which was granted. She was in daily contact with Amanda, talking through ideas to capture Elliott. Rachael was satisfied with the doctor's prognosis of Meg's improving physical health. Her mental condition was another matter. The doctors revealed that Meg had been heavily drugged and the result of that alone could cause depression, recurring flashbacks, and sometimes respiratory problems.

After obtaining permission from the FBI, Rachael boarded their chopper heading back to Los Angeles. Once in the air, a series of arguments ensued. Rachael wanted to be dropped off at Santa Catalina Island, but the flight plan didn't include a stop at Avalon. Since Amanda was in good standing with the FBI, they agreed to land at Catalina and leave Rachael there. Flying over the twenty-six miles to the island, she had time to reminisce about happy island days. In addition to their regular trips to the Colorado River, the family had spent three weeks each summer vacationing on Catalina. Rachael knew that spending a month on this magical island with her mother would do Meg a world of good.

Since it was a privately owned airport, the FBI followed protocol and called ahead to state their intention to land. They were advised that it cost twenty-five dollars, and Rachael agreed to pay the bill. Her mother's golf cart was waiting for her at the airport.

Catalina, a truly unique piece of paradise, only allowed a limited number of cars on the island. A waiting list was established and held by the mayor, but historically, no one ever got a new car unless someone died and willed their car permit to a close friend or relative. Gas and electric golf carts were the usual means of transportation, and they numbered somewhere between two to three hundred. Everyone shopped, dined, and socialized with their carts.

As Rachael climbed into the driver's seat, the memories flooded over her. How long had it been since she and her sisters would fight over who would get to drive? Amanda, being the oldest, usually won the battle, but sometimes they would let Meg drive. Days were so simple then. The puppy-love affairs would come and go, but they always ended on a positive note. Except one time.

The summer cottage had been cleaned as requested, and at three o'clock, the security company arrived. Every door and window was wired, along with the installation of motion detectors. Surveillance cameras were mounted and direct wired to a DVR placed in the attic of the house. Rachael purchased three handguns. The nine millimeter was placed between the pot holders in the kitchen, the Glock .40 was in the master bedroom behind the Harlan Coben collection, and the snub nose .38 was in the bathroom, midway between the stack of blue towels. Each was loaded. An extra clip or stash of bullets lay alongside. Leaving the gun in the bathroom was a small attempt at humor. She knew both her mom and Meg spent a lot of time in front of the mirror and would enjoy the size of the Saturday night special.

Convincing Grace and Meg to go target shooting with a firm commitment to kill would have been an impossible task a month ago, but now…A sudden sadness filled Rachael. While she and Amanda had seen their share of blood and despair, that sort of trauma should never have touched Meg. Rachael was burdened with guilt.

Rachael walked through the house, checking the security installation and its cache of weapons. All passed the test—mission accomplished. Next came the PR part of the plan. Rachael's first step was to visit the local police department, where she met with the captain and her old friend from summer vacations, Josh Meyers.

"Well, look at you," Josh began. "All grown up and carrying a gun. Far cry from the old days of cops and robbers on the golf course."

Rachael laughed. "As I recall, I kicked your butt then, and, well, some things never change." She gave him a second look.

"Some things never do," Josh said.

Instant eye contact, and then it was gone.

Rachael shared the details regarding the serial killer in Bullhead/Laughlin and continued on through the kidnapping of Meg and the subsequent escape of Elliott. "Meg and Mom will be arriving within the week, and I'd really appreciate it if you would spread the word. Don't treat her any way other than you used to. Pity or sympathy will just mess her up more. Our little bird really had her wings clipped."

"Jeez, Rachael," said Josh. He was visibly shaken by Rachael's narrative. "Tell me she's going to be OK, for God's sake. She's just a kid."

Rachael was touched by Josh's concern but didn't show any emotion. "Mom is working with her; we're all trying to help. Shit. The rainbow that used to come up every morning for her, well, it's disappeared. We can only try to be there for her and hope for the best."

"Meg is part of the island's family. She'll be safe if she doesn't wander off our radar screen. She used to be pretty sneaky about getting her way. She always listened to a different drummer."

"How well you remember." Smiling at his accurate read of her younger sister, Rachael continued, "I had a complete security system installed today, including a surveillance camera. Put in new deadbolts, along with rekeying the whole house. I hid three loaded guns in the house for their protection. It's going to be a real trick to get them ready and able to use them."

"Do they know how to shoot?" asked the captain.

"Sadly, no. If possible, could they use the police firing range? Josh, you know Mom and Meg trust you. Maybe you could help so they don't shoot themselves in the foot. And maybe stop by for dinner now and then? Even take Meg out sometimes? Get her used to social situations again?"

"No problem there. She was always like my kid sister. My pleasure."

Rachael flashed a heartfelt smile his way. Josh responded by grabbing her hand. Rachael pulled it back. "What are you doing?"

"A bit jumpy, I'd say. Come on. You're going for a ride with me." He yanked her off the chair. "The captain and I will brief the guys, all fifteen of them. May sound like a small group to you city folk, but these officers are handpicked to handle all situations. A better bunch you couldn't find."

"Great," Rachael said, still a little unnerved by the touch.

"I'll take Meg to the range on Middle Ranch myself. The locals'll know you're back by morning. You know how that goes. They'll pitch in and watch out for Meg. But now, we'll start our own networking. Come on. Let's go."

Rachael smiled at the thought of a diversion and didn't hesitate this time. Josh opened the squad car for her. She was impressed. "Wow, just how important have you become? A car of your very own on the island? Pure bliss."

"Not quite so monumental. Six black-and-whites only, but we have a bunch of golf carts and

T-threes. That's all, and we have to share. I thought you'd like to be treated like royalty for one day. Wave to everyone when we pass by. Seeing you sit next to me—ha, tongues'll be wagging all day. Poor telephone operator will have a cow."

He drove through the alleys and circled around to Wrigley Road, parking the car at the ridge. "Well, has anything changed from four years ago?"

To her surprise, Rachael found herself fighting back sad feelings. *What the hell is going on with my emotions?* she thought. Her grief had never had a chance to escape. Her eyes scanned the horizon and then looked down to the yachts moored in Avalon Harbor, the Holly Hill House, the old Casino Ballroom, and the pier. All was as it was supposed to be. It seemed so unaffected by the real world.

She simply replied, "No, nothing's changed." A silent moment passed, and she leaned on Josh's shoulder in gratitude. "Nice to be home."

They finished the tour and ended up at the station again, where Rachael picked up her golf cart. Arrangements were made to go out to dinner, and Rachael felt happy and safe. Quite a new experience.

The reverie carried over until she arrived home and punched in the code to the security system. She called the hospital for an update on Meg's condition. Her left kidney had been severely bruised, but the doctors felt there would be no permanent damage. Healing the body was the easy part, the doctor said. He made no comment on her mental condition. Rachael called Grace, and they both agreed on the day that Meg would begin her island rehab.

The night was balmy. Rachael and Josh enjoyed eating at Steve's Steak House, which afforded a spectacular sunset mandated by the Chamber of Commerce. Small, twinkling lights framed the windows, adding a magical tough to the ambience. When they talked about Meg's case, conversation came easy, but when that topic was extinguished, they both seemed a little shy about their interim history.

"Last I heard about you," started Josh, "was three years ago. I heard you were going to get married."

"Sad and long story, I'm afraid," said Rachael. "Would you settle for an overview, or do you want the gory details?"

"Overview is fine. I'm not into gore tonight."

"We were partners in narcotics. He got shot during a sting operation. He didn't make it." She turned away from Josh for a minute. She didn't feel it was necessary to tell him about the miscarriage she had that night. "And you? What's going on with your love life?"

"Rachael, I'm so sorry. It takes a long time to get over a shooting, let alone, when it's someone you love."

"Thanks." She didn't want to dwell on the subject, so she returned to her former question. "The love life? How's that going with you?"

"Oh, plenty of dating, but after a while on this small island, you've made the rounds. I did come close last year, but she ended up being a psychotic nurse. Glad I realized that before it was too late. Otherwise, sometimes in summer I find a partner, but I really haven't been in love with anyone since you left. So there. How's that for honesty?"

Rachael was overwhelmed. "Josh, you jest." *Or do you?* "How was I supposed to know? You only kept in touch with me for a year during college. I thought you had found someone else. I thought I was just your summer girlfriend."

"For five years, I told you that I loved you and that you would always be my first and last love. Guess your hearing wasn't too good."

"But Josh, we were sixteen years old. Kids... just experimenting. Of course I thought I was in love with you, but we were kids."

"Everybody says that girls mature quicker than boys, but I guess we blew that theory. I knew that you were the one. So how about it? Do you want to get married and settle down on this island paradise with me?"

Rachael slugged him and laughed. "You idiot. You can't just bowl me over with one dinner and a quickie proposal. Where's your white horse?" She was loving the moment.

"Got him stabled down by the golf course, as a matter of fact." He waved to the waiter, paid the bill, and pulled an incredulous Rachael to her feet. "Come on, I'll show you."

"I heard they closed down the stables. No?"

"True. Still haven't developed the area yet. But, well, that's a long story."

The squad car left the small town behind and rumbled around the curves of County Club Drive to Cabrillo Road. Josh stopped the car in front of an old but well-maintained home and jumped out of the car. "Come on, brat. You want to see the white horse? I've got a matching pair."

Rachael was confused by now but enjoyed every moment of it. "Don't make so much noise. You'll wake up the owners. How long have you been boarding your horses here?" She was trying to tiptoe around while Josh trampled ahead, smashing leaves and debris as he went. He grabbed her hand and yanked her around the corner of the frame building. Out in back were a two-stall barn, tack room, and lighted riding arena.

"Wow, this is great," said Rachael. "Let's see the horses."

Standing in separate pipe corrals were two chestnut quarter horses, a mare and a gelding.

At the sight of Josh, they both began to neigh. "It's a his-and-her combo," he said. "You can name yours whatever, but mine is Rex."

"What do you mean, 'mine?'" asked Rachael.

"Figured you'd come back someday to get me, so I bought one for you. My sister rides her to keep her in shape. Good trail horse. I'll get the tack, and you can go change out of those shorts. There's clothes in the house that ought to fit you."

"You crazy fool. What are you talking about?"

Silence. Rachael turned and looked at the neat ranch house and realized that it belonged to Josh. "Well, how about that. You jumped up and bought a house on your favorite street on the island. Congratulations. But what's with the clothes?"

"They belong to Kelley. You remember my sister, don't you? She rides after work some days, and I keep a room for her. Go on in the back door. No one locks their doors in this neighborhood."

Rachael walked up the steps and opened the door. She smiled at what Josh had accomplished in the years they had been apart. There was a definite masculine feel to the room. She noticed antiques that he had collected, along with some vintage quilts. Kelley's bedroom was feminine, with a full entourage of stuffed animals. Rachael rummaged around in the closet and found some faded jeans and a Grateful Dead T-shirt. She changed and came clomping out of the house, ready to ride. The high heels were a joke.

"Do you like the look?" she asked as she strutted down the steps. "Shoes don't fit, so I guess I'll go barefoot."

Josh was cinching up the second saddle. "Can you still ride, or did you turn into a wuss in the city?"

"I can still ride better than you any day of the week. And…by the way, did I tell you that I'm ready to test for my green belt in Krav Maga? What level are you now?" Rachael asked with a smirk. "I can still whip your scrawny butt. Now who's the wuss?"

They took off at a slow walk, the horses knowing each step of the trail. Rachael recalled the days when they had saved their pennies to rent a horse for an hour.

"I'm surprised those old nags survived us," Josh remarked, "especially when we were racing. Remember when you urged that mare to jump the ravine? She stopped dead in her tracks and skidded to the edge. And you, graceful as usual, went flying over her head. Really smooth, Rachael."

"We did have some good times. Ah, the innocence of youth."

"More important than that, the experimenting. I remember the first time I tried to cop a feel. You decked me on the spot."

"Hey, I was only twelve with no boobs and didn't know how much fun it could be. My mama raised me right." Rachael laughed.

Both riders fell into a warm silence. When they reached the shoreline, the horses were facing the pier, a little more than a mile away. Reining up, they established the rules for a race. "Winner gets to cop a feel," said Josh.

"Winner decides if she'll allow it," said Rachael. Lifting the reins, she yelled, *"Yee-haw!"* and took the lead.

Heads down, they raced toward the finish line. Rachael pulled ahead and, tossing her hair in the ocean breeze, yelled, "Look at me, I'm Kevin Costner." She dropped the reins, spread her arms wide, and laughed to the heavens.

Josh pulled his horse to a stop and became a silent witness to the miracle that was unfolding in front of him. *Enjoy your moment, Rachael. God knows you deserve it.*

Realizing that Josh wasn't by her side, Rachael reined in her horse and turned back. She saw him watching her from a distance. She knew he was smiling. All the pent-up emotions came tumbling out. *God, he gets me.* When she reached him, stirrup to stirrup, she merely said, "Thank you."

The two headed back to Josh's house and eventually got off their horses and walked the rest of the way home. "Now about that bet," started

Josh. "Since I was gentleman enough to let you win, I think we should reexamine the terms. I think you owe me."

"Bullshit," said Rachael. "I had you beat by a mile, but if you think you won, then collect your prize now." She squared off in front of him and pushed up her 34-C's, a movement not missed by the flabbergasted Josh. "It's now or never, and I'm not removing a stitch of clothing, nor my shoulder holster that's hidden under your sister's blouse."

Josh roared with laughter. "A little more sassy and forward since the last time I tried."

"And bigger?"

"Looks like it, but I'll wait," said Josh. "It won't be long before you're pleading with me to molest you."

They both laughed and continued on in silence, each extremely happy within the confines of their own memories.

The moon was waning when they finally cleared the horse trail and arrived back at Josh's house. "Sorry, but it's curtains for me," said Rachael. "I've got a lot to do tomorrow. Work called, and they want me back in three days."

"I have a better idea. Stay the night. Your golf cart'll be fine at the station, and I'll take you there really early so you can go home and change. With only three days, I can't help but be selfish with your time. If I promise not to attack you unless you ask, how about it? We need more catch-up time."

"I'll stay, but don't worry about..." The sentence went unfinished because she was in his arms. *Oh, God, thank you.*

64

"Hey, you guys. How are you?" Amanda asked. She had returned to the hospital to check on Meg before her discharge.

Grace looked up, shrugged, and gave a "who knows" look.

"How the hell do you think I am?" Meg hissed.

"Well, toots, it looks like you're back to your old self. Ready to depart these morbid walls?"

"More than ready, but as usual, Mother has the rest of my life planned out. Not only can I not get back to Bullhead and to my job, but now I have to go to Catalina for two weeks. She wants to get my hair done. Like they don't cut hair in Bullhead. Jeez, I've really had it with this family. I'll be OK as soon as you lazy FBI people nail the bastard. I'll be more than good."

Amanda knew it was the pain and fear talking, so she dismissed the ranting. "We have tapes, prints, and witnesses from Las Vegas. The Coast Guard and FBI chased Elliott to Mexico, and we're working on extradition with the Federalese. They know Elliott's a serial killer and don't want him on their side of the fence, either. We'll find him, and we'll drag his wicked ass home. Or maybe he'll just disappear forever with a bullet between his eyes. Who knows? We may get lucky that way."

"Don't feed me any of your psychobabble. He's smarter than all of us. Probably working in the hospital as a doctor...waiting his turn to get me when you're not looking."

"Is this why you're not sleeping?"

The room fell silent for a minute, and then Meg rolled over and looked at her sister. Amanda tried not to show any reaction to the swelling and bruising of her face, but Meg was watching her closely and caught the initial despair. Amanda hadn't noticed all of the bite marks and hickeys before, but now the bruises were fully developed and were a formidable sight. *They probably cover all of her body. That sick bastard.*

"Not too pretty, huh, sis? Mom says there's no permanent damage, and I guess I could use a few days off." She nibbled on her raw lip, pulling at the loose skin. She didn't know how to start because their relationship had been so strained. All that hatred over a misconception. "I want to say thank you for saving me. It was quite a spectacle we created, I hear. One person thrown out of a seaplane and one crazy FBI person jumping in after. As I recall, you never really liked to swim in the ocean. Sharks and all."

Amanda crossed the room and sat on the edge of Meg's bed. Taking her hand, she smiled. "You're welcome. No one will ever hurt you again, Meg. I promise you that. I have loved and adored you my whole life. I know that I've been tough on you sometimes, but it was always tough love."

Meg didn't say anything, but Amanda could see the love well up. That was enough.

Now it was Grace's turn to take the floor. "OK, how long can you stay, and what's going to happen with the FBI and all such things?"

"Oh, Mom. You sure know how to screw up a nice scene. The chopper will be heading back to Los Angeles in two hours, and I'm going to be debriefed. Wrap-up of the Laughlin investigation will be handled by Nevada. The bureau is assigning me to another case with the understanding that I get to finish up with Elliott when the time comes. I'll be stationed in Texas for a while."

"Texas?" argued Grace. "Why not stay with us on Catalina and go back to Bullhead with Meg? Stupid FBI."

"Meg, don't think I'm deserting you. My partner, Matt, is staying in Laughlin, and I'll talk to him daily."

"It's OK, sis. So does everyone believe he'll come back to get me? Will I be on his calendar? I mean, are we looking at August first again?"

Amanda didn't want to go there with Meg. She needed to be free of Elliott. Finding the neatly packed box of human hearts—his trophies—on the train tortured Amanda. She knew Elliott's intention was to add Meg's to the inventory. Now was not the time to share her find.

The situation of Elliott's return needed to be addressed. "We have split opinions on this, but I'm voting on the conservative side and planning for the worst. I believe Elliott can't let you go at this point. You're his unfinished business. From how you've described his mannerisms, he's tipping over the edge. He's a perfectionist, and his plan failed. He'll try again. Probably a more involved plan. But Meg, serial killers make mistakes when the crime gets personal. Knowing this puts us in a better position to protect you and take him out."

"I'll be comfortable knowing that your Matt will be in town for the time being. Rachael'll be there too. I know I've been fighting you about going to Catalina, but I guess that's where I need to be right now. Right again, Mom, damn it." Everyone laughed.

When the time came for Amanda to leave, the three women passed knowing smiles around. All the years of animosity were erased. Nothing more needed to be said. Taking a taxi to the pier, Amanda thought about her relationship with Meg. *If I had to pick one person in the world to be my best friend, I would pick Meg.* When the helicopter arrived to take her to Los Angeles, the crew found a tall, upright, focused, and gorgeous FBI agent ready and determined to kick butt.

65

By the eighth day of hospitalization, Meg was antsy to leave, so she fully cooperated with her physical therapist and doctor. She learned to maneuver with her walking cast and with her arm in a temporary cast that would be removed within a week. When the wheelchair arrived, Meg eagerly hobbled to meet it.

The *Catalina Flyer* left hourly during the high season, and the trip took an hour, shore to shore. Once on board the ferry, Meg declared she needed a Bloody Mary, and Grace was quick to agree. Laughingly, Grace ordered two for each, with extra olives for nutrition. The women toasted with a solid clink of the glasses. "Here's to the Pennington women."

"Rachael will be waiting for us on the pier. She has a surprise for you," said Grace.

"She found my long blonde hair and can magically reinstall it on my head?"

Grace frowned. *The mean Meg is back again.* "No, even better than that. I can guarantee you that you'll be smiling for a long time."

"Like that's going to happen." Meg turned away and stared out to sea.

Grace didn't know whether to laugh or cry, so she just took a sip of her second drink and contemplated having a third. This trip was certainly not going to be like the fun-loving trips the family used to take.

The summer vacationers pushed to abandon the boat, so Grace and Meg waited. No use risking the herd knocking over the wheelchair of a slow-moving cripple. Since Rachael had brought over most of their luggage earlier, they only had an overnight bag each and Meg's wheelchair. Grace tossed the bags on Meg's lap and pushed her down the boat ramp. As they departed, a suntanned Rachael and Josh came rushing toward them. "Hey, sailors, welcome home"

Meg broke out in laughter at the sight of Josh. "Holy cow, where did you find that piece of junk? Thought you'd be somewhere in the Ozarks, you old hick."

"Love you, too, Meg," Josh said as he leaned over and scooped her out of the chair. "Since when are you such a wimp? Thought you'd be signed up for soccer by now." His words were fun, but his heart ached to see one of his favorite people so physically trampled.

Josh had parked the patrol car at the end of the dock, and the four climbed in.

"Same cottage, Mom?"

"Same one, honey. Close enough to town to walk, but far away enough so the boisterous crowd doesn't bother us. The cruise lines still stop by, Josh?"

"Same as ever. You get up in the morning, and thirty locals are milling around town. Then the *Catalina Flyer* arrives. There are three takeoff ports now, and along comes the Carnival Cruise line with three thousand people. You can't find an empty barstool in town. Same old, same old."

"I'll enjoy watching the crazy weekenders try the scuba and kayaking. They are so spastic," said Meg, "trying to cram a week's vacation into one hour."

Within minutes, they arrived at their summer rental. Nothing had changed. Same furniture, same landscaping. The sameness brought a sense of security. Rachael knew she would need to address the new security system but decided to lie and say the owner had installed it. The guns were a different matter. Later. Rachael made sure she'd covered every aspect of safety for her mom and sister. The citizens and police would be on the lookout for any newcomers that might look or act warily, especially if they showed an interest in Meg. The men at the airport would keep track of unusual private planes, along with any seaplanes. Rachael worried there might be a crack in the foundation of her plan, allowing Elliott to squeeze in, but for the moment, she couldn't visualize what that might be. She would review the changes with Amanda when they got back together.

The sisters both believed that Elliott's next encounter would not take place until August in Bullhead, if it took place at all. Like other criminal experts, they waffled between believing his obsession would drive him to try to recapture Meg at any cost and believing that his sense of self-preservation would prevail. He had come so close to getting caught. It would be suicide to try it again.

Meg, hobbling around the cottage, was the first to notice the security system. She seemed satisfied with Rachael's explanation. "Josh, come on over here and help this poor maiden to the ladies' room," said Meg.

"Now, Meg, that's my job," said Grace as she hurried to Meg's side. Rachael shot a curious glance at her mother, a glance that was returned with a curious shrug. Was Meg hitting on Josh? The thought whizzed in and out of Rachael's mind. There was no way that Meg would be interested in Josh, especially after what she just survived. She was just a natural flirt. It was embedded in her DNA. And yet…

Rachael wasn't the only one curious about Meg's behavior. When lifting Meg out of the wheelchair, Josh felt she hugged him too passionately. Surprising. But after all, they were longstanding friends. He dismissed the feeling.

Grace was the smart one. She sensed what was going on and would put a stop to it. Josh's presence would be limited until Grace had time to help Meg get her head screwed on right. Further complications in any of their lives were totally unacceptable at this point.

Rachael spent five days on Catalina helping with Meg. Once the walking cast came off, there would be physical therapy, along with swimming at the calmer beaches. The three women took turns cooking and enjoyed shopping for groceries and driving the golf cart. After dinner, Rachael would excuse herself to visit Josh.

Meg suggested Josh come over for dinner and TV, but that idea was thwarted by Grace. "Rachael and Josh need this time to themselves. Maybe something will come of it this time. Lord knows Rachael needs someone special in her life."

Meg just grunted. "Forget it, Mom. There's no such thing as love, if that's what you're talking about. Besides, Rachael is just leading Josh on, like she always did. She'll love him and leave him. She did the same thing to Hal."

Grace observed Meg closely as she rattled on about Josh and Rachael. She didn't like what she saw or heard. Meg seemed so agitated, so very agitated. It was as if she were having an out-of-body experience. Worrisome. Grace postponed discussing the rape with Meg. She would wait until Rachael left. When the time was right, she would lead her daughter out of her despair. Grace was not a psychologist, but for years, she had worked for one who specialized in patients overcoming trauma. She had also taught school and listened to thirty girls an hour in her dance classes discussing love, friendship, and hatred of their peers and parents alike. She counseled kids toward practical solutions to their situations, including her own children, when they would listen. Another career had infiltrated her normal life, one she was still unable to share with her girls. Now, in her career as a novelist, she was exploring the inner workings of the human mind. She knew that accessing and adapting Meg's inner thoughts to the real world would be her greatest challenge.

For Rachael, nights with Josh were pure heaven. They spent every evening riding along the shore of the Pacific. This was Rachael's favorite time. She knew Josh wanted to move forward with their relationship, but she wasn't sure their timing was right. She had loved him as a young girl—had been thrilled with her first kiss. But he lived in a world of her past. She had put down roots in Bullhead, and she wasn't sure she could pull them up and ride off into the sunset with him. The recent episode with Hal and his daughter also weighed heavily on her mind.

It was ten thirty when they finished riding and eventually walked the horses back toward the stables. "Well, am I going to get lucky tonight? You know…a midnight omelet overcooked by my favorite chef," Josh added.

Rachael stopped and took the reins of Josh's horse in her hands. "We need to talk, Josh. I don't know how to feel about us. Is this just a continuation of our summer puppy love? I know you're not looking for a one-night stand, but I'm leaving in two days and won't be back for a while. And that will be a temporary visit again. A lot depends on Meg's progress. I'm not sure if that's enough for me, or if it's enough for you." They continued walking in silence.

Reaching the stables, they unsaddled their horses, removed the bits, and turned them out into the arena. Josh took Rachael's hand and walked her into the house. She was surprised to see that his small dining room table was already set for dinner.

"Go take a shower while I finish dinner," Josh said.

Rachael was smart enough to leave the room without questioning him like she would a suspect. He had bought her favorite shampoo and body gel. She took a long, steamy shower.

Drying off, she found some new thong underwear with the labels still attached, a pair of white shorts, and a beige blouse just her size. No bra? An oversight? She dried her hair and let it fall around her shoulders.

Josh was waiting for her with a glass of Merlot. "Give me a minute, and I'll join you. I want a quick shower, too."

He left the room, and Rachael rummaged through his CD collection and selected an oldie by Nat King Cole. On the patio, she watched the moon's reflection move across Avalon Bay. Her thoughts took her to the other body of water that she loved—the Colorado River. Dreadful heat, and even more dreadful heat, was most of what the area had to offer, and yet she loved it. But standing here on Josh's balcony with the moonlight and water, she felt she might be able to discover another life for herself. Island fever could always be conquered with a quick trip to the mainland. She relaxed into the chair, enjoying the island magic.

Rachael recognized the scent of his scrubbed body before he stepped onto the patio.

Josh pulled a patio chair next to Rachael and sat down. He took her glass of wine away and held both of her hands in his. "Rachael, I have been in love with you since the first time you dunked me in the Pacific Ocean, twenty years ago. My life stood still through all the winters and springs until summer would come and I could see you again. There have been women in my life, but there has never been another love in my life. I made a commitment to love you then, and I'm making a commitment to you now." He leaned over and gave her a warm, loving kiss.

When their mouths were finished exploring each other, Rachael pulled back and reached for her glass, not willing to meet his eyes with hers. "No," said Josh. "Talk to me. You have to talk to me now. I know you share my feelings, but are they enough for you to make a commitment to me? I love you, Rachael. Can you say those words to me?"

Rachael pulled loose from his hands, stood, and turned away. He stood and turned her around. She was crying. "Oh, God, Rachael. I'm so sorry."

Rachael tilted her head up and looked into his eyes. "Just shut up, will you? I have loved you as long as you have loved me. I'm frightened to death of loving you, but I do. Now quit screwing around and take me to bed. We'll figure out the rest of the stuff later."

This response was unexpected. They kissed and laughed as they peeled off their clothes, heading toward the bedroom. Their newly rekindled love, which was initially consummated with a huge surge of urgency, now relaxed into a sensual, slow-moving rhythm of lovemaking.

Afterward, she lay in his arms for a long time, quiet and reflective. Eventually, Josh's growling stomach demanded food, and they returned to the kitchen to eat the dinner he had prepared. There was no more talk about the future that night.

***

Two days passed. Rachael and Josh were inseparable at night. During the day, she spent her time with Meg. Meg seemed angry all the time. She was depressed one moment, and then within seconds, she seemed to reach a high point where the music wasn't loud enough and she wanted to dance around the house in her underwear. Looking in the mirror, she would proclaim, "Look at you. Scarface with ugly, brown, short hair. No one would bother kidnapping you now."

The outbursts were usually short-lived and followed by an onset of depression or sleep. Rachael and Grace did what they could to turn the moment around.

"Mom," began Rachael, "are you sure you're going to able to deal with this by yourself? I'm thinking Meg needs professional help."

"Might be," said Grace. "I'll call Meg's rape counselor. Maybe she'll have some suggestions. I thought she'd start coming around by now, but, well, I don't need to tell you. Next week will probably tell the tale when you're not around for her to pick on. Maybe I should go to the library and get a current book on spells and cast a few like your Grandma Nora would have done."

They both laughed. Just like her mother, Grace had always played the role of resident witch when any black cloud bore down on her children. Anything from removing warts to casting out evil spells from broken mirrors was fair game to her. While the family retained its skepticism, they still withheld complete judgment with regard to her talent—a little worried that she might have powers inexplicable to them.

"This is your last night with Josh," said Grace. "I won't tell if you don't make it home, and since I'm your mom, who's left to tell, anyway?"

Rachael hugged her and headed out the door to meet her lover.

66

Since the early jitters of sex had been eliminated, Rachael and Josh decided to spend their last night together at his home with a simple dinner, lots of conversation, and more than lots of sex. The sunset at 8:05 was magnificent, laying long lines of disappearing sun on Josh's patio. A mild breeze floated across the perfect evening.

"Have you decided to cancel your return to Bullhead and stay here with me in the land of paradise for the rest of your life?" Josh asked.

Rachael took a sip of Merlot and turned her face to meet his gaze. "Let's not start the evening off that way. You know why I have to go. I've got a job, a partner, a house—all of which are screaming for attention right now. Mom needs her privacy with Meg. She has a huge job to handle. I really have to go. I'll miss you like crazy, but we'll talk every day. Promise."

"Talking is nice but not really what I had in mind. As a kid, I'd always mark my calendar and hate it as the day came when you'd go back to the mainland. We didn't have a choice in the matter then, Rachael, but we do now. Either one of us can quit our job and join the other, or else we could both quit and find jobs together in some other location."

"I'd get claustrophobic living full-time on the island. I don't care that you can see the mainland; it's still surrounded by water. And you, I can't see you living in Bullhead when the temperature reaches one hundred and twenty-eight degrees."

"Well," said Josh, "we could find someplace around a lake, river, or ocean, 'cause I know we both need the water. And, ya know, we both like small towns. Let's research some ocean cities and see what we can find. Hopefully, you don't want to go to Northern California. Too cold for me."

Rachael looked away. "I think I got left out on part of this conversation. Did I make some kind of a commitment to you when I was drunk last night? I didn't think I had that much to drink."

Josh sat quietly for a few minutes. He knew this was a pivotal moment. If there was ever to be a future for them, it had to be decided now. More time passed. Finally, Rachael got up and headed to the kitchen to refill her glass of wine. When she returned, she found Josh standing at the edge of the deck, leaning against the post, deep in thought. Rachael went to his side and took his hand.

"I have played this scene over and over, Rachael, and it never looked like this. I'll say this again. I've been infatuated with enough women to know that I've only been in love with one. This is the real deal. I bought this house with us in mind. I knew you'd love the view, and when our kids came along they'd love living here with us. So I was wrong thinking you could live on the island. If that's true, then I'll sell my house, quit my job, and move wherever you like if you'll marry me. God, Rachael, I have waited all my life for this moment. This time I need an answer, please."

While speaking, Josh had turned to Rachael and searched her eyes for some sign that she shared his commitment. When he finished speaking, Rachael dropped her gaze and released her hand from his.

Her silence crushed him. "I guess that was my answer. You may think there's someone out there who'll love you more, but there isn't. Maybe more money—more prestige, probably—but I never believed that was important to you. I'm so very, very sorry, Rachael, that you don't or can't love me like that. This is the last we'll speak of it."

An awkward silence fell, and the thought of dinner and romance drifted away with the breeze. Josh smiled at Rachael. "I'll take you home."

***

Rachael was up before sunrise and went for a three-mile run. The rest of the house stayed cozy in their beds. When Grace crawled out, she noticed that while Rachael was gone, her bed had been slept in. She cooked pancakes and sausage for her daughters, and they chattered while Rachael finished her packing. Dying to know what happened, but considering the rumpled bed, Grace hesitated until finally she could stand it no more.

"How did it go last night?" asked Grace.

"Actually, not too well," replied Rachael. "We have a few issues that will probably never be resolved." She didn't want to talk to anyone about last night. She didn't know how she felt about the abrupt parting. Josh certainly was marriage material, but she had been so close to getting married before, and then…well, then her life had been shattered when her fiancé had been killed. "Josh and I will not be seeing each other again, Mom. End of story."

Silence. Meg looked at her mother, and they both raised their eyebrows and shrugged.

***

Waving good-bye to Rachael as the *Catalina Flyer* departed from the Avalon Bay pier was a sad moment. Rachael kept looking up the dock to see if Josh would come to say good-bye, but he never showed. The boat pulled away with long faces and short waves.

"Well, she's gone. Guess we'll be in charge of taking care of Josh now."

Grace watched as Meg's mood turned from sullen to enthusiastic as she watched the wake of the boat disappear. As usual, Grace had other plans. "Surprise," she said. "We have an appointment at ten thirty with Tim at the Apple Haircutter Salon. He flew to the island just to see you. We'd better get a move on."

Meg acted surprised but actually had answered a call from the salon confirming her appointment. "Yeah, I love Tim. He's so radical in an innocent sort of way. Hmmm. Is that an oxymoron? Let's go."

The other stylists at the salon had been forewarned about Meg's recent trauma and were cautioned not to question or gawk at her ugly hair and bruises. Unfortunately, they went overboard and almost ignored her upon arrival.

"Meg, darling," said Tim. His large frame, dressed in a traditional Hawaiian shirt and walking shorts, nearly blocked out the florescent lights. "My God, girl. Hurry in—you look like shit." That broke the silence, and all stylists chuckled quietly and returned to normal. They came over and hugged or teased Meg that she was trying to establish a new fashion statement with wicked hair. The levity helped.

First, Tim had to bleach out the ugly dark brown hair dye, and then they decided on a new shade for Meg.

"This Champagne by L'Oreal is really hot right now. It has a little more red in it than your original color. Or, of course, we can use the Ultra Sunlight, which would be almost identical, and there would be no touchups required. So...what'll it be?"

"I've had so many changes in my life lately, Tim, I think trying to return to an original me would help a lot." She had returned to passive.

Tim turned away to regain his sparkling composure. *I will kill the man myself if I ever meet him*, he thought. "So be it. Good choice. Be right with you." Tim went to the back room to mix the color and returned with the magic formula. "While the color takes, we'll have Marie start your manicure and pedicure. Meg, my dear, you're going to be your old, ravishing self. There's too much underlying beauty there to have been messed up with a botched haircut and a gruesome dye job."

After the color change, Tim said, "OK, do you trust me enough to let me pick a style for you? I know every little wavy strand of your hair, and I have an idea."

"Go for it," sighed Meg. Tim recognized that she was tiring and hurriedly began with a modified wedge cut. Elliott had hacked off her hair with no precision or finesse, like a machete chopping through a jungle. While Tim wanted to give her as much length as possible, he finally gave in to a shorter style. He entered into his usual discourse on the stock market, changes on the island, his daughter's college days, and finally the latest radical diet he was trying. He was a fountain of chatter.

Years ago while in Bullhead, Tim had volunteered his salon and services to a shelter for battered women. Because of their traumatic backgrounds, the women would not make eye contact with him. It would prove to be a difficult beginning—allowing a man to touch their hair—and while they were thrilled with the results, many women would leave without uttering a thank you. He knew what Meg was feeling. She couldn't look at him.

The mousse was massaged into her hair, the blow drying finished, and "Voila!" exclaimed Tim as he turned the chair around.

Meg stared in the mirror at the style. *So this is the new Meg...whoever that is.*

Everyone in the room stopped their work to catch a glimpse of Meg. She sat transfixed for a full two minutes, staring at her image in the mirror.

"Thank you," Meg whispered. The tears came. The room was suspended in time. No one spoke, but everyone looked as the ugly duckling was replaced by the fair, although bruised, swan. "Well, I...thank you." Her hand drifted over her raw lips and brushed away the tears.

"The pleasure was all mine, darling girl." Trying to lighten the moment, Tim continued, "If you have any trouble with that style, just drop by anytime."

When trying to pay for the transformation, Meg was informed it had been covered, which she knew was a little white lie.

"Well, tell my rich benefactor thanks a lot. I owe him." Meg hugged Tim for a long time, and he could feel her gratitude. She felt safe in his hug but finally let go. Once Meg had left the salon, the other stylists gave Tim a standing ovation.

The hair was step one in Grace's plan to revive Meg's verve. The following two weeks on Catalina were filled with carefree days of shopping and people watching, while in the evenings, the two would talk gingerly about Elliott. Those evenings were painful, and Meg would only discuss a little at a time. She never wanted to recall all of the torture. Grace believed that Rachael and Amanda would catch Elliott, so she had no trouble trying to convince Meg of that fact. If her daughters were not successful, then Luke would finalize Elliott. He would pay with his life for his crimes, both for Meg and for all the women he had killed. Grace didn't doubt that for a minute since she had witnessed similar situations before she retired.

Meg's job was to decide which direction to go in her own life. Did she want to go back to a life

in Bullhead City, living with Rachael and working for the Bureau of Reclamation? Was college a
viable alternative? Did she want to come back and
live in Yorba Linda and go to Cal State Fullerton?
What might interest her as a major? All of these
questions needed to be addressed, but a little at
a time. Meg didn't need any more pressure in her
life.

Meg initially turned to alcohol to relieve the
pain but gradually backed away from depending
on the booze. Finally, she was able to get a good
night's rest without the aid of sleeping pills. Now
that the nightmares had reduced in frequency
and intensity, she seemed able to enjoy the island
and the island people more. "I think I'm finally
on island time, Mom," Meg said with a smile.
"Encouraging, huh?"

During the healing process, Josh came over
to visit daily. He took Meg and Grace to the police
shooting range and introduced them to their new
guns. Josh was pleased with the progress that Meg
demonstrated when she practiced the quick-aim-
and-shoot technique. He ignored Grace at first,
but when they checked their targets, he had to
comment.

"Grace. You nailed it. Wow. Are you sure this
is your first time out?"

Grace feigned a problem with trying to reload. "Just beginner's luck, I guess." She clumsily laid down the gun and shrugged.

Josh didn't believe that for a minute. Krav Maga also came naturally for Meg, even the first week when her foot was still in a cast. Josh kidded that she would be catching up with Rachael before long. When Josh got a day off from the department, he and Meg would ride the horses along the beach. Meg turned more and more to him after Rachael left.

"Did you know that I asked Rachael to marry me?" said Josh.

Meg was not surprised. "She didn't say anything to us. She just got up on her last morning and said something about how it was over between the two of you. Mom and I knew you probably had a lover's spat. But no, she didn't tell us you proposed. What happened? Oh shit, it's probably none of my business."

"Well, since I thought you were going to end up as my kid sister, I guess it is partly your business. And that's why I'm confiding in you now. She couldn't answer me. She just froze up. I gave her alternatives about where we could live, and I even said I'd move to Bullhead. I guess she knew that I really didn't want to do that, but, Meg, I really love Rachael. I would have moved for her. She didn't say yes or no—just stood there and almost cried. I was hurt, and I got pissed. I felt I deserved an answer. And that's how we left it. Dumb, huh?"

The horses were walking through the surf now, and the two pulled them to a stop.

"There might be something missing in our DNA. Mom's trashed and burned men all of her life. She's been married two times, but she never really could bring herself to a full commitment. I think Mom fell in love when she was around twenty-eight, but something happened. She won't talk about it. Mom's got a lot of secrets. Amanda backed away from what she thought was the love of her life when he started using drugs. She might've been able to salvage the relationship, but she ran away instead. Rachael's partner in Bullhead has it really bad for her. I think he just asked her to marry him last month, but she froze up with him, too. She's still not over the death of her fiancé."

"She told me about him."

"Did she tell you she was pregnant and had a miscarriage the night he died?"

"No." Josh was disturbed by that. "I wish I would have known."

"And then there's me. God, I've had a thousand boyfriends, but not one of them have I really loved. Do you see a pattern? It must be in our genes." She was wistful for another moment, and then she gave him a wicked smile. "And I haven't even gotten around to Grandma Nora."

"I don't believe it's in her genes. I know that Rachael loves me. We need to find the right place to be together. Shit, I thought love was supposed to be easy," said Josh.

"'Fraid not, my friend. Change of subject. OK?"

"Fine. Except just know I haven't given up on Rachael yet. We'll have our moment in the sun; I know it. Maybe we'll have to go to Australia or somewhere, but I plan on being her husband."

"It would be nice if one of us rode off into the sunset. I know that Mom would be relieved, because she needs to get back to her life. The whole family has done a lot of sacrificing for me. I don't think they know how much I love them for it, even Amanda." She paused, searching for the words. "I've been given a second chance to show my love and a chance to grow up a little. Maybe not take my life for granted anymore. Guess I'd better do something about that."

"Meg, that's what we all love about you. You've always danced to a special drummer, and lately you've shown a renewed thrill for living each day. It gives us hope that you haven't lost your passion for living. The world would suffer without your magic sparkle."

"Josh, some of that is still there, but I have this burning rage right now. It's replaced the fear and shame that I was first experiencing, and I'm not sure where to go with it. I think I want revenge. My family will shit if they think I'm going after this guy, especially since you've shown me how to shoot. That's Rachael's and Amanda's department. But that son of a bitch raped me, and he did it in such an utterly devastating and demoralizing way that I could kill him for it with my bare hands."

"Then make a plan with your family and do just that. You'll have my support all the way. You're right. You need to be involved, and when this Elliott guy is captured or killed in the process of trying to get away, you need to be there to kick the asshole in the slats or wherever. But Meg, my darling, this is not a one-man job. You have to involve the family."

Meg smiled at that. "You're so great to talk to," she said, reining her horse around. "I feel so much better every time we're together. Rachael is so stupid. Hey. Race you to the pier?"

The sentence struck a sad chord in Josh. How ironic. His horse felt the nudge of his heels, and they were off to the races.

Convincing Grace and her two sisters that Meg wanted to play a role in the capture of Elliott started as an impossible task. Finally, after many phone calls, the four decided to meet back in Catalina for two days and invite along the FBI and the Bullhead PD, as well as a representative from Metro in Laughlin, to lay out a plan to capture Elliott.

Josh wanted to be involved with the planning and also to be instrumental in the implementation of the plan. Since the case was now a federal issue, the FBI would coordinate with the local agencies. They located Elliott in Mexico, and while he was under their surveillance, he was seeing a plastic surgeon. The last time their agent saw him, he entered the clinic with bandages and wasn't seen exiting. They had pictures of all incoming and outgoing patients for six days but never captured a shot of Elliott. Somewhere along the line, he had evaded them again.

The consensus of the investigative team was that he was still infatuated with Meg, and if she returned to Bullhead, he would follow her. The question was if he would kidnap her between now and next July 30 or if he would wait until August 1 of next year and keep to his pattern. The FBI profiler, along with the other professionals, decided that the dates were significant to Elliott, and that August 1 of next year would be his target date. The FBI would set up shop in July in Laughlin. Meg was included in all of the meetings and understood she might be playing an integral role in the scenario.

Rachael and Josh were moderately friendly to each other during the meetings. But Hal was also on the island now, representing the Bullhead PD, and when he made his entrance into the meeting room, the tension could have been sliced with a knife. Hal had no idea what had transpired in Catalina between Rachael and Josh and would not have cared. He had moved on and was already looking for a job in Tucson. Josh knew all about Hal, thanks to Meg, and he watched every connecting look made between the two. Not wanting to show any jealousy, Josh spent a lot of time joking with Meg.

"Hey, Rachael," said Hal. "Something going on between Josh and Meg? They look real cozy together."

Rachael snorted. "Hardly. Josh is old enough to be her father." She said it so everyone in the conference room heard it. Josh hid his smile.

The Mexican Mafia was no longer flying to the Davis Dam area of the Colorado River, but the FBI knew they were continuing their money-laundering business in Las Vegas. Black-market body parts were also showing up, indicating that Elliott was still in business. His deliveries were taking place at Lake Mead instead of Katherine's Landing. Amanda's partner, Matt, stayed on at the Oasis Casino and was actively working as a dealer. The suites that used to be occupied monthly by the Mafia were not being utilized anymore. The case involving Beckett was being evaluated.

With the finalization of the temporary master plan, each agency had their role to play in the drama. Grace and Meg would return to Yorba Linda and stay until after the Christmas holidays. When January rolled around, Meg would return to Bullhead City, start college at the College of the Desert, and also work part-time for the Bureau of Reclamation. No change in Rachael's life. She would continue on with the Bullhead Police.

Amanda would return with the FBI in July. Improved security would be installed at the river house, and Meg was instructed in self-awareness at all times. She didn't have to be persuaded on that point. With the plan in place, the enclave of police officials meshed their calendars and set their sights on July.

When it was time for Meg to leave the island, saying good-bye to Josh was more difficult than she had anticipated. Josh was special—very special. Why couldn't Rachael return his love? Josh and Meg discussed just that point the evening before she headed back to the mainland.

"You know, while Rachael seems so sure of herself and can handle any police situation, she's a mess most of the time in her personal life," said Meg. "When she's got time off from the department, she doesn't go out and enjoy life. She just sits in her inner tube in the river and drinks beer. A real loner."

"Well, how about her partner, Hal? You told me they had something going."

"He had something going on with her, but Rachael didn't love him back. She loved helping out with Hal's daughter but would've been happy to be an aunt to her or a sister. She certainly didn't want to sign up for mother. He totally misread their relationship. The only one she seems to moon over is you, and yet she won't let it happen. Beats me. Maybe she's the one who needs the shrink."

Laughter erupted between the two, and they gulped down a portion of the beers they had been toying with. Downtown Avalon was really noisy at night with the tourists trying to make up for lost party time. The two pushed their way through the crowd and headed to the end of the pier. Another windless night wrapped around them, and a serene bond encompassed them as they dangled their feet in the warm Pacific Ocean.

"What chance do you give me for finding my someone?" asked Meg. She started pulling wood splinters from the dock and stacking them neatly next to her.

"As far as I can tell, Meg, you could have your pick of any guy you meet. I know you've been through a lot and the wounds are still pretty fresh, but look how far you've come. And you look great. Your hair is cool. At least I think it is. Not really up on that sort of shit. You don't have any physical scars that I can see. You're not one hundred percent yet with the mental scars, but we all know how resilient you are. You're passed the fear, remorse, and guilt trips. You're fine."

"Not so sure about that, Josh."

"Do you think you'll have a hard time committing like your sisters?"

"Don't know. If I could find someone like you, I'd grab on tight and not let go. You know that you're very special to me, don't you?"

Josh nudged Meg on the shoulder, almost tossing her into the water. "Are you hitting on me, little sister?"

Meg, regaining her balance, shot him a fierce look. "So what if I am? Turned down by one sister and turned on by another. Doesn't that work for you?"

Josh was speechless. "Shit, Meg, don't pull that crap on me."

Meg broke out in laughter, and she stood up, giving Josh a huge push. "Gotcha."

Jumping up to meet the challenge, Josh took a beginning stance for Krav Maga. Responding quickly, Meg squared off in front of him.

"First one to score five points wins. The other has to strip naked and jump in the water," yelled Meg.

"You're on," said Josh.

The two sparred for five minutes. Josh was surprised that Meg had learned the technique so quickly, but he pulled his punches, not wanting to hurt her.

"Don't you dare let me win. Come on, Josh, gimme all you got—bring it on," Meg taunted. She circled around him, and to the casual observer, she looked like a well-toned cat ready to strike her prey.

Josh was as gentle as he could be with her. No more pain was going to be inflicted on this girl. He realized Meg was beginning to tire, so he encircled her with his strong arms, picked her up, and threw her off the pier into the seventy-degree water.

When her head popped up, she spit some salt water out and said, "You creep. I could've taken you in another minute." With sure strokes, she swam toward the ladder and started climbing up.

"Sorry, chickadee. No match for the brown belt yet, but there's definite potential." He reached a hand forward to help Meg. She grabbed his wrist, positioned her right foot at the top of the ladder, and yanked with all her might. Josh went flying over her head into the water, letting out a huge bellow on the way. It really wasn't a surprise, but he gave a great impression of shock.

"Serves you right, asshole," said Meg. "That's twice this month I've been thrown in the ocean, and I'm getting tired of it." She flew up the ladder and stomped off, leaving him alone, swimming to shore.

Josh caught up with Meg at El Galleon Bar. She was wrapped in her Hawaiian mini skirt. Beads of water reflected off her skin as she teased the patrons with a poor interpretation of the hula.

The bartender found a towel in the back room and handed it to Meg.

"Good thing these nights are warm here on the island; otherwise, I'd be freezing my tush off by now."

Josh grabbed the loose end of the towel, and together they laughed off the moment. "Sorry about the toss. Guess I'd forgotten about your earlier problem. Are we OK? If not, I'll drop my pants and you can spank me."

Rod, the bartender, came rushing over. "Oh, no you don't. If anyone gets spanked by Meg, it's going to be me. My bar. My butt." Rod bought a round of beers for his friends and then told them to go home. "Last call coming up, and you don't want to be around when I try to get rid of these drunks. You're off duty, Josh, so get out of here. Have a safe trip home, Meg. Come back soon."

It was late, and Josh steered Meg toward her home. She seemed to be enjoying the evening and especially his company.

"Let's go to your house and have a nightcap. I'll be going home in a few more hours, and all of this magic will disappear. Come on," said Meg. She grabbed his hand and pulled him in the direction of the police station. "We'll pick up one of the carts and drive up now. I might even want to go riding for a while."

Josh felt this spelled trouble, but he finally gave in. They walked the three blocks to the station. "We'll pick up the cart, but no promises on the rest."

Meg insisted on driving but got overruled because it was a police vehicle. "Don't want to get me in trouble, do you?" He laughed.

They turned up Eucalyptus Avenue, where the street became rural with no streetlights or sidewalks. Meg reached over and turned off the ignition.

"What the hell are you doing, Meg?" Josh put on the brakes and stopped the cart.

She turned around in the small golf cart seat and faced him. "I had this all planned out, but you just won't cooperate. We were supposed to go to your house and make love. So now that you've spoiled all of the seduction stuff, I'll plain old tell you that I'm in love with you. I want...well...I want some sex tonight."

Josh winced. Earlier, he had mentioned to Grace that Meg seemed to be coming on to him, but it was in such a playful way that he hoped she was just role-playing to see how it fit. Now the truth was out. She was still screwed up, and he knew that the outwardly healthy attitude was a cover-up. He sucked in a deep breath and began. "Meg, honey. You're confusing love with security. You feel safe with me. You want to make sure that I'm not going to leave you. You're just confusing your feelings."

"Bullshit. Don't start with that secondhand-store psychology. I've had my fill of shrinks. The first time I saw you on the pier I…well…wow. What a hunk. I remembered you as Rachael's pimply-faced summer boyfriend. But when she left and turned down your marriage proposal, you finally noticed me. I know you love me. Don't be bashful. I'm not a virgin, you know."

Josh put his arm around her and pulled her close. She mistook that move and closed her eyes. "I do love you…in my own brotherly way. But it's not the kind of love you're looking for. That kind of love is reserved for Rachael. She may have walked away, but we aren't through. I promise you that you'll always be safe as long as I have a breath left in my body. Elliott won't hurt you again."

"You're turning me down? Why? You look at me as damaged merchandise now? Is that it? I know that's what I'm going to be facing in Bull-head—that's why I don't really want to go back. All the guys will think I'm easy. A throwaway lay. I want to marry you and stay on the island. I'll make you happy. I know I will." She was tugging at his shirt now, her face distorted with hurt and despair. She pulled at his clothes and reached between his legs, searching for his erection, but found nothing.

"Meg, stop. Look at me. Meg."

She was pleading with him now. "Love me, Josh. God. Please love me. I can't do this without you." She was losing it. Her voice fell into a deep chasm, and piercing, guttural animal sounds erupted. Then, the tears came like a gushing flood.

"Meg, you have to face what happened to you. It wasn't your fault. You met up with a maniac. Not your fault. Hold your head high and admire your own fortitude. You're a survivor, and nothing or no one can ever break your spirit. Bullhead guys will have some pity for you, but that'll soon be overcome with admiration when they see that the old Meg is back in town. Don't let Elliott win. You be the winner."

Meg was openly sobbing now. "But you don't get it, Josh. He hurt me. Oh, God. He hurt me in ways I can't talk about. I don't remember all of it, but each time I get a flashback, I see him. He was raping me and chewing on me and stroking me and putting strange things inside of me and…oh, Josh. He ruined me. I'm ugly and used up and…" Huge tears accompanied by body-wrenching moans followed. Josh held her tightly as she raged on. "Oh, Josh, I've made such a fool of myself. Jesus, what am I going to do? I don't know what to do. I need someone to love me. Help me—please help me."

He encouraged her crying with soothing words and knew that finally she had hit bottom. Now, the upward climb could begin. He switched his approach. "Hey, sweet girl. It was an honor for you to consider me as a lover. Maybe not a mate but a strong, sacrificing, macho man with huge pecs. You chose well." He waited a minute to continue, hoping Meg was climbing out of the abyss. She was still shaking within his strong hold. Silent moments passed, but now he felt her strength returning. The tears were subsiding, and a partial smile crossed her lips.

"I will always be around to take care of you. Come on, twerp, let's go home now. Your mom will be getting nervous."

Meg didn't break the embrace but rather drew in closer. "You pick the damnedest time to be a smartass. Here I pour out my soul to you, and in return you want to talk about your testosterone. Well, all-helpful one, do you happen to have a tissue?"

"My girlfriends have learned to supply their own. I've broken so many hearts, you know. Use the bottom of my shirt if you like. Only the best for a Pennington girl."

Meg let out a snorting laugh. "You know, I have the same DNA that Rachael has, just rearranged a little. Sure you don't want to change your mind?"

"We're not going there again. A guy can only say no so many times." He smirked at his own humor, and Meg sat and looked at him with an incredulous expression on her face.

"No wonder Rachael turned you down. You're a real asshole." She was smiling.

They drove in silence for the remainder of the trip. This had been a sobering and exhausting experience for both of them. Although their heartstrings were tugging for different reasons, both Josh and Meg were feeling relief.

The porch light was on when they arrived, and Meg saw the curtains move in the living room.

"Mom's up to her old tricks, spying. How about you give me a huge kiss good night and see how long it takes her to ask me about it?" asked Meg.

"No tongue."

"God, you're such a party pooper. OK, bro, no tongue." They jumped out of the cart and headed for the front door. "OK, she can see us from here. Lay it on me."

Josh grabbed her with a gigantic sweeping motion, swinging her around in a circle while she laughed out loud. Carefully returning her to the sidewalk, he took her face in his hands. She threw her arms around his neck, and they kissed and kissed and kissed.

"I thought you said no tongue," Josh said, finally breaking away from her. A deep blush washed across his face. "You owe me big time for this. Be sure Rachael hears about the kiss—not the conspiracy plot against your mom." The porch light began flashing with increased urgency. Time to go in.

Grace had disappeared when Meg went into the house. That spoiled the subterfuge, so Meg went to bed with solid thoughts on life. Grace received a call later that night from Josh. He explained the whole scene she had witnessed in the front yard. He knew she would be devastated by their actions, but once she understood that the show was for her benefit and was a culmination of humor and compassion, she was ecstatic. It was so Meg. Their Meg was finally back in full force.

"Josh, I'll never be able to repay your kindness. Thank you."

"De nada."

Meg's attitude and general persona had shown marked improvement since her emotional evening with Josh, so now it seemed right to pull up stakes. Catalina had performed its magic on her, and now it was time to return to Yorba Linda and take the next step toward normalcy. The women did laundry and packed all day. They made charity baskets for Josh with food they didn't want to transport and invited him over for the last supper. The three guns were unloaded and wrapped inside their clothing for transfer. Meg seemed surprised that she was so ready to leave. She loved Catalina, but it was more like a fairyland for her. It was not reality. *I guess I'm really pulling it together. Who knew?* she thought.

Josh lugged the suitcases down to the boat dock, struggling with the weight of them. "What?

Are you stealing the silverware?" He helped them board the *Catalina Flyer* heading back to the mainland.

"Come on, Josh, give us a kiss," said Grace, smiling, beyond happy.

"Not you, too," he replied, winking at Megan. "You Pennington girls are all alike. Horny. I have to pass on the kiss. I think I'm already in enough trouble. Have a safe trip home. I'll think about Christmas. Can't make any firm commitments right now."

"Bring your sister, too, if she'd like to come. It might be fun to share a Christmas on the mainland. We're very festive," said Grace. "All of the Penningtons will be there for a change."

Meg jumped into the conversation. "You might get another shot at Rachael, or if she's still all stuffy, maybe you could give Amanda a whirl. You still haven't tasted that flavor."

Grace swirled around and took a swing at Meg. "You are really a mean little scruff. Better watch it. If Rachael finds out you and Josh have been kissing, she might take you down a peg."

"Never happen. She's getting old, and I can outrun her."

"Get out of here," said Josh. "I can't take any more of you crazy women."

69

Christmas at the family home was always special. Rachael came home on December 22, and the two sisters immediately started shopping. Grace was glad when she could shove the girls out the door. She needed some alone time. Keeping Meg busy was wearing on her. Knowing the shopping would be an all-day event, she dialed Josh and asked if he had decided to join them for Christmas Eve and Day.

"Wow, Grace, that's really thoughtful of you, but..."

"No buts," said Grace. "I cook a damn good turkey, and the girls would love to spend the day with you. Amanda is even going to sneak in for Christmas Eve and part of the day. Make our day special and say yes, please."

"Rachael and I didn't end up on the best of terms, you know. Did she tell you?"

"Didn't have to. I saw her the next morning, and she didn't want to talk about it then...in fact, she refuses to talk about it to this day. Rachael doesn't know how she feels, Josh. You know she loves you. Can't get a picture in her head about her future. If and when she does, that will include you, I feel sure."

Josh smiled at the phone and said, "Well, yes, I'd love to spend Christmas with your family. What should I bring, and when should I appear at your door?"

Grace had two other phone calls to make before dashing to the drugstore to buy stocking stuffers. She smiled at her own ingenuity and really hoped it was not going to blow up in her face.

After spending Christmas Eve at the Friends Church, enjoying the choir's awesome rendition of Hallelujah Chorus and, of course, eating Chinese dinner at Wings Restaurant because no one wanted to cook on Christmas Eve, the four women headed home. They watched *It's A Wonderful Life* for the umpteenth time, and the girls headed for their old bedrooms, still decorated with high school memorabilia and handmade quilts. It was no surprise to Grace that they were all melancholy before retiring and questioned her on the finer points for the morning.

"Are there still some roosters in the neighborhood, or should we set the alarm for four a.m.?" asked Rachael.

"If you brats get up before eight o'clock, I'll tell Santa not to fill your stockings," replied Grace. That was a huge threat with serious repercussions, so the women hugged and went to their own rooms, feeling content and safe as all Christmas Eves in the past.

At 6:00 a.m., the front doorbell rang. "Oh, my God, it must be Santa," yelled Grace as she went flying down the hall. Amanda, Rachael, and Meg were on her heels. "Mom, don't open the door," yelled Amanda, who had grabbed her .38 special on the way out of her bedroom. "Don't open the door before you find out who it is, Mom."

Grace was there first and threw open the front door. The three girls came sliding across the wood floor to an abrupt stop at the entry and exclaimed, "Oh, my God. What are you doing here?"

"Just met coming down the driveway. Heard there was a party," said Matt. Standing on the front porch with smiles and presents were Derek and Matt, Amanda's partner. Amanda quickly disposed of her gun and joined in the hugging and scolding of Grace. Just as the men came in and the door was partially closed, an SUV came flying down the asphalt drive.

"Mom, did you invite the whole town? There's someone else arriving," said Rachael.

"Better go check it out. Don't take your gun. He's friendly, I hear."

Rachael started down the brick sidewalk toward the car. She could tell by the plates that it was a rental. The car was angled to the left, obscuring the driver's identity. When Josh stepped out, she stopped.

"What the hell are you doing here?

"And a Merry Christmas to you, too. I'm an invited guest, thank you. Think I deserve a better salutation than that. 'Happy holidays' comes to mind." He took some presents out of the car and walked toward her.

Rachael still didn't move, not knowing what to do. Awkward? Yes, awkward came to mind.

"Well, I guess I could help you with some of the packages," she said. Josh was getting closer and closer, and she saw a huge smirk begin to cross his face. When he reached her, he put down the presents and pulled her close. She struggled to get away, but not all that hard. Sensing a reluctant withdrawal, he pulled her close and lifted her off the ground. "Now, be a good little girl and kiss your husband-to-be." Before she had time to complain, he planted a huge kiss on her lips. "Now let's go enjoy Christmas. I can't wait to see the family."

Rachael gave up. She knew her mother and sisters were behind this, and while she hated to admit it, seeing Josh was the best present she could ever hope for.

Grace loved the day more than any of them. Being fifty-five years old, she knew that these moments weren't destined to last forever. That's why this year the turkey was bigger and juicer, the presents more awesome, and the wine more potent. These were the best of times for her. The never-used dining room table was sagging with food and cluttered with chatter.

Derek was trying to fit into a seemingly well-connected family scene but was somewhat intrigued with the presence of Amanda and Matt. He pulled Meg aside and whispered, "Is Amanda a lost relative or something? Wasn't she the cocktail waitress at the casino? Didn't she leave the Oasis and go to New York? Dancing in a Broadway show? I didn't know that you were friends, like, well enough to invite her to Christmas."

Oh, shit, thought Grace. She had overheard Derek's question as she was heading toward the kitchen. "Oh, Derek, you just don't know the family well enough. Rachael and Amanda struck up a feminist relationship after Meg was kidnapped. And Amanda has been dating Matt now, so there's the picture. Actually, it's usually Meg who brings home the strays for the holidays. Nothing personal, Amanda. We are really delighted to have you and Matt spend the holidays with us."

Amanda had picked up on the ruse by then and chimed in, "Thanks, Grace. The timing was perfect. I was going to travel to New Hampshire for Christmas, but my folks decided to go abroad for the month, leaving me stranded. Thanks again for the invite."

"Works for me," chimed in Matt.

Grace smiled and went into the kitchen. *Cool—yes, very cool—are my Pennington girls.* Grace was disappointed with herself for not realizing this potential problem. Getting sloppy. Might need a refresher course with the agency, came to mind.

All was jolly on the Pennington front until near the end of dinner when Meg mentioned the kiss. "Kissed anyone better than me since I saw you last, Josh?"

Grown men don't blush, but Josh's ears were burning. "Just did in your front yard, brat," he replied.

Everyone in the room turned and looked at Rachael. Her eyebrows shot up in surprise, and she shot a quizzical look at Josh.

Grace quickly changed the subject to what was being served for dessert. "I'm taking orders for dessert. We have pumpkin pie and whipped cream and, oh, pumpkin pie and whipped cream. What'll you have?" Now she really regretted not telling Rachael about the kiss that culminated in Meg's breakthrough. Amanda looked back and forth between Rachael and Meg.

"Anything I should know about?" asked Rachael. *Oh, my gosh, I'm jealous.*

"Wow," said Meg. "Josh, I'm proud of you. I had you figured for a kiss-and-tell kind of guy. You're one classy hunk." She was having so much fun. She had never seen Rachael squirm over a guy. This was priceless.

Derek and Matt leaned back in their chairs. "How about those Sun Devils? Headed for a good year, I hear," said Derek, trying to steer the conversation away from a huge train wreck.

"Rachael. To the kitchen, now. I need help with dessert." The bossy mother took over.

The dinner party saved their laughs until the two left the room. It took only six sentences to let Rachael know about the kiss, and she looked at her mom and said, "I'll get those two for this. Maybe not today, but soon." War was on.

When they returned to the dining room, they were short a guest.

"Where's Derek?"

"Down the hall. Boys' room."

Ever vigilant, Amanda headed to her bedroom. Turning the doorknob slowly, she entered and found Derek checking out the pictures in her room.

"Get lost?"

"No, just checking out some more of the beautiful quilts your mom's made. I really like this one on your bed. I'm assuming this is your room."

"Grace calls it her guest room. Where she puts up all the strays that Rachael and Meg bring home. Come on. Dessert's waiting." *Mental note: Don't trust Derek. Found him snooping.*

Gifts were given and received. The most hilarious gift was from Josh to Rachael. She kept unwrapping one box inside another, inside another, and so on until the final box was found.

She glanced nervously around the room. The small package was black velvet and shaped like a ring box. Her eyes darted back and forth between Josh and her mother. With a nervous laugh, she opened the box and found a handwritten note. "A ring of your choice when you're ready. I love you."

No one was privy to the note. Rachael jumped up and waded her way through all the paper wrappings and sat on Josh's lap. "You get a real kiss from a real Pennington girl for this. Love you, too," she whispered.

70

The day after Christmas, everyone left Yorba Linda. Grace and Meg followed Josh to the car rental company and took him to the *Catalina Flyer*. Derek made excuses about a difficult lawsuit he was working on and rushed off. Amanda shared the bedroom story with everyone and told Meg to be careful around him. She headed back to LA to continue working on a new case assignment. Rachael and Matt shared a ride back to Bullhead but made arrangements for Hal to pick up Rachael in Barstow. Matt was scheduled to work the floor at the Oasis the next day.

Rachael looked forward to the one-on-one with Hal before starting back to work after the holidays. The captain had assigned them separate cases since last August, and they hadn't spent any time together. They met at Taco Bell for lunch and then hit the road for Bullhead. They talked about their work, ignoring what was really on their minds, but finally, the conversation turned to Sarah.

"So, the transplant's OK? No more dialysis? God, she must be so happy to be able to go out and play with her friends like a normal kid."

"She's perfect, Rach. Happy; color's good. No questions."

"Speaking of that, my friend, any fallout about the missing container? Are you OK?"

"No one's said anything," said Hal. "I'm not doing a very good job of handling it, Rach. My whole life with the department, I've been a good cop, but now since the kidney thing, I can't look the captain in the eye. I think he knows but doesn't want to call me on it. But if he does, then he's lost all respect for me, and I can't handle that. What should I do?"

Nearing Bullhead, Rachael said, "Hal, pull into the River Rat Bar for a minute, and we'll talk about it."

Hal turned down the dusty dirt road. The bar was almost empty, and after talking to Bill for a few minutes, the two settled down in a corner booth and ordered draught beers.

"First of all, what you did was for love. You were protecting the most valuable person in your life. No one can fault you for that. I haven't heard any scuttlebutt from the ranks, but the guys probably wouldn't talk about it around me. If you tell the captain, he'll have to make a decision that he doesn't want to make. That could be a disaster, especially if the DA gets involved. You know he's an ass. Would like to nail anyone in our department."

Hal nodded, "Yeah, but—"

"No buts. Given the opportunity, the captain would probably prefer to let it go. Those were stolen body parts. Useless. The kidney that you took was the only organ that got to be used. Hal, those parts were pirated. They were going to someone who skipped over the list and paid big bucks to butt in line."

"I know all of that, Rach. The problem is I did the wrong thing for all the right reasons. Still doesn't make it OK. I'm thinking about moving to Tucson. Sarah is still young and can make new friends. My sister lives there and really likes it. No traffic, no smog, really good schools."

Rachael remained quiet, thinking through his remarks. She held up her hand and ordered two more beers. Folding her napkin into an origami bird, she searched for the right words.

"Hal, I know that you had plans for us—a future with probably more kids and the like—and I'm really sorry that I let you down. But now, you talk about leaving, and I get panicky. You've been my rock for the last few years, partner."

The beers arrived. Rachael's face reflected her sadness. Hal looked like he had just run over his dog.

"If you leave, will you tell the captain the whole truth?"

"I've thought about that. If I tell him, I'll feel better, but I can't risk the fallout. I was planning on writing a letter to him—a personal one." He took a long swig of the beer. "Maybe tell him what I did and tell him that I'll answer guilty as charged if he wants to pursue it. I could seal the letter and tell him it's up to him to open it. Is that too chicken shit?"

"Totally. Just quit. Leave town, Hal. Don't screw up your life with this anymore." She reached across the table and held his two sun-baked hands. "Go to Tucson. Find a job. Be happy. You're no criminal. You're a warm, loving father and a special friend. If you're looking for forgiveness, go see a priest. You just need to forgive yourself, Hal—the rest of the world doesn't give a damn."

Hal stood and walked to Rachael's side of the booth. "OK, partner. Got the message. I'll give the captain notice today. It'll take me a month to get out of my lease and find a new place to live. Means we'll still be working together. Are you OK with that?"

"More than OK. You know I'll miss you like crazy. I hate all these changes. Ah, shit, let's go catch some bad guys."

71

After Hal resigned and left for Tucson, Rachael worked on her own, deciding not to partner up with anyone. Crime in the city consisted of the normal car heists, petty theft, spousal abuse, DUIs, and drug-addiction-fueled crimes. The crazy summer vacationers and weekenders chopped through the water during the day and filled the casinos at night. The usual round of events and festivities continued into spring and on into summer. Harley Week came and went with thirty thousand motorcycles roaring through town. This year, no one died.

The Fourth of July festivities presented minimal problems for Rachael. She kept in touch with the FBI through Amanda and Matt. A fair amount of kidding from the home branch of the FBI was dished out to Matt because he was promoted to pit boss on the night shift, a sought-after position. "A new career move?" they would ask.

Grace had gone back to her writing, but there was one significant change in her life. Elliott sent pictures of Meg to her each month. In January, the picture showed Meg with her short haircut boarding the Oasis water taxi with friends. Month after month, a picture arrived showing Meg in a different location. The FBI collected the envelopes and worked on the photos. It was decided that a great deal of effort had gone into the Photoshop renditions. Meg was asked to keep a daily diary listing all of her moves, the clothing she was wearing that day, and who was with her at the time. The FBI and Meg would then meet and match the pictures with the date and her wardrobe. They could determine who was present on the precise day of the picture. Now it was believed that an accomplice might have been involved all along, and the FBI was getting closer to uncovering the unsub.

With some reservations, Meg returned to her job at the dam. Jerry and Mike were ecstatic to see her. She strutted around, showing off her new hairstyle, and when she finally calmed down, they did a three-way hug, and everything returned to normal. Her best friend, Paula, had been counting the days until her return, and the social scene commenced immediately. Meg made the rounds at all the casinos and talked to her favorite bartenders along the way. Don, at the Oasis, concocted a new drink in her honor, the Meg Manhattan. She started feeling good about herself.

The only noticeable change in her behavior was observed by her three closest friends. While the drinking and laughter seemed normal, Meg would falter sometimes when meeting new men and would leave the scene if left alone with them. Once her friends realized the problem, they made sure that she was never alone in public. It was an easy job, and the brat pack carried on as usual. Derek came to visit Meg twice a month, and they continued to enjoy each other's company. Derek was Derek. No romantic gestures on his part.

"I've given up on him," Meg confided to Paula. "Give him a turn if you like. There's something about him. We don't click like I thought we might." She mentally questioned his sexual orientation, since he hadn't tried to get her in bed, but she finally dismissed the thought.

Meg enrolled at Mohave Community College, changing her major to forensic medicine. No one argued with her decision. In fact, no one argued with Meg about anything. She kept up a good front, but everyone was aware of the pressure that defined her life as the clock slowly ticked toward August 1.

Amanda returned to the Oasis in early July. Beckett had pleaded guilty to income tax evasion and remained under house arrest. Financial restitution was made to the government. He had helped the FBI scan the Mexico film, hoping to ID Elliott. There was one condition left of his plea bargain. Beckett had to wear an ankle bracelet and work in the surveillance room at the Oasis from July 15 to August 2. No one knew Elliott like Beckett. The FBI believed if anyone could spot a disguised Elliott, it would be Beckett. After August 2, he would be on parole for three years.

"Well, cookie, looks like we'll be working on the same side of the law for a change," said Beckett when Amanda entered the monitoring room. "How about dinner tonight?"

Amanda just shook her head. "Give it up, Beckett. As far as I'm concerned, you got off easy. I hope you make it worth the Bureau's time. Think you can spot Elliott?"

"No problem. It'll give me pleasure to help you nail his ass."

THURSDAY, JULY 31

Elliott had not wasted the year-long hiatus. His plastic surgery in Mexico transformed him into a much younger version of himself. He dropped twenty pounds; worked out in the gym to transform his previously chubby waistline into a well-defined six-pack. The rather bulbous nose was reshaped into a more Grecian style, hair implants replaced the comb-over 'do, blue contacts masked the brown eyes, and a final hair color change from sandy to dark brown completed his disguise. He purchased an expensive pair of designer sunglasses, which gave him a suave look. Women were beginning to notice him, which only exacerbated his self-esteem. Now he could turn a few heads in the casino. *I'm back*, he smirked to himself.

Elliott selected a new girlfriend for the occasion. She was blonde, like Meg—same body type and height. *Yes, Brenda will do nicely when I make the switch.* She was totally oblivious to his maniacal history and actually felt fortunate to have such a handsome sugar daddy taking her to Laughlin for the weekend. They stayed at the Desert Palms for three nights and now, July 31, they switched over to the Oasis. Driving from the Desert Palms to the Oasis thrilled Elliott. His overall plan was simple, and his exit strategy was borderline genius.

Rachael was talking to the head of valet parking when Elliott and Brenda pulled up in their white Cadillac with stolen plates. The attendant quickly opened the door for them, sensing a good tip would be in the making. Voice lessons helped change the pitch of Elliott's voice, and he had developed a nice Texan twang. "Here ya go, partner. Take good care of our buggy for us, will ya?" He slapped a fifty-dollar tip in the attendant's hand.

"I'll watch it like it was my own," the happy employee said.

Rachael glanced his way, but her gaze didn't rest on him. Her eyes moved around the remaining people as they were entering the casino. His mind filled with gratifying thoughts. *Good. You didn't recognize me. If I had more time in town, I would like to perform a duet with you and your sister. You have been a formidable opponent.*

437

After checking into the hotel as Mr. and Mrs. Wright from Austin, Texas, the two went to their room to unpack. Elliott needed to ditch Brenda for a few hours to put his caper into play.

"Brenda, darlin'. Here's some gambling money. I've got a little business to take care of in town. You get us some tickets for tonight's show and make reservations at the Riverside Gourmet Restaurant. It'll have to be early if we want to see the show. Now, you go ahead and take care of that, sugar. Go win some money on the slots."

"How long you gonna be gone, baby?" she asked, rubbing the two Ben Franklins like they might not do the job. "I don't like to hang around by myself."

Sensing that his little gold digger wanted more money, he dug a little deeper. "Not long. Here's some more cash. Go to the spa and get a massage or something. You know how to spend my money, and I love to see you happy. I want us to get out on the river tomorrow. Right now, I need to make the arrangements. How about a nice boat ride through the gorge? We can spend part of the day in Lake Havasu. I hear they have great shops there."

"Well, OK. But get back to the room by six o'clock. We've gotta get dressed for dinner."

Elliott left the room and walked through the casino to the elevators leading to the water-level entrance. The water taxi ran every ten minutes between Laughlin and Bullhead, transporting employees to the various casinos. Local gamblers not willing to get hassled for a parking spot in the 112-degree temperature also used the taxi. One was idling at the dock, and Elliott boarded. The ride took two minutes, and when Elliott stepped off the boat on the Bullhead side, a taxi was there to pick him up. "River's End Bar," Elliott said, and the driver took off.

73

Josh made the trip to Bullhead by air. One of his cop friends owned a small Cessna, and they flew from the Catalina Airport directly to Bullhead. Hal came to town, bringing Sarah to visit her friends. Derek also arrived to be there for the projected finale. While the other two men planned on playing an active role in the anticipated abduction, Derek preferred to stand on the sidelines for Meg's moral support. The FBI had lost track of Elliott, but the profilers concluded he would arrive in Laughlin in time to find and attempt to kidnap or kill Meg.

By now, he would have a master plan in place, and historically, the kidnapping would have to be tonight. Plainclothes FBI and Metro cops were stationed at all entrances to the Oasis Casino, since it was the location of the previous kidnapping. The FBI and Bureau of Reclamation helicopters were on standby at a ground-level position adjacent to the casino. New surveillance cameras were placed in strategic spots covering the vast parking lot and launch ramp.

Rachael, Josh, and Hal decided to take turns watching Meg. Amanda would be serving drinks and would watch the crowd. It was the floating regatta weekend, and the casino was packed. Matt, the FBI pit boss, rotated between the gaming tables.

Meg, Paula, and the three guys met at the Oasis around four thirty. It was still sweltering outside, and beads of sweat glistened on everyone. They headed toward the river bar to cool off. Their favorite bartender, Dan, was slinging the booze around when they sat down in front of the video poker machines. He was assigned an integral part of tonight's business. His role was to make sure that no one would tamper with Meg's drinks.

"What'll you have? A Meg Special?"

"Sounds good," said Derek, Mike, and Jerry, who were all eager to get some alcohol flowing.

Rachael came by to visit with the gang and mentioned, "Cameras have been placed in your room and hallway. They're in the vents, so they're not noticeable to the naked eye."

"You know, Rachael, Elliott's not stupid. Don't you think he'll know this is a setup? I mean, give me a break. I check into the hotel where he kidnapped me last year. How smart is that?"

"I know it smacks of stupid, but Elliott thinks we're stupid, so we're playing into his plans. We know he thinks it's a setup, and that's part of our plan. His kidnapping will have to be very involved this time. He assumes the place will be crawling with the FBI and cops, so he'll be very careful. Diabolical shit, isn't he? The true genius of the plan is that he has underestimated the power of sisterly love."

Rachael borrowed Meg from her group. Since neither had taken time for dinner, they decided to share an early meal at the Panda Express. Meg dipped her egg roll in soy sauce and said, "Rachael, it will be OK, won't it? God, I don't think I could go through that again and come out sane. Don't really want to say it out loud, but I'm scared."

Rachael reached over the table and touched her sister's hand. "I promise, Elliott will not hurt you. I promise."

"I wish Josh could stay with me. I really need him right now."

"What?" said Rachael. "What's this new attachment to Josh? Why not Hal, or even Derek?"

"I suppose this isn't the right time to bring this up, Rachael, but, well, Josh and I really got close in Catalina after you left."

Grace had already told Rachael the story about Josh, the meltdown, and the kiss. Rachael knew Josh had totally dismissed it as grief pouring out, but what was this? Was Meg still looking for a relationship with Josh? Rachael had to resolve this misunderstanding. "Look, Meg, Josh is mine. Whatever you think was going on between you two, well, it was nothing more than brotherly advice—nothing else. Were you trying to make a move on him while I was gone? That pisses me off. How could you?" Rachael regretted her harsh words the minute they came out. *God, Meg was traumatized. Get a grip.*

"Nothing physical happened. I could talk to him. He didn't judge me. And why should you act so indignant? The poor guy asked you to marry him, and you didn't even give him an answer. You might as well have kicked him in the balls."

Rachael glared down at her sister. Maybe she hadn't heard the whole story. "We'll discuss this tomorrow, and Josh'll be there for the talk. Tonight, I have to save your wreck of a life." Rachael grabbed her purse off the small table and turned to leave. "You bus the table. I've got business to take care of while you go off and play and the whole town sits on high alert to save your worthless ass."

She stomped off.

Meg stayed another ten minutes at the table, fingering the remnants of an egg roll. That wasn't really how she wanted the conversation to go.

A small rubber boat tied up to the Oasis boat dock at 9:00 p.m., a little after dark. The boat driver went up the escalators and disappeared into the crowd of gamblers. He had been paid handsomely for such a small task. He was dressed in cut-off jeans, a saggy T-shirt, and flip-flops. That was one nice thing about Laughlin: any type of dress was appropriate at any hour. He wondered why a guy so overly dressed for the casino with shiny black shoes followed him around for a half hour. A second boat—much larger, much faster—arrived shortly thereafter. It too was tied to the Oasis boat dock.

Elliott and Brenda enjoyed a wonderful steak dinner at the exclusive Riverside Gourmet Restaurant and then watched the Smothers Brothers Tribute performance at the Castaway Theatre. Next, the handsome couple headed for the Oasis Casino to try their luck at the gaming tables. The casino was packed, but they managed to find adjoining chairs at the twenty-dollar blackjack table.

Elliott had spotted Meg earlier and was pleased with the resemblance between Brenda and Meg. The hair color, height, and weight were close, but their clothes were different. Brenda was overdressed. Two dealers came by and said, "Hi, Meg," but, realizing their mistake, apologized and left. Other than that, no one paid any attention to the Texan couple as they played their hands. Hal walked by several times, and Elliott watched as he checked out the male players, looking for some similarity to the old Elliott.

Amanda dropped by the table where Meg and Derek were playing three-card poker.

"Cocktails?" she asked.

Meg looked up and ordered an apple martini. "And be sure they use the good vodka this time, girl. The last one was watered down. Tell Dan that the drink's for me. He'll know how to fix it. Three green cherries."

"Wow, Meg. I though Amanda was a family friend. You're a little rough on her, aren't you?"

"Nah, just playing my role. And hurry it up. My sister and I just got into a huge fight. I need a stiff drink right about now," said Meg.

Amanda finished taking drink orders and looked for Rachael. "What's going on with you and Meg? Hell of a time to get into a fight."

"She made a move on Josh when I left Catalina. That's really not OK with me, but don't worry. It's over for now."

"Oh, for God's sake, Rachael. Mom already told you about that. Josh was just helping with her rehab. Suck it up. Do your job." Amanda walked off.

Swell, Rachael thought. *Now both my sisters are mad at me. Too bad Mom's not around to make it a threesome.* She took off for the main entrance, frustrated with the recent events.

Josh came up to Rachael's post and gave her a wink. "How's it going? All's quiet so far in my area."

"How's it going?" Rachael sputtered. "Why don't *you* tell *me?* I hear you and my baby sister hit it off pretty well after I left the island. Why didn't you tell me?"

Josh was taken by surprise. "God, I'd sure be happy to think that you might be jealous, but I know that's not the case. Nothing happened. We put on a show for your mom. I know she told you. But you know, Rachael, you've no right to interfere with Meg's life or mine. You haven't cashed in my Christmas note yet. We had our chance, and you didn't want it. So get off it. Don't be pulling any jealous shit on me. It doesn't look good on you. I'm watching the south entrance for the next two hours. I'm out of here."

She was ruffled; he was pissed.

74

Bundles of C-4 were hidden in the casino. The first mini-explosion to detonate would be in the south tower casino by the food court. Five minutes later, another blast would shake the valet parking area. The final explosion would be in Meg's room. That mini-bomb was the most challenging to hide.

Elliott changed into a maid's uniform, pushed a cleaning cart down the hall, and entered Meg's room. He spotted the surveillance cameras and kept his head down. With the devices well hidden, Elliott went to the laundry supply closet on the seventh floor, pushed the cart inside, and pulled out the change of clothes he had hidden.

When the door from the supply room opened, an FBI lookalike emerged, complete with his Glock. Next stop was the bar. After flashing his fake FBI credentials, Elliott informed Dan that he was the only agent to handle Meg's drinks. Dan hurriedly inspected his bogus badge and agreed. With a sleight of hand, Elliott added ipecac and a light shot of Rohypnol to her drink.

"Did Dan give this drink to you?" Meg looked toward the bar. Dan waved to her. She smiled his way, feeling reassured, and took a sip.

"Yes, Miss Pennington," answered Elliott.

Minutes later, she excused herself from the table. "Sorry. Gotta hit the ladies' room." Her stomach was heaving. Leaving her chips, Meg was escorted to the restroom by Agent Kearns as Elliott watched. Soon it would be time to make his move.

***

Beckett was nervous. The FBI had briefed him regarding everyone's assignment for the evening. Six busloads of senior citizens arrived, and Beckett greeted each one, looking for a disguised Elliott. Next, he was escorted to the check-in window, where he scanned the surveillance footage as guests registered.

"Wait—back up." The digital images reversed in slo-mo. "There. That guy doesn't resemble Elliott too much, but look at the girl. Is that Meg?"

A face scan was completed. "No, sorry. Different markers."

"You sure?"

"Yeah. Let's move on." The FBI agent took Elliott by the arm and headed toward the casinos.

"I'm taking this very seriously," said Beckett. The FBI man looked at him. "That son of a bitch ruined my life. I'd like to be the one pulling the trigger." They continued their search. All of the slot banks were filled, and the sound from the jackpot winners was deafening. The craps table gamblers were getting raucous, and the roulette wheel was finally paying off. For such a noisy, smoky room, everything seemed quiet to Beckett. *Maybe Elliott won't show up. God, to think he was my partner. He killed Angie and Carlos...and poor Sasha. What a monster.*

As they passed the blackjack table, the first explosion erupted in the south tower casino. Josh was only twenty feet away. The explosion knocked him against the blackjack table, sending the chips flying. Patrons grabbed for the black chips while dealers yelled for security. People rushed for the exit doors. Hysteria and mass confusion robbed the guests of common sense.

Josh pushed the button on his shoulder mic and yelled, "We've got injuries. Send the medics now. South tower. Casino." Some gamblers were bleeding, but there were no fatalities as far as he could see. As he raced to the door to make sure no one was leaving with Meg, he called for backup to handle the exit door to the pool area.

"All task force members, hold your positions. This may be a decoy. Be alert," announced James, the special agent in charge. Sirens were heard as emergency vehicles approached the casino. Agents and police took charge of the public to keep them from panicking.

The FBI agent assigned to Beckett pushed him to the outside entrance. Beckett resisted, turning back to his beloved casino. "My casino. What's happening? Damn Elliott." His emotions were bursting. His life was shattering as the second explosion, placed under the valet's podium, discharged. The force of the blast threw Beckett into a plate-glass window. His decapitated head rolled under a waiting limo.

Three cars were tossed violently in the air with their drivers inside. A young woman waiting for her car looked at the glass shards sticking out of her chest, not seeing the one penetrating her neck. She passed out. A Chevy caught fire. The remaining attendants ran with fire extinguishers. They drove the adjacent cars out of the way to prevent more fires. People pushed past security and poured out of the casino, screaming.

Amanda was yelling through her mic. "Hold your positions. He's just trying to cause a diversion. You know who his target is. Who's got Meg?"

Agent Kearns answered, "She's with me. Went to the bathroom before the first explosion. I'm outside the door. It's the one by the cashier's, mid-casino area, north tower."

"Are you sure she's still in there? Did you look away at all during the explosions?"

There was no answer. When she realized the FBI radio system had been jammed, Amanda started for the casino.

"Wait," said a technician. "There's a fire showing on the fourth floor."

"What room?" Amanda yelled.

"Your sister's room. Looks like a small one. Security is on the way. Jeez, the FBI lines have gone dead. We have to use the house phones or cell phones from now on."

Amanda yanked open the door to the emergency stairwell and sprinted the four flights to Meg's room, checking her Glock. Evidence of blood mixed with the singed sheets greeted her, but it looked planted. She grabbed the house phone and rang the security office. "Lock down the casino. Don't let anyone else out. Make sure all of the cameras are working. Get some of your security walkie-talkies to the task force. Hurry. We can't let him get away again. Watch Meg."

**

Elliott rapped Agent Kearns on the shoulder. "I just talked to Field Agent Blake. He needs you at the front entrance by the marquee. Looks like they finally caught the bastard. I'll wait for Miss Pennington to come out and then bring her to the command center. Blake wants to do this by the numbers."

Kearns nodded and started backing away. He clicked his shoulder mic to verify the change, but the mic was dead. He acquiesced. "There are two other women in there. She should be out any time now."

As Meg left the ladies' room, she was still rubbing her mouth, wishing she had some mouthwash or at least some gum to handle the sour taste. She was feeling queasy, almost drunk. That seemed absurd. She hadn't had that much to drink. The commotion in the casino surprised her. She fought against the crowd, trying to find Agent Kearns. Elliott approached. He flashed his FBI badge and took her gently by the arm.

"Miss Pennington, there's been three explosions in the casino. They think they've caught this Elliott guy at the front entrance. I need you to come with me down the escalators to the boat dock. Need to get away from the crowd."

Meg tried to pull away. "I don't feel real good." She put her hand to her mouth. "Take me to my room. I think I'm going to get sick again."

"Sorry. There could be other explosions. We have to leave now. This way. Hurry."

Meg hesitated again. "Where's Rachael? She should be with me. I don't think I should go with you. Where is she?"

Elliott feigned a communiqué through his shoulder mic. "Oh, Detective Pennington has identified...who? Oh, Elliott. Great. OK, she'll meet us where? At the boat dock? Ten-four."

Woozy, Meg gave in and allowed Elliott to lead her toward the escalators. When they passed the three-card poker table, the dealer was scrambling to retrieve his chips but asked if she was OK.

She slurred, "Yeah, I'm going for a boat ride." She felt sick again and tried to pull away from Elliott.

Elliott gave her one more shove, and they disappeared into the crowd. Dan saw Meg leaving and yelled, picked up the house phone, and dialed the command center. The lines were busy.

Hysterical patrons heaved and pulled at each other, clawing their way to the escalators.

Elliott yelled, "Let us pass. FBI." The crowd parted somewhat, but terror had deafened most of them. Enough space opened to allow Elliott to pull Meg to the glass exit door, where a security officer stood, holding a rifle across his chest. Showing his FBI badge, Elliott convinced the guard that he was following orders. The guard recognized Meg from her pictures and allowed them to pass. The fresh air wrapped around Meg's senses.

"Do I know you? Something's familiar," she mumbled. She still felt faint.

He shoved her down the boat ramp and pulled out his gun. Startled, Meg tried to pull away but he held on.

"Oh, you know me, sweetheart. I said I would come back for you."

***

Amanda was in Meg's room when security called. "Check the boat dock. Looks like we spotted Elliott."

She rushed to the window and saw Meg being dragged down the boat ramp. She yelled through the receiver. "Find Rachael and Josh. He has Meg. Heading for a boat. Tell the helicopter to warm up. I'll meet Chris there. Call water patrol. Hurry."

Rachael ran for the river bar escalators. Knocking people aside, she muscled herself to the bottom. Heightened panic paralyzed the crowd. She yelled at the guard, "Don't let anyone out except FBI!"

Josh threw civilians out of the way. He and Rachael charged through the door.

"He's got her. Heading for the boats."

They ran across the parking zone to the ramp. Elliott had knocked Meg into the bow of the boat and was untying the ropes on a sleek power boat. Rachael stopped, took aim, and fired. Elliott felt the bullet pierce his left shoulder. He returned fire and hit Rachael in the chest. Her vest shielded her, but the impact threw her against Josh. They fell. Elliott fired again, nicking Josh in the neck. Blood spurted across Rachael's face.

Rachael rolled his body over as blood gushed from his neck. "Officer down, officer down! Get help." She pressed her palm against the open wound, trying to stem the flow. *Not again. Please, God. Not again.* With her free hand, she took aim at the fleeing boat. It was out of range.

Rachael tore off the bottom of her T-shirt and held it tight against Josh's spurting artery. Blood gushed for a minute more and then evened off as he passed out. A guard relieved Rachael as Amanda reported in on the walkie-talkie.

"Water patrol says there's only one boat ripping down the river. Must be Elliott."

"Elliott doesn't know the sandbars. If he hits one…" Rachael couldn't finish. She spotted a Wave Runner tied to the dock. Untying it with one motion, she took pursuit. "Amanda. Where are you?"

"With Chris. We're airborne. Rach, we got him. Follow the spotlight."

Rachael spotted the light and roared down the midnight river. Elliott had slowed because of the uncertain water conditions, so she rapidly gained ground. Meg, seeing the chopper, wrenched away from Elliott and turned off the ignition.

The bow of the boat dipped abruptly. Rachael's Wave Runner smashed onto the swim step. She catapulted into the backseat of the boat. Elliott grabbed Meg and threw her against the starboard side. He turned the ignition key, shoved the throttle forward, and jumped into the river. The boat lunged. Rachael went sprawling. Meg scrambled to her feet and helped Rachael.

Rachael grabbed the walkie-talkie. "Elliott bailed out. Find him. He can't get away."

"Have you got Meg? Is she OK?"

"Yes. But find him. He should be on the east side of the river."

Amanda was not the only person following the helicopter's search light. A black SUV swerved into the parking lot as the chopper descended.

"Got him. He's almost to shore. Chris, land on the street," Amanda ordered. "He's crawling up on the bank. Maybe wounded. He's mine."

The chopper landed. Amanda ran through the trailer park and smashed through the mesquite and scrub plants. *Damn, where is he? There.* She sprinted toward Elliott.

Slumped forward, bleeding, holding his head, he mumbled, "Damn, I almost got caught. You're late, De—"

"Sorry to keep you waiting, Elliott." Amanda's Glock pressed against the back of his head.

"You."

"Yeah. Recognize me, you asshole? Amanda Pennington, FBI special agent. Meg's sister."

Elliott stared in disbelief. "You slut."

"Now, now, Elliott," she said, forcing his hands behind him. Knowing the gunshot wound was painful, she wrenched them back a bit harder. Her smile said it all. How satisfying the moment.

"Amanda. Did you get him?" asked Meg.

"Right on, little sister." She holstered her gun as she wrestled him to his feet.

"Mandy. Don't turn him in right away. I want some payback time," snarled Meg through the walkie-talkie.

"Sorry, kiddo. You'll have your day in court."

With a stealth-like motion, Derek slipped up behind Amanda and slammed his Beretta against her head. She slumped to the ground.

"Mandy." Rachael paused. "Mandy?" She turned off the engine and pulled Meg close to her.

"Anything wrong?" asked Meg.

"Just lost reception, I guess. I'm sure Chris is right there with her." Thoughts of Josh flooded her mind, but she knew Meg needed this moment. They huddled in the back of the boat, floating down their river. Casino row slid by as the tiny slice of moon steered them downstream. And, as always, the river began its job of washing away the pain.

Upstream, wounded and leaning against his brother's SUV, was Elliott, smiling.

—The End—

16647770R00249

Made in the USA
Charleston, SC
04 January 2013